# SPELLCRAFTER — SOHRANN

## BOOK TWO IN THE SPELLCRAFTER SAGA

### CHRISTOPHER J. KIRKLAND

# CONTENTS

*This book is dedicated to you, the fans of Spellcrafter. Because of your love and encouragement for the first book, when I was not confident in my own work, I pushed myself to complete this title. Without your support, I would have most likely given up on the series. I cannot wait for you to all see where this story goes and where the characters take us. Thank you.*

ISBN-13: 978-1-7360165-2-7

Printed in the United States of America
Visit the official Twitter: @SpellcrafterO
Visit the official Instagram: spellcrafterofficialpage
Visit: www.facebook.com/SpellcrafterOfficial/

## AN EMPIRE AT WAR

The Imperial capital world of Shadehedge was shrouded in temporary but seemingly endless darkness. Most of the civilians of this planet were asleep or indoors, but some still roamed at this hour. A lone man wearing an orange and black cloak with red rank tags could be seen heading toward a manor that loomed large further along his path. Its large pillars and stone steps that led upward toward its entrance were daunting but awe-inspiring.

Behind him were three individuals who could be identified as his personal guards. They wore black armor with purple ranking pads and black helmets. Their visors appeared to be continually updating with markers and data, possibly on threats, as they glanced around themselves wearily. The escorts talked amongst themselves and shared information as they marched behind their escortee, their large rifles in hand.

He placed one foot in front of the other as he proceeded up the steps, the dim lighting of the path's lanterns guiding his way. Two guards stood before him; their weapons attached to their belts. Their faces were shrouded behind the black and red helmets matching their armor, but one could almost assume they were human.

"Name, identification, and rank," the guard on the left commanded, stepping forward. He raised a hand to tell him not to move any further. "If you'd please, sir."

"Of course." the man obeyed, removing a holographic identification card. It flickered to life with a bright red color. A man with grey, swept-back hair; a thick, grey mustache; and a wrinkled face appeared on the screen along with the name "Emmanuel McCarthy." His name was quickly followed by his rank: Director of Imperial Intelligence. He turned off the device once the guard stepped back to clear his path, replacing it into his uniform.

"Am I cleared?" he asked with a poker-face like expression.

"Yes sir," the guard told him, his voice just as mechanical and soul-less. "Lord Chaos is expecting you in the council room; however, he asks us to remind you that you are an observer only."

"Understood," he responded. He moved into the manor gardens, his personal guard in tow. Over time, they branched off to split into different directions to keep watch in this plant-covered zone as the Director of Imperial Intelligence continued into the grand building. The large, wooden, black doors opened as two more guards appeared before him. These men and women stood at attention and watched, their helmets turning to follow him as he slowly moved through the foyer.

The main hall was grand and immaculate, with a massive golden chandelier lightly swinging above his head as lit candles danced in the draft from the door, ceasing as the door shut. The individual proceeded up the long set of stairs that spiraled upward in either direction; today, he would go right. This led him to another hall of guards that stood in a line, preventing him from entering any other room except the one at the very end of the long hallway lined with pottery and paintings of individuals he recognized as members of the Dreadful family line. The entrance was metal with an electromagnetic lock to prevent those without authorization from entering, and of course, to protect them from danger.

Emmanuel removed his identification device once again as he

reached the door and inserted it into the slot near his hip. He then pressed the button that allowed the mechanism to read his credentials. Eventually, the door let out a hiss as the circular lock holding the two sides of it together rotated a few times before splitting, releasing the magnet, and allowing entry. He replaced his device inside his utility belt and entered a dark room, the door closing behind him as the magnet reactivated.

The room was lit only by the dim, red-white lights on each corner of the room. Red Imperial banners lined the massive room, boasting the Imperial crest. A long, round table with a shiny top resided in the center of the room, its marble top shining in what little light there was. Exactly twelve individuals were sitting in the chairs planted into the ground. Most of them seemed relatively young. In fact, most of these members were new. The Shadow Council elected its own members, but Chaos had every right to remove a member. In the past few months, he had fired a total of eight, leaving only four senior members.

At the very end of the table, a man called out and gestured for him to come to sit in the place that was set out just for him. This individual was one of the few old brasses still among the Shadow Council. He had thin, white hair, a white mustache, and a black button-down military shirt. The Director approached the table, passing by the eleven other council members whose eyes followed him to his seat.

"Director McCarthy," he began, his German-like accent thick and clear. He extended his hand to the Imperial Intelligence Director, who shook it firmly. "It is a pleasure to finally meet; I've heard much about you."

"Same to you, Mr. Schneider. Thank you for putting in a good word to Emperor Chaos about my project."

"Of course, I'd be remiss to have him ignore one of our best and brightest. We need individuals like you if we are to survive the Great Universal War." Schnieder released his hand and turned his chair forward, facing the other councilmen. The room was silent for a few minutes as members exchanged glances before a parade of honor guards wearing red and black caps, black military service uniforms, and red pants marched in. They moved to all sides of the room and stood at attention, weapons ranging from swords to rifles in their hands. Soon, footsteps followed as a rather imposing individual entered.

Their host wore grey and white damaged armor with severe scorch marks, bullet holes, sword scratches, and blood. His armor also featured a long, black cape burned and torn at the seams but still flowed behind him. He had red pants with grey lines heading up toward the hips, and he wore black and grey boots. This was none other than Chaos Dreadful: Emperor of the Empire, as if the intimidating unnatural red sword at his hip wasn't enough indication.

"Lord Chaos!" the Director spoke suddenly and without thinking as he stood up with the other twelve members of the meeting.

"He is the Emperor, and you will address him as such. Do not address him as Lord again." the female on the right side of the table hissed as a warning.

"Eslena, please," Chaos raised his hand as he brushed back his greying hair to reveal wary, brown eyes under shaggy hair. "I don't care what I am called."

"You earned that title through hard work and strategy, sir. With all due respect, it is only natural." she continued, sitting down as her compatriots did the same. This woman was rather young. She had short, brown hair placed in a ponytail with a few strands of it covering the left side of her face, obscuring her green eyes. Her white and yellow top with frilly sleeves was small and revealing in the chest area. She wore white and golden gloves with what appeared to be a communication device on the right hand and a long skirt, which was a swansong of colors ranging from white to yellow and purple.

"You'd think she'd keep her mouth shut." the man next to her muffled through his thick, greying beard. "Especially after the embarrassment of her apprentice failing, then running off, and then attacking an Imperial squad trying to apprend-" he paused once he saw Eslena's glare, taking it upon himself to not finish this statement (which was probably wise). The room was quiet enough to hear the man gulp as he sank back into his seat. His attention was now fixated on Chaos, desperately hoping for him to speak.

"Director McCarthy," Chaos began as he sat down in his seat on the far side of the table with the senior members. "Who would you recommend for the Sohrann project?"

"Sir?" the Director's attention snapped up from the table as he looked across at the Emperor, unsure if he was allowed to speak. Schneider nodded to him without making eye contact, assuring him he could give input. "I recommend a knight, sir. I do not believe a Shadow Council member is necessary, or your own presence for that matter. The planetary forces are not organized and should crumble almost completely under the might of a small Imperial invasion." The other council members were focused entirely on him now. "If this is done correctly, we will have what we need before the Alliance arrives and have a strong foothold on the planet for their counter-attack. I already have an Imperial agent planetside."

"When were you cleared to do this?" another council member asked. He looked much like Eslena, but his hair was short, and he wore almost entirely grey. "You must consult us before-"

"With all due respect, we are in a war with a majority of the Light Realm Universe as well as a few pockets within our own." His eyes dragged across the table to each member, respectively. "Sending a spy preemptively was the best choice. Imperial Intelligence must be able to operate independently of the council."

"If IA needs more freedom, I will grant it," Chaos agreed with a nod of his head. "But what makes you think a small military force will be enough?"

"Sir, the Empire is already stretched far as it is...it is a risk, but we must take it. The Empire has tens of thousands of young men and women willing to risk their lives for our cause. There would be enough volunteers for this, and frankly, not all of them need to come back."

"I don't know if I agree." Chaos admitted. He sat forward and cupped his chin and mouth in his hand.

"Sir, I'll be blunt. If we don't make a significant move, we're doomed. If we can't gain ground and we're stuck in endless skirmishes, we're doomed. And if we can't innovate our military, which is outdated to begin with, mind you, we are never going to stand a chance. There is no reason why we shouldn't try at least given our enemies clearly have the advantage."

"If you can coordinate with the military division to prepare this invasion, I will clear it personally. I'll give you my personal knight: Vedi. If anything goes wrong, I will send more, but most of our forces are still engaged in fighting elsewhere." Chaos said this as his eyes shut. He was a little bit unsure about this decision, but it was made now.

"Are you insane? You'd throw countless Imperial lives down the drain for a chance?!" the man who objected earlier had stood up and knocked his chair back slightly. He leaned over the table and pointed at the director, who raised an eyebrow. Across from him, Eslena had lowered her head and shook it very slowly as if out of embarrassment. "If we get them all killed, who will follow us?! They're not fodder."

"Devonix, please take your seat," Schnider asked him as kindly as possible, but it was hard not to hear the hint of irritation in his voice. "We are in a war. Death will be a common occurrence and at this point there is no other option. We need to get our projects rolling if there is any hope of survival. The only reason we haven't been crushed is because the Alliance hasn't pushed into the Shadow Realm."

"We don't need to put them out there like lambs to the slaughter! Sir," Devonix turned his attention to Chaos, who watched him, a hint of compassion in his expression. "Please allow me to go."

"Devonix, the decision has been made. Your concern is admirable, but we have no choice. If we don't make a move, we will continue to lose this war. As it stands, the Alliance does not even need its full military to deal with us, and at the Battle of Terminus two years ago, which by the way was a surprise attack, we were forced to retreat and lost a considerable amount of our forces."

"So when it's an important military move that could make or break us, you send...not even a fleet, but one damn ship with possible back up, but when it's your daughter-"

"Brother, sit down." Eslena hissed, her hands dropping from her face as her expression changed from embarrassment to concern. "Now."

"No, this needs to be said." Devonix pointed an accusing finger at the Emperor. As he did so, the guards in the room seemed to react. The ones with guns removed their safeties and aimed at Devonix; the ones with swords became antsy.

"You claim to be focused on the war effort, but you'll stop everything to try to get your daughter back. And when the other daughter *died*, you almost completely stopped giving orders, and we had to scramble to pick up your mess." he continued. "You send-what, an entire army because you heard your daughter was on some backwater planet, but this? You just say it's whatever, huh?!" Chaos stood up as Devonix spoke without a word. "Your family is important, but the Empire is relying on you, and you're wasting resources trying to capture your daughter when the runaway child is a traitor and has fully committed to the enemy."

By this point, Eslena had wholly given up on getting him to listen, as did the other members. Chaos was standing right in front of Devonix as he continued to rant. The Director watched anxiously and was unsure of what would happen. Chaos extended a single hand and gripped Devonix's entire mouth. His hand began to glow red before bursting into flames. By now, the guards had lowered their weapons or put them away entirely, and the only sounds were that of the raging fire that illuminated the room, and Devonix's muffled screams. Director McCarthy lowered his head and attempted to drown out the sounds. The others simply watched, minus Eslena, who was sitting back in her chair with her eyes rolled. A less than pleased look painted her face; there was very little concern for her brother now.

In the end, Chaos stopped and released poor Devonix, who fell back into his chair, knocking it over as the sickly-sweet smell of burned flesh circulated around the room. Chaos regained his composure and stared down at the weakened man. Devonix moved slightly, showing clear signs that he was not dead. Those on the far side of the table could see his mouth had been fused together by the heat.

"Prepare my ship." Chaos commanded his guards, who hurried out of the room. He continued. "I'm leaving for Penrose. Clean this mess up and inform Vedi of my new orders. Give him whatever he needs. The rest of you have your orders." Chaos calmly walked out of the room as the door sealed behind him, leaving the council members sitting in silence either out of respect or fear.

# 1

# REMNANTS

The sound of planes echoed through crippled buildings and the deserted city streets. Sand dunes and vast stretches of the desert surrounded a city cluttered with destruction and death. There were destroyed homes, office buildings, dead plants, ruined streets, and abandoned vehicles. The entire scene was littered with debris, and of course, the occasional unidentifiable body, which was hard to spot from this height. Not a single living soul could be seen - animal, humanoid, or otherwise. The sky on this planet was a thick veil of black which light could barely cut through; there was no moon to speak of here, but the stars remained.

Three planes entered from the atmosphere, breaking the sea of clouds as they soared rapidly through the sky. There was a red fighter with jet-like features, a cockpit with a black and red theme, and two seats that were placed side by side. This plane also had yellow markings on it signifying it as a lead vehicle, although in this case, the aircraft took up the rear- left position. To their right was another fighter, this one in the style of a heavy fighter combined with a light bomber; its black paint job made it difficult to see in the darkness, but the cockpit lights made their two pilots, who were sitting back-to-back, visible. The final vehicle of this flight was black and purple. It took up the front and was in the style of a fighter jet. The three planes emitted a bright, blue light from their underbellies as if searching for something on city level.

Chris sat forward in his seat, warranting the attention of Penny. She leaned over to see if he had found something only to return to her controls once he shook his head and cursed quietly. Chris had emerald-green hair, blue eyes and was about fifteen by this time. He wore a white bomber-style jacket with a vibrant, blue Ice symbol on the back, grey pants, and black shoes. His partner, Penny, was wearing a black, long-sleeved top; a black skirt that fell to her knees; grey and black style leggings; black gloves; and ankle boots that were, of course, black. She had straight, black hair that fell to her lower back and brown eyes.

"Are you okay?" Penny finally asked after some time of silence, her eyes still fixated on the sky above them and Violet's trail.

"Yeah," Chris lied, returning his attention to the console. "I'm good."

"Radio check." Violet, who was the pilot of the plane in front of them, called over comms.

"Roger," Penny responded, confirming that she could hear loud and clear.

"Weak, but readable, I guess," Ian answered from the plane to their right. "It's probably on my end."

"We'll get it checked out later. Have your computer do a diagnostic and see if that does it."

"Alright..." he replied. As he did, another transmission came in on all of their comms. An audio bar appeared on the canopy.

"To all deployed pilots searching for survivors, please be advised that you have one hour to conclude your searches before you are recalled to Salvation." the voice was male and sounded reasonably young. "Once you return, have mechanics fuel your plane, restock, and repair any damaged systems for the coming ground invasion within one planetary rotation. Station commander out."

"Well, you four heard the man. After we clear city limits, we are turning around." Violet told them. "Don't get your hopes up. New Hope got hit pretty hard, but many of the cities did evacuate."

"Still no signs of life?" Megan's image appeared on their plane's canopy between Chris and Penny. Megan had her pink hair in a french braid. She wore a green shirt with a thick, black line traveling down the center and a black jacket. "We have nothing here. Ian, try a little more to the right. Do you see that residential area?" Ian could be seen in the background, but the only thing that could be made out was his hair and the lights from his monitors.

"Yeah, I see it," he responded.

"Try there."

"Negative on the square and surrounding areas," Violet informed them, her image appearing on the canopy next to Megan, who seemed to be focused on her terminals. Violet was a woman with lightly colored lavender hair, which was currently in a messy bun. The curly strands protruding from her head fell on both sides. Her one-piece pilot outfit was black with a blue Alliance phoenix symbol on the right side-arm. "New Hope appears to be wiped out."

Penny noticed the expression that Chris had on his face, so she decided to say something. "If there's a chance that someone is still alive in New Hope city, we need to keep looking. Once the fighting starts, they could be killed." Penny implored, hoping to invoke a response from Violet, who shut her eyes and shook her head.

"We need to get back to the station and get these birds ready for the coming battle." Violet declared. "We've flown over ninety-four percent of the city and found nothing. All we're doing is making ourselves a clear target for Imperial flights and ground crews."

"Well, that's cold," Ian told her; his cockpit image appeared, causing the other two to shrink and move aside. "I figured you would be trying to look a little longer, Violet."

"Orders are orders, and if we get attacked, we'll likely be outnumbered, Dreadful," she said, referring to Ian, who did a very subtle eye roll. "Now, form up." As she said this, the two planes began to move back into their tight-flight formation. Penny gripped her controls and scrunched up her face a little as if something was bothering her. It wasn't her own feelings necessarily, but close enough. She had not spoken much throughout this entire mission but became more vocal as talk of leaving continued.

Penny turned her head to check on Chris, believing that the cause of her discomfort was from his own emotions, and sure enough, he was away from his console and looking out of the side of the plane with a doleful expression. She continued to stare blankly and only stopped once Violet spoke again, snapping her out of it.

"It's time to head back," Violet announced as her plane began to climb. "Let's get out of here."

"But if anyone down there is still alive..." Chris objected, shooting up from his position like a bullet. "Violet."

"They're either evacuated or dead, Spellcrafter," Violet told him simply as her image distorted and then vanished from the canopy.

"Regrettably, Chris," Megan started, her expression similar to his own, but with a hint of anger in her voice. "She's right. We've been out for a while and found nothing. The scanners would've detected the survivors. We have to go. Don't worry." she lowered her head, her expression becoming darker and more serious. "We'll make them pay, I promise you."

Chris turned to face Penny, hoping for her to take his side. Penny was focused on flying but could still see him from the corner of her vision. She was trying to formulate an appropriate response but couldn't find it. Instead, all she could do was whisper the words: "I'm sorry."

Chris thought about the people who were probably still down there, waiting for help that would never arrive. His hands slipped off of the controls once more as he shifted in his seat to face the window. His arm came up as his head laid on top of his hand. There was no way he could stomach leaving without being entirely sure. Penny sensed that something was wrong and looked over at him again, but quickly stopped after remembering that she needed to focus on flying. Her heart sank a million miles into her chest. Penny couldn't bear to see him like this. Not again.

"This is Penny to Violet."

"Violet. Go ahead, Penny," Violet answered but sounded a little bit irritated. "I told you to form up."

"There's something wrong with the plane's engine. It sounds bizarre, and there's this tapping noise that started during the search." Penny lied, continuing to make up the story as she went. "I'm wondering if it's something serious. We'll land somewhere safe and check it out." Chris lifted his head to look at Penny, completely bewildered.

"Do you need us to land and cover you?" Megan asked.

"No, we'll be fine. It should be an easy fix. It's probably related to drainage or something." Penny continued. "You go ahead. We'll catch up."

"...Don't take too long." Violet told them; her tone filled with suspicion. "If you don't hurry up, I'll-"

"Yeah, yeah..." Penny groaned to herself as she pressed the red disconnect symbol on the canopy. Violet's ranting ceased before she could say anymore. Penny could not help but smile softly at Chris, who was staring at her with a baffled look on his face (which she found somewhat cute). She removed one hand from the controls then raised her hand before bawling it up and raising her thumb. Chris turned a slight shade of red as she did this. She a very proud expression on her face as she continued to pilot like nothing had happened.

"Why?" Chris raised his eyebrow. "You know this is going against orders. I don't want you to be chewed out by Emily..."

"Well, you've kind of gotten me used to breaking the rules..." Penny shrugged her shoulders and giggled. "And I'm sure there are quite a few people down there waiting for help that will arrive."

"You read my mind?"

"A little, but honestly, I could just tell," she admitted as her hand returned to the steering device, her smile dropping a little. "By the face you were making..." she pressed a few buttons in front of her as she continued on.

"Penny?"

"Yeah?"

"Thank you..." he said as they both watched Megan and Ian's plane, as well as Violet's, pull away and disappear into the clouds. Once they had gone, Penny began to fly lower to search the ground more thoroughly and at a slower speed. There was no movement and no signs of life, but still, they continued to search. Penny had suggested that they search the center of the city once again where Violet had been and then move to the very outskirts. It would take more time, but it was worth combing every single zone. Sure enough, searching at the center of New Hope was fruitless.

Penny then directed their plane toward the outskirts, continuing to fly on their set path to allow Chris time to scan every building, street, and alleyway. The scanner was strong enough to detect life-forms in the sewer (if there were any to be found, of course). They searched for a few minutes, still headed in the same direction before Chris started to lose hope. After about fifteen minutes, the scanner began to emit a loud mechanical tone, flashing an approximate location on screen. The light just outside of the plane changed from blue to green.

"Penny?" Chris started as he displayed the map on the canopy as well as an approximate safe landing zone. She said nothing but smirked confidently as they circled around to land on a very long strip of road leading to the town center. She dropped the landing gears and carefully brought them down on the damaged street as the plane jumped and skidded. Once, twice, three times before finally smoothing out and coasting slowly on the sandy streets. The fighter came to a halt and the two of them removed their safety restraints.

"Wait, what are you two doing?" their plane's AI named 'Cornellius' appeared on the screen between them, represented by a holographic frowning face. "I don't think these are our orders. It's dark out, and those...things will be coming out soon. Besides, isn't this still technically Imperial territory?"

"No, they're not; yes, it is; yes, they will; and yes, this is Imperial territory..." Penny responded while she rummaged just behind her seat.

"Got the flashlight?" Chris asked her.

"I do," Penny held up a white flashlight and shook it lightly. "But maybe we should take the smaller ones."

"Those die quickly."

"But they're more portable if we need to fight. Don't worry," Penny handed him a small round flashlight meant to attach to clothing specifically on the torso. "I'll protect you, and if something goes wrong, I'll get us out of it. We'll be back before you know it."

"What about the Spark?" he asked, referring to their fighter.

"It'll be fine here for now."

"What?! You're leaving me?" Cornellius protested so sharply that Chris ended up covering one ear. Penny was ultimately unfazed by his temper tantrum. "The Empire could still be around! They probably saw us land too! Are you crazy? You're crazy."

"Relax, we'll be quick, and honestly, with the demons out and about, I doubt they're moving too much. If they do show up, we'll be long gone." Penny pressed the button on her side of the plane near her hip. This caused the canopy to rise up and allow them to exit.

"What if they do attack, huh?!" Cornellius was becoming more and more outraged.

"Lock the cockpit, shoot them, and don't fly off," Penny answered, climbing out of the plane, her boots making contact with the fractured road. "We'll be back."

"Sit tight, okay?" Chris hopped down as well, placing his bare hand on the cold metal as he swung over on the right side. He stumbled for a moment as he hit the ground, but steadied himself as he looked out at the dreary, dead city just ahead. He could hear something crumbling and crashing to street level ahead.

"As if I have a choice," Cornellius shut the thick canopy glass behind them and powered down the lights slightly so the plane would be harder to see, but not enough to where it would attract...other things drawn by pure darkness.

Chris and Penny stepped out in front of the plane's headlights and studied their very dark surroundings. It was freezing, but his jacket helped a little bit. Penny didn't really react to the cold, but he was sure she felt it. After a moment of looking at the destroyed city, Penny went ahead and walked over to the storage compartment on the left side of the plane and removed a small emergency backpack. Once she resealed this storage unit, she returned to his side.

"Want me to carry the backpack?" Chris asked, his flashlight was already attached to his person and online.

"If you want to." Penny extended the hand holding the bag, and once Chris took it, she got to work on her own flashlight. Chris fished in the back and pulled out a pair of high-tech binoculars as she did this. He studied them for a moment to ensure they were needed and then handed them off to Penny. She pressed a button on the right side to activate them and then held them up to her eyes. For a while, she just stood there scanning left and right with such small movements, it looked as if she was standing still.

"No body temperatures," Penny explained as she continued to pan her body.

"None at all?"

"Wait," Penny pointed down the very dark street ahead of them to somewhere he couldn't seem to make out in the night. "There's a skyscraper with some kind of orange logo on it that looks like a...hotel or something." she hesitated as her vision panned upward as if searching the floors. "I've got...one on the first floor and five on the second floor."

"Anything else?" Chris asked, looking around warily.

"It seems like one is injured on floor two from how he's moving, but I'm not fully sure."

"We should've brought Megan and Ian." Chris thought aloud as

Penny lowered the binoculars, turned them off, and handed them back to Chris, who replaced them in the bag.

"That would've just been suspicious to Violet...we'll find a way. Ready?" she asked.

"Yeah, let's go!" Chris responded as the two of them took off into a sprint, full speed, side by side. They made their way through the ash-covered streets, being careful to watch their step. Chris ignored as much of what he saw as he could, but some of these disturbing sights still caught his eye. Still, they had a job to do, and the horrors of war could wait. A brown fedora blew gently in the wind, coming to a stop in the middle of the street, until they ran by, causing it to fly up and become displaced once again.

Black birds took flight as they interrupted their feeding on the dead lying forgotten, making a loud, raucous cry as their wings carried them into the sky. There were about thirteen of them, all flying in the same direction. The flock eventually vanished behind the tall buildings, but their loud calls could still be heard in the distance, echoing along the destroyed city. The two of them continued onward, and by now, were nearing this hotel.

Chris stopped for a moment to pick up a newspaper and look at it. It read: *The war between the Alliance of the Light and the Empire of the Dark continues to escalate as more and more planets decide to join the Alliance or the Empire. Penrose's battle enters its second consecutive year as the fighting appears to be in the Alliance's favor.*

Further down, in the planetary news section, he read: *Alliance forces are a few days out to reinforce the planet but will not arrive for another week. An evacuation by Resistance personnel is expected for the following cities: Grandham, New Hope, Towle, Tyese, Conyers, and Carter. Other cities, towns, and settlements will be updated as the situation progresses, but please follow the directives of the Resistance when they arrive. They are here to help. Evacuate in a calm and timely manner and take only the essentials. Free medical supplies, food, and water will be provided to all who need it. In other news, the mysterious ground quakes continue planetwide, toppling structures, causing disturbances in wildlife, and concerning Sohrannian Resistance Director Elias Borne.*

Chris lowered the paper and peered out into the endless darkness. He was overhearing what sounded like voices, "IA sent out a warning that the Alliance might be arriving on the ground soon. I saw some of their planes pass over, I guess looking for neutrals." One said.

"...Or us." Another said in a dark tone. "One or the other."

"Anyway, keep an eye out. Obviously, don't shoot any medical responders, but if they make any militaristic movements, just fall back to the outpost. We're way too outnumbered to risk being picked off." a man with a slight German accent told his subordinate. Chris moved to react only for Penny to take him to the ground, land on top of him, and cover his mouth. She shut down both of their flashlights and let them sit in total darkness. The soldiers passed, their lights flashing to and fro on their weapons. Once they had passed, Penny got up and pulled Chris to his feet. It was amazing that it could be so dark that just not moving was viable.

"We can't risk confrontation until we get these people out," Penny told him as she reactivated their light sources. "Just watch yourself, okay?"

"Okay." Chris nodded and dusted himself off. "So, how do you think the search in Towle city is going?"

"Poorly," Penny said while moving on, making sure that they were in the clear as she did.

"Well, that was positive..." he mumbled sarcastically.

Penny stopped to address this comment. "Think about it," she said. "If the two had found anyone, we would not be in the dark about the situation. We'll know more once we actually have a presence on the ground. I'm not too worried about the other searches, though. We can worry about it once we're back on Salvation."

Eventually, they came to a stop at the building Penny was referring to, and it was indeed a hotel. The survivors had barricaded the front door, presumably to slow down any curious Imperials and prevent entry. The structure was heavily damaged but sound enough.

No light could be seen from the outside, and no indication that anyone was alive in there.

Chris suggested climbing in, but Penny reminded him about the glass from the shattered windows. According to her, the best way was the main entrance where the lone survivor on the bottom floor would be located. Penny walked up the once beautiful steps on the dusty and burned rug that ran down them and studied the entrance. For the most part, there was no way in; however, she explained that they could squeeze through the part of the door with a large wooden bookcase blocking it. Chris watched as Penny placed both of her gloved hands onto the case's body and tried to push it back without much success.

*So, are you going to ask for help?* Chris asked her mentally, trying not to laugh.

*No, I figured I'd do this all by myself,* she responded sarcastically, her head turning to look at him.

*Oh, okay, I'll keep watching. You are doing great!*

*Get over here.* Penny shook her head and grabbed the case one again. Chris joined her, and together they were able to push it back enough to slip through the small opening. Penny slipped through the small gap horizontally, and once she reached the other side, she stopped to wait for him. Now he did the same, cutting his flesh occasionally on the sharp glass shards. Once he had cleared the debris, he checked his hands only to find that they had already healed, but the stinging sensation remained. Once he was sure he was okay, he studied his surroundings. He stopped for a moment when Penny grabbed his wrists, checked his hands, and let go when it was determined that he was fine.

The hotel interior was hard to see due to the lack of lighting, but Chris could make out basic things such as a receptionist desk, mailroom, luggage carts, and the lobby with various potted flora. Chris also made a mental note of the various makeshift barricades along the walls and windows on this floor. He moved over to turn on one of the lamps, only for Penny to remind him about their briefing earlier.

"The power was knocked out here, remember? So, don't be surprised if it doesn't turn on," she said.

*Click click click.* Nothing.

"...Told you."

"Yeah, well, I had to try, right?" Chris laughed awkwardly as he did a very animated shrug, only for Penny to just shake her head and continue to slowly proceed through the room. The moment she heard one of the chairs in the darkness fall over, she summoned her shield and stepped back toward Chris. Standing before them was a male figure wielding a rifle. He appeared to be wearing a tan dress shirt, torn up dress pants, and black shoes. The man was not advancing on them, but Chris thought he saw very subtle shaking.

"Who are you two?" he demanded as he quickly trained the gun between them. "Talk fast, or I swear I'll shoot!"

"We're Alliance Wizards," Penny explained calmly. She did not lower her shield as she felt that he may shoot anyway. "We're here to get you. Can I have your name?"

"I'm the one asking questions. Don't move. I'll take both of your weapons now," the man told them, his eyes studying them up and down.

*Should we do what he says?* Chris asked Penny.

*No,* she answered.

"We can't do that, but I can show you some identification if you'd like."

"Your weapons. Now," he aimed down the iron sights at Penny's head. "Last warning. I know who you are Dreadful." Penny said nothing and did nothing.

Chris made a move to defuse the situation by stepping forward. The man stepped back in that instant and fired at Chris and Penny. In one motion, Chris summoned his sword, swung his arm, and effectively blocked all three shots sending them flying elsewhere around the room. The man flinched as one of the bullets whizzed by and hit a vase behind him. He fired again, but this time Chris did not need to move. Penny stepped in front of him and blocked every attempt to harm him with her round shield. She then spun as he was reloading and released her shield, allowing it to fly away and slap into the weapon, knocking it free of his grip and leaving him with just the ammo. Once she caught the shield, she summoned her small sword and pointed it at him, stepping forward slowly and cautiously.

"We've got trouble!" the man called as he took off up the stairs to their right and vanished, leaving his forgotten weapon behind. Chris moved to follow him and calm him down, only to be met with two people standing at the top of the first set of stairs. The newcomer wore dress attire, had slick brown hair, and similarly colored eyes. He wielded a rifle as well. The second on the right was the man from before rearmed with a pistol and his composure.

"Bafair, we got the Sorcerers!" he called, but the newcomer made a face as he said this and lowered his weapon.

"Edmon, what are you doing? Put your gun up. They damn near took off my arm a second ago. Put your gun up, or you'll be next, Ed."

"These aren't Sorcerers. Look," he pointed at Chris. "That one has green hair. Who else has green hair that we've heard of, Syff? That Wizard girl that's usually shadowing the Terminus Headmaster!"

"Spellcrafter..." Syff's eyes widened in the darkness as he ever so slowly lowered the pistol in his hand until it dangled at his side. "I don't believe it. You're really Wizards? Even her? The Emperor's freaking daughter?" he gestured out a hand toward Penny, who nodded subtly one time. He flinched a little as if expecting Penny to do something after this. "Gah. What is this world coming to?" Syff turned and proceeded upstairs, mumbling a mix of 'I don't believe it' and 'The world really is ending.'

Chris didn't really have time to watch Syff leave before this man named Edmon took his hand with both of his own and then immediately swapped to Penny, who seemed just as lost.

"Edmon! Edmon Harper!" he said, introducing himself so fast that neither of them had a chance to comprehend what he was saying. "Alliance Wizards? Thank God! Thank-!" he turned around toward the staircase and celebrated silently as if controlling his excitement before turning back. "You're our rescue? I knew it!"

"Yes. We were the ones that passed over not too long ago," Chris explained, which only furthered Edmon's excitement. "Is anyone here injured?"

"Nothing too serious! Bafair has a banged-up leg, but he said if rescue ever came, he could make the trip! So, how many of you are there?" Chris and Penny exchanged glances. "Wait, is it just you two?"

"We'll be fine," Chris assured him. "Here, uh, why don't you sit down until we get a headcount, okay? There are five of you, right?"

"...Four. Um, Mary died from a bullet wound. We found her not too long ago and brought her into the group. She's...gone, but she had a baby. I don't even know how many months old Joseph is."

"So, you have five?" Chris asked. "Okay, that's what I needed. Hold on," he stepped away and lifted the arm that he had his black watch strapped to. After pressing a few holographic buttons, a call started. "Cornellius? Cornellius, respond. This is Delta two."

"Oh. You didn't get killed then," Cornellius responded in a very monotone way. "That's wonderful. I suppose."

"What? No." Chris looked back toward Penny and Edmon, who were conversing as a few more figures descended from the stairs before returning his attention to the device. "I need you to be ready to take off. Don't fire up the engines yet. I think it will draw too much attention, just be ready. Penny and I will be headed back that way soon with civilians-"

"You do realize there is no space, right?" Cornellius questioned. "You fly a fighter, not a commercial airliner."

"What do you mean?"

"Are you forgetting that the Spark is a two-seater?!" Cornellius sounded like his artificial patience was wearing thin.

"No, I haven't. I have an idea, actually. It won't be comfortable, but they'll be out of here. Could five people fit in the storage compartment? And is it safe during a flight?"

"I can't believe you're actually asking me this..." Cornellius went silent as if mentally contemplating hanging up. "Five people is pushing it. There are no safety restraints, and on the off chance that we crash-"

"There are four adults and one infant." Chris went on like Cornellius wasn't still talking.

"Are you even listening? There is a forty-five percent chance of a successful escape with no injuries," he answered. "But the little one could be killed, surely you know that? ...Surely you care?" He asked hysterically.

"If it was left here, the baby would die regardless. Leave that part to us. Penny will get every last one of us out of here safe and sound. Just smile a little, buddy!"

"This is a horrible idea. This is a very bad idea," Cornellius continued to rant as Chris reached up to shut off the call. "This is one of your ideas."

"I get it from her." Chris smiled to himself a little and approached the group that had gathered by the staircase.

With them was a woman who appeared to be in her early twenties with black curly hair, brown eyes, and multiple injuries on her face and arms. She wore a light blue dress with black shoes. In her arms was a baby wrapped up nicely in an ash-stained blanket. Chris couldn't make out if it was a boy or a girl, but regardless it would grow up without a mother, so part of him didn't want to dwell on it. Chris nodded at her and then diverted his attention.

There stood a man - well, partially standing. He was injured on his right leg, and so he was using Syff for support to move. He wore a tan poncho that covered down to his waist that had very expressive designs on the back in the shape of an eye with weapons for eyelashes. He had short black hair with stains of blood, green eyes, a thin brown beard, and wore multiple makeshift bandages assumedly from articles of clothing left in this hotel. This man was a member of the Sohrann Resistance force.

"Sir, are you able to make the trip?" Chris asked him, but as he did so, the man just nodded and gritted his teeth as Syff pulled him upward.

"Just gotta watch the leg. I'm fine. A few broken bones never hurt anyone." he managed through grunts of pain and short breaths inward. "So, are you our savior?"

"That's us," Chris nodded. "I'm Christopher Spellcrafter, and this is Pennelopie Dreadful."

"Wizards, huh?" the man managed a dry laugh. "Got here a bit late, wouldn't you say? Doesn't matter. You're here. Don't worry about me." He extended a hand to everyone who was now on this floor. "This little group here are civilians that didn't get to make it out before the attack on New Hope hit. They're the priority. If I slow you down, keep moving. Got it?"

"With all due respect," Penny raised her eyebrow and folded her arms as she walked over to Chris's side. "My partner calls the shots here. Make no mistake, you are a civilian too. We can all make it out if we do this right. That being said, you won't be giving any orders. Is that okay?"

"Fine by me," Bafair said, his expression that of someone who crossed a line he didn't know was there.

"Nowhere is safe with you. Bafair, we shouldn't trust our lives to the Emperor's daughter of all people, man." Syff started in a cautious tone. Penny raised an eyebrow at this statement.

"If she gets us out of here, I don't care." Bafair drew a pistol from his hip and nodded at Penny, who did the same back. "She could be the literal devil. At that point, she's good in my books."

"Ready?" Chris asked Bafair, who had now managed to his feet and once again grabbed onto Syff. "There's no rush."

"On the contrary. I'd love to see one of your...what do you call them? Life Wizards? Right about now."

# 2

# ESCAPE

Chris, Penny, and the other survivors moved carefully and quietly through the deserted streets, taking cover as they went. The two Wizard's flashlights shined brightly in the thick barrier of darkness that was the night. Syff was still helping Bafair walk, but they moved so slowly that the group had to keep stopping and waiting for them. Bafair would sometimes collapse onto the ground, and Syff would pick him back up. After a while, Chris decided that they should just move at a slow pace to ensure they stayed together. It would be hard to defend themselves as this street was very open with many angles of attack.

"No Imperials," Bafair observed as he grunted and continued hopping on his left leg shakily. "I don't blame them. I don't want to be out right now either. During the evacuation, we knocked out the city's power to slow them down when New Hope was lost. Those demons will keep them busy until we retake this city, but I don't imagine that it'll be easy. We'll have the same problem if we don't hurry."

"We'll worry about it later," Penny told him as she took cover near an alley and looked down the long dark path before moving on.

"Maybe you should let Syff use your pistol." Chris tried, referring to the firearm Bafair had in his left hand.

"I'm capable. Edmon already makes me anxious with that rifle."

"You're the one who taught me how to shoot it." Edmon turned and pointed back through the darkness, the rifle flashlight switching on as he aimed down. "I hope we're not being followed."

"I taught you for a few minutes. Focus, buddy. I don't need you freaking out again."

"Keep your voices down," Syff reminded Edmon and Bafair. "Hey, girl, where is this plane of yours? Assuming there is a plane, and this isn't a trap."

"Not far," Penny answered briefly, completely ignoring his mistrust.

Chris's watch began to illuminate. He pressed a button and listened as Cornellius started to speak to them, "I should probably warn you that I scanned multiple hostiles heading toward your position. They are most likely a patrol."

"How many?" Chris asked as he looked up to try to see through the darkness.

"Three for now, but you are almost completely surrounded. Combat would be suicide."

"Alright."

As the call ended, these three soldiers they were warned about came around the corner and spotted them. They were in black and red armor and appeared to be carrying light weaponry. Chris and Penny drew their weapons, and the soldiers raised their guns to fire. Before they could act, three loud shots sounded behind them as the soldiers collapsed and fell to the ground. The two of them turned to see who it was, only to find it was Bafair. He lowered his arm and winced, gesturing to keep moving.

"We need to move." Bafair reminded them. He gripped onto Syff, who transitioned to a half run, gesturing his head for the woman carrying the crying baby to move first. "I'm fine, go Syff. Try to keep the baby quiet!"

"We'll hold them off, get to the plane," Chris ordered them as he pointed straight ahead. "Run! Move!"

"I'll stay with you," Edmon told them as he raised his weapon. His determination faded when Chris pushed him away and pointed toward the others.

"Protect them, okay? Penny and I can't worry about you and ourselves! We'll be right behind you. Cornellius,' Chris called to the AI as loud as he could. "Prep the engines!"

"You've attracted a lot of attention," Cornellius warned them as a swarm of Imperials charged at them from the darkness. Chris deflected and reflected bullets with his sword, occasionally firing out an Ice spell to slow the incoming wave of soldiers and Sorcerers. Penny was to his left, fighting a Sorcerer who was foolish enough to challenge her. After a few seconds, she had defeated him with a decisive blow to the chest using her small sword. She fell back and blocked what she could.

We should move, Penny told him mentally as she backed up in tandem with him. Right now.

"Yeah, okay!" Chris agreed as he blocked a few more bullets and took one shot to his left arm before turning and breaking into a run. The pain only hit him a few moments later like a sharp pinch. Penny was just behind him. After a few moments, the wound had healed. "Cornellius, shoot them!"

"You're in the way." Cornellius reminded him. "Do you have a death wish?"

"Just do it already!" Chris ducked under a bullet that was meant for his head and spun for a moment, firing an Ice spell at one of the Imperials who fell back, an Ice shard planted in his kneecap. The Spark fired its forward machine guns, and as it did both, Chris and Penny took cover behind a car. Many of their attackers were cut down by the heavy machine gun fire, but now they were placing down portable barricades to take cover behind to avoid the Spark's assault or hiding in the buildings. Still, many of them were blown away by the power of the Spark's guns like the cover was not even there.

"We have to move. They'll call for backup" Penny told him as she stood up and leaped over the destroyed red car in front of her, sliding over the hood as she did. Chris ducked out from the vehicle and kept running until they had reached the spark.

"Command, this is R272 reporting in from New Hope town square. We're pursuing two Wizards and need close air support or back up, do you copy?" the Imperial trooper nodded to himself before leaning out of cover and firing his submachine gun. "Air support inbound boys. Hang tight!"

"Yes, sir!" Someone cried out in response.

"I'm getting shot at..." Cornellius muttered as he opened the storage compartment on the side of the plane. Bafair went first, biting his lip so hard that it bled due to the sheer pain of sitting in such an awkward position with a busted leg. Next was the woman who was with them holding the child, and finally Syff. Chris and Penny arrived to see Edmon firing back into the darkness at enemies he couldn't see, but he was helping to some extent. Gunshots began to ricochet off of the plane's armor and fly all around them. Chris dropped down once they had reached the plane to make himself a small target. Penny grabbed Edmon by his shirt and dragged him to the aircraft's rear to avoid the barrage.

Chris yelled as loud as he could over the gunfire but still could barely be heard. "Cornellius," he called out. "Close the compartment!"

"What about Edmon?" Bafair tried before the compartment closed, leaving them in total darkness but protected from danger. Chris did not have time to answer before the door sealed.

"This is all your fault," Cornellius complained. "All of it!"

"I know. I know. Just keep shooting and hang on!" Chris said over the loud gunfire. He climbed up into the plane and sat in his usual seat on the right side. He then prepared the advanced weapon systems and manually fired on the enemies, taking control from

Cornellius. Now they were forced to remain in cover. The few that continued firing directly at them were killed or seriously injured.

"In. Now," Penny told Edmon as she assisted him in climbing up onto the wing and into the cockpit. "Get behind the seat. There's a little bit of space back there. Move whatever you need to, just hurry." As she said this, she took a plasma round to the leg and winced but still kept moving. She only needed a moment to hold her wound and reset. As soon as Edmon was in, she climbed onto the wing and swung into the pilot's seat. She sealed the canopy behind her and ducked down to avoid gunfire until it was completely shut.

"Are you okay?" Chris asked abruptly.

"Fine," Penny assured him as she started to mess with the different buttons and mechanisms of their plane. Sorcerers and soldiers charged toward them, and despite Chris's efforts, they were getting closer. "Set that gun of yours to safety and hang on," Penny told Edmon as she strapped in; Chris did the same. Penny started the take-off sequence. As they rolled forward, enemies stopped attacking and leaped out of the way, continuing to fire at their rear once they were clear of the path. The plane's wheels left the ground after a few moments, and once they had gained the necessary altitude, Penny pulled up and raised the landing gears. As they traveled upward, the plane smacked an Imperial soldier on the head. Chris even thought he heard a metallic 'ting' when it happened.

"We made it!" Edmon cheered, laughing as if he was the happiest man alive. "I can't believe we made it!" he calmed down once he noticed Penny had been injured. "Are you okay?"

"Just...hand- me one of those white tubes on the back of the seats. Do you see them?" Penny held her wound and winced. She flew with one hand and pressed the wound with the other. The plasma had cauterized her injury, so there was no blood, but due to their partner link, Chris could tell she was in immense pain and just forcing herself to be bare it. Plasma was always something to avoid, especially as a magic-user since it prevented the wound from healing for quite a while on its own. Penny continued to tightly grip the controls in an effort to ignore the pain.

"Enemy aircraft in pursuit," Cornellius warned them.

"Is this it?" Edmon asked as he handed Penny the white circular item. She nodded and gave it to Chris, who pulled it apart and pushed the button on the side to reveal a long needle. He then handed it back to Penny, and once she had prepared herself, she injected it into the wound and let out a breath none of them knew she was holding in. Penny relaxed in her seat for a moment before grabbing the controls, regaining her focus. She dodged an Imperial jet, which soared by and circled around to give chase.

"You ready?" Chris asked her.

"Always. I'll take us low around the buildings." Penny decided, flying the Spark down toward the many city buildings.

"We'll crash!" Edmon protested, grabbing both of their seats and trying to pull himself forward from the cramped space. "You can't!

"Sit back!" Penny told him as she smiled to herself. "I'm going to remind them who they're messing with." Penny increased the throttle and began taking tight turns, moving around the skyscrapers with ease. Two of the Imperial fighters broke off for a moment, flying upward to avoid crashing. Still, two others continued to match Penny closely, their machine-gun fire cracking glass and destroying the city's structures.

"There is a baby in the back, by the way..." Edmon reminded her.

"I know," Penny answered. "Which is why I can't do what I usually do..."

"What do you usually do?!" Edmon asked in a sudden outburst. He was forced backward by the force of Penny accelerating.

"Those two are coming back!" Chris updated her as he pointed through the canopy at two planes in a nosedive. As he said this, she nodded but remained focused on the terrain. "It looks like a small squadron was sent after us." Penny increased her speed even further, relying on split-second reactions to maneuver them through the narrow openings between the buildings and roads. Chris could see

30

her eyes darting every which way; her breathing changed almost every turn. "Incoming!"

"Yeah, I see them." Penny pulled up suddenly, performing a loop before coming out of it early and leveling them out low to street level. There were small groups of Imperial soldiers on the street level who watched in shock for a moment before opening fire. Chris returned fire to the ground units with the Spark's underbelly gun and then focused fire on the two persistent planes after them. He then watched as one of the aircraft discharged an object with a long smoke trail and was rapidly approaching them. A few more were fired soon after. Warnings flashed on the canopy.

"Missiles!" Chris told her.

"Look what you've gotten us into!" their AI sighed.

"Missiles?" Penny smirked and sat up. "Good."

"Don't you dare-!" Cornellius threatened although they knew he wouldn't do anything. "Not again!"

"Calm down. It worked the last time." Penny began to press a few buttons on the plane while Chris continued constant fire on the enemy. The missiles were getting uncomfortably close, but Penny seemed unconcerned.

"Hey, don't forget there's a baby in the back." Chris reminded her. "Just another reminder, in case you didn't hear him..."

"It's not like I can forget," she responded. In unison, Chris stopped firing, and Penny cut the engines as they fell back past the Imperial fighters. Seconds later, two explosions were heard, and large balls of fire and flying debris enveloped the sky where they had been. Penny reactivated the engines, regained control, and changed direction as the chase continued. The two remaining fighters pursued them at high speeds, firing and even landing a few hits on the Spark (presumably upset at the loss of their comrades).

"I hate you, and I hate it when you do that!" their AI protested.

"It worked, didn't it?" Chris laughed nervously and looked over at the screen where Cornellius displayed a frowning face on his screen. "Penny has kept us alive so far."

"I hate you both so much."

"I feel sick." Edmon covered his mouth and sat back. He looked pale and dizzy. He gripped onto Chris's seat for support as he flew forward again, his head coming between them.

"Try to sit back." Chris reminded him.

"Oh, I hope he gets sick, so you have to clean my seats, or it gets all over you...." Cornellius hissed.

"Aren't they gone yet?" Edmon said, pale as ever.

"Nope. Sit back." Chris repeated.

Penny focused straight ahead as she dodged left and right through narrow openings between buildings, turning the plane so its wings were angled vertically before leveling them back out. The enemy fighters were close on their tail but couldn't really line up good shots with Chris's constant firing. Eventually, one of the planes started to trail smoke as Chris struck the underbelly.

"Is he-I got him??" Chris used his computer to get a better look and zoomed-in to see a small fire building within the enemy plane.

"Are you relaxing now, Cornellius?" Penny asked a rare smile painted on her face as they flew through the air gracefully.

"Never with you," he answered. "The plane that you damaged is having internal combustions. If they continue at this speed, they'll likely-" *Ba-boom!*

Behind them, the plane that had previously been shot by Chris exploded from the inside with a bright red and yellow flash, sending shrapnel and fire everywhere. The remaining plane dodged around the fiery explosion and continued relentlessly after them.

"Patch me through to his communications," Penny told Cornellius, who connected her almost immediately. The Imperial crest appeared on the canopy instead of a video of the pilot. Chris assumed Penny was going to try to negotiate with the remaining pilot. "Back off or get shot down."

"Ah, so it's the traitor we all used to look up to, huh? I suppose it makes sense that you're the one who took down my squad." It sounded like he was pressing some buttons on the other end. "That changes things."

"Does knowing that make you want to disengage?" As she posed the question, he opened fire with heavy plasma rounds, forcing Penny to barrel roll out of the way. Her lips quickly formed a straight line. "Cornellius cut the comms. I'm done talking."

"Did you really think that would work?" Edmon asked.

"No, but you can't say I didn't try. Still Imperial."

"I don't think I can hit him," Chris told her as he gritted his teeth. "Do you know this guy?"

"Nope, but I know how to handle him. You just sit back." Penny smirked once again. Chris could tell she was about to have fun. She raised her thumbs to the forward gun buttons and flew a bit higher. They passed through a parking deck's third level, coming dangerously close to the walls and cars. Chris watched warily as the enemy pursued with a rain of plasma, bullets, and the occasional missile. Suddenly, Penny opened fire and stuck a brightly colored red pipe, which released heavily pressured water. Water spewed from the line and into their path. The Spark flew through no problem and pulled straight up to avoid crashing into the skyscraper, which was right in front of the garage. She then leveled out the Spark and flew slowly to watch her work unfold below them.

The Imperial plane could be seen flying up vertically, trying to perform the same maneuver Penny had done, but due to the spray of water that had hit the cockpit, he was having trouble. There was damage on the underbelly and on the plane's right-wing, so Chris deduced that the pilot must have reacted late. Even so, he managed to save himself, but the damage was too extensive. The plane was now scraping against the skyscraper as it tried to turn away from it, sending sparks and rubble everywhere toward the ground. Eventually, the right wing fell off from the impacts as the fighter finally broke away from the building and descended toward the top level of the parking deck. It crashed down onto the open top level and slid, smashing through the concrete barrier before coming to a halt with the nose dangling from the edge.

The cockpit of this plane opened up, and the pilot could be seen getting out. He stood on top of his ruined vehicle, watching them fly away from his position. His plane began to catch fire near the engines, allowing the man's figure to be seen more clearly in the darkness. He wore a black pilot outfit and helmet with red rank markings. The man ripped off his helmet and threw it down angrily, revealing brown, wavy blond hair. Chris sat up in his seat and looked back at him. This pilot must have been at least moderately impressive if he was able to survive that crash landing.

Chris turned back and sat up straight as they flew out of his view, only to see Penny with the biggest grin on her face. She was relaxed and clearly pleased with her performance, resisting the urge to laugh. Chris was about to ask if Penny was okay, but her wound would most likely have healed by now. He stared at her for a moment before smiling and thinking: *She loves doing that, even if she doesn't want to admit it.*

"Does-Does she do this often?" Edmon shook Chris's shoulder lightly to get his attention, his hand shaking from fear.

"You could say that," Chris responded cheerily. "Yeah."

"I'm sure you have quite the strong stomach then..."

"Nope." Chris laughed. "Not at all."

"You should probably call the advisor and let her know we're on our way to Salvation with civilians. They can prepare the medbay." Penny told Chris as she directed the Spark up toward the sky, breaking through the clouds and flying into the upper atmosphere.

# 3

## THEIR SALVATION

The hum of the surrounding machinery was soft and consistent and yet did not disturb anyone sleeping. There was a shifting sound as pure white sheets ruffled and huffed as a figure tossed and turned. For a few moments, their body remained curled up in a half-ball before stretching. Penny sat up slowly and observed her surroundings before rubbing her eyes. She was still a little sleepy but knew she had slept long enough. Before getting out of bed, she lifted her purple nightgown to confirm she had fully healed from her injury before turning to swing out of the narrow bed space, sliding down as her bare feet touched the cold floor.

"Chris?" she muttered, her voice grumbly and rough as her body tried to wake up further. Her vision focused on the bed across from her only to see partially made-up sheets and no sign of Chris where he should be. How long had she been asleep? She always woke up before him, so it must have been late, right? "I wonder where he went." She thought aloud.

"System administrator Thompson. System administrator Thompson," the automated announcement system called over the many speakers set throughout the station on the ceiling. The speakers in each of the quarters were a little quieter to avoid startling soldiers and Wizards unless necessary. "Please report to the server room two for routine satellite dish calibration. Thank you."

Penny stretched with one arm up and the other holding onto it before turning and facing the bed. She then got on her knees and pressed the dark blue 'eject' button on the white drawer before it hovered out to her. She didn't feel creative whatsoever, so it was probably best to just wear what she usually did. Who knew what would get done today? They only had a few hours left before the ground invasion began.

Penny took both sides of her nightgown and pulled it over her head, tossing it onto the bed without a care as she reached in and put on her black short-sleeved top with the light blue colors on the sides. She then went for her similarly colored skirt, stood up, and stepped into it before securing it. *Shoes, shoes,* she repeated to herself internally. Finally, Penny's eyes locked onto her boots, slightly hidden under the bed platform. She reached underneath her bed and pulled them to her feet. *Tap tap,* the shoes sounded as she took the front of both shoes and lightly kicked them onto the floor to ensure they were also secure.

Time to go and find her partner again. Penny walked toward the ovular door and was about to open it before noticing her watch sitting on the nightstand embedded into the wall. Once the purple and black smartwatch was securely on her wrist, she returned to the door, placed her hand on the right-side panel, and watched it slide open with a soft 'puff.'

*Wait, I forgot my gloves-* Penny reminded herself. She made a move to turn around and get them, but instead just rolled her eyes and kept walking, allowing the door to close behind her and lock with a small red flash around the door outline. *I guess I'm not doing anything dangerous or messy right now.* The hallway wasn't bustling at the moment as most of the crew, Wizards, and soldiers were asleep or at their stations. Penny turned right and walked down the smoothed-out, white interior of the station. As she passed by one of the large, reinforced windows, she looked out at the stars and the tan planet they were orbiting.

Penny stopped dead in her tracks and stared at her own reflection in the window. It stared back, and as she pushed a strand of hair back behind her ear, it did the same. Her breathing fluctuated as she continued to stare. *I look a lot like you now, huh, Tori?* She thought to herself, assuming her sister may have been listening. *It's not really fair...I never thought about it before, but...I never thought I'd be the same age as you or outgrow you. Or even-* She paused as another announcement came on the intercom about more civilians being brought onto the station. Turning, Penny continued on her way down the hall, ultimately pushing those thoughts to the back of her mind.

Penny located the white elevator marked with the words 'Quarters level three' further down the long stretch. There was also a black screen above the doors, which curved around the shape of the elevator. Sometimes words would drift across this display with things like 'current temperature of New Hope city three degrees Fahrenheit. Two and a half hours until sunrise. Penny placed her hand against the sizeable black reader next to the elevator and let it read her biometrics.

"Pennelopie M Dreadful confirmed." the machine said aloud. "Calling lift."

A few seconds later, the doors opened to a cylinder-shaped elevator. Penny entered and pressed the button to head to the command deck. She was alone in this elevator, so she didn't see any issue leaning against the hand railings placed on the walls. From where Penny was, the elevator opened up to space, and from there, she could see the General's black and blue capital ship: The Tenacity. Just before this view was gone and she had reached her destination floor, a few Alliance fighters zoomed by the station very close to where she was.

"Arrived—level twelve. Command level." the voice told her again. Penny sat up and exited into a dark room with a large golden map of the entirety of Sohrann being displayed. Three men stood around it, along with two women. Penny didn't look long, but they seemed to be discussing tactics for once they were on the ground. She couldn't really hear what they were saying, but it didn't really concern her, so she wasn't trying to. At best, Penny could make out the word 'battalion.'

As she moved to the right of the room through one of the station's many tube-like hallways, she found where she was going. After passing by numerous entrances from the briefing room to the interrogation room, she found what she was looking for: the command center. She proceeded toward the door with two large white doors featuring pulsating blue lights to signify that it was powered on. They slid open and allowed entry with a loud, hissing sound.

The room was very dark aside from the many screens around the room, and the individual screens in front of each of the figures shrouded in darkness. Salvation's command center was round with a few deformities here and there in its shape. There were three levels to this room, not including the very bottom floor. The floors were a shiny grey color that reflected all light coming from every direction. The station Commander, the Wizard squad advisors (including her own), Overseers, and station technicians were all located here.

Almost anyone could tell who did what based on their outfits. The female advisors wore a military-esque dress with black shoes and a blue bandana around their neck, unlike the male advisors that wore a black outfit that covered their whole body and that same blue bandana. All of these men and women had a white communication device in their ear. These individuals were responsible for telling squads of Wizards in the field what to do, informing them of situational changes, and dispatching help in the event that they are in danger.

The technicians wore blue overalls and were responsible for the upkeep of the station's machinery. Overseers were typically much older and wore navy blue overalls with a dark blue beret featuring a golden Alliance symbol. They wore a red handkerchief around their neck, and some had implants to communicate faster. These overseers were armed in the case of an emergency and contrasted the advisors the most, seeing as they could not typically defend themselves.

Penny stood there a moment until she had found who she was looking for. Using the stairs, she walked down to level two and turned left to find an advisor named Evangeline. She sat on the second row toward the very edge where the glass barricade railing was. Evangeline had blonde hair, hazel eyes and was wearing the advisory attire. She leaned over to place her elbow on the armrest and stared blankly at her screen, Chris's report scrolling as she read it. Advisors had this weird ability to read faster than most brains could comprehend, but Penny knew that a person could be trained to do almost anything if it was from a young age.

"Hello, Evangeline. Is that Chris's report?" Penny asked her as she approached and stood to the left of her seat. She knew the answer to this question but pretending to not know would probably be best. *Who knows what he wrote?*

"Yes, this is Delta Two's report. Good morning, Delta One," she responded in an almost American-like accent. Evangeline was known for being very formal, so Penny did her best to do the same. "A question, Delta One."

"Yes?"

"Why did you two disobey direct orders from command? In the report, it states that you were repairing your plane, and civilians approached you. You were then forced to 'evacuate them in the Spark's storage compartment.' Please be truthful."

"Chris and I continued scanning the ground because we felt we didn't do a thorough search and found some civilians as well as the Resistance member he mentioned."

"You know this report is required to go through Emily, correct?" she asked, turning away from her screen to look at Penny, who made a slight face.

"Uh, yeah, I know," Penny admitted. "She's going to kill us both. Sorry for not telling you sooner."

"...I'll modify the report details to be more believable. Delta Two is a poor liar, and I do think your actions were just. As he put it, they came to you. You had no intention to stick around longer than you were required but managed to save survivors regardless. Is this information accurate?"

"...Sure, yeah." Penny smiled a little at Evangeline, who nodded and turned to change the report before sending it to Emily. "Thanks for that."

"Was there something else, Delta One?" Evangeline asked Penny. "I assume that wasn't the only reason you came to speak."

"I was wondering if you knew where Chris-err...Delta Two is?"

"Where he is?" she repeated, her eyebrow gradually raising. "You lost your partner?"

"No, I didn't lose him. I woke up, and he was gone. I can't use the partner link to know his exact location yet, so I was wondering if you might know." Penny explained, progressively slowing her speech as she became more embarrassed.

"You're starting to act like him."

"I'm what?"

"I'm studying the cameras to locate him." Evangeline pressed on her multiple screens before a set of camera feeds appeared from all over the station. She slid her finger across to the hanger twelve footage and dragged it to the center screen. After a few moments, the size increased so that Penny could see as well.

"Delta Two is in hanger twelve servicing the Spark with new parts. Do you need to know where the rest of your squad is?"

"I don't need to snoop," Penny made a face and waved her hand a little. "Thanks, though. It's still weird having you here in the station and not on the Tenacity."

"I'm not in the habit of working here either, but the communications here are stronger all across the planet. Let's not forget that I have a lot more at my disposal to help you and your squad, including real-time planetary updates, imagery, and satellite strikes." Evangeline slid her finger across the central screen to close out the camera footage and bring up the invasion details. "Still, I can't wait to return to my normal station."

"You seem busy, so I won't distract you," Penny told her as she turned to leave.

"Delta One?"

"Yes?" Penny turned around partially with one foot on the first step.

"Please ensure that you are cautious during the ground landing operation. The fighting will be violent, and unlike you, Delta Two has a tendency to try to do more than he's able to try to save lives. I need not remind you of how likely he is to get himself killed. I'm counting on you to keep him leveled out."

"I know," Penny responded. Internally she was a bit peeved that someone was telling her how to take care of her partner, but she knew Evangeline had a point. "I will."

"Thank you. We'll speak over comms later. Good luck." and with that, Evangeline rotated in her chair and returned to the mission details. She had to be prepared perhaps more than them for every situation. Advisors had it rough, but they still never had to see combat. As Penny exited this room and proceeded back to the elevator, her thoughts admittedly lingered on what Evangeline had said. This was their squad's first active deployment in a large-scale battle. They had participated in small scale battles, sure, but a full-on landing was something else. Luckily, they would be assisting only in the air according to their orders, so she wasn't too worried.

"Pennelopie M Dreadful, confirmed-" the machine chimed again as Penny stepped into the elevator and took it down to the appropriate level. After waiting a few short moments, she stepped out into a white hallway with bright lights lining the ceiling and floor edges. She went left and continued heading in that direction until she reached a large hangar. Planes here were being fixed, assembled, and disassembled for scraps.

The hangar was large and impressive with a white and grey color scheme and the occasional golden line. The Alliance Phoenix rested proudly on each of the three walls here and in the floor's center. The hangar shields were a very pale holographic blue. This shield occasionally hummed when space debris tried to enter, or a ship passed through. The barriers allowed Alliance transports to enter and vessels with cleared identification, but little else. Everything else was treated as if it had hit a wall. If your ship did not have the proper credentials or clearance - boom.

Penny scanned the hangar for the Spark and her partner, but there was far too much going on here to easily find them. She did, however, notice Chris's sister Emily marching into the hangar. Penny knew that face, so the ensuing conversation likely wouldn't be too fun. Emily's green hair was in a bob cut held together by a black hair-band. She wore a black dress that fell to just past her knees with a white necktie. The back of the dress was cut out in the shape of a leaf. She also wore similarly colored gloves with white knuckles, black leggings, and knee-high boots. As she moved, Penny followed.

As Emily and Penny approached, Chris's legs could be seen sticking out from under the spark as bright blue sparks flew out from the underbelly. Penny tried to get to him before Emily, but Emily arrived first anyway. She had to warn him regardless, so she contacted him mentally again.

*Hey, incoming,* she told him.

*Incoming what?* He asked as he continued to work.

"Chris," Emily started in a somewhat loud tone. "Chris. Christopher. Come out here, we need to talk right now, okay?" After not receiving a response, presumably because of the sounds of sparking, Emily decided to reach down and touch his leg. Chris reacted by trying to sit up and ended up smacking his head on the bottom of the Spark's armor before sliding out from under it, his hand on his forehead.

"Oh, hey, Em." He managed.

"Are you alright?" Emily asked as she reached out and pulled him to his feet. Her tone had changed entirely from being upset to concerned. Chris leaned back against the Spark and nodded like he had heard this a million times. "I read your incident report about those civilians."

"Yes?" Chris raised his eyebrows. "That was fast. I submitted it like an hour ago."

"I've been wanting to talk to you about it." She told him.

"Was something wrong with my format?" he asked playfully. Emily wasn't having any of it.

"Well, yes and no. I'm just concerned that you withheld some of the details. Is there anything you didn't tell me? It just seemed like there was more to it."

"No." He lied.

"Chris," Emily sat on top of the plane next to Chris and placed a hand on his shoulder. Penny continued to listen in, remaining as hidden as she could within the busy hangar. "I understand to a degree why you went down there to get those people. I know you kept searching despite orders to return because you have a good heart, but I don't think you understand the environment you're in." She placed both of her hands in her lap and took a breath. "It's natural to want to help others that are suffering, but your orders are there to protect you. They also come directly from me nine times out of ten. Like what have I taught you about disobeying orders?"

"You taught me when to do it," Chris responded with a smirk. "And how to do it without getting into trouble."

"That wasn't one of those times. This was dangerous. So, tell me, honestly...Did you land to make repairs, or did you land on a rescue mission?" Chris didn't respond, but upon getting a pat on the back from Emily, he went from lowering his head to raising it back suddenly and looking at her. This look was enough to give her the answer she expected. "You did good, but please be careful. Don't get me wrong, I'm proud of you, and it's what I would have done, but this is an active war zone now. You being a Wizard matters a lot less here. Especially to the Imperials."

"I'll be careful," he promised. As Chris said this, Emily placed her hand against his back and patted him a few times before sliding down off of the plane.

"I need to go speak to the General, but we'll talk more later, okay? The operation might be delayed by a few hours since sandstorms are ongoing, so you should get some rest. Eat if you haven't, and don't do anything crazy."

"Like you?" Chris retorted smartly.

"Do as I say, not as I do." Emily sighed while holding her nose.

"Or I could keep working on the Spark." Chris smiled and pressed the lever on the torch-like device he was holding, causing a small blue flame to erupt from its exhaust.

"Don't play with that." Emily rolled her eyes as she turned left out of the nearest exit to the hangar and disappeared. Chris released the button he was holding and turned back toward their plane.

"Cornellius, try to fire up the engine three, okay?" he told the plane's AI. Cornellius activated the Spark's third engine, which resided just below the tail. The machine came online as blue exhaust poured from the thrusters. "Okay, now try the other two engines." As Chris asked the computer to do this, the engines roared to life through the smaller exhausts lining the area under both wings. Chris smiled and nodded to himself, patting the armor of the Spark. "We're good! Shut it off."

Penny approached Chris, unable to keep herself from smiling as she did a small golf clap. Chris noticed her finally and decided to play off his excitement by taking a little bow. Penny couldn't help but notice the smudges of oil on his cheeks and forehead as he raised himself up. He raised his arm to try to wipe his face with his arm, only to smudge the oil further along his face. Now it was also on his arm.

"Well, I suppose it's a good thing you're not wearing your jacket," Penny remarked. "I see you got us up and running."

"Yes, your Spark's ready, ma'am! That'll be three hundred dollars plus the labor fee-"

"You don't even have the courage to hold my hand. I don't think you're going to charge me." Penny smiled and drew closer to the plane. She placed her hand against the armor and stared at her reflection before speaking again. "You cleaned it too?"

"I repaired it, filled the bullet holes, repainted over damages, and also had the mechanics bring over a new canopy.. just in case. We did get shot at a lot, and there were way too many cracks."

"You did good," Penny smiled and moved her hand across the smooth surface, which made a squeaking sound as she did. "Hourev really did teach you a lot. I like having a portable mechanic. It looks like when we first got it."

"I just touched it up," Chris told her. He was modest, but Penny could absolutely tell he was proud of himself. "It'll just get messed up during the battle, but it looks nice for now, right?"

"Hey, Spellcrafter-" one of the station mechanics approached them with a thin white tablet. He wore a grey jumpsuit and a hardhat with goggles. "I was told to bring this to you."

"What have you got there?" Chris raised his eyebrows a little and extended a hand for the device. "System update?"

"Uh...that and uh," the mechanic moved, so he was beside Chris and swiped along the screen until he got to what he was looking for. "The Spark is getting some new machine guns. The armor is also getting a slight overhaul in the coating material. Fuel consumption is being improved, and finally, the tracker is being completely swapped out for the new version-"

"So, you mean to tell me that I have to take the Spark apart again, install all the new stuff, and put it back together?" As Chris was talking, Penny stood up on the Spark, sat on the armor, and watched from near the cockpit.

"Yes, sir, that's correct." the mechanic nodded only to seemingly notice Chris's glare. "Uh, at least the armor doesn't need to be repainted. So long as we are careful, it'll only need an outer coating. So, you won't need to wash or repaint it again."

"I've been at this for three hours, Gilbert," Chris said, his eye twitching.

"Well, I can take over the swap if you want me to. I'm not working on any other planes, so I've got time. Just let me take my break and-" Gilbert paused as Chris took the tablet, pressed the power button, and surrendered the device by pushing it against Gilbert's chest with his head lowered.

"Yup, sure." Chris's tone was dull and frustrated. "All you."

"Are you sure? I know you don't take repairs on the Spark lightly. The last time I tried to fix it, you told me I did it wrong."

"Yup. Whatever. You've got it. I'll go back behind you," Chris smiled through gritted teeth. "Anything else?"

"You'll be happy to know that there's a new payload function we'll be adding! You can drop a bomb on any ground target without much-added weight-" Gilbert paused upon seeing Chris's twisted expression and took a step back. "Oh, that was...sarcasm, wasn't it?"

"Mhmm."

"I'll just let you breathe, go on my break, and come back to fix it, yeah?" Gilbert tapped the back of his tablet and smiled as kindly as he could, despite being afraid.

"Walk away," Penny said from on top of the Spark, her voice showing hints of suppressed laughter. Gilbert nodded with a smile and backed away. Eventually, he turned around and walked off entirely. Penny smiled as Chris turned to focus on her, sliding down the armor until her boots hit the wing. Then she climbed down from that too and came face to face with him. Chris opened his mouth to speak but was silenced by Penny. She took her thumb and purposefully smudged the oil on his cheek further. "We should get you cleaned up, you know?" Chris grunted a little and reached for her wrist only to pause, turn a shade of red, and lower it again. Maybe he thought she wouldn't notice, but she absolutely did.

"I'll deal with it later," Chris gave an embarrassed smile before doing a little eye roll. "I really wasn't intending to get covered in oil, but there was a busted-" Penny walked over to the tool cart sitting beside the Spark, took the clean white cloth lying on it, and started to dab the oil off of his face. "What are you doing?"

"Helping," Penny told him simply. She stood up a little on her toes to reach his forehead and clean that too. They were about the same height, but he was still a bit taller now.

"When did you get so-"

"So what?" Penny paused and removed the cloth. Their eyes locked for a moment.

"Girly?" he finished. Penny, deciding not to show that she was flustered, took the cloth and placed it over his head.

"I'm not girly. I just wanted to help." Penny returned her heels to the ground and flicked his nose as he removed the cloth. "Why didn't you wake me up?"

"You got shot."

"Okay?"

"So, I let you sleep it off. That was plasma." Chris told her honestly as he replaced the cloth on the cart. "Are you okay now?"

"Yeah, of course. It's not the first time. I've had worse," Penny explained, her head tilting a little. "At best, it stung. You know I can take a hit."

"I'm still glad you got some rest." Chris gave a warm smile, and Penny returned it. "Hang on," he told her as his watch began to flash and beep. "Hey, Eva."

"Advisor Evangeline to Delta Two," Evangeline's image jumped out as a holographic projection. "Have you completed maintenance on the Spark?"

"...Kind of." He replied, glancing back at Penny, who shrugged. "I've got someone finishing it up for me. Some upgrades came at the last minute, so I guess I'm starting over. Why?"

"I have been informed by the General that you are to report to hangar nine just before dawn for a scouting mission. Some of our scouts have gone missing, and so you will be the one to complete their tasks. You will also search for them."

"What? Isn't that a job for...you know, more scouts?" Chris made a face. "Also, don't you mean Penny too?"

"No, I'm afraid your partner has not been listed for this mission.

Delta One is a Tank and would slow you down. Time is of the essence."

"Okay, fine, but..."

"If you're worried about getting rest, the ground operation has been pushed back one day due to sandstorms. I understand you don't want to do this, but I need your confirmation that you've received the message." Evangeline told him as she turned her head to face the camera.

"Yeah, yeah. Okay." Chris grumbled to himself. "What happened to the scouts?"

"We haven't been able to get in contact with them over the last forty-eight hours. You will need to check out their last known where-abouts. I don't think I need to tell you a measure of caution is needed. Advisor Evangeline out."

"Wait, you haven't told me-" Chris stopped mid-sentence as she shut off the call. He turned to face Penny, who nodded to him. "She always hangs up on me!"

"You'll be fine. Just be careful. If something happens, I'll be right behind you, orders or not." Penny told him. "Let's head back to the room, okay?"

"To wash my face?"

"So you can rest beforehand, and so we can talk," Penny told him, grabbing his hand without further input from Chris. She then pulled him toward the exit.

# 4

## SIMPLE SCOUTING MISSION

"_And so because of this, those are your objectives. You can't waste any time," Emily's voice spoke loud and clear through Chris's watch. The blue and grey Alliance dropship that had brought him here lowered him as close as it could to the dunes below; the engine's exhaust sent sand flying to and fro. Chris leaped out and slid down the dune he had landed on and then took in his surroundings: dunes for miles. The dropship took off as he waved to give them the all-clear. "Any questions?"

"So I'm supposed to scout out what the enemy has to stop us from landing, hack targets that you tell me, and find the missing scouts, right?" Chris responded as he observed his surroundings, the heat waves causing distortion a few feet in front of him. "That doesn't sound hard."

"That's right, good job, Chris!" Emily praised. Truthfully this embarrassed Chris more than anything despite being the only one who could hear her.

"I'm supposed to wander around the dunes and hope to find something here?" Chris asked her as he raised his hand up to block the sunlight coming from the horizon. "That doesn't seem like a good idea."

"No, you're going to get a general idea of where to go from me, but from there, you'll need to find the targets. Daytime is only four hours, so you need to hustle." Emily's voice took on a grave tone as she said this. "No playing around. I don't want you out there at night. Move quickly. It is also important that you avoid any form of combat or engagement that could-"

"I'm not afraid of the dark, Emily," Chris interjected.

"You should be. Did you not read up on this planet like I told you to? The demons-"

"Here we go..." Chris continued walking through the desert while half-listening

"Christopher-" she started to go into a rant.

"Gotta focus, Em..." Chris told her. She worried way too much in his mind. He was capable at this point, not perfect, but still capable. "So, uh. Where am I going? They dropped me off in the middle of the desert."

"It was just to ensure that you wouldn't be spotted by any Imperial patrols. Head east from your current position, and you'll find New Hope city. You'll find one of our missing scout's last known location on the way. From there, you'll proceed to the city and your first target."

"Okay," Chris responded as he broke into a light run. For a moment, he went down on all fours to climb up the large dune in front of him before reaching the top and sliding down on his side.

"Listen carefully, okay? At night there are these creatures called demons that will come out and attack anything without an extremely bright light to ward them off." Emily paused for a moment. "They have thermal vision, so they can likely see you before you see them and are smart enough to ambush you in groups."

"I'll deal with them-" Chris responded without thinking, only to be met with a loud 'no.'

"I don't think you'd be able to, Chris."

"Why not?"

"The people who live on this planet are killed by them frequently. We lost a partner group to them last night, and I honestly feel like that's what happened to our scouts." Chris didn't respond to this, but internally he was a little unsettled. "Be careful. It's not just the Imperials out there."

"Noted..." Chris mumbled.

After about ten minutes of wandering through endless sands, Chris was nearing New Hope city. As he ran, Chris noticed what appeared to be some sort of clothing lying in the middle of the desert. This was strange to him, and so Chris decided to investigate. Upon approaching the fabrics, he noticed that they were slightly red in color; although, their initial color was obscured by the blood. Chris knelt down and lifted what looked like a torn-up shirt.

"Em? Are you there?" Chris asked aloud as he pressed a few buttons on his watch.

"Yes, of course. Is something wrong?" Emily answered.

"I...I don't know what I'm looking at, but it looks like someone was..."

"Was?" she repeated.

"Eaten? Or-or maybe they took off their clothes?" Chris knew it was probably the first one, but part of him really hoped it wouldn't be true.

"Okay, I need you to look for dog tags," Emily explained. Chris began checking the clothes only to find a set of very much intact dog tags. He raised them to his watch and scanned them with it.

"Okay, coming your way." He told her. "Wayde Fenider. Was this one of the scouts? He has Alliance ID tags."

"Yes. He is." Emily answered after a minute had passed. She was speaking slowly, as if she was thinking. "Did he have anything on him, and is there anything that could lead you to a body?"

"I...don't think there is a body to find," Chris admitted as he stood up a little and looked around. No blood trail to be found. Whatever happened to this man occurred right here, and it could not have been pleasant. Chris started to sort through the left-behind clothes again. He was glad that he was wearing gloves like usual. Eventually, he dug out a black device that was flashing a location on repeat. Following his training, Chris dismantled it, took the thumb-sized chip, and let his watch scan it.

"Hey, Em?" Chris spoke again. "Looks like he was trying to send a distress signal to the other scouts. I've got one here that seems to have responded as of five minutes ago. It's moving."

"Yes, they're not far from you, but I suggest you move on."

"What?" Chris's voice raised for a fraction of a second before correcting. "Why?"

"I'm watching the signal move, and it's unnatural. You're going to be walking into trouble, so carry on with your mission. I'll have someone else check it out, okay?"

"Like hell. If there's a chance the other scout is alive, I'm going."

"No, you're not," Emily told him sternly. "Move on and get to the city. You're already wasting time, and you're going to need to do some climbing." Chris didn't respond as he stood up to look in the signal's direction, only for Emily to follow up one more time. "That is an order."

"Sorry, Em," Chris told her as he pressed a button to shut down the call.

"Chris, don't you dare-!" Emily's voice silenced as the watch on his arm informed him that the call had ended. He then tracked the signal to its source as fast as he could. There was a long trail as if someone was being dragged by someone else or something else. Blood could be seen along the trail, as well as a few shotgun shells. By now, he was right on top of the response signal's approximate location.

"That looks like them...I was afraid I might find this," Chris muttered to himself as he slid down another dune, his eye-catching a female body lying forgotten in the sand. "How did she get here?" he looked around warily in case he may be in any danger himself, but upon seeing nothing, he decided to approach. The woman wore attire similar to Alliance soldiers, but was doused in her own blood and covered in sand. She also appeared to be missing an arm from what he could tell, though he really didn't want to confirm this.

Reaching down, Chris removed one of her gloves and slid her sleeve up. Then he pressed two fingers to her wrist and sat there for a moment. *No pulse*, he said to himself. *Is she breathing...?* Chris tilted her head up and brought his ear close to her lips only to hear nothing at all, and if there was something, then it was so faint that he couldn't listen to it. He then checked her airway by opening up her mouth to look inside, only to see nothing there either. Chris tried performing CPR for two minutes before sitting on his knees, his jaw clenched as he did. A strained 'damn' left his lips.

"She doesn't even have her dog tags on her. Great." Chris said to himself as he brought up his watch's interface and pressed Emily's name.

"Satisfied?" Emily asked him.

"No," Chris admitted in a crestfallen manner. "She just died. I almost made it."

"You can't save everyone, little brother. I'll get someone out there to identify her, but you need to move." she reminded him. "You haven't got very long."

"Sorry," he told her, his voice low and frustrated.

"I understand why you did it, but I tell you these things for a reason. Are you okay?"

"I'm fine." Chris lied, his voice nearly a whisper. "I just can't get the image of her- she was missing an arm..."

"The wildlife on this planet is...interesting, isn't it?" Emily asked him with worry in her voice. "We weren't prepared for this. All the more reason to coordinate with the Resistance since they know this planet far better." Chris stopped just outside of the city and informed Emily of his location. "Okay, little brother. You're looking for an anti-air turret. It's automated, so don't worry about dealing with any Imperials. If you hack this one, every turret in this sector will target Imperial ships and planes when activated."

"Got it..."

"Chris, are you sure you're okay?" Chris ignored this question from Emily and entered the city. "Well, you're getting close..." she sounded concerned now. "It should be at the top of an apartment complex. You'll need to do some jumping."

"I figured..." he grumbled. "Okay."

"What's wrong? Oh- right, you hate heights. Better be careful then." Emily said shortly.

"Really now? Yeah, I'll get right on that." Chris stared up at a damaged, rusty exterior stairwell that ran upwards. The only way to reach it was to do a little magic. He jumped once, and at the height of this jump, he jumped again, his body performing a flip as he went higher. Then, using both hands, he pulled himself up onto the staircase and walked up like normal.

*Hey,* Penny's voice entered his mind loud and clear yet again. Even from the station, they were close enough for her to contact him.

*Hey,* he responded as he leaped onto a ladder and began to climb it.

*I just wanted to check on you. Something felt strange, so I thought something may have happened to you.* Penny explained. *Are you alright?*

*I don't know. I'll explain later.*

*Oh, okay. Tell me if you need anything. Emily is trying to keep the line clear to keep you focused, but she didn't say anything about partner link conversations.* Chris couldn't help but smile as Penny noted this, but it melted away again pretty quickly. *Anyway, I won't distract you, but whatever it was, I'm sure you're doing everything you can.*

*You know exactly what happened, don't you?* Chris asked her.

*I do,* Penny admitted before going silent. At this same moment, Chris reached the mostly destroyed rooftop of this building. In the center was a round device with a massive turret on top. One part of it had missile silos, and the other part had large guns. It rotated ever so slightly and beeped every few seconds.

"Hey, Em? I found the turret." Chris raised his watch to just below his mouth as he spoke. "Wanna walk me through this? It looks complicated, but I see an electrical panel."

"Don't worry, you don't actually need to do anything. Just take out the device that you were provided and attach it to that panel."

"Question?" Chris asked as he removed a flashing white device from his red jacket and placed it on the circuitry. "Why didn't they shoot us down last night?"

"I don't think you were in range of the turrets. It could be any variety of things, but if that wasn't it, then perhaps they didn't want to risk shooting friendly fighters. That's just a guess, though." Chris could hear typing on Emily's end.

"Can I remove it yet?"

"Nope, sit tight." She told him. "Patience is a virtue, little brother. Haven't you heard that before?"

"Only as many times as you've said it."

"It won't take long. The information we received on this was solid. So, I can just log into the turret- like I'm an Imperial." Emily seemed to be enjoying the 'sibling bonding time.'

"Uh-huh," Chris responded, admittedly half listening. He sat down on the edge of the building and leaned over a little. "Cool."

"Don't act interested or anything." Emily laughed a little when he blew air out of his mouth. "Okay. Nearly done. I just need you to remove the device in a second."

"Okay, but won't they notice if the turrets start firing before they attack?"

"Don't worry, they're only going to become Alliance turrets when the general activates the override. For now, we'll just avoid their range or shut them down."

"Oh, okay. Can I remove it yet?" Chris asked, his voice hinting at his boredom.

"Yes, little brother," Emily responded. He could tell she was shaking her head just by the tone of her voice. "You can remove it and stop asking me."

"Well, when you say it like that, I almost don't want to." Chris smiled to himself as he removed the Alliance hacker from the turret. A brief spark of blue followed as it was taken off. "I'm lucky I didn't get shocked just now..."

"Did you forget to hit the button on the side? That's a security measure."

"Thanks for reminding me," Chris muttered sarcastically.

"It's what I'm here for! Now head back to the- hang on. A distress call," Emily told him. "It's very faint. I actually just lost it, but it seems like another Wizard."

"Am I close?"

"Yes, but- they mentioned Imperials, and the sun is about to set." Emily paused; her finger sounded like it was tapping on a desk of some sort. "You get to the transport, alright? I'll go."

"No way, you said I'm close. I can make it, Em. Send me the coordinates." Chris begged. Turning, he leaped off of the building and let himself fall in a spread position toward the ground before landing on both feet, tucking and rolling. "Where?"

"...I'll send you the coordinates." Emily sounded conflicted, her voice lowering a little. "Listen, I'll dispatch the transport directly to you. Just...I can't promise that the demons will not reach you before I do."

"That's fine," he promised her.

"No, it's not." Chris could hear Emily standing up from a chair. "If the Wizard is not fit to move, you'll have to leave them. I am not losing you to those monsters. I'll be there in ten, do you understand? Ten minutes."

"Ten minutes." Chris echoed, his eyes trailing off toward the horizon and the sun lowering behind it. He took off into a sprint to locate his downed comrade. Chris wasn't sure if he would know this person, but regardless they were Alliance, they were a Wizard, and he failed to save two others. Someone was coming back with him.

Chris's boots sank into the sand as he climbed up one of the many dunes in this seemingly endless desert. A mole-like creature became startled from this sudden disturbance and burrowed to avoid him. His panting could be heard as he hurried off in one direction, his footsteps leaving a clear indicator all the way from New Hope as to where he had been. All the while, Emily was briefing him.

"Dion Lucetta is a part of a squad called Just Mother Nature. She's a damage specialist like yourself, and a mace wielder," she explained as Chris continued to sprint and nearly slip on the sand. "Together, you may have a chance, but without a Tank or Healer, the clock is ticking."

"Anything else?" Chris spoke through breaks in his breathing.

"She was injured by an Imperial Sorcerer, but she's healing up now. According to the call, she escaped from the confrontation. Dion doesn't believe our plan was compromised, but she doesn't think she can make it back to the transport."

"Roger."

"Listen, Chris...they're for you, but I placed some medicine in a vial. You'll find it in your jacket. It's meant to speed up fast healing and boost mana production. It'll tire her out, but you'll need to work together."

"Thanks, Em. See you soon. I'm coming up on her now." Chris explained as the call ended, the mechanical sound of a shuttle taking off could be heard on Emily's end just before the disconnect. In a small, flat area, Chris found Dion. She appeared to have light brown hair but could not fully see her facial features. She wore a long dark blue top with black bolt designs, dark blue leggings, and tan colored boots. She sat in the sand, holding her bleeding shoulder, which progressively made her top more of a pale blue color.

"Dion," Chris said, referring to her by name as he approached. He looked at her, but then back at the now darkening horizon as the pitch-black darkness began to develop the sky and the world around them. Dion jumped a little and made a move to summon her weapon, only for Chris to catch her wrist and lower it. "Calm down, okay? I was sent to find you. Command got your distress."

"Another Wizard? Oh, thank goodness..." she lowered her head, closing her gold-colored eyes as she did. A sigh escaped her lips before reopening them. "Help me up."

"Let me check you out first. Is it just your arm?" Chris asked, pulling her by her other shoulder to get a good look without hurting her.

"It's just a stab wound."

"No," Chris thought aloud. He'd seen something like this in his classes. "It's not. It's more than that. I think they poisoned you." Before Dion had a chance to speak further, Chris had already lifted his watch and attempted to call Emily back to receive no response from her.

"Advisor to Spellcrafter," was the answer that came instead as Evangeline's image projected from his watch, illuminating the darkness around them. "Your sister is inbound."

"I know, but I need your help. Dion was attacked with venom and I'm not sure what it is. Emily told me to give her a vial to boost her fast healing and magic, but I think that might kill her faster in this case, right?"

"That is correct. Do not administer the drug. It will speed up her heart, increasing the travel of the poison inflicted upon her. It is best if she does not heal fully until help arrives and tries to use her magic as much as possible." Evangeline's hologram looked directly at him, her expression stony and read like usual. "Do not attempt to leave your current position if you are going to protect her."

"So, we have to just fight and hope for the best?" Chris asked, concern littering this sentence. He looked up at Dion, who nodded. "Okay. We'll try."

"I have complete faith in your survival. You have just seven minutes until assistance arrives. I will, of course, be in contact if the situation changes. Advisor Evangeline out."

Chris lowered his head and shut his eyes for a moment. This was his decision, and whatever consequences came, he would take them. Regardless, there was a chance for both of them to survive this. He would just have to watch her. Chris reached in his jacket pocket and removed a small clear vial with blue liquid; after staring at it for a few seconds, he replaced it and took a deep breath.

"Are you okay to fight?" Chris asked her as he stood up and extended a hand.

"I'll manage," Dion answered, taking his hand with the arm that was not injured. He pulled her carefully to her feet. "Thank you for coming. I don't think anyone else would have responded. It was already getting dark, and you were the closest, so..."

"I wasn't leaving you," Chris told her as he flicked his right hand to the side to summon his green hilted sword. "Besides, I like our odds together."

"You have a cheery disposition considering the situation, but hey...I don't mind." Dion swung her arm around and clasped her hand around her mace. The purple and blue handle firmly in her grasp. She then cast her magic into the weapon, much like Chris did at times, and stood at the ready. Her weapon sparked and hissed with bright yellow lightning. "You don't just have one sword, do you?" Chris smiled and summoned his second blue sword for his left hand. "Figured."

"So, have you fought these things before?" Chris asked her as they backed up against each other. Both glanced around warily as the sand below and around them shifted ominously.

"This is my first time on the planet too. I imagine we're both going into this blind." Dion explained. "From what I read; these things regenerate."

"Regeneration-" Chris made a growling noise in his throat.

"Regretting your life choices already?" Dion asked

"Maybe a little, but so long as you and I make it out of this, I can give a definitive 'no.'" Dion laughed humorlessly as he said this and responded with an 'okay.'

"So," Chris continued, watching as the sand shifted and left trails under the surface that rose and fell. To them, it looked like sharks circling their prey. "Do-do you think they've spotted us yet?"

"I don't want to answer that," Dion told him as she backed up more against him. The sand below where her feet were placed sunk inward, revealing a pair of mangled hands which became buried seconds later. She placed both hands on her mace and shifted her stance. Chris readied both swords. His right hand was in reverse grip, and his left was being held in a standard grip. There was silence for a moment or two, and the only thing that could be heard in the night was their nervous breathing. Then, it happened.

"Dammit!" Chris bellowed as his right leg, was yanked violently into the sand. "Dion, something has my leg!" He tried to kick at whatever it was, but the weight of the sand around his leg made it impossible to do so. Just as he was about to panic, Dion's hand wrapped itself around his left arm and pulled. He was yanked clean out of the sand, and before he could even get to his feet, Dion had advanced on the hole where he just was. She pointed her mace downward and fired a bright bolt of lightning into the small abyss, likely killing whatever was down there with any luck.

"Stay calm." Dion reminded him. "I know it's hard, but we have to try."

"I am calm!" Chris responded as he tightened the grip he had on his swords. Truthfully, he was terrified and wished his squad were here. "What had me...?"

"Probably a goblin," Dion told him, her gaze shifting upward toward the darkness where multiple yellow eyes could be seen staring back at her. Too many to even fathom counting in the short time they had to prepare. Every second made it seem like a different set of eyes were blinking, so it was impossible to tell just how many creatures were in the darkness or where one ended and another began. "Oh geez..." she whispered. Even from here, Chris could tell she was shaking, but she still summoned her resolve and brandished her weapon. This was enough to inspire him to get to his feet and do the same.

# 5

# DREAD OF THE NIGHT

C hris dodged to his left, unknowingly drifting toward another demon lurking in the darkness in his attempt to avoid the first attack. A brilliant purple bolt of lightning shot through the night, illuminating the area as the attack hit home. The small grey and black goblin flew back into the dark, its body surging with electricity, but very much still alive. With the foe behind him dealt with, Chris turned his attention to the first demon. Two quick slashes with both swords to the large brute in front of him, and then a sidestep as a large wooden club was brought down into the sand where he just was. As the troll-like creature made an effort to lift its club and attack again, Chris took this opening to swipe at the creature once to knock it off balance, and finally delivered a critical blow by running up onto its leg. Springing from the creature, his foot came up and collided with the creature's chin, with his sword followed suit. A thud was heard in the sand as the head of this horrid creature rolled down, with the body following shortly behind.

Just behind him, Dion was backing away from another demon. This one had the appearance of a large spider. Taking her mace with both hands, Dion brought the weapon above her head and brought it back down, squashing the creature beneath the spikes of her weapon as black blood spilled from its body. Then, she placed her boot against the furry body and removed her weapon once again. Dion turned to move to the next enemy, her hand shifting from her weapon to her wound as she sucked air through her teeth. The mace impeded itself into the sand with a soft *thump*.

"Are you holding up, alright?" he asked her over the various growls and hisses around them.

"I'm still alive," she answered while panting heavily. "Pretty sure it's been more than ten minutes. Or I can't count anymore..."

"It has. I don't know what's taking Emily so long, but maybe they can't see us very well out here."

"I'm getting tired here," Dion huffed as she blasted yet another opponent with lightning, it's bee-like body flailing uncontrollably from the sudden current. "You might be fighting alone soon."

"Stay with me, alright?" Chris encouraged as he retreated back to her position. "We'll make it work."

"That personality will only get you so far. Still, it's keeping me moving."

"Don't tell her, but I think I may get it from Emily," Chris raised his arm and fired Ice magic at the shifty shadows coming toward them. "I wish she would hurry up, though. They're getting kind of close."

"What do we do if we get surrounded?" Dion asked him as the small circle of breathing space became smaller every few seconds.

"I thought you may have a plan."

"Uh- well. Not really, no." Chris shook his head. "I don't really know any good spells for this. If Ian were here, I'd just have him keep their attention." Dion turned her head to look at him, her facial expression clearly showing she didn't know who he was talking about. "He's one of my tanks."

"You're a squad leader?" Dion's mouth went agape for a moment before closing. "Never mind. I can see it," She shifted her shoes in the sand and squinted through the darkness. "Listen. I can knock a couple of them down for you and buy us time, but I might be out after that." As she said this, Dion knelt down for a moment to shake off a sudden rush of pain. The demons remained relatively passive for the moment, but it was likely because they were regrouping. Even in the darkness, Chris could see that some of these things they thought they defeated had regenerated and rejoined the fight.

"You don't have to do that," Chris explained, reaching behind himself to touch her shoulder. "Don't kill yourself just to buy time. That's pointless here."

"What's pointless?" Dion asked him suddenly, her voice slow and staggering between the two words. "Oh-right." she shook her head lightly and held it. "Right. The demons. Sorry."

"Dion, I need your head here. I can't do this alone!"

"I know. It's just tough to focus on your voice right now." Dion staggered to her feet, stepping backward and then forward again, her balance apparently thrown off. "Screw it." As she said this, Dion raised her mace to her eye level and slowed her breathing. Her weapon sparked and surged violently, illuminating the ground around them.

"You are going to drain your mana." Chris protested.

"I know!" Dion cried out as she powered the weapon up further. "Down!" she warned as she swung her mace around suddenly. Chris ducked in that instant and watched from the ground as three hundred and sixty-degree electrical waves traveled over him. The unseen demons were either injured or just outright fell back from this intimidating attack. Chris stood up slowly, a bit worried that there may still be remnants of the attack. As he did, he saw that she had indeed bought the two of them time. Even if only a few valuable seconds.

"That worked, Dion!" Chris cheered loudly. "Nice!" he paused after noticing Dion just lying on the ground, barely attentive. "Dion?!"

"I don't matter right now," Dion told Chris as her weapon sparked and hissed from the aftermath of that attack. "Wait."

"Dion, you used too much mana. How will you heal yourself?"

"Healing isn't important right now when I'm poisoned, and you know it." Dion reached out a hand for him to help her up. He took it and lifted her to her feet as best as he could. "I'm fine, Chris, but-" Dion paused, seemingly noticing the utter silence around them.

"What? What's wrong?"

"Where are they?" she asked once, very silently like a whisper.

"Where-" he began.

"Where are they?" Dion repeated, much more concerned than the last time. "Where did they go-?"

*Foosh!* The sand between Chris and Dion separated suddenly when a creature that had the body of a scorpion and a stinger resembling a snake crawled out. It had a black and green body that was somewhat shiny in Dion's very dim lighting. Chris scrambled to his feet, and after realizing that the surprise had made him lose one of his weapons, he flicked his hand and resummoned it. Around them, the Demons were regrouping, but this time they were a lot faster to attack. First priority: help Dion.

Chris moved to the scorpion quickly before it could attack Dion with its long-serrated tail resembling a mouth. He dashed forward, raising one blade in the air as he twirled and cut the creature clean in half from its bottom all the way down to its mouth. Then, once Chris had both feet on the ground and had slid a little in the sand, he prepared to fight once more. Dion couldn't really fight anymore, which was troublesome for him because that just meant he would need to fight harder. Placing one of his swords under his arm, Chris fished in his pocket for the stimulant that Emily had mentioned. It appeared as if it would be used for him anyway, which he found humorous in an ironic kind of way. Removing the vial once again, he unscrewed the top and dumped the blue contents of it down his throat. Not long after downing the fluid, his heart was racing, and his mana worked hard to heal his body.

"It regenerated!" Dion warned from behind him. Chris turned to raise his swords once again to deal with the scorpion before he was rushed by the other demons only to see it leaping directly at him, its small legs dangling in the air and its tail raised. He angled his left sword to block it, only to hear a familiar voice in his head warning him. *Don't stop it. Take the hit or dodge.*

*What? Why?* Chris asked. Though he was concerned, he lowered his sword anyway and turned to try and roll out of the way.

*Trust me. I read up on these Demons, and the scorpions typically carry corrosive venom. Your sword would be destroyed, but your body can take it.* Penny explained urgently. *We're having trouble finding you; just hold on a little longer.* It didn't take longer than a few seconds for his body to register the pain of the scorpion's venom eating through the skin on his left shoulder – it was a clear sign that he'd failed to avoid the attack. He screamed out and once again cut the creature down. Chris had no time to look at the wound, but he could tell that his jacket's fabric on his shoulder was eaten clean through as well as the shirt underneath. This wound would need to be tended to, but adrenaline could keep him going.

"Are you okay?" Dion asked him, pointing her weapon into the dark as she did. Every time her weapon sparked, faint shadows could be seen advancing toward them.

"Fine," Chris said through painful breaths, the stinging sensation transitioning to something more like a burn. As he said this, a demon with a lion's body and three snake-like heads approached. As it charged to snap at him, Chris sidestepped, delivered a great kick to its left side, and cut clean through the chimera. Then, in one motion, he brought the blade back up and through the body. *Starting to fight like her*, Chris thought to himself. Three more were coming toward him, but he didn't waste time trying to see what these things were. Instead, he extended both hands and slightly let go of his blades. An immense blast of snow and ice flew from his hands, sending them flying away and freezing them a little ways back.

"You can't keep that up," Dion warned him. Chris hunched over a little as she said this. Even now, he wasn't used to using so much magic at once. Typically, he would cast in short bursts.

"Look who's talking..." Chris groaned. "Can you fight yet?"

"I can try," Dion's tone was not very assuring.

*Bang! Bang! Bang! Bang!* Four Demons paused as an equal number of gunshots rang in the night. Then, after a few moments, they fell over and shriveled up without a trace that could be regenerated.

"The hell was that?" Dion asked quietly.

"...Someone who can help." Chris decided after some thought. He knew exactly who this was.

"Well. Well. I'm flattered that you can remember me just from my pistols," a voice responded shortly after. It was accompanied by slow clapping. "You seem to be in a tight spot. It's not every day that I stumble upon two Wizards who were dumb enough to stay out at night. Sohrann isn't a very nice planet."

"Tori, are you going to help or not?" he asked reluctantly.

"Where is she?" Dion asked. Chris could tell she was a little unnerved as she was looking around herself. "Who is this?"

"A friend of his." The disembodied voice responded. "Also of course, I am. I can't have you dying on me. That just wouldn't be very fun for either of us."

Chris turned his head quickly to his left. A female figure had appeared with a loud warping sound and shoved him to the left just as one of the demons launched a spiked projectile. Then, she turned and fired one of her pistols as they fell against the ground and damaged its inky body.

This newcomer had long flowy black hair, brown eyes, and what appeared to be a purple and black dress with frills flowing in the night air. The dress only came to her shoulders, but she also had articles of clothing that went with her dress on her wrists and a purple and black fabric headband. Eerily enough, she looked a lot like Penny now.

"So," Shadow Victoria began as she stood up and extended a hand for Chris. He took it hesitantly and was surprised by how easily she could yank him to his feet. "What's a little boy like you doing in a dark, scary place like this? Wanna tell me what this is all about?"

"I came here because Dion asked for back up. We have help coming, but they're having trouble finding us." Chris told her truthfully.

"Dion, huh?" she asked, her gaze shifting to Dion. "She's nearly dead, you know? I'm sure you could have survived alone "

"We know," Dion responded. She made a move to stand, only for Victoria to push her back lightly. She fished in the side pouch on the side of her dress and removed a small needle, then she stuck it into Dion's arm. "What did you just-"

"Now. Now. Morphine is always helpful. Sit tight." Victoria gave a sly smile as she stood and took up her pistols again. "You can fight if you won't get in the way, but otherwise, leave this to the healthy ones, yeah?" Chris could tell Dion was bothered by the condescending tone from Victoria but was at least a little appreciative.

"It doesn't matter how long we hold them off if they can't find us-" Chris made a face. "These things don't stop coming."

"Yeah, I know. I've been watching for a while, but I didn't decide to do anything until I noticed your help hadn't shown up. You Alliance types really do need to learn-" she pointed one of her pistols at a charging Ogre. A single shot went through where the heart should have been as it collapsed onto its knees and shriveled up. "You have to do your research before you come to a foreign planet. Not everything wants to play nice."

"I...can't even deny that." Chris shrugged.

"Now, as for your rescuers?" Victoria handed Chris her pistol and flicked her hand to the side, summoning an orange stick. She then snapped it, threw it to the ground, and watched as it illuminated and sparked. Red smoke was also emitting from the device.

"A flare?" Chris questioned in disbelief. "Why do you have a flare?"

"You can never be too careful, and it wards these things in a pinch. Now-" Victoria's lip curled as she extended her hand. "I'll take that back, thank you. I will need it to save you and your damsel."

"I can fight." Dion's voice sounded exasperated, but she was back on her feet all the same with her weapon in hand.

"Well, good for you. I've got one more flare before these monsters are on top of us. Honestly, simple light, and they back off?" Victoria blew out air from her lips as if amused.

"Shouldn't you worry about yourself too?" Chris asked. "You aren't coming with us, are you?"

"No, I'm not. Thank you for the concern, but these things don't really phase me. Unlike you, I don't have to be afraid of the dark." Victoria paused and active the flare, this time white in color. As she did, her thin smile could be seen. As soon as she knew it was ready, she tossed it to the ground along with the other red flare.

"How long have we got?" Chris asked her kindly as he could.

"Your ride has already spotted you, so I wouldn't get all worked up." Victoria pointed a finger at the horizon as a large hovering aircraft flew quickly toward them. Bright lights were emanating from the front of this vessel as well as the bottom. What appeared to be flashlights could also be seen from the right side. "Shame. Guess we don't get to dance."

"Wait, Tori?"

"I wish you wouldn't call me that, but yes?"

"How do we kill these things?" Chris asked earnestly, his swords lowering toward the ground.

"I'd like to know too," Dion admitted.

"Wizards asking about killing? My my." Victoria holstered her guns on her hips. "It's the exact same way you kill anything with regenerative abilities," Victoria shot one of the more humanoid demons in the distance. It appeared to be a shot through the heart, just like the last few. "You go for their blackened beating hearts and check things off from there."

"Makes sense," Dion shrugged and sighed. "I'd thank you, but part of me doesn't want to."

"Well, that isn't very polite. And here I was feeling charitable..." Victoria raised a hand as the luminous lights of the Alliance troop transport obscured their vision. The gentle whizz of the ship's engines was interrupted by gunfire as soldiers who were dangling from the right side opened fire. Their bright flashlights illuminated the patches of darkness as they circled them twice over.

"Drop the countermeasure flares!" Chris heard Emily order loudly.

"Yes, ma'am." The pilot responded as bright orange and yellow light sources ejected from the transport and littered the ground.

"Save your ammo, boys." one of the soldiers ordered. This most likely was their captain. "No need to kill em all. Just pick off the important ones."

"Penny," Emily began over the gunfire. Penny turned her head to acknowledge her. They were both standing inside of the transport and holding onto the ceiling straps. "Get down there and secure those two." Penny nodded and leaped from the circling gunship, performing a flip before touching down and going straight for Chris and Dion.

"Penn?" Chris questioned, a little surprised that she had come along.

"I did tell you I'd be here," Penny reminded him as she ushered them toward where the transport appeared to be coming down. However, upon noticing that Dion was so injured that walking was a miracle, she took her left arm as Chris took her right.

"Watch your fire, boys." The captain, who sat in the middle of this squad, lowered his weapon from its aimed position. They wore blue and white combat gear; with white helmets with light blue, glowing visors that barely showed their eyes. "Get in here!" He called out to them. As they approached this sizable blue and white Alliance ship hovering just above the ground, Emily disembarked and walked past them. Chris opened his mouth to speak, but she passed right by them.

"Come on, kid," the commander said from behind her as he and the other soldiers stood to a crouching position and assisted Dion onto the shuttle. They had to turn her around, take both of her arms and gently pull her up, while Chris and Penny pushed her legs. "Hey, Joker? Assess her injuries and relay them to home base."

"You've got it, captain," the soldier to his right nodded and stood up, his red cross clearly visible on the right side of his armor. "Go ahead and sit there, kid."

"She gave me morphine..." Dion managed before blacking out. Chris assumed this was because she realized she was safe now and relaxed for a bit too long.

"What about Emily?" Chris asked the captain, who extended a hand to both he and Penny as he said this.

"She'll be back," the captain assured as he pulled the two of them up effortlessly. Chris nearly fell because it was a very high step up, but regardless they were safe now. He turned and stared at Emily, who was face to face with Victoria. The two of them stayed like that, their clothes flying in the wind caused by the troop transport. They appeared to be talking, but Chris couldn't hear much of it. Whatever it was must have rustled Emily's feathers because the next thing he knew, Emily had summoned her weapon in straight sword form and brought it to Shadow Victoria's neck.

Victoria took a step forward, unphased by this empty threat. Emily's grip seemed to loosen even from here.

"You can't do it, can you?" Victoria's voice came suddenly over the howl of the wind and the hum of the engine. Emily kept her weapon in the same position but didn't reply. "Hesitation? That's not like you from what I hear."

"If you hurt my brother, I will kill you." Emily declared a very determined expression on her face.

"I saved him. A simple thank you is customary, isn't it?" Victoria called out to Emily, who had now turned and was stomping back toward the shuttle. Chris extended a hand for Emily to use, but she climbed up into the vehicle without any help, leaving him to slowly lower his hand out of embarrassment.

"Oh, and don't forget, your little brother there still owes me." Victoria's eyes cut toward Chris. He quickly looked away, feeling uneasy and troubled by their interaction, but understanding why Emily reacted the way she did. Once she was on board, the captain gave the pilot a thumbs up. The pilot did the same and lifted the craft up and away from the ground, leaving Victoria alone with the flares dying out. Chris poked his head out from the ship as he sat down in one of the many seats attached to the metal walls. He could see her calmly walking away from where they were and into the darkness...the demons did not attack her. They didn't seem to want to...

Chris's thoughts were suddenly put on pause, interrupted by a smaller gentle hand interlocking with this. These hands were gloved, but all the same, the warm feeling put him at ease. Looking over to his left, he found Penny staring at him from her own seat. The doors around them closed and left the interior completely black, but after a few seconds, the dim lights kicked in above them. He could barely see Penny now, but even so, he could make out her face; it was a mix of concern and relief.

"-General. I'll have an update for you when I arrive back at my quarters. I'll contact you again. It seems things are becoming more complicated on the planetside." Emily said in a hushed voice. She used her right arm to hold onto the ceiling strap and her left to press an earpiece. She nodded, assumedly meaning that the general had answered. "Understood. Speak soon." Chris's attention drifted to Emily as he overheard part of what she was saying. For a moment, he just stared at her despite clearly seeing she was facing away. She appeared shadowy in the dim lighting, but her similarly colored hair was still effortless to make out.

"Are you okay?" Emily asked him suddenly, her head turning slightly to look over her shoulder.

"Yeah." Chris nodded his head as he said this. "Thanks." Emily's eyes locked in on his injured right arm.

"Can you even feel that?"

"What?" he asked. "My arm?" Chris reached up to touch the spot where a hole was burned clean through his clothes and skin. Only just now did he notice that bone could be seen. "Not...really..." Emily tightened her grip on the strap and turned away.

"Okay," was her response.

"Will Dion be okay?" Chris asked the soldier beside Dion. She was currently lying down on a hovering stretcher.

"Yeah, of course. Dion was lucky this time... fortunate." the soldier known as 'Joker' explained. He lifted a tablet, which he was holding in his left hand. "Essentially, during her fight with the Sorcerer combatant, she was stabbed one good time in the arm. This was enough to disperse a poison you might be familiar with: hemo-toxin. It's common in some serpents but can be used on a magic-user to disrupt rapid healing facilities."

"So...what needs to be done?" Chris asked.

"Well, I can't do anything myself, but she'll be seen by someone who specializes in removing toxins. Likely a Life Wizard. Don't worry, she'll be fine, but she could lose a limb depending on how quick we get back." Joker told him, his voice raspy and mechanical in his helmet. "You did well keeping her alive in this sorry state."

"I had help," Chris admitted. "Dion held her own, but if Victoria hadn't turned up, I can't say we still would've been there."

"I believe you would have." Penny squeezed his hand hard suddenly, but not hard enough to hurt him. "I'm sorry we took so long. We were having trouble locating you from your last known positions, so instead, I took the controls for a bit and tried to sense where you were. That's when we found the flares." Penny placed both of her hands in her lap. "By the time the second flare went up, I had already found you."

"You can sense where I am already?" Chris asked her with a raise of his eyebrow. "But we're still practicing that."

"It was only faintly, and I kept losing it, but yes. I can't really describe the feeling."

"It's okay. I'm sure I'll understand eventually." Chris gave a smile as Penny nodded her head and agreed.

"Pilot, how long until we break orbit?" Emily asked abruptly.

"About four minutes, ma'am." He responded as the sky in the cockpit view rapidly turned dark.

"I'd recommend you grab a seat and strap in." the copilot told Emily. "It's going to be a bit bumpy in a moment."

Emily lifted her head, made her way over to the seat on Chris's right, and sat down. Penny reached up above her head and pulled down a harness that hugged her torso, thus locking her in place. As she did so, Emily had pulled Chris's safety harness down over him and then done her own. This, of course, caused her to receive an embarrassed look from Chris. Emily didn't really tease him this time. Instead, she reached up to ruffle his hair and then returned both hands to her harness to prepare for the sudden change in force.

"They're all locked in." the copilot said as he reached above his head and yanked a large lever forward. As he did this, Chris felt a massive force suddenly grip his body just like the last few times they went up into space; after a few minutes, this feeling subsided. "Setting an automatic course for Salvation."

"Shuttle 33-7B, please transfer clearance codes on this frequency," a female voice said over the comms as two fighters took up positions on either side of their ship.

"Copy. Transferring now. Lovely night on Sohrann, Ellen. You should see it. The wildlife was so active." The pilot chuckled as he pressed a blue button near the yoke. Then, he entered a long string of numbers before waiting for a response.

"Lovely, huh? Got a death wish there?" Was the response from her. "-And I've got your codes...you're clear for landing in hangar twelve."

"To be fair, we just got aquatinted with the local demon population. Lovely bunch. Be safe out here, Specter seven."

"Copy," the fighter pilot responded as she and her wingman pulled away from them and flew off somewhere behind them.

The ship moved toward the sizeable conal structure that was the station. To Chris, the station just looked like one of those top spinning toys from Earth that he used to play with. As they approached, more fighters and transports passed them, traveling to the General's ship or just returning just like them. When they got closer, the pilot disengaged the automatic guidance system and brought them in for a landing.

"Welcome back to Salvation station, boys. Your home away from home." The pilot announced as the vessel phased through the shielded hangar and brought them down for a landing. There was a man with yellow flashing lights signaling them on the dock. Seconds later, there was a soft thud as the engines powered down. "Thank you for flying air rescue."

"I want my money back," one of the soldiers joked as he unhooked himself and removed his helmet. The other soldiers burst into laughter, and even Chris thought he heard a little snicker from Emily. "Miss, I don't think I can survive another ride with him making puns all the time. Can I transfer?"

"I'm afraid not, James, but not to worry-" Emily stood up and smiled a little bit. "I'm sure he'll be easy to tune out over the sounds of battle."

"It's not that easy," James responded, standing up and moving toward the door. The doors on both sides of the shuttle flew open, and he as well as his squad departed. The only member left was Joker, who was carefully bringing down Dion on the hovering stretcher. He removed his armored tablet from his armor's chest area and pressed a singular button, causing Dion to float off beside him. Chris made a move to follow, only for Emily to shake her head and gesture toward Penny.

"Hope you feel better, kid." The pilot told him with a nod, watching Penny and Emily assist him in getting off. "If you're really her brother, you'll be fine. I've seen her take some nasty hits and shrug them off."

"Don't encourage him, please..." Emily sighed. "Here," she pointed just ahead of them at a stack of metal crates, which she ushered Chris toward. "Sit him down here for now."

"I can walk, you know." Chris rolled his eyes a little.

"Oh, really?" Emily asked as she let go for a fraction of a second, only for Chris to tetter backward. She regained her grip on him and continued walking soon after. "See? The shock hit you."

"I'm just a little tired," Chris insisted, but neither Emily nor Penny seemed to believe this as they made him sit down and stay put. "Really, I'm okay."

"Even still, let's get you looked at. Then you're resting, understood?" Emily asked as she turned to walk away. "I've got a few things to take care of before the operation, but Autumn should be here soon. I informed her about your situation before we left."

"I'm okay," Chris started. He attempted to stand only for Penny to gently push him back down. "I need to get ready for the ground landing, right?"

"You still have a few hours before then," Emily tried persistently.

"Em, I've rested enough..."

"That's an order," Emily told him very sternly as her head cocked back toward him. He jumped a little. "Understood?"

"Yes, ma'am..." he responded under his breath. He felt very uneasy at this sudden shift in her tone.

"Thank you..." Emily said in a far more relaxed manner.

"She's just stressed and worried about you," Penny reminded him quietly, her hand sliding onto his shoulder. "Don't take it personally."

"I know. I'm just not used to that."

"She has a lot on her. Besides, you're a handful and tend to get into trouble." Penny smiled down at him. "I should know."

"What's that supposed to mean? I can take care of myself!" Chris sat back against the crates and looked up at Penny, who just covered his eyes to mess with him.

"Aww, so you don't need me?" was her response. "We both know that's not true."

"I never said that." Chris pouted a little, only for Penny to lightly pop him in the mouth with her hand. "Hey!" she giggled and uncovered his eyes.

"Just cheering you up a little," Penny admitted, her heels tapping against the hangar floor. "...Like always." Her attention changed as the hangar doors which Emily had exited through reopened. "Here comes Autumn."

Autumn wore a red cloak and black boots; she also wore a red wizard hat and a golden ring on her right arm. Her curly hair fell to her shoulders and was always a signature way for him to single her out in a crowd. The moment she was close enough to speak, Chris tried to explain what happened to him, only for her to extend a hand. A soft white glow emitted from her hand, and a few shafts of light touched him and seemed to even penetrate his skin.

"Hurt again..." Autumn said to herself with a smile, a short laugh escaping her. "I've grown used to this."

"It's not my fault that there were---" Chris started but was soon interrupted.

"Scorpions," Autumn said lightheartedly with a kind expression. "You were fighting scorpions. Only arachnid demons have the ability to use acid from what I've seen."

"Have you been reading?" Penny asked.

"Somewhat? Grandfather always trained me to learn everything possible about a planet before landing. 'Be prepared for any situation' and all that." she lowered her hand and moved closer to take a look at Chris's arm. "You know, you should probably read up on the places you visit so you're prepared for the dangers, Chris."

"I learn as I go," Chris shrugged a little only to feel a very sharp pain.

"Stop moving." Penny reminded him.

"Don't be like Ian," Autumn smiled a little wider. "Are you always so distracted?"

"Uh..." Chris looked over to Penny only to blush and nod. "Lately, yes...sorry...."

"Mmhmm..." Autumn made a noise in her throat, and when Chris looked back, he could tell that her expression had changed to a disinterested straight face. She placed her hand over his arm and began to heal him, which gave off a golden color. Within a few moments, his injury had already started to regain feeling, and he could see his skin reforming. Bones also appeared to be repairing themselves. The feeling was actually quite tingly and relaxing. "Anyway, acid is a big no-no to Wizards. You need to watch yourself."

"She's right. I'll help you be more prepared. We already have to worry about the Empire," Penny began, kneeling down beside Chris as she did. "I don't need you injured or killed by planetary nature."

"This next part is going to hurt," Autumn warned Chris. "Like really badly. I'm just going to fix the nerves and then close your skin."

"You make it sound like it's not that bad!" Chris protested.

"Do you need me to hold your hand?" Penny asked kindly.

"Well-" Chris turned a bright shade of red. "I'll be alright."

"He does." Autumn corrected under her breath. Autumn made a low noise as if she was clearing her throat or showing disapproval. Her hands emitted a bright green light as she continued. As this went on, Penny took Chris's hand and squeezed. However, after a few minutes, the pain subsided, and it was around this time that Autumn was retracting her hands and standing up. Chris opened his mouth to speak, but Autumn turned on her heel before he could and started to march off.

"Autumn?" Chris called out to her. She stopped and stood still without turning around. "Thanks again! You're always so good at that."

"I try," Autumn turned her head a little, showing her partially hidden smile. "It's nice to be thanked."

"Plenty to thank you for!"

"You really are strange," Autumn commented. "I'll be seeing you." She said before her smile melted just a little. Then, she left.

"Now then, partner of mine," Penny began, emphasizing the word partner as she stood up and effortlessly pulled him to his feet. "I'd say you need to rest. Tomorrow isn't going to be very colorful."

# 6

## CALM BEFORE THE STORM

The constant gentle beep of hospital machinery filled the small room, which housed a medical bed and various tools. The reflection of a green haired young man sitting in a chair on the left side of the bed could be seen staring at the window. He wore a white bomber style jacket, a white and blue shirt, and jeans. Chris's eyes transitioned from the space-facing window back to the bed. For a split second, he thought he had heard Dion speak, but it was actually just a noise she had made in her sleep. He had come to talk to her and check to make sure she was okay, but whatever anesthetics that Dion was given had her out cold. Chris had been sitting here for about twenty minutes, hoping for her to wake up, but that would likely never happen while he was here.

His attention was drawn by the sound of the white sliding door. Chris could already sense who this was, but seeing her brought a smile to his face. Penny wore a remix of her usual attire. There were small spaulders attached to her shoulders, a large silver and brown belt that ran around her waist, but upon further evaluation from Chris, it was clear that this was armored. Penny still wore her skirt like usual, but underneath it was a pair of leggings. In a way, he honestly found her very attractive like this from an 'I can kill you without trying' sort of way, but really, Penny was harmless to him.

"It's almost time," Penny reminded him as she leaned against the door frame. "Are you okay?"

"Yeah," Chris nodded as he stood and turned to look back at Dion. "I was just hoping she might be awake."

"She's alive because of you and what you did. I'm sure Dion will thank you a million times when she's awake. If you want," Penny folded her arms and laid her head against the frame. "After the battle, we can come to see her if she's not already back on the ground."

"I'd like that, but I figured she'd be okay by now..." Chris mumbled.

"If a poison is allowed to fester in your system, you'll be in a terrible state. That's why some Sorcerers choose to sever the affected limb." Chris cringed as Penny told him this dark fact, and a thought occurred immediately after. "No, I never had to do that, Chris!"

"Oh, okay, good."

"I'd rather die with my limbs where they should be.'

"So you'd prefer to die to poison?" Chris asked as they left the room and proceeded down the busy hallway. "That's dark."

"Yes, but no one has to clean up the mess at least." she continued. "It doesn't really matter either way. I want to be cremated." Penny shrugged as they turned the corner and waited for the elevator at the end of the hall. Chris made a noise in his throat at this statement, which prompted Penny to punch his shoulder lightly. "Joking. Again."

"Your jokes aren't too funny..." Chris shook his head and entered the elevator with Penny. "Please be careful out there."

"I should be telling you that. I'll only be in danger if you are." There was silence after she said this. The floor numbers continued to count as the elevator chimed each level. The ride felt endless, and part of Chris hoped it would be.

"So, uh..." Chris tried before going quiet and sighing.

"Yes?" Penny pressed on. She stepped toward him and locked

eyes for a moment. They were about the same height, so this wasn't hard.

"Just...please be careful out there, yeah?" Chris reminded her awkwardly. Penny reached up and cupped her hands on his face. "I know you should be saying that to me, but now I'm saying it. I don't want anything to happen to you."

"So, you're worried?" Penny continued. She could try to pretend that she was looking directly at him, but her eyes were darting from mouth level to eye level every few seconds, and part of her wasn't really sure why. "I'm not."

"Of course, you're not." Chris continued as their faces grew closer. "I'm usually the one getting hurt, but we won't mention that time in the clocktower, right?"

"No, no, we won't," Penny agreed. She smiled and shifted her hands to his shoulders, which transitioned into her arms, coiling around his neck. Their faces close, and breathing slow...hearts beating, and unsure of what would happen next. As it happens, the elevator would decide for them.

"Arrived. Level-" the elevator voice began, but whatever came next was ignored since the two of them were entirely embarrassed. They had gotten off of each other and moved to their separate sides as the doors parted.

"Oh, hey, you two." the Alliance soldier standing before them said, his face hidden behind his helmet. Chris recognized the voice of the rescue pilot that came to get him. "Feeling better?"

"Oh, I-Yes, thank you." Chris cleared his throat and nodded as Penny exited the elevator without him, the moment ruined. The man entered the elevator and gestured at Chris to warn him that Penny had gone on. "Thank you...Sorry" Chris repeated as he moved out of the elevator, having to stop the doors from closing before he could get out. After escaping from this small room of awkwardness, he found himself back in the familiar tube that led to the hangar. Penny had slowed down enough for him to catch up, and together they entered the hangar. The lights were dimmed slightly, and a small group of

Wizards and pilots was huddled together staring at a clean holographic map.

"So, do we all understand the plan?" Violet asked her helmet under her right arm. "Ian, were you listening?"

"Honest answer?" Ian asked, a small laugh escaping from his throat.

"Yes."

"I heard the beginning parts, but after that-" he didn't get a chance to finish before Megan's elbow collided with his gut causing him to complete his laughing out loud.

"Ian..." she hissed. "This is important."

"You can tell me on the way. I'd rather hear it from you," Ian declared, his eyes drifting to the hangar's left side, where Chris and Penny had entered. "Besides, we have two lovebirds coming in late." The others in this group began to 'ooh' and talk amongst themselves, but a stern glare from Penny and the sound of Violet clearing her throat was enough to regain collective focus.

"Lovebirds, Ian?" Penny asked. She was genuinely confused from what Chris could tell, but he wasn't really sure why.

"You're late," Violet said simply, the holographic glow casting a shadow under her face. "Something more important?" Chris blushed and shook his head without a word. Penny did not feel the need to answer, as the plan was shared with both of them already. In fact, Emily had pushed Chris to memorize the entire battle plan 'just in case,' so even if he wanted to forget, he could not.

"Penny? Anything to add?" Violet pressed on over Chris's thoughts. "About why you missed the briefing?"

"My partner needed me, and I was there," Penny replied to her without looking. "If you have a problem with it, you can always take it up with Emily. Though, I don't expect you to since you know what the response will be."

"Well, if you get killed, I guess I'm going to have to." Violet snapped her fingers, ending the projection which appeared to emit from the ceiling. She was the first to walk off toward her plane, but not before yelling at the top of her lungs about how they had less than five minutes.

"All the same, I'd rather get my orders from my squad leader," Ian said a little louder than he probably should have. He wrapped his arm around Chris's neck and tugged. "I've got your back out there, buddy!"

"Agreed. This will be our first real conflict, so we will need precise orders-" Megan paused as if a thought dawned on her. "Right. Sorry. No pressure. I'm working on it..."

"Bit late!" Chris protested, his hands fruitlessly trying to pull Ian's muscular arms off of himself.

# 7

# THE BATTLE OF SOHRANN

The Alliance orbital station's hangars were filled with planes, shuttles, and tanks finishing up preparations for the attack. Heavily armored tanks were being loaded into the larger transports, soldiers were packed into shuttles, pilots leaped into their planes. They locked their helmets to their flight suits as their canopies descended. The first wave deployed quickly, launching out of the station's hangars and the General's capital ship, proceeding toward the surface.

"All phase two pilots, on deck!" the intercom blared. "Repeat, all phase two pilots, if you are not already, report to the hangars immediately!"

"How do you think phase one is doing?" Chris asked Penny. He climbed up the rest of the ladder, which was leaning against the Spark's wing.

"I doubt many of them will make it given the demons active this morning, but with any luck, it won't have been for nothing. They tend to linger when the sun is rising," Penny told him truthfully as usual. She took his hand and pulled him over her seat. Chris then sat down on his side and secured himself with the safety harness. Penny did the same and began activating the Spark's core functionalities.

*Knock! Knock! Knock!* They heard from the left side of the plane. One of the Alliance mechanics was standing on the left side. He placed both hands on either side of his mouth and called out to Penny. "Wheels up in two!" he yelled out. "We've detached the ladder! Go ahead and roll onto the ramp. They're getting hammered down there." The man then took a step back and started to move one of his arms in a circular motion and pointing with another.

"Here we go..." Chris said. He could feel himself becoming progressively nervous as the seconds dragged on. He was so deep in his thoughts and nerves that Penny had enough time to roll them onto the ramp and tap his shoulder to make sure he was okay.

"Are you still with me?" Penny asked, her voice filled with concern. "I can do this on my own if need be."

"No. I'm okay." Chris insisted. "This is too important - besides, I'd rather not give Emily ammunition to say she was right."

"I'll get us both back here in one piece, and then we can talk about what happened earlier," Penny told him with a smile. She gently knocked his shoulder with the back of her hands before reaching above her head. Chris nodded, instantly going from nervous and scared to calm and shy. "Rebreather."

"Right." Chris nodded, turned to his left, and opened the compartment that resided just between their seats to remove a black mouth-shaped device. He then placed it over his face and recoiled slightly as it attached to his face. A few seconds later, the rebreather gave off a soft blue glow to indicate that it was working. "I'm good," Chris told her, his voice much more mechanical and filtered than before. Penny did the same and gave a courteous nod as hers activated with a purple color. On the canopy, their vital signs and breathing rates appeared together, along with their names. He couldn't wait to reach the surface and remove this uncomfortable device.

"Cornellius?" Penny asked him as she continued to mess with the controls. "Run a quick diagnostic to make sure we're okay. I don't want to get into space and find out something is wrong because my co-pilot didn't do the repairs."

"You're implying that Chris does repairs correctly?" Cornellius replied in a dull tone. "Oh. Alright, then."

"I'm implying I trust him more than anyone else."

"That's a mistake" Cornellius paused as a buffering symbol appeared on his screen. Penny gave his screen a quick smack as retaliation. Seconds later, he appeared once more as his smiley face image. "Ninety percent."

"Only ninety?" Penny growled under her breath. "Dammit. Chris what did that mechanic-"

"That's not too bad. It's better than that one time when the engine shut off on us." Chris began.

"I don't want anyone to fix this plane other than you or Hourev. They always do this." Penny protested. She regained her focus when the lights ahead of them flashed yellow and their platform began to vibrate. "Please fix it later?"

"I will," Chris promised. "Once...I figure out where that ten percent is. I may need to ask Hourev for some tips."

"We'll worry about it later," Penny took a deep breath, which was made much more apparent by her rebreather's filtered sounds. "Okay, here we go. Remember, we're probably going to be surrounded, but focus on the targets."

"All craft ensure that your data is synced with the station, so we can have full coverage," Violet's image appeared on their canopy for a fraction of a second before vanishing. Multiple aircraft names appeared on screen before shrinking to either side of the canopy, small enough to not get in the way, and following this, green markers were given to each of the planes in real-time. This made it nearly impossible to commit friendly fire and helped to avoid collisions, but also prevented splitting up.

"Launch!" a deep, commanding voice came suddenly as Penny fired the thrusters, and the Spark was propelled not only by itself but also by the launching pad. The wheels came up soon after as the stars surrounded them on all sides, as well as other planes and ships. From this point, all Penny had to do was follow the others.

"Bombers stay in formation. Fighters, you are going to circle and protect the bombers. Support and transports ships cover the rear." Violet reminded them over the comms. "We're sitting ducks already. Let's not make any pointless mistakes."

"Having a little trouble with my right-wing over here," one of the pilots said. On the canopy, it showed the pilot of this plane to be 'Blue Rose.' Chris peered out of his side of the aircraft to see them trailing smoke. They were flying almost right next to each other, so it was easy to see the damage.

"I have eyes on smoke, Blue Rose. You should pull back and get that checked out. Deploy with wave three." Chris explained over comms. "I think your engine coolant either wasn't replaced or is leaking. You would not survive atmospheric reentry."

"I have to miss all the fun?" was the response he received back. "Okay, I'll pull back. Thanks, Delta Two. Are you sure it's the coolant?" Chris watched as their plane ascended and performed a flip to turn around and head back to the station.

"Yes, I am. Turn around before your engine overheats."

"Well, look at you," Penny commented with a smirk as their end of the communication ended. Chris turned to look at her.

"What?"

"Nothing." Penny laughed a little as she made a slight adjustment to their flight path.

"No, tell me."

"You just know a lot about planes now. Hourev really did teach you a lot." Penny faced them toward the planet and followed just behind two of the lead planes labeled 'Dreamcharge,' which was Emily, and 'Slipstream,' which was unironically Violet's craft. The two of them flew far ahead of the others to guide them in, but Emily seemed to speed up and slow down based specifically on the Spark's position. She was keeping an eye on them again. Chris wished that she could just trust him with something.

"Beginning atmospheric reentry," Penny muttered to herself as she gripped the controls tightly. "Chris, are you strapped in?"

"I am," Chris answered while checking each flight instrument one last time.

"Copy that, Delta," a grizzled old voice replied over the coms. "Alright, everyone, remember to keep it tight and stay in formation. You all know your tasks, you know who you take orders from, and you know not to break off unless you're told. The bombers take priority: if they go down - I don't know what happens next."

"What about those fighters? If those hacked ground turrets try to hit them, they could hit us," a younger female pilot asked. "Just a thought."

"Stay well out of their way if you can; if need be, the order will be given to get on those fighters. The first step is to protect our bombers," Violet answered. "If you don't fly like an idiot, you'll be fine. They don't have the numbers to take us on for long."

The plane started to rattle and shake violently; flames enveloped them and made seeing outside impossible. A message popped up briefly saying 'comms unavailable.' The interior did not get hot at all. In fact, it stayed cool during the entire process. All the while, the two of them were forced deeper into their seats by the sheer force. Penny seemed to be making slight adjustments to their trajectory as they flew down. The flames stopped after a time, and the plane cooled its exterior. The other planes could be seen all around them in a tight formation with a few layers of puffy white clouds separating them. A notification popped up on Chris and Penny's canopy hud: follow the Slipstream. The black plane just ahead of them was marked with a large purple circle, and the word follow printed in small text below it. Penny moved to follow just as instructed. Just below them, the bombers soared.

"Bombers, get your payloads ready. We're going to be in range soon. Teams one and two go ahead and break off. Remember your targets. Your job is to keep enemy reinforcements from arriving and cut off their supply line." Emily ordered over comms. "Spark and Nighturge, move up with me.

"Moving up! Don't worry Em, you've got two aces behind you," Ian's image appeared on their canopy. Megan and Ian flew up alongside them as the two planes increased speed to match the Justice.

"Ian." Megan's voice silenced him almost instantly. "How are you two looking?"

"All clear. You?" Penny responded as she glanced over at Chris. He gave a nod to tell her that he also was picking up nothing.

"No enemies on the scanner. Strange." Megan muttered. "I expected a hornet's nest."

"All the same, don't let your guard down," Emily instructed them.

All was silent until Cornellius suddenly spoke out and broke the silence, "Enemy aircraft tailing."

Without any more warning, machine-gun fire broke the peace. The blue and yellow plane behind Chris and Penny was hit multiple times from above; the canopy glass was riddled with holes. The brown-haired female Wizard in the back was fine, but it appeared as if the Wizard pilot in the front was hit and judging from the blood that was now painting the glass, pretty badly. The young man slumped against his controls, their plane veering off entirely from the group and falling in a nosedive toward the ground before vanishing through the clouds. The female pilot in the back screamed out, but moments later, there was silence as a fiery explosion took place below.

"They're gone!" Ian called out over comms. "We've got fighters, but I don't see them!"

"I've got two here." Another pilot said. "No, wait, three! Ah-!" Static followed.

"Break, break now!" Violet called out as she yanked her plane upward to avoid a missile that narrowly missed her wing.

"Draw them away from the bombers!" Emily told them, referring to rather sizable planes and shuttles flying just below them. Penny suddenly gripped the controls hard and forced them into a hard right turn. Soon, Chris realized why as two fighters soared overhead and came close to a collision with them. He turned the belly gun on them and opened fire, just narrowly missing the one farthest to the right.

"Are they crazy?!" Chris questioned.

"No, we were in their way." Penny corrected shortly as she changed their direction. "Violet, they're headed for the bombers. Can you see them?"

"I see them. Meet you there." Violet answered back. "Hey Hal? You and your boys have company! Make sure your guns are scanning the skies!" Violet said. Penny steered them back on course and dove down after the fighters who were swarming the bomber formation. Chris could see them flying around the much larger planes like an angry hive of bees.

"Where? I don't see 'em-" Hal responded. However, he stopped answering once the lead bomber was stuck in the right engine by two missiles. The wing separated from the body as it spiraled out of control and sank to the ground.

"Hal?" Violet questioned. "Hal, you better be alive. You still owe me."

"I'm alright. Losing altitude and - bail out!" His line on the comms went grey before vanishing entirely from their canopy.

"Violet, watch your rear!" Megan cried out. The Nighturge soared overhead and shot down an Imperial fighter, which was headed straight for her. "Ian, they're still chasing."

"Pulling away to help." Penny declared.

"No. Focus on the bombers," Ian said as he and Megan soared by.

"Ian, I have this." Penny increased the throttle and allowed them to climb a few feet before attempting to line up a shot. Chris peppered the planes in pursuit of the Nighturge but he could do no good from this distance without accidentally hitting Megan and Ian. "You've got two on you. Turn left on my signal. I'll be coming from above."

"Penny, the bombers." Ian continued dodging his plane as much as possible.

"Turn, Ian!" Penny shouted.

"All I'm seeing are enemy fighters and none of ours-!" one of the bomber pilots said over comms. "Could really use some support!"

Ian turned hard as a volley of rounds clipped into their cockpit and left wing. Penny opened fire, and Chris fired two heat-seeking missiles. Penny shot down the plane nearest to the Nighturge, and Chris destroyed the one furthest away. One of the fighters exploded while the other spiraled out of control toward them. Penny and Chris ducked down as she performed an evasive maneuver, but even so, the ashen body of the fighter slid over them and screeched along the metal. The sound was terrifying to Chris, but he willed himself to sit up in his seat once Penny had done the same.

"The Spark's hull capacity is at eighty-five percent, and the far-right engine is at twenty. Beginning automatic repairs." Cornellius told them. An artificial sarcastic slow clapping sound concluded this statement. "Nice flying, Dreadful."

"If he says another word, mute him." Penny sounded irritated. "Ian, Megan, are you okay?"

"They're smoking," Chris told her with a pointed finger. Penny flew closer to check on them. "Are you two, alright?"

Penny spoke warily. "...Cornellius, open a video link."

"Opening a direct channel." Cornellius only needed a few seconds to bring up two cameras of Megan and Ian side by side. Ian was unconscious with his head slumped against the glass but seemed mostly unscathed, and Megan was still with them. However, she was breathing hard and holding both her right arm, which was extensively bloody, and her chest, which appeared to have been hit directly as well. On her face, she had cuts presumably from glass and an impact wound on her forehead.

"Meg, you guys don't look so good." Chris started. "You should head back."

"We're okay," Megan sucked in air through her teeth, her hands glowing green as her wounds started to heal. "Get back to the bombers. I'll have Dara autopilot for a while until Ian wakes up. Dara? Ian is out. Can you pilot."

"Autopilot engaged! I do hope he's alright," their AI responded.

"We'll stay with you." Penny decided, but as she said this, a bomber just below them detonated and sank downwards, falling apart as it did. From here, they could see small specks, which appeared to be the crew bailing out. Multiple fighters were swarming around them, but none seemed to fire on them directly. All the while, the other bombers continued toward their target, firing their guns and staying in formation for protection.

"No, go ahead." Megan sat up slowly, wincing from what could only be incredible pain. "Dara, get us higher and out of the fight. Defensive flying. Also, run a diagnostic. I'm climbing to the front to tend to Ian."

"Affirmative." Their AI responded. The Nighturge flew higher into the clouds to avoid conflict and appeared to back off for a while. "No enemy fighters are pursuing at this time. Beginning diagnostics."

"Heading toward the bomber formation-" Penny said in a very dark and bothered tone. "Coming from above." A few moments later, they were flying deep in their bomber formation of about fifty planes, weaving in and out to protect them. The dogfighting continued above, but the priority had to be the bombers. Once they had landed a clean hit on the enemy defenses, it would be a reasonably easy march onto the Imperial base.

"I see more coming in toward our bombers," Emily said over the comms. Chris could see her plane, the Dreamcharge, leaving the bombers to engage.

"I'm with you," Penny responded, her eyes darting from Emily's image on the screen to the open sky. "Chris, are we good? I don't know if we've taken any serious damage." As she said this, Penny launched a missile from afar and scored a hit on an enemy.

Chris swapped back to the interface, which would allow him to control the rotating belly gun. "Yes, but I'll keep watching. For now, though, we're flying fine."

"Okay, going in. Be ready." Chris nodded to inform Penny he understood. He then slid his finger up to activate the rear guns and take manual control. Behind them, the machine gun looked up and focused dead ahead.

"Be sure to keep your speed up, Emily. We can't let any of those Imperial Burst Fighters catch us off guard. They'll tear us both apart." Penny reminded Emily. "If there are any good pilots, they will pose a threat."

"I'm not really worried about them," Emily answered shortly.

"Even so, I'm just warning you," Penny explained. "It would only take one burst to tear through either of us."

"Okay," Emily paused before speaking again in a more uncertain voice. "...Is Chris okay?"

"I'm okay," Chris answered himself. "Penny is flying, after all." He gave a thumbs-up, which warranted a small smile from Emily. Chris couldn't tell if it was real or just her trying to hide her concern again. "Let's get in there, Penny."

Penny nodded and placed her hand on the throttle to increase speed once again. They were now going so fast that Chris could not sit up, but he could still reach his controls. Penny turned slightly to avoid enemy fire and then again to dodge gunfire coming from below. Upon looking out of the canopy, Chris noticed they were flying upside down relative to the planet. From here, he could see a violent ground battle raging on, endless sands, and bombs dropping on a helpless enemy base lying in the middle of it all.

Metal trenches were created seemingly randomly around this fortress, and it was not hard to make out the battle lines. Soldiers crawled out of the trench from the Alliance lines and charged forward, and although some were cut down, most made it into the next trench and began to take it over. He only looked away when a bright yellow flash erupted to the far right and sent sand everywhere. It happened multiple times as the bombers passed over and even hit a few trenches on the way.

"Confirmed hit on Imperial fortifications! We're pulling out!" a bomber pilot told them all. "The rest is up to you guys! Returning to orbit."

"I'm looking at the destruction now!" Chris said over comms. "Good job!"

"Keep the fireworks going for us, would you, Spellcrafter?" the pilot continued. "We'd like the party to keep going once we're gone. I'd hate for this masterpiece to be ruined by a loss."

"You bet!" Chris replied. Penny lowered her head slightly as the fighting continued. She was thinking about something.

"What's wrong?" He asked.

"This is just going too well," Penny admitted as she leveled them out, yet another enemy fighter exploding from her attacks just ahead. "Small numbers or not, they should be putting up more of a fight. Stay alert, okay?"

"Got it." Chris nodded. He trusted Penny, not only because she was his partner, but also because she would know better than most as an ex-Imperial. And more than that, Penny was the Emperor's daughter.

"Delta," Evangeline appeared on the canopy. Figures could be seen rushing to and fro behind her. It was as much chaos there as it was planet side. "New orders from the general. You're going on foot once a majority of those fighters are eliminated. Your squad mates from Echo will join you soon after that."

"Any particular reason?" Chris asked.

"Delta One's tanking abilities will assist in the efforts to push the fortress, and once inside, she may be able to provide insight on the interior situation and Imperial tactics. It is much the same for Echo one."

"Understood," Penny answered, diverting the Spark toward the ground. "What are our orders on the ground?"

"The orders are simple so I can't tell you how to do your job, but I do recommend you act as a guerrilla unit to ambush the enemy. Reach the fortifications at all costs and aid the Alliance forces on their way." Evangeline explained like she was staring at a map. "If possible, rescue what remains of a squad that should be on your way at this location I just marked." a marker appeared on the ground with a flashing green circle. "They're getting surrounded and need help urgently. I'll update your objectives as needed. In the meantime, I'll just be watching your progress."

"Got it." Chris shrugged and glanced out of the canopy once again to look at the vicious ground battle.

"I'd rather you two come back in one piece, so do what you can and forget what you can't. You've got an hour until sundown. I suggest you either reach the objective or extract before night falls. Good luck." Evangeline cut the line, but the objective marker she set remained and a list of objectives.

"There's nowhere to land down there," Chris said as he removed his breathing device. He was scanning the ground with the under-belly gun camera to find a safe place, but there were only trenches or long stretches of gunfire. Some zones were just wild west firefights with no clear winner at all. Penny directed Cornellius to take over flying and assist the ground forces as best he could and 'not wreck their plane.' She then started to unhook herself and slow the speed of their craft. Chris unhooked himself and popped the canopy, and watched it slide back, the hot desert air blowing in their faces. They would not be able to communicate verbally over the howling winds, but luckily they didn't need to.

*Climb onto the wing*, Penny told him mentally. *The skies are clear for now, and since the turrets lining the perimeter are ours, I'm not worried about getting shot at trying to jump. Let's take our time. We'll go for a trench and work our way forward from there.*

Chris stood up in his seat, climbed over the side, shimmied onto the right wing, and grabbed onto the edge. He was unable to stand up like Penny was on the left side. She crouched down and held onto the front of the wing, while Chris hung on and lay flat on his stomach. When Penny said, he would let go, but not a moment before. This was absolutely terrifying. Not only were they dropping at speeds faster than usual, but they were also going into a real warzone for the first time. Needless to say, he was running on autopilot himself.

*Jump!* Penny's voice sounded in his head, and as she said it, his fingers unlatched from the Spark. He watched as it soared away high and above and then cut his vision down to see Penny a few seconds from the ground. She hit the dune feet-first and slid down straight into the Alliance held trench. He did the same, stumbling a little as the rolling sand carried him down, but was ultimately caught by Penny waiting at the bottom inside of the dugout path.

"Are you alright?" Penny asked, her gloved hands brushing sand off of him. "Other than being a little dirty."

"If I say no-" Chris began with a half-smile. Penny rolled her eyes and turned away, making her way past squads of Alliance soldiers rushing to change position.

"We're in a war zone right now, but if we weren't?" she stopped to look at him and beckoned Chris to follow. "I'd answer that question happily. Now come on- and keep your head down. These trenches are deep, but that doesn't mean they can't hit you," Penny moved her head in such a way to gesture at the walls, which could have been four or five meters high.

Chris and Penny made their way through the winding trench until they could go no further. They were forced to use the stairs to exit near the very edge of the trench line. From here, they could move into the open sands. Gunfire whizzed to and fro seemingly at random, with the occasional flash of plasma discharging from a specialized rifle. Soldiers dashed from cover to cover and hopped over and into trenches. Craters littered the sand with bodies lying inside, both mangled and un-mangled, and shouts were heard from either side. Occasionally a Wizard could be seen melee fighting a Sorcerer alongside their partner. Sometimes they win, sometimes they were killed, and others were just shot in the middle of their duel by the advancing soldiers on both sides. There were medical responders dragging forces from both sides into trenches or behind dunes to tend to them.

*The Imperials are stalling,* Chris thought to himself. *All they have to do is hold back our assault until night falls.*

"Chris," Penny said suddenly as they looked out over the battlefield. "No matter what you see, you need to stay focused, okay?" Chris could only turn to look at her in confusion. "We need to get up there, and there's no time to stop." Penny crawled up and over the dune in front of the trench and slid down with her shield raised. Chris followed her, dodging gunfire not intended for them as he did. A hand coiled around his ankle and pulled to keep him in place. Upon turning, Chris realized that it was an Alliance soldier bleeding to death from his stomach and lying on his back, staring at the sky.

"Can't help him," Penny told him. "Keep moving."

"Yeah, but-"

"Megan isn't with us right now, and I have nothing to draw from to heal his injuries. I bet there are medics up ahead, so if they left him, it was for a reason."

"Can't I stay and comfort him?" Chris tried as the soldier's grip loosened to barely even touch.

"Not right now." Penny stepped back as a grenade tumbled down toward them. Her foot moved before he could even think of what was happening. The grenade flew up and away into some barren part of the battlefield not too far from them, the explosion sending shrapnel and hot sand everywhere. She raised her shield just in case some of that might come back on them. Penny took Chris's hand and forcibly pulled him into cover alongside about seventeen other Alliance soldiers trying to stay low behind a portable metal barricade.

"W-who's in command here?!" Chris asked the group over the sounds of battle.

"I think you are now, sir." The soldier, on the far right, responded. "Our squad leader was killed leaving the trench; we tried to help him but had to leave him behind. I don't think we can stay here either, but every time we try to move, they light us up!"

"Do any of you recognize where we are in relation to the base?" Chris continued on. This time the medic to his left responded.

"Right where we're supposed to be just before the tank line and the Imp base. No one else is, though! They're all back there!" he cried out as he sat up to point as far back as he could. "The few that did push up got cut down by the enemy tanks and machine guns. Then their Sorcerers are up there too! We can't go anywhere."

"Where are our tanks?" Chris asked the advisor using his watch. "Advisor?"

"Wave two tanks are pushing up but have no way to advance with so much anti-armor ahead. You'll need to take them out." Evangeline responded on his watch. She was clearly still listening in.

"...Ah!" Chris grunted in frustration and turned to look at Penny on his right. She just stared at him, calmly as if the situation was under control, and she was under no stress.

"Okay..." Chris covered his head and slid backward to avoid gunfire traveling overhead as well as what appeared to be fire magic. "Okay, so medic I want you to head back and get your squad leader back to the trench!" No response. "Medic?!" Chris rolled over to look to his left only to find the medic's face was burned to a crisp to an unrecognizable degree, his helmet and face mask burned off completely.

"We can't sit here." Penny reminded him. "They won't move up until we do." As she said this, her right hand flicked to the side to summon her small sword. "I'll help us move up."

"Okay," Chris responded, his mind unable to unsee that man's face. He slid down the small sand mound and began to speak to everyone around him. "Okay, listen up! We need to push up, overrun those trenches, and stop sitting here waiting to die. So, um-" Chris racked his brain, trying to think of a plan.

"Form up on me and use my shield for cover. I'll cast a spell to move us up. Pick off any stragglers we pass to make way for the rear." Penny ordered. She then lifted her watch to talk to the company just behind them. "The rest of you push up when we do! If you stay there, you're dead anyway. The best chance for survival is forward."

"Hell yeah." the soldier to her right responded. *Maybe she should give the orders*, he thought to himself. What was he supposed to do? Penny was the one keeping everyone together while he struggled to figure out what was going on.

"Chris, you lead, okay? I'll move when you do." Penny said with a nudge. "You're okay. I'm still here with you." This was enough to bring back Chris's confidence. Without giving it a second thought, he stood up and pointed a finger forward. Then he summoned both swords and calmly walked on. Penny moved with him, her shield raised and at the ready. Moments later, a large and ghostly conical barrier formed around her shield and enveloped everything in front of them. The color was hard to see, but anyone who was paying attention could tell it was a shade of purple.

"Come on!" Chris turned and gestured at the remaining sixteen men. They nodded and reluctantly stood up, but eventually came to the realization that they were safe behind Penny's Soul Barrier. The eighteen of them were the only ones brave enough to move forward onto no man's land. The other Alliance soldiers behind them seemed to take notice and provided covering fire. Others crawled out from behind cover to charge up but sometimes were shot down anyway. Bullets, plasma, and magic that impacted Penny's shield were absorbed like objects sinking into a body of water. Every dozen or so hits caused her to flinch slightly, but she marched onward anyway.

"Delta is moving up, push! Push!" an Alliance soldier just behind them cried. "We have Wizard back up! Push up with the barrier! What are you doing? Go!"

"How are you doing?" Chris asked Penny. He could tell Penny was sweating and straining herself now. All around them, what remained of this platoon were firing at exposed Imperials or those they passed. Penny allowed their bullets to pass through her barrier, but none from the enemy could pass.

"I need to put this down soon." Penny's voice sounded very strained, but she still continued on at the same pace. Even absorbing a tank shell did now slow her down.

"Be ready to take cover!" Chris ordered. "Set up portable barriers!"

"Yes, sir! Hunker down!" the soldier closest to him removed a gadget from the back of his armor and placed it down. This device erupted a holographic barrier, which became solid after a few seconds. The other platoon soldiers did the same and took cover behind them. The rest made their way into the trench just past Penny's barrier and began to raid it.

"We'll cover you," one of the soldiers with a sniper told him. "She can put it down!"

"All units," Chris, Penny, and the soldiers all her their devices go off with Autumn's voice. Chris and Penny turned to take cover behind the barriers. Chris felt one or two bullets cut through his left arm and one of his legs, but seconds later, it healed after getting to cover. "I do not believe you will reach the base before nightfall. We have less than thirty minutes before the demons emerge, and it's too late to retreat. I'm coming to assist from another battlefield. Continue your approach. I'll clear a path."

"The Terminus Headmaster's trainee is coming this way?" one of the soldiers asked while looking at Chris and Penny. Chris couldn't help but smirk and nod.

"Emily, get on the ground and deal with those anti-tank crews. I'll deal with the tanks. You can clean up after me."

"Okay, I'll be there." was Emily's response. Chris was about to return to what he was doing before suddenly sensing a change. Penny and Chris looked to the sky at the same time as the other Wizards and Sorcerers. They all felt it. She was approaching so fast that it was hard not to sense the sudden surge of magic enveloping the air. A loud crackle followed as a blinding red flash soared over their heads; it was so powerful that they all had to duck down.

"Was that her?" Chris questioned, a nervous laugh following the question. "Oh, wow."

"This should be interesting," was all Penny said. 'Let's go ahead and move up. Take advantage of the panic she causes, okay?"

"Hey, Autumn, hold on. I wanna get a good look at this!" Ian said from the air, clearly recovered now. "It's not every day I get to see you in action!"

---

"Sir," an Imperial soldier pointed up toward the sky at the single figure coming toward them. "Picking up a magical signature approaching at high speeds!"

"I've got eyes on her," the Imperial squad leader he was talking to responded. "Wait- she's going for the tanks! Intercept her! Fire!"

Autumn dodged left and then right again in the air effortlessly. Their bullets could not keep up, and she was even faster than their plasma. By now, the many Imperial soldiers were ignoring the Alliance forces and trying to fire on Autumn. The tanks tried to fire on her, but even their machine guns could not touch her. Even the times they almost hit her, she shielded it with what appeared to be Ice magic.

"Kill her!" the squad leader uttered with a finger in the sky. "What are you doing?! Kill her!"

"Imperial tank crews," Autumn's voice rang across the battlefield like a loudspeaker as she continued forward. "I need not harm you. I am destroying your vehicles. Evacuate now if you wish to survive."

"Ignore her. We must keep the enemy back at all costs!" one of the tank commanders said, only to turn and see his crew escaping from the belly of this metal beast. "Where are you going, cowards? Operate the guns! You know what you signed up for!"

"Sir," one of the crew members returned. "She's right on top of us; we have to go!" Autumn appeared next to this man and placed him on her shoulder. She yanked the commander from the tank using her magic and threw them both out of range. After ensuring that all tanks were unmanned, she flew high into the air and fired a bright yellow and red beam of magic. It roared for a moment before causing the surrounding area to go silent, and then finally, there was a massive explosion. The entire tank line of over twenty armored vehicles detonated, and all that remained was a scorched crater of sand. In the center of this crater was no longer sand but solid glass. Not a single scrap of metal left to be found, and not a single Imperial killed.

Next, Emily descended from her plane. Chris could not see what happened after she landed, but from what he could tell, she used an Imperial Sorcerer to break her fall then proceeded to go to town on everyone else that happened to be nearby. Needless to say, the two of them were doing a great job, and all they had to do was pick off the stragglers and push onward to the base.

"So, are we pushing up?" one of the Alliance soldiers asked Chris.

"Well, would we not after that?" Chris asked sarcastically. "Let's move."

"Channeling your inner me?" Penny asked with a smile.

"Maybe," he answered with a smile as he pushed onward past the barriers.

Ahead were small groups of Imperials attempting to hold their ground with what ammo they had left. There were also a few Sorcerers, but they were exhausted, so Chris figured they wouldn't put up much of a fight. Still, it would be best to avoid an outright conflict if possible. Chris climbed up the dune along with Penny, requesting that the platoon stay back at the bottom while he took a look. Explosions still rang all around them, but the enemy did not seem to know they were here. Chris could see about ten Imperials. Seven were soldiers, and three were Sorcerers. They were all gravely injured but still very much in the fight like it did not matter.

"Autumn, we could use a hand." Chris gestured at the explosive specialist behind him as he spoke on his watch. The soldier pushed up to lie down beside his two leaders. "Can you make a sandstorm for me? Just a brief one at my location."

"Why?" Autumn asked curiously.

"Improvising."

"One desert storm, coming up, I guess!" Autumn flew over and raised both of her hands. The sand around the group of Imperials and Chris's forces took to the air. It blew every which way, making it hard to see, but this would still be possible. "Be careful."

"How many grenades do you have?" Chris asked the man.

"Five, sir. Two fragmentation, one implosion, and two concussion."

"Better go with an implosion to be sure," Penny told them over the wind. She had her head down and was trying to cover her face with her arm. "They'll die either way if left out here. We need to get past them."

"Implosion. Yes, ma'am." The man removed his backpack, and after fishing in it for a moment, pulled a small round ball. He then pressed a button on the side to prime it, then chucked it where Chris was pointing. Seconds later, yelling could be heard, but it was very apparent that they could hear the device but not see it. A powerful suction noise came first, then a fiery explosion in the shape of a ring. When the sand cleared, the Imperial bodies were strewn together unexpectedly. That was probably one of the deadliest grenades.

"Chris," Emily's voice emitted suddenly from the watch. The sounds of battle could be heard from the other end but were also echoed in real-time. "Move up but keep your head down. Autumn and I are drawing their fire as well as keeping their frontline on the run. You may still have stragglers."

"Okay, Em," Chris responded over the explosions around him. He stood up alongside Penny, and after pressing a few holographic buttons projecting from the watch, spoke loudly. "Everyone listen up! Autumn and Emily are clearing us a path up ahead, so we have the easy job: running. We have literal minutes before nightfall so let's hustle!" Penny could be seen smiling to his right, clearly proud of his sudden confidence. "Let's go, move it up! If I beat you there, you're doing it wrong!"

"But I'm wearing heavy gear, sir. You just have swords." One of the soldiers with a machine gun and a heavy backpack said.

# 8

# ONSLAUGHT

The Imperial mortars continued across the night sky as planes continued to screech above to provide air support. Flares and magic were some of the few entities lighting the pitch-black environment, but occasionally plasma would also fly. Flashlights were frantically moving toward the Imperial base. They were out of time. Already, some of the Alliance soldiers and Wizards were succumbing to the demons. The Imperial defenders had managed to hold the outer perimeter, but soon the two armies would clash with only seconds to go.

"Watch your left!" Penny warned Chris as she continued to sprint forward. Chris ducked under sword attack coming for his head and immediately spun while crouched, deflecting their sword and cutting them across the abdomen with the other. Seconds later, the attacker was swallowed up into the ground after being incapacitated. Chris tried to make a grab for the Sorcerer's body before the demon could drag them under but failed to react in time.

"You need to keep moving!" Penny bolted past Chris, grabbed his arm, and dragged him onwards. Countless footsteps roared across the desert toward the base. "Get a rocket launcher up here on the double!" Two soldiers ran up beside Chris and knelt down, rocket launchers on their respective arms. "Fire!"

Two yellow streaks followed the projectiles a short distance before crashing into the base's large walls, collapsing them almost instantly. Likewise, other entrances were blown open around this one. The Imperials were barricaded inside, but Chris knew it would not take long for them to be overwhelmed. Another wall was blown out somewhere on the other side of the base by a tank. The enemy was surrounded.

"If they're smart, they'll surrender," Chris stated as they walked inwards through the smoke and halation.

"It's not about being smart or not." Penny corrected as they drew closer and closer. "For the Imperials, the most dishonorable thing anyone can do is surrender. They're fighting for their homes and families. They will throw their lives away if it draws them closer. I was the same." Penny told him as she looked around warily. "So, don't expect them to. It's very rare."

"Then will we have to kill them all?" Chris asked in an alarmed tone.

"Or incapacitate them, so they cannot fight," Penny told him intuitively. "They will only fight harder now that they are cornered."

Entering the courtyard of this Imperial fortress revealed an ongoing set of skirmishes with Wizards fighting Sorcerers. Dead soldiers lined the floor, outmatched by the magic users clashing on both sides. Alarms were sounding all over, and bright lights were coming online the darker it got. Autumn was high in the sky, casting a spell to keep a bright light on a majority of the battlefield to keep everyone on both sides safe. Chris only knew it was her because of how brilliant the spell was and how long it was going. She might have made a wonderful sun for this planet and could probably stick around longer too.

"Delta two," Evangeline said over his watch. "Hang back and wait for your other squadmates to catch up. Echo two is flying them from high in the sky. When they arrive, take the command center to your far left. No Wizards are pushing that direction - only troopers."

"Are they going to be okay?" Chris tried.

"Don't be silly. Echo two is an expert healer and combatant; her partner, Echo one, has sustained more grave injuries. Do not worry about them and compromise their focus. I'm sure Echo two and Delta one would agree."

"Well, Ian would agree with me, so ha!" Chris countered, but the call had already gone silent on the other end. "Stop hanging up on me!"

"Well, I assume she hangs up because she cannot keep up with your chaotic personality." Megan's voice said from above him. Her flower touched down on the sand just behind them and then faded away into bright green pollen. "I am very sure that Penny does too, but finds it charming."

"Charming?" Chris quickly glanced at Penny, who was conveniently looking away like she was focused on something else. "Oh, okay. I think I get it."

"Just like Megan is captivated by mine, buddy!" Ian pumped his fist in the air. "You should've seen how she reacted when I got shot up there."

"Ian," Megan extended a hand outward toward him. "I can send you flying back out there into the desert to be eaten."

"Ah, you wouldn't do that." Ian placed his hands behind his head. "You could be nice to me like Penny is with Chris, but we all know you won't when other people are around."

Chris interrupted this bickering by speaking up to ask the two of them if they were okay. Both Megan and Ian seemed surprised by this question and turned to focus on him. Megan smiled and nodded her head, and Ian did a dramatic turn, followed by a thumbs up. He figured they should have been used to his caring nature, but somehow it still caught them off guard. Even Penny had grown used to it.

*It's because they're always checking on you, not the other way around,* Penny answered his thoughts mentally. *They appreciate it.*

*Even you?* Chris asked. Penny did not answer. To Chris, this meant that the answer was probably yes.

"Anyway," Chris began by pointing to his right where the battling was not as bad. "Our job is to secure the command center right over there. I want to take it a step further and turn the base defenses on the Empire."

"And the demons?" Megan asked quizzically.

"We'll turn the defenses on them. Maybe we can give our people a chance to get out there and help anyone stranded out there. I'm sure the trenches have defenses too, but I won't know what's possible until I get a chance to see those controls."

Chris turned and gestured for his squad to follow. The four of them carefully made their way through the courtyard. It was mostly secured by this point. Chris explained their goal to the Alliance lieutenant, who stepped aside and ordered his men to do the same. Chris's squad proceeded alone, approaching the sizeable automatic door which slid downwards to open and allowed them to descend into the dark base. The lights here were a bright white color to prevent demons from entering and killing them all. Further ahead, Chris could see Imperial forces behind makeshift barricades and hiding behind walls.

"The Alliance is sending Wizards to break our defenses, but we must hold!" an elderly gentleman said as he adjusted his black officer's hat and pointed forward. "Cut them down!"

"Hey, big guy!" Chris called out as he broke into a run.

Ian took point, charging forward a few feet and summoning his broadsword. Then he leaped into the air, clearing most of the gunfire which came his way. He then landed in the thick of the enemy lines, drawing their attention and ignoring any hits that he suffered. Chris ran on the wall to join him, gesturing at Penny to protect Megan and attack from the front to surround them. Chris leaped off of the wall to land on top of an Imperial combat medic, then promptly froze the person he was about to attend to.

"What are you doing?" The Imperial officer cried out to the three individuals approaching from further in the base. "Defend the facility! We're under attack by Wizards!"

"Wizards?" one of the Sorcerers asked in a dry laugh. "It's been too long."

Chris had just enough time to roll away from a lightning spell that struck the barricade just behind him. The Sorcerer placed his hands together and then charged up another blast to send Chris's way. He countered by raising an Ice wall and then advancing rapidly. This time though, he did not see the follow-up spell which struck him in the chest. Typically, this would be a fatal mistake, but Megan was there to patch him up as always. A bright green aura enveloped his body and then faded as soon as the injury had gone.

"Fool, Calel!" One of them yelled, drawing back his hood to reveal jet black hair. "Kill the Life Wizard if you want this to end."

With that, this individual faded into darkness using his magic. Chris tried to focus on finding him to protect Megan, but he still had to concentrate on his own Sorcerer. Ian was still clearing the crowd of grunts and would soon be done. It would have to fall to Penny to protect their squad's healer. Chris didn't even need to tell Penny to fall back to Megan. Her eyes seemed to be following a set path which was indirect but clear. She stepped forward, raised her shield to block an indivisible strike, stabbed forward, and kicked hard to remove her blade, which was now covered in blood. The Sorcerer reappeared on the ground, wounded and frustrated. He raised a hand to try to cast, but Penny gave him a quick kick to the head to finish him off.

"So very loud," Penny said under her breath.

"I can protect myself, you know?" Megan asked. "Get in there with the boys and do some damage."

"Yes, please!" Chris guarded another spell against the Sorcerer attacking him. The lightning arced across the blade violently before impacting toward the floor where he had pointed it. "Can you do something other than magic?!"

"Wizards are so pathetic at doing anything other than defending.

Perhaps if you would attack me-" the man fired another violent bolt at Chris. "You'd stand a chance!"

Now, he summoned his second sword and began to rapidly deflect further attempts. Chris had had enough. He swung his right sword forward, casting a spell as he did to send an arc of Ice magic at the man. Then Chris advanced on him quickly to try and strike a blow. Clearly, the man was not expecting him to close the gap so quickly. He had just enough time to try and prepare another spell before both of Chris's swords struck him across his stomach. Chris then finished him by freezing him to the ground.

"Yeah, shock me now!" He taunted cockily. "You just...sit there."

"Nice work, bud." Ian dusted his hands off, walking away from the Imperials he had dispatched. The last one slowly fell to his knees before falling forward after having his head slammed against the wall. His ears were probably ringing in his helmet.

Now the fighting would fall to the Imperial officer and the final Sorcerer. The officer raised his gun to fight, but the Sorcerer did nothing. Instead, he threw his weapon aside to give up and raised his hands. Not tolerating surrender, his officer aimed his pistol at the Sorcerer before Chris or anyone else could react. A shot through the head with a plasma bolt was enough to kill the young Sorcerer. The officer then turned to fire on Chris and Ian, only to be smacked in the face by Penny's shield.

"He killed his own man?" Chris grunted a little as he stared at the fallen Sorcerer. "Horrible."

"Like I said." Penny stepped back away from the man to rejoin the squad and shook her head.

"The command center should be in the next room," Megan noted.

"I wonder how many will be held up in there," Ian asked, drawing his mask down from his face for a breath of fresh air. "I'm already sweaty."

"Well, let's hope they're tired or ready to give up. A few of them seem to be" Chris folded his arms as he approached the door which would lead to the command center. It began to open automatically, and so he readied his weapons. The squad did the same around him, ready for almost anything. Megan had already prepared a healing spell in case gunfire came through the door immediately. Instead, when the door opened, the four lowered their guard slightly and looked on, horrified at the harrowing sight.

Dead Imperials lay randomly across a bloody floor. Screens were shattered, computers were trashed, and weapons lay not far from their owners. Most of them had been shot, but some had clearly taken their own lives with a blunt weapon or firearm. Chris slowly proceeded forward with a disturbed and twisted expression. His feet only moved because his mind subconsciously told them that they had to. Chris was careful not to step on any of the bodies, occasionally pointing one of his weapons down to ensure that he could react if there was movement.

"Don't--- Don't bother. They're all dead." Megan breathed heavily from behind him. She seemed a little affected by the smell but cast a spell on herself to nullify it. "I'll check further into the room, but I am honestly not sure if there is a point."

"Did they start fighting amongst each other or-" Chris tried, hoping to be right just once.

"No," Penny said to his left.

"You either kill yourself to prevent capture and stop the enemy from learning about the Empire's plans...or," Ian pointed to a soldier who clearly did not shoot himself. "Someone does it for you. I've just never seen this many."

"Yes, they've also destroyed all of the consoles. Not only can we not do what Chris suggested, but any chance of learning more just went up in flames." Megan sounded a little irritated. "Damned maniacs."

"These 'maniacs' are still my people." Penny shot back very quickly. Chris could sense a little tension in the air because of this comment.

"Yeah, and mine." Ian joined in.

"I didn't mean it like that." Megan tried. Ian seemed to accept this resolution, but Penny was too focused on the dead to care. "Still, they wasted their lives, and for what?"

Chris continued walking into the room to check on each of the destroyed instruments. Almost nothing could be salvaged, and just trying to interact with the communications terminal caused a violent volley of sparks to shoot up at him. He figured something must not have been destroyed, but now was reevaluating that thought. Chris pressed a few quick buttons on his watch and then raised it to his face.

"Evangeline--" he began, though he was unsure what to say.

"Yes, I see you." The Advisor told him, her voice far calmer than he was anticipating. "I have eyes in the room. Just breathe."

Chris quickly glanced up to see one of the Imperial cameras glowing red and fixated on him. "Then you see what I'm seeing?"

"Yes. I'm contacting medical assistance and trying to get some mechanics down there." Evangeline said. Chris watched as the camera panned the room. "Your voice is shaking. Do you need to step out? I can bring in another squad."

"You know why. I'll be fine." Chris ripped his eyes away from one of the bodies and moved on.

"How is your squad?" Evangeline went on.

"They're fine," Chris answered again. "I think we'll need to replace all of these machines, though. We're not getting any info off of these. We'll be lucky if we can even use the base defenses."

"Agreed. For now, Delta Two, I'd like you and your squad to keep the area secure and wait for reinforcements."

Chris diverted his attention upon hearing a shuffle on the other side of the room. He set one of his swords on the communications terminal and then prepared the one he had in his grip. Megan was moving much faster than him, extending a hand forward to cast a spell. Chris figured it was better to trust that she had seen something that the rest of them hadn't. Penny moved over the left side of the room while Ian moved right. Either someone was alive, or a demon managed to tunnel in; regardless, they needed to find out.

"I can see you, so you might as well come on out." Megan pointed her sword directly at a set of supply crates jumbled together. She then stood there to wait for whoever was there.

A pair of hands poked out from behind the crates. They appeared to be small and feminine in nature. These brown gloves waved back and forth over and over. "Wait, wait!" A voice said from behind the crates said. "First, I need to know: Imperial backstabbers or Wizard do-gooders?"

"Are you really in a position to ask?" Megan asked impatiently. The hands placed themselves on top of the crates and began tapping. "Wizards. Come on out."

The woman sighed and gave a thumbs up. Chris watched as her silhouette stood up from the objects and began to walk into the light to meet them. Megan backed up slowly, keeping her sword at the woman's neck. The woman wore a white leather jacket with a brown neck collar, black pants, and similarly colored cuffed boots. Chris also noticed a pistol at her side as well as a few other trinkets on her belt. Her hair was short and red in color; the woman's eyes were green.

"If I had a Lumen for every employer that screwed me over, I wouldn't need this job," the woman held her nose and shook her head. "Note to self: crazy warmongering Imperials make lousy business partners."

"So, how are you not dead?" Ian asked in a very blunt manner. "Either you're that impressive or fortunate."

"More like I have the sense to not shoot myself in a bad situation like these idiots." The woman shifted her weight awkwardly. "So while they were blasting each other or themselves, I was shooting them, you know? I like breathing."

"Can I have your name?" Chris asked her as kindly as he could.

"Ha, okay. See, if I tell you my name, I feel like I won't be allowed in Alliance space for years, so maybe not? Thanks for the rescue and all, but since I'm not one of the Imperials and I helped you take them down, maybe you can let me go?"

"I can't, and I still need that name. Once you're cleared by us, you're free to go." Chris continued. "It's that or get arrested for no reason."

"Or I could - hey, I could tell you who my employer was! I didn't get paid the full amount for what I did anyway," She said quickly.

"-And now you'll be telling us that and everything else my partner asked you for." Penny leaned against the wall on her side of the room and shook her head slowly. "Another thing? Don't reach for that gun of yours."

The woman scoffed and shook her head, "Okay, look, I don't shoot toddlers. You guys look like you're barely into your teens. What are you, twelve or thirteen?" Chris rolled his eyes at this guess. "Not only that but again, I'd like to continue flying in Alliance space without getting shot."

"Seriously, your name." Chris pressed on, his eye twitching slightly. "You're making me feel like a robot, and I do not appreciate it."

"Fine. Captain Aiem'y Lendard, professional businesswoman." The captain gave a soft wave to Chris. "For hire, by the way."

"Smuggler." Penny connected from the other side of the room.

"I prefer professional transporter of delicate specialized goods." She tried.

"Illicit." Penny chimed in again.

"Is it my face? Do I just look shifty?" Aiem'y seemed very annoyed at her situation.

"You have no idea," Megan answered to her left. She lowered her weapon and relaxed. "Just cooperate, and you'll probably be free to go."

"I guess."

Megan pointed to the left toward the exit to lead the captain back outside. She must have been trying to act cute or stall to get out of it but quickly dropped it when Megan raised her weapon again. This time, the captain raised her hands slightly and strolled out of the room with Megan. This left Chris, Penny, and Ian to attend to the destroyed terminals and dead Imperials. Alliance soldiers came pouring in after the gunfire ceased outside of this room, so Chris assumed they had won the battle.

"I better see about getting these machines out of here and repaired. Maybe some of the technicians can have a look." Chris decided after a moment. "Can you two-?"

"You leave us the grim job?" Ian asked with a jaw drop. "Gee, thanks."

"I'll come back and help you, but I might go assist outside too. I just...need some air."

Penny agreed with a simple, "Alright."

# 9

## ONE STEP CLOSER

Chris and his partner stood together on the top of the damaged Imperial base's wall. Chris leaned against the wall's railing and watched as the many lights of Alliance soldiers continued toward the base. Tanks and trucks hummed in the distance. They were picking up the injured or stranded, bringing them onward toward the base, and then going back for more. Penny likewise was leaning against the wall but was hunched over, her eyes panning over the endless sands. From this height, they could see everything from their fallen and forgotten troops and rescue attempts to demons claiming the injured who were overlooked on the battlefield. There were even soldiers hunkering down in the trenches with bright lights.

"We should be out there," Chris said again for what was probably the third time. "Instead, we're here where it's safe."

"Do you want me to go out there?" Penny asked, her tone lighter than usual. "I can. Emily said you can't. She didn't say anything about me. If that would help you relax, I'll do it."

"Not without me..." Chris looked over at her. "I appreciate it, though, Penn."

After a minute of silence, Penny spoke again, "I'd be fine."

"I know you would, but still," he returned his gaze to the effort taking place further out in the desert surrounding the base, and the wounded being assisted toward a triage area. Bodies were also being brought in to be identified from both sides. Still, there were very few Imperial prisoners as most of them either died or decided to end their own lives to avoid being captured. Penny, after sensing his stress and frustration, moved closer and placed her hand over his. His grip loosened moments later, his hand reversing to allow Penny's hand to rest in his.

"How much longer do you think it will be until those lights get figured out?" Chris asked her awkwardly.

"I'm not sure, but at least the lights around the actual base are fine. It was smart of them to sabotage the base defenses and try to get the demons to kill us, though." Penny scoffed a little. "I can't say I wouldn't have done the same a long time ago."

"Can you tell me something you did?" Chris inquired out of genuine curiosity.

"Well," Penny placed both of her arms on the railing and looked up at the sickeningly black sky of Sohrann. She sucked on her teeth and finally answered, "I held Megan hostage one time. Not my worst act, but hey, I apologized...Gatchi did most of the violent acts."

"Gatchi?" Chris repeated with a quick turn.

"Yeah."

"I haven't heard that name in a while. I wonder where she is."

"You almost sound worried about her. Just how much do you know about her?" Penny questioned with a curious head tilt. "I've known her for a long time, but you-"

"I didn't know her for long, but honestly? I still think she can change. Just the look in her eyes the last time I saw her was enough to tell me..." Chris answered vaguely as he watched some of the lights activating out in the trenches. "I just hope she's okay."

Penny paused without speaking. Her eyes darted from him to the rolling sands out in the distance, "Me too, but I hope she stays away. I'd rather not fight her."

Chris's expression fell to a grimace at this declaration from Penny. It was true. She could still come back as a potential threat. He just sat there staring at the soldiers and magic users being brought in for treatment for what felt like forever. The lights above and within the trenches came online as more engineers rushed out with escorts to protect them from potential demons. The occasional roaring boom of gunfire was further out in the desert, but it was not demons battling. The Resistance forces were still assaulting the Imperial outpost not too far from them, placed in some ruins. It went on for what felt like forever, so he was almost sure that he wouldn't sleep tonight.

"Chris?" Penny said to his right. He jumped and slammed his elbow on the railing, cursing under his breath as he did. "You look tired."

"No. I'll be fine. I couldn't sleep anyway. What about you?"

"I'm fine." She answered softly. Chris squeezed her hand. "Well, maybe I'm a little tired, but if you're staying up, then I will too. Besides, our lovable squadmates are out there protecting those soldiers."

"Hey, Penn?" Chris started absentmindedly. Penny made a noise to show she was listening and turned her head. "How come this whole thing isn't a big deal to you? Like the fighting, I mean?"

"Sorcerers go to war with one another all the time. If we weren't fighting another faction, we were fighting each other in power plays. I guess it's just something I really am used to. The only time I reacted to...any of this was when-" Penny trailed off. Without her voice to maintain the sounds around them, the only things that could be heard were gunfire and voices.

"Was Tori used to it?" Chris pressed on without meaning to. "I just feel like it's just me."

"Tori—was different." Penny breathed out as if she had gathered the wrong words. "Tori was a good fighter and used to it just like me, but she broke easier. Seeing someone beg for her help or for their life always made her stop and think. Even when I was so mean to her, she was just always so considerate and fair. If anything, when she became one of the Mages, she started just being a goody-two-shoes."

"And what about you?" Chris asked.

Penny stared blankly at their connected hands before removing her own and placing her hands together. She shook her head and did her best to smile with the most vacant expression he'd ever seen. This was a silent answer to him - an answer Penny would prefer not to speak. He nodded, and she lowered her head once again. They needed to sleep, but somehow the stress of everything was keeping him up. Penny wouldn't even consider resting without him either. Perhaps Megan and Ian were faring better in the trench lines further out.

"So, how do you think Em and Autumn are doing?" Chris asked. Emily and Autumn had gone without the rest of the army to push back the Imperials with a small assault force during the night. Their goal was to gain ground and make it easier to move forward once the sun rose.

Penny snickered. "Ah, you should be asking how the Imperials are doing."

"Still, I'm worried," Chris said honestly. "She's still my sister even if she's kind of insane in a fight..."

"She can drop all four of us without even trying when we practice with her." Penny reminisced. "I'd say she'll be alright!"

"Yeah, I guess-" Chris began to trail off as his eyes caught sight of something ridiculous.

A woman was wearing a black and purple tunic with a robe just over it. She had short brown hair that was currently curled, ghostly green eyes, and a pale face. She was just wandering back and forth in his cone of vision. Chris sat forward and waved his hand to get her attention, but he called out instead when he received no recognition. Penny blinked and gawked at him curiously.

"Chris?" Penny began.

"Ma'am! You should come into the base. It's not safe! There are demons." No reply. "Hey!"

"Chris?" Penny asked very slowly to his right. "Who...are you talking to...?" She placed a hand on his shoulder and tugged gently. Chris slowly looked away from the woman's creepy grin, which betrayed her innocent appearance. He felt like he was being pulled toward her somehow now. "Chris!" Penny finally spoke up louder.

He turned to face her, breathing erratically for what felt like no reason, "Penn, what's up with this lady?"

"What lady?" Penny inquired curiously.

"The-" Chris pointed a finger only to lower it back to his side. There was nothing there but an empty stretch of sand lit by the base's lights. "I guess I'm tired."

"Let's get to bed." Penny declared with a concerned stare. "Come on."

# 10

# THROUGH THE SHADOWS

The dimly lit Imperial command center had now been rebranded with Alliance flags and systems. New security was installed, technicians were brought in to set up new devices, and a few Resistance operatives joined them. The machinery's constant beeping and hums were only softened by the various voices discussing their own business. The general was one such person here and was speaking to Chris.

The general was a man wearing a black and blue military uniform with various metallic insignias. His beret lay just beside him on the terminal he was standing next to. His black hair was rapidly greying either with age or due to his job's stress; his beard was thick and covered most of his face. He was developing more wrinkles, seemingly by the day. Currently, the general was briefing Chris on a list of tasks to accomplish.

"Can your squad handle that?" He asked while pointing at the holographic map of New Hope. "It's a tough job, but if you can secure a route, I'm sure New Hope can be taken quite easily. You've been on the ground there already, from what I hear."

"What exactly did you hear?" Chris inquired with a nervous smile.

The general chuckled as if this question should have an obvious answer, "You and your partner improvised again. That's all. I won't question it, considering the results. You should be allowed to think for yourselves sometimes."

"Well," Chris hunched over the terminal and stared at the map intently. "If we can take this outpost," He pointed and allowed the map to zoom in on a small outpost with a checkpoint blockading the road. "I think we could get at least a few tanks and soldiers through the city. It could also work as a refueling depot."

"That's what I was thinking, but we can't risk a forward assault."

"No, there's no need." Chris declared confidently. "Let my squad go in. We'll take it tonight without any resistance. From there, we'll wait for reinforcements, and if any Imperials arrive, they'll have a nice surprise. I bet we could launch the attack from there too if we coordinate with the Sohrann forces."

"You don't need any soldiers?" General Delore raised his eyebrow a little.

"Only if they can stay quiet and take out a base of bad guys without a sound. I'd rather take this without a fight." Chris swiped the map to zoom out. "Megan flies us over tonight, we surprise the base, and you send an attack force out as soon as the sun is up."

"And if they detect your squad?"

"...I do what I always do! My team can handle it." Chris answered with a chortle. The General lowered his head as if he were afraid of what that meant, but still agreed to the plan.

---

The night sky was pitch black with dim twinkling stars in the distance. Even with no moon, somehow, the sky still looked at least a little pleasant to Chris. The cool desert breeze was refreshing, but even with a jacket on, it was somewhat chilly. He sat back on the center of Megan's flower and shut his eyes. To his left was Ian, who was doing much the same. Penny was in deep thought from what he could tell, but still enjoying the ride. Megan flicked Chris with her finger and glared a little. "What?" he asked.

"You still haven't told us the plan." She clarified. "Are we really doing a direct assault?"

"No, I'm taking your advice and going about this carefully." Chris did his best to mimic her voice as he continued. "We'll strike at them before they even realize what's happening."

"I'm disappointed in this plan. I was looking for a fight, but you want to sneak around!" Ian complained loudly. "Boring! Hey, Penny, what do you think?"

"If we get forced to fight, then we will," Penny answered wisely. "I don't really care either way. If it goes wrong, you'll have your fun."

"Bah. Whatever." Ian shut his eyes and started to relax. One could almost think he would fall asleep, but there was no reason to, as they were almost there.

The city was gradually coming into view. The empty skyscrapers loomed over the streets below. There was no light to be found, so a person would have had to strain their eyes to even register it. If there was light, then it was hidden by the countless buildings. Chris sat up on Megan's flower and observed their approach. His watch pinged precisely on cue, and he began a call with his advisor.

"Advisor Andrews to Spellcrafter. The satellites are telling me that you are nearing New Hope. I have information to convey." She said. A question came to him internally while she was talking: when did she even sleep?

"I'm all ears, Eva," Chris answered. "Is there a problem?"

"No. I'm warning you that I've done a scan of the location you intend to capture and have found what looks like non-combatants. It should not be a problem, but I believe the Imperials are using them to deter us from attacking."

"Can you tell me what they have?"

"A few tanks and lookouts, but nothing serious. I suggest you split your squad up and attack from multiple sides. Do not touch down near the base as you will be spotted." Evangeline marked a location on Megan's watch. She immediately lifted it and changed their trajectory. "Please watch out for scouts and demons."

"Can do. Thanks. What would we do without you?" Chris asked her. "I really appreciate-"

Evangeline's hologram, which was projecting out of his watch, flicked her hair to the side and huffed, "Probably charge headfirst into danger needlessly. Advisor Andrews out." And with that, the hologram retreated back into his device.

"I didn't even get to finish my compliment," Chris said with an astounded look.

"Well, maybe she didn't need one," Penny said with a weird smile. "She probably thought you were flirting with her."

"What? I wasn't!" Chris said louder than he meant to. He turned to face Penny as his jaw dropped.

"Mm," Penny muttered, her attention drifting away.

"The jealousy is strong with this one," Ian said in an overly dramatic deep voice. "Strong indeed. I sense her frustration!"

"And yet you can't sense mine." Megan's words probably cut his silly attitude into pieces with just five words. "We're getting close. It would be in your best interest to stay quiet."

Megan landed their flower on top of one of the shorter buildings. They were hidden behind the taller skyscrapers around them, so it would be difficult to detect them. Still, having flashlights would expose them regardless. The four of them would have to shut off their devices if trouble came too close. Ian stood up as soon as the flower vanished, and the back of his head smacked against the cool concrete.

"Lead the way, oh leader of ours," Ian said in a pompous voice. "We'll follow you, my liege!"

"Whatever." Chris chuckled. He checked his watch for the base's location then hopped down onto the street level, his flashlight illuminating the objects just around him.

The four friends made their way toward the Imperial outpost, not only marked on their devices but also clearly found in the night due to the bright lights. Occasionally they would come across a patrol, take them out quickly, and move out without a hitch. Once they were close enough to the Imperial fortifications, they removed and deactivated their flashlights. Chris went first, peeking around a corner where an Imperial tank was softly purring. It appeared to be part of the defenses. He could see some lookouts in the buildings surrounding the outpost, a skeleton crew of soldiers on guard duty, and a few mechanics.

He returned to his squad and signaled for them to follow him. They would take the tank first. Ian climbed up the chassis' side as slow as possible, opened the hatch, and slipped inside. A soft 'tong' sound could be heard, like the sound of two people slammed against metal. He then climbed out but left the tank running, as usual, to make it appear as if it was still being crewed. Ian could be quiet when he wanted to be.

"I can't wait to get off of this dust ball. It's either super hot or super cold." Chris heard a female Imperial soldier talking just ahead. "No in between."

"I get what you mean. Still, it's better than being on Polaris or Penrose. I'd take this station over that mess any day!" Another replied, this one being male.

"Here here." the woman concluded.

Chris watched as the two soldiers began to walk their separate ways. The woman was coming toward them and the tank. She was just about to see them until Penny grabbed her by her shoulders, kneed her in the chest, and then backhanded her with the shield. Penny then hid the body just in front of the tank and moved on in her own separate direction. Chris directed Ian to follow her and for Megan to follow him. They would just split up and make this go by faster. This would also probably prevent Megan and Ian from butting heads.

The two of them were able to crawl under some left behind Sohrannian cars and reach an outpost area that looked like it was once a market. However, the first thing Chris found notable about this area were the citizens of Sohrann who were being held captive. There were a few Imperials here, mostly regular soldiers, and a damaged tank. He moved to find cover but was pulled by Megan, who grabbed his shoulder and forced him to crouch down. As she did this, an Imperial soldier shined their flashlight where he was just standing and, upon seeing nothing, went back to patrol.

"Slow down." Megan urged him in a low voice. She moved onwards by herself, avoided the light as much as she could, and silenced the civilians she passed to not give her away. She stopped mid- crawl and held up another finger to warn Chris of the soldiers up ahead. Megan crawled out from the shadows slowly before standing up in a half-crouch. As soon as the soldier in front of her turned his head away to look at one of the trembling civilians, Megan slammed her foot into the back of his leg. As he fell to his knees, she removed his helmet, covered his mouth, and pinched his neck hard until he collapsed. Then, she slowly let him fall to her feet and dragged him into the darkness.

"You've got moves, Megan." Chris smiled and nodded. "Remind me not to cross you."

"You don't do that already?" She whispered back, jokingly. "There are two more ahead. I'll move when you do."

Chris crept up alongside her and then started moving toward one of the soldiers. Megan did the same to his right. He jumped onto the soldier's back and held his neck tightly with his arm. When the man had fully sunk to the ground and stopped squirming, Chris let go. The Sorcerer on the right was about to go for his weapon, but Megan came from seemingly nowhere and threw him hard into the damaged tank nearby. He then slid down slowly onto his back, unconscious at the very least.

"What about them?" Megan asked him, pointing at the prisoners.

"Stay here," Chris said. "Keep your heads down and don't make a sound if you can help it." Most of them were too scared to speak, but Chris assumed that they understood his directions. Once the outpost was taken, they would just have to remain here until the morning.

"Do you think the other two are okay?" Megan asked, just behind him.

"Whoa," Chris answered in a half-whisper. He just had to mess with her now. "Amazing."

"What?"

"You're worried. That's new. Oh my gosh, I should document this!"

"...Sorry I asked." she finished in a groan.

Minutes passed, and it felt like they had cleared more than half of the fortifications, and yet still more soldiers were discovered. The looming concern of those that were subdued waking back up was looming in the back of Chris's mind. It was not supposed to take this long. They would just have to work faster. Though it would be easier to kill them, merely being a Wizard made this a big no-no. Truthfully, he was glad that there was usually a way to not kill. Pushing these darker thoughts aside, he kept moving.

"Penn? Status?" He whispered into his watch.

"I've locked some of the sleeping Imperials in their quarters. Even if they wake up, they have nowhere to go."

"I feel like someone will discover a mess soon," Chris told her. He heard a quick slamming noise on the other end and assumed Penny had dealt with another straggler. "God, for once, I wish Em was here."

"Don't let her hear you say that," Penny replied.

"I don't know; it just might brighten her day," Chris said. "Anyway, I think-"

"I think someone may have discovered my handy work." Ian chimed in wearily. "One moment."

Megan turned back to face Chris and crouched to make herself less visible behind one of the Imperial portable barricades. "Do you need help? Ian?"

"I'm fine, but there are way more people coming."

"How many?" Chris inquired.

"Too many for just me," was Ian's response.

"We'll meet up and take them together. Quick and hard, okay?" Chris pulled up his watch, quickly marked a location near the market, and began running with Megan to meet the other two.

Penny and Ian had actually arrived first. The two were hiding in the shadows next to some of the freed Sohrann citizens. They had armed themselves with guns from fallen Imperials and were hiding for their lives. If his squad played their cards right, these people wouldn't even need to fire them. From here, he could see about fifteen Imperials coming in and pointing their weapons every which way. It was too dark to see, but it looked like two Imperials were leading them.

"Penny, you go first. Do your thing." Chris whispered to her as he ran up beside her. "Ian, take four on the left. Meg, same for you. I'll work on anyone still standing."

With that, the four split up into separate directions. The patrol was becoming suspicious. It was time to act before the enemy called it in. Penny's shield ricocheting off of three heads was his signal to go in. Megan came next, using her magic to launch two Imperials into the ground. She then deflected bullets that came her way and backed up into Penny, who raised her shield to protect her. Ian picked up another enemy, smiled wide, and threw him as hard as possible into two others. Penny cut down another after advancing toward him, so this just left six.

Chris summoned as much mana as he could from within his body. Then he extended both hands and called forth a blizzard. Four out of the six Imperials had been frozen within blocks of Ice. His spell completely ignored his allies, and Chris had to internally pat himself on the back for such an expertly used spell. The only two still standing were the Sorcerers. At least, they thought they were both Sorcerers. As it turned out, one of them was once a Wizard.

This traitorous Wizard drew back his hood to reveal distinct short red hair and red eyes. He wore a white cloak with star designs and kept his sword, a saber at his side. His counterpart was a man of at least thirty with jet back hair, purple eyes. He wore lightly armored black robes with purple designs along the edges. If his appearance did not strike you, the following laughing fit would undoubtedly have been a clue.

"Been a minute, Hunter." Chris sneered, drawing a sword to point at him from thin air.

"You look well." Penny followed up as if finishing his thought.

"Not long enough, it seems." Hunter placed a hand on his sword, but his counterpart's hand came across and stopped his arm.

"Now, now. We can be diplomatic. They are at a severe disadvantage." He said with a strange and overplayed gesture. "I assume we all know each other, so we can skip the introductions and skip straight to-"

"Shut it, Vedi." Chris snapped suddenly. Vedi drew his sword and pointed it at Chris's neck, prompting the others to draw their own weapons and stand on guard.

"Uh-uh-ah. No toys. I'm just reminding him how to show respect. Still, very dutiful to protect your over-glorified leader."

Chris could see Hunter gripping the hilt of his own sword. When Vedi lowered his sword, Hunter loosened his grip and subtly returned himself to a relaxed state. This left Chris to wonder why, but soon filled in the blank with the most likely reason: he was going to join in. Hunter had no good intentions. There was no way he ever would. Chris rubbed his neck a little and stepped back once before holding his sword defensively in case Vedi tried that again.

"Enough games." Megan cautioned them. "Surrender or die. We will not warn you again."

"I'm out of patience," Vedi muttered, effortlessly breaking Megan's defense and sending her sword flying away. He then grabbed her by the throat and lifted her effortlessly into the air at this side. Ian cried out and tried swinging hard, but Vedi blocked it, moving Ian's sword aside before elbowing him in the chest. "Now then! It seems I have your attention." He spoke loudly to be heard over Megan talking.

"You want trouble?" Chris asked, summoning his second sword. This took a slight toll on his body. He'd used a lot of magic just now. "You got it."

"Oh, calm down. I just want your 'partner,' and her brother, boy." Vedi laughed a little. "It's not about you two. I'm running an errand for his royal highness. Now come along Ms. Dreadful. Your father misses you."

Chris stepped in front of Penny, but she clearly didn't need the protection. She was just calmly, staring down Vedi and focusing on her next moves. The people they had saved were now scrambling over and pointing their scavenged guns at the Sorcerers. Chris appreciated it but wished that they had stayed well out of the way. The Imperial soldiers had also broken out of their quarters and scrambled to back up their superiors.

"It seems we're at a stalemate!" Vedi exclaimed loudly. "I'm offering you a peaceful solution to this conflict! Take it." Chris could see Megan shaking her head lightly, only to receive a tighter grip for it. "Alternatively..." he squeezed tighter. Megan's gasps for air became all the more frantic.

"Wait!" Ian stepped forward and was quickly pushed back by Penny. "We can talk about this."

Chris raised his arm toward his face, pressed a button, and waited. Vedi seemed amused. "Calling for help? Is it your murderous sister or your brainwashed soon-to-be leader?"

"Delta two? What is-" Evangeline maintained her trademark calm voice despite the situation.

"Eva? Can you hit my location?" He asked loud enough for everyone to hear.

"I have a station satellite near you, but it may be better to call in reinforcements-" Evangeline reasoned.

"Prepare an orbital strike on my position. Hold fire." Chris maintained with a death glare aimed at the two Sorcerers. The Imperial soldiers behind them exchanged glances. Behind him, he heard both Penny and Ian make a noise. Megan's jaw dropped despite being held in a death grip.

"Nice bluff." Hunter snickered. Vedi said nothing.

Chris pressed a button on his watch's map and then spoke again. "Shoot here, short, controlled burst. Watch your fire."

There was a crackling sound like a jet flying overhead. Briefly, the sky illuminated red and blue. Soon, bright bolts fell from the sky and crashed into two Imperial tanks, destroying them immediately and eviscerating everything around it. The death rain stopped shortly after, and the sky returned to darkness. Vedi nodded to himself as if impressed by this display but still had not let Megan go.

"Target my location exactly. Maximum firepower." Chris said this as a threat directly to the enemy this time. "I want the total destruction of the target-"

"Buddy? Have you lost your mind?!" Ian blurted out suddenly.

Penny nodded to herself before chiming in to help, "An Imperial knight and a traitor all in one shot. Not to mention all of these soldiers. Frankly, it's a fair trade."

"Do it." Megan gasped helplessly while kicking at Vedi weakly. She was starting to go limp.

"Spellcrafter, I can't say I agree with this," Evangeline started.

"I'm calling your bluff." Vedi smiled.

"Screw it. Eva, I need you to-" As Chris was saying this, Vedi suddenly dropped Megan and began to clap. Ian scrambled to pick up his partner and drag her away from this maniac.

"Ah, it was a bluff." Vedi clapped even harder. "But wow! The fact that you were even willing to threaten the total annihilation of everyone here for your squadmate? I like your moxie! You grew up."

"You should have told her to fire!" Megan scolded through heavy breaths.

"Focus on breathing," Ian told her while rubbing her back. "Don't talk crazy."

"To any of you sorry excuse for soldiers who are still breathing,"

Vedi said from his diaphragm. "Pack it up, and let's go! We'll fall back to base command."

"You're just leaving?" Penny vocalized her concern quite clearly at these actions.

"After that display, how could I not? There are other objectives I must meet, and we're done with this outpost. Oh, yes, that reminds me." Vedi clapped his hands twice. The soldiers behind him quickly shot down their comrades who were too injured to come along or were still unconscious. "I can't have you interrogating them, you know? Enjoy the lovely weather."

Hunter nodded at them and walked away first, closely followed by Vedi and the rest of their army. The four friends were left there with the civilians. The base was captured one way or another despite the complications. Now the only thing left was to tend to Megan. Chris asked his advisor to stand down and alert the home base of the outpost's capture. All the while, though, he wondered what they would do about this new problem. A traitor who tried to kill himself and Penny was here - along with the man who killed her sister. He turned to address Penny and found her shaking slightly, her eyes locked onto to Vedi.

# 11

# BLITZ

Chris looked over his attack plan one more time before forwarding it to Evangeline. Once it was approved and the sun had fully risen, they'd attack. He'd been sent a heavy Alliance tank and a light hovering tank. A reasonable force of Alliance soldiers joined them. They would also be receiving reinforcements from an Alliance major's battalion, resistance soldiers, and two independent Wizard squads would be assisting in their own ways. It was a fair attack force to take the city, but it would still need to be nearly perfect to avoid disaster.

His plan was simple and had been a strategy he'd seen used throughout history. Their forces would hit the Imperials with a decoy force supported by a tank and a few Wizards. From there, they'd hit the enemy from all sides and box them in. Part of him was actually hoping they'd surrender, but it was never that easy. Now that he was receiving a call from Evangeline, he'd finally know if it was feasible. Chris answered the call, staring out at the rising sun on the orange desert horizon.

"Advisor Evangeline to Delta Two. I have received your attack strategy and have run it by the General and the Headmaster's Hand. I have an update to convey."

"Good morning, advisor!" Chris said as cheerfully as he could. "It's a nice almost day down here. The killer monsters are finally going back to bed so we can move."

"Considering all that's happened, you're still you." She commented with a surprised tone. "Yes, I'm sure it is a nice day - as nice as it can be in a desert." Evangeline cleared her throat and then continued. "Your attack was approved by both of your superiors."

"That's great! Well, when the other groups arrive, we'll-"

"I haven't concluded my statement. I was performing a deep satellite scan while you were sleeping through the night and discovered that the Imperials have captives." She explained. "They are civilians, but not what you are used to. It appears they have about a dozen captured officers."

"Like police officers?" He asked while walking forward to look into the distance. "So, hostages?"

"I don't believe they're hostages, but I'm starting to think that New Hope was being used as a sort of prisoner of war camp. I don't think I need to tell you to be careful but do so. Bafair Kai also contacted me and told me he is onsite and ready to assist." Evangeline was once again typing. *How can she do so much at once?* He wondered. "I will be available for assistance if you need it during your assault, and I'll be coordinating all fronts of this attack with the major."

"Awesome. Thanks, Eva-"

"There is one more detail. Please be more careful to avoid situations like what unfolded last night. I noticed your over-exaggeration and obviously did not fire. My orders are to protect you, not to kill you," Evangeline took a breath and then continued on with her rant. "So I'd kindly ask you to not ask me to shoot your position and kill your squad."

"You know I was bluffing, though." Chris paced awkwardly. "I just needed some sort of advantage over them. If I'm honest, I'm just glad it worked."

"I'm aware, and it was admittedly clever. But neither your sister, the General, nor I would approve of that. I've lost far too many Wizard squads to stupid decisions." Evangeline went utterly silent.

"Uh, Eva? Are you-"

"Good luck with your attack. Advisor Evangeline out." She concluded abruptly. The call ended just after she uttered the last letter.

"She keeps hanging up on me. Still," Chris said to himself. "That wasn't like her."

Chris turned to head back to meet his squad but stopped in his tracks. Something felt...different - off. What was it? He could hear voices around him like a woman's laughter. Chris pivoted himself back around to look at just what it could be. It was so unsettling that it just couldn't be anything good, but he was also overtaken by an unnatural calm. How could one be so anxious and yet so calm all at once?

A woman was standing in front of the sunlight wearing that same black and purple attire. She had short brown hair that was currently curled, ghostly green eyes, and a pale face. This time he could make her out much more clearly because she was closer, but he had not met her before, so it didn't help. Chris decided to do the one thing most people wouldn't: walk toward her. It was not because he wanted to, but because he felt compelled to by some unnatural force. Just what was this?

"Good morning," she said in a surreal and calm voice. "You seem to enjoy days like this as much as me."

"Who-" he started.

"Who am I?" She finished for him. Chris nodded. "Who I am is inconsequential. What I bring you is more important." She smiled. "Would you mind if we have a short conversation?"

"I - suppose. But why are you following me?" He inquired very directly.

She laughed softly to herself, "Really now? Following you? If you can believe it, I'm not. At least - not intentionally." The woman proceeded toward him gingerly and smiled. "You see, I don't often invite others to speak with me directly. They also rarely agree like you. Very interesting."

"Can I have your name then?" Chris tried. Her expression shifted but was still hard to make out.

"Call me - Pixie Mitchell." She decided after a pause. Chris's expression shifted as he began searching for any breaks in her character.

"Pixie...Mitchell." He repeated. "I get the feeling that's a fake name. I swear I've heard that last name too..."

"Maybe it is! Please respect it as my name." She seemed amused. "I'd like to give you a friendly warning about your attack." Chris waited for her to continue on with his arms folded and a weird feeling in his gut. Something was really freaking him out about this woman, but he just couldn't bring himself to panic or show concern. "The leader of the Imperials in this city and the surrounding area is an Imperial Knight, much like Vedi, named Aarlam Vass. He is quite powerful with his Death magic and uses two swords. To kill him would be an amazing feat."

"An Imperial knight?" Chris repeated slowly. "Like...Vedi?"

"An Imperial knight either follows his own agenda or serves a Shadow Councilor." Did she sense that he was confused, or was it just that obvious? "It just so happens that this one serves a Shadow Councilor who is quite powerful. Though I am unaware if she is on Sohrann, it cannot be good if he is here. Draw him out, kill him, and this sector should pretty much fall to the Alliance. If you survive, maybe we'll speak again!"

"You seem optimistic."

"I've just heard a lot about you. Besides, I have something of a steak in this-" her eyes suddenly cut past Chris, and a smile formed on her face. Chris turned quickly to see what she was looking at. Ian was standing there directly behind him with his hood drawn back to reveal messy hair. Behind him, Penny was walking over as well.

"Uh, buddy? Are you okay?" Ian asked. "I think the stress of everything is getting to you. You were just talking to yourself."

"No, I-" Chris glanced behind himself, and no one was there. Was she even real? "I guess. I'm sorry."

"No worries. I talk to myself sometimes." Ian joked with a smirk. "Megan never listens to me, but I listen to me!"

"Can I ask you two a question?" Chris asked since Penny had now come close enough to speak.

"Why not?" Ian asked sarcastically.

"Of course," Penny said in a tone that put him at ease. She was always sweet when he needed something.

"Uh- do you know someone named Aarlam Vass?"

"No," Penny responded curiously. "I don't think I've ever heard that name. Why?"

"Well then, maybe you can tell me what a Shadow Councilor is?" He tried again.

Silence and the air of uncertainty took over. For the first time in what felt like forever, Penny's jaw had dropped and then shut. She turned her head to look at Ian, who looked back with a similar expression. Ian grunted a little like he was not excited to give the answer. The two finally looked back at him slowly. Penny opened her mouth to speak, but Ian was first.

"A Shadow Councilor," Ian began hesitantly. "...Is one of the leaders of the Empire. They govern territory and basically enact the Emperor's will. They're like the most dangerous people in the Empire just under the Emperor, and they typically have knights to protect them."

Chris rubbed his chin and nodded. He accidentally made eye contact with Penny, who promptly spoke up, "I've never mentioned them to you before. How do you know?"

"Oh, I uh - just heard it somewhere." Chris figured if he told the truth, they'd call him a liar. Penny stared at him for a moment like she was concentrating.

"He was talking to himself," Ian muttered to Penny.

"Chris," Penny said in a slow and careful tone. "I don't sense anything different about your mental state or thoughts, but I am asking you to be honest with me."

"I am Penn." He said. "If there's something to tell you, I will. I was just curious."

"...Okay," Penny answered with clear disapproval. She turned back toward the outpost and didn't say a word further.

"Penny," Chris outstretched his arms to either side with a bit of frustration.

"I'm just going to check on Megan." She responded. "We'll talk after the battle."

"Chris," Ian said in a far darker tone than he was used to. "Be careful. Those people are no joke. I won't force you to tell me how you know about them, but I'd really prefer you to spill it."

"You'd call me crazy," Chris told him. "I'll try to explain later."

"Alright, well, even if you don't tell me, you should tell her. I know it's bad coming from me, but you have no reason to hide it." Ian said this subtly and directly. Chris knew what he was talking about immediately. Ian probably knew just how hypocritical it was for him to tell Chris to open up to Penny. Yet, telling Penny about how he is hearing and seeing things is far better than telling Megan what he'd done.

"Alright." Chris agreed with a nod.

"Now...let's go so I can get out of this armor!" Ian said, suddenly snapping back to his usual fun-loving self. "It's hot!"

As Chris watched Ian leave, a thought occurred. What would he do if he ever gave Penny a reason to want to harm him? It was a silly thought because Chris knew that he'd never do something like that. But Ian had - and he still continued to protect her despite the only possible outcome. Megan would find out, and most likely, she would not react well, but Ian wasted no time trying to save her from Vedi. If they turned on each other, what would he do?

---

The sound of a tank could be heard humming toward his direction. It did not roll or roar, so it was hard to detect, but when he saw the floating fortress moving alongside the soldiers, he knew. About eighty soldiers, seven Wizards, and the floating Alliance tank were approaching along the highway. They soon entered the once Imperial checkpoint and stopped just short of entering. An older gentleman walked in front of the soldiers and placed his arms behind his back. He wore a black and blue officer's uniform and had greying brown hair.

"Spellcrafter?" He asked as Chris approached. The man wasted no time in extending his right hand. Chris took it and shook hard. "Major Kaden Lawson. My battalion is ready and willing for a fight. I analyzed your battle plan, and I have to say it is old school, but it will work. I have already broken off part of my forces to perform the encircling movement."

"Did you hear about the prisoners on-site?" Chris asked him.

The two began walking toward the outpost with the moderate attack force following them. "Yes. It will make the battle difficult, but it's not the first time I've dealt with a POW camp."

"I'm sure you know about the Resistance helping us here too?"

"Yes. I welcome their support, but I am concerned about a... civilian outfit assisting in a strategic military attack." He sighed a little. "So long as they watch their fire, I'll be glad to have them."

"Sir!" An Alliance soldier was rushing toward them and panting heavily like he had run from quite far away.

"Trapper. What are you doing here?" the Major asked him directly. "I gave you an order to scout out the path ahead."

"I did, sir, but a local force consisting of what looks like law enforcement is attacking the Imperial line. They're being torn apart, sir!"

"Why would they even try that?" Chris asked with wide eyes. "That's suicide."

"Then, we need to mobilize and engage early. Now." The Major signaled for his troops to move forward, and they began to hurry through the checkpoint.

# A FLASH OF GREEN

Chris flinched at an explosion that rocked the side street that he and his squad were taking cover in. He covered his head as rubble fell from above and landed around them. A few of the blunt objects impacted his hand, but his head was perfectly fine. Despite the stinging sensation in his hand, at least he was able to still think. The others did the same. When a larger piece of the building started to fall, both Penny and Megan reacted. Penny used her soul barrier to catch the giant piece. She was grunting like it was cumbersome. Megan pushed the rubble off of the spell, using her own magic. It crashed next to them and laid there, crumbling the rest of the way from the force Megan had thrown it.

"I hate this." Chris cursed and returned his back to the concrete. Penny held his shoulder and peered out from cover to the battle going on just ahead. Alliance forces were moving on the highway just above them. The war was also going on around them. Just because they were boxed in did not mean that the Imperials would surrender. All he could hope was that the police officers caught up in this mess were going to be okay.

"We should move," Ian suggested as a tank shell impacted not too far from them. "Now would be good."

"Yeah. Okay." Chris agreed. He then gestured for the others to follow him across the street. They were moving away from the battle lines now to a quieter area of the city. While the Alliance was battling the Empire in this flanking maneuver, perhaps they could help somewhere else. "Eva?" Chris raised his watch. "I want to know where those officers are."

"You are actually nearing their position. Proceed on your current path toward the courthouse and you will reunite with your main forces. Bafair Kai and a handful of Resistance agents are also en route." She concluded. "If you require assistance, contact me."

"It'll be good to have Bafair's help!" He said with enthusiasm as the call severed.

Penny agreed from behind him, "He is an excellent marksman."

The scene Chris came about was that of about a dozen or so police officers in varying levels of armor taking cover behind a line of cars they had set up. The doors were open, so he assumed that they had driven these here to use for cover. The windows were smashed out and being used for cover while they tried to keep low. A swat van was on the left with a small squad returning fire on the Imperials. A few of these men and women were injured. These few were lying down behind their cars, but most were actually doing okay.

"Meg, see if you can help them out." Chris pointed at the injured officers as he made his way to cover. She broke off a short distance away and began to heal them. He had looked away for but a moment, and she was already nearly done.

"Kids...?" one of the officers asked with his mouth agape. "Oh, Wizards. Your timing is great, but we have no way forward. Sorry."

"You should fall back and let us handle this." Chris tried.

"No way. No how. These people have some of ours." He reloaded his rifle and shook his head. "We aren't going anywhere, but I'm still glad to have the help. Right now, we're trying to get into the courthouse to save Deputy Haye."

"How about you leave that to us then?" Chris offered. "I bet we can handle it."

"Okay, what about these guys?" he asked while attempting to move to a kneeling position to fire, only to nearly be hit. "Damn!"

"Hey, Oddball?" Chris pressed a button on his watch to connect to the comm frequency they were using and smirked. "Can you give us an assist?"

"Yes, sir! Moving to intercept." A man with an English accent responded back.

"Oddball?" he asked.

"Just keep your head down." Chris gave him an open mouth smile. Then, he vaulted over the car while deflecting bullets heading in his direction. "Ian, come on!"

Ian was quick to not only act but also overtake Chris entirely. He was now the one in front, taking the brunt of the damage and soon met the enemy frontline head-on. Chris always appreciated his ability to just soak hits like that and not even react. The Imperial soldiers did try using plasma on him, but his armor resisted it fairly well. If it was going through, then Ian just didn't bring himself to care. Chris summoned a singular sword, rotated it to reverse grip, and cut clean across two Imperial soldiers. Turning, he then froze them in place, their guns forever aimed between one another to try and shoot him - at least until they were unthawed.

"Ian, be careful. Our tank should be coming soon," Chris informed him over the battle. He dodged a plasma round aimed for his head and retaliated with a shard of Ice. Penny shoved him lightly to block another incoming round meant for his heart and then fired a spell that instantly killed the soldier just by clenching her fist at him. Her hand quickly turned to Ian, who recoiled from being stabbed by a Sorcerer's blade. A light purple spell shot out from her hand and healed his injury rapidly, allowing him to defeat the opponent with relative ease.

"I forgot you could do that," Chris commented playfully.

"Stop playing around." She turned her head to the left and stared off blankly. "I can hear the tank coming."

Chris focused his ears but could not hear anything at all. What was she talking about? "You have better hearing than me, I guess!"

He only heard it when the tank burst through the building's interior on the far end of the road and opened fire on the Imperials with a tank round and then a hail of bullets. It then hovered out into the street to take on the Imperials further down the path. The crew kept their tank well out of harm's way and low profile to be able to shoot at an enemy that could barely attack back. Then it would progressively move forward. It was quite nimble too.

"Sir," the tank commander said from within the metal beast. "It appears neutral forces have engaged the enemy up ahead."

"Neutral?" Chris inquired.

"Ah. It appears to be three Resistance soldiers and one law enforcement officer." He said. "Moving to cover!"

"We're right behind you," Chris said. He then pointed to the right side of the street. "Ian, you and Meg head that way. We'll hit them from two sides to help out Oddball. Let's clear a path."

"Yes, bossy man!" Ian said sarcastically. "Come on, Meg. We get busy work again."

"He probably is just trying to get time alone with Penny," Megan was playing around now. It was rare for her to go along with Ian's teasing. "Have fun you two."

"Hey! No-!" Chris called after them. "I'm not!"

With that, Megan and Ian sprinted down the street, using Oddball for cover until they eventually moved past it. He could already see them fighting. He moved with Penny along the left side toward Bafair and the officer that was mentioned. They were held up behind a car. Bafair had his gun on the hood and was using it to control his gun better. The officer was peering out from the vehicle's side near the truck and firing a pump shotgun. This newcomer was a man with a clean brown beard, a tan shirt with the text: *Shenneld County Deputy*. He also wore dark blue jeans, and from here, Chris could not tell his eye color because they were hidden by his sunglasses.

"I'm glad to have the tank and all," Bafair began. "But there still are a lot of them. You okay, Dep?"

"I'm fine. We just have to get to that station. They'll kill the other officers and my partner if they get desperate." The Deputy ducked back behind the car when a fire spell flew out at him. The magic missed him but struck one of the Resistance members behind him. The woman rolled around for a moment before going limp. Bafair was quick to pull her to cover, but the deputy yanked him back by his collar when more gunfire came. He would have been killed there if this officer had not saved him. "She's gone. Worry about you right now."

Chris rushed in, deflecting bullets with his sword, and even countered a fire spell with one of his own Ice spells. He swung his sword hard, casting as he did, allowing his magic to pass through the weapon and send out an arc of Ice. The bright blue shockwave froze two soldiers solid before vanishing into thin air. Penny was closer to Bafair, the Deputy, and the only other surviving Resistance fighter. She had dropped one of the Sorcerers trying to advance on them and stomped his head with her boot. She then turned, kneeling as she did, and stabbed another who was rushing her to avenge his ally.

"Are you two okay?" Chris tried.

"We'll talk after I get to that station!" The deputy answered back, sprinting forward past the tank, taking cover as he did. "Bafair, let's go! My colleagues need our help! *Now!*"

"Right behind you," Bafair said, sparing one last glance at his fallen friend before following with his other ally slowly. He spoke to Chris as he passed. "Hey, kid. Thanks for the save. We could really use more, though."

"We were headed this way anyway. I'm guessing you freed that deputy, then?" Chris inquired.

"Ha!" Bafair snorted as if this was a bad question. "He freed himself before I even got close." Bafair took off running with his gun lowered slightly.

Chris followed Bafair without a second of hesitation. Penny was close behind, and so were Megan and Ian. They encountered very little opposition ahead, though. The only one Chris could see was the deputy, who was really a killing machine. Chris figured he had received some military experience or something because he did not move like the other officers. Even when he ran out of shotgun ammunition, he just attached the sling to his shoulder, swung it around to his back, and drew a revolver instead. It was actually embarrassing to be outperformed by an officer.

"Penny, there should be a knight leading this attack," Chris said, catching his breath between his words. "So hopefully, we're headed right to them."

"How would you know that?" she asked him. This was an honest question. What was he supposed to say? Chris decided to just not say anything yet. When the city was under their control, they would discuss it. She was not trying to read his mind, so he figured she must have agreed that now was not the time.

"Anyway, we need to get to the station regardless. Megan, can you fly us? It sure would be nice." Chris tried, briefly turning his head as they jogged forward. Megan was in the very back, trying to keep up with them.

"I would not recommend it. There are so many vantage points to shoot us down from." Megan responded intuitively.

"Looks like we're hoofing it," Ian commented.

"I guess so," Chris answered back. A loud notification went off on all four of their watches. Upon checking, one could immediately see the bright orange 'air support inbound' message with a caution sign. Three allied fighters. "I sure hope they're careful not to shoot randomly."

Penny gestured for him to keep moving and stay focused, "They will be." She said over a loud 'boom' in the distance.

"Delta Two," Evangeline could barely be heard over the sounds of battle. "I scanned an Imperial Knight in your vicinity just headed and alerted command. You have support coming to help your squad."

"Air support?"

"Yes, but the Headmaster's Hand is also accompanying this force. She will temporarily be joining your squad to ensure the swift elimination of this threat." Evangeline must have noted his silence because she spoke up rather quickly. "Please acknowledge."

"Yeah, okay." Chris agreed. She was right. Emily would probably be more suited to dealing with one of these knights if they genuinely were that dangerous. Did he really want another repeat of what happened with Vedi? Risking the lives of his squad just because they were closest was probably not wise. "We'll wait for her."

"Understood. She will be there in two minutes. Advisor Andrews, out."

"So, Em is coming down?" Ian asked, hunching over and holding his knees to catch his breath. "Niiiice."

"While she deals with the knight, we can clean up around the city," Megan suggested smartly.

"She might still need help." Penny added smartly.

"It's up to her, I guess," Chris told them all with an uncomfortable face. "I thought she was helping in Towle city, though?"

"I guess they're done." Ian laughed. "I almost feel sorry for the Empire. Autumn and Emily showed up to shut this whole thing down! Uncle! Uncle!"

"What do you know about that phrase?" Chris asked with genuine curiosity.

"Okay, just because I'm not from Earth doesn't mean I don't know a little, buddy."

The loud boom of the sound barrier being broken silenced their conversation. Alliance fighters came in from the west, opened fire across the city, and then soared off. They were probably going to come back around for another couple of runs. Another flight of fighters was coming from the west, this time with one fighter spearheading them. This craft broke off and flew low to the ground, almost at street level. The engines died down slightly and instead suspended the plane just at the height of the nearby buildings.

The pilot ejected from the plane's belly and fell downwards while their seat, still attached to the plane, returned to the cockpit. The fighter flew off at incredible speeds. The pilot flipped once to reorient herself and then landed on her feet in a crouched position. She stood up slowly and took in her surroundings before speaking to Chris. He couldn't help but notice that Emily was covered in bruises that were still healing and was boasting a few damages to her attire. Just how much fighting had she done today?

"What's our status, little brother?" Emily asked, wasting no time at all to treat her injuries even though she very well could.

"Our stat-" Chris stumbled over his words for a moment before regaining them. Maybe if she didn't shove 'little brother' into the question, he'd be just fine. He thought he had heard a little laugh from Penny too. "We're pushing toward the police station just this way. Bafair, Oddball, and a county Deputy were already headed in that direction. A few soldiers too. Uh..." Chris cleared his throat. "So far, we're fine. They can't exactly put up a fight when they're being hit from basically all sides..."

"Very good." Emily rubbed the back of her neck and stretched. "Time to move. I will face the Imperial knight. Your squad will free the hostage."

"What?!" Chris spoke up without meaning to. "We can help you."

"No. You can free those people who are sitting ducks for either executions or crossfire. You will get to that station and free them." Emily said, pointing a stern finger at him. "I can handle this without any help. Just wait for me to lure him away, okay?"

"...I guess," Chris muttered as she sprinted off. Megan and Ian were close behind.

"Don't worry," Penny said, placing a hand on his shoulder. "You know Emily is scary. Now come on. We're missing all of the stress and fighting."

Chris and his partner caught up with the other three when they had arrived at the police station. Emily was staring down at a man who Chris assumed was the Imperial knight Pixie had mentioned. He had slick swept-back hair, tan eyes, and appeared quite fit. Aarlam Vass had two sword holsters just under his white and purple cloak. This man definitely gave off the same level of threat as Vedi, and their outfits were quite similar. Chris guessed that he could not have been that much older than thirty-something.

"Are you the big man in charge?" Emily asked in a loud voice. "I'm assuming so since I was told that you had carved through our soldiers from the other district."

"Hold fire until I say so," the knight raised his hand to the soldiers behind him, using the police cars and portable barricades to conceal themselves. "To answer your question, yes. I also destroyed the pathetic tank you sent to flank us."

"That just means you might just keep me occupied for a while, but I'd rather not resort to violence. Surrender, and you will be treated fairly."

"Do you think I don't know who you are?" He scoffed and placed a hand on his forehead. "If I let you go here, then I might as well kill the entire Imperial army. You're too dangerous to just surrender to, and as a knight, it would be an insult. Now, what do you say we put an end to this?"

Emily scowled a little. "I guess I don't need to introduce myself, then. Chris," she started. "Take your squad and free the prisoners inside the station." She pointed to the building on her left next to the parking garage. A bright badge illuminated above the building with the letters NHPD. "There is no need for you to drag these children behind me into this. You and your men will face me and me alone. Will that be a problem?"

"Not at all." The knight smiled and waved his hand as if shooing the other four. "Men, stand down and allow them to pass into the station. If I am to fall, do no harm to them, but still target your efforts to her when I give the signal."

"Em, you can't be serious." Chris objected angrily.

"I am. This is not the first time I've done this, and you know it." Emily pointed toward the station again. "Now go."

"If you will not leave, then I will not attack you," the knight said, referring to Chris directly. "But I ask you to take cover and don't come out until this is over. I'd rather not go back on a fair agreement." Chris figured that this was perhaps the most polite and well-mannered Sorcerer he'd met so far besides Penny and Ian. It was almost...chivalrous. "If you were to enter the station, you would most likely be safe."

"I'm staying, Em, but I won't jump in unless you're in danger," Chris muttered, stepping aside. "Penn, Ian, Meg? Go on and help the prisoners. I'm staying with her."

"Just don't get yourself killed." Ian nudged Chris's shoulder and then hurried inside.

Megan nodded before following too. Penny did hesitate but accepted this. Instead of arguing, she removed her shield, put it in his free hand, and entered the station as well. It was out of character, but she must have understood his reasons. On the other hand, Emily did not say anything and only stared at him with great concern. Why couldn't she accept that he would be just fine and was looking out for her? He still did as he was told and moved to a safe distance with his sword and Penny's shield.

Would they just stand here staring each other down? He sat there thinking to himself with the shield partially raised. Emily happened to move first, extending both hands outward, launching all Imperial soldiers in her cone of vision multiple feet away from herself. She then outstretched her hand, summoned her green weapon in its halberd form, and took up a relaxed stance. She held the weapon behind her, laid the blade against the ground, and waited. Her injuries had healed by now, and so any advantage he could have had was gone.

"Well, I see you're back at full strength!" He called out to Emily confidently. "I was hoping to fight your best. If you don't hold back, I'd appreciate it."

"I wasn't going to." Emily watched as he took a step forward. She was quite ready for his next move.

Aarlam charged forth at blinding speeds, sending some stray sand up into the air behind himself. He then changed direction to strike from Emily's left. Chris's eyes couldn't keep up, but Emily did need to. She swung her weapon around her slender body, using her life magic to speed up to rate at which it moved, and smacked him clean across the hip with the halberd rod. She then returned the weapon to resting behind herself and stood relaxed again. Aarlam flew back a few feet before recovering and landing on all fours. He raised to his feet and spit out a decent amount of blood.

"That was quite the hit!" He praised with a cough as he rubbed his hip. "You're just as good as the reports say. Maybe a little better."

"I can assure you that those reports are flawed," Emily answered indifferently. She continued to stare at him. "Not many people walk away from meeting me without at least being captured. One way or another, the same will be true for you."

"Aren't you going to attack me now? I'd really like to see what you can do."

"Right now, I'm just letting you exert yourself, honestly," Emily answered sarcastically, brushing her hair back and away from her face. "I'm actually thinking about what I have to do after I'm done here."

Aarlam scoffed loudly. "Oh-ho! My, you're cocky. I feel underestimated."

Emily rolled her eyes, "If anything, I'm giving you a chance to prove me wrong."

"I'd hate to disappoint!" Aarlam charged forward and drew both swords. Leaping into the air, he spun like a tornado once and struck Emily's halberd, which was once again ready to guard. She then converted the weapon to a mace mid-swing, catching one of his blades

149

in the momentum. As it crashed to the ground, the steel severed, leaving only the guard. He swung again, but Emily cartwheeled out of the way and converted her weapon to a ninja sword and blocked. *I kind of want one of those now*, Chris thought to himself.

"I suggest you surrender. I'd rather not kill you in front of my brother." She mocked him.

Aarlam ignored her and just stared blankly. Emily raised an eyebrow and lowered her guard a little. Perhaps she saw no risk in it, at least not right now. Chris suddenly realized what he was doing: casting a spell. *Maybe it's the spell Tori used that one time*, he wondered to himself. It would probably be best to say something. He sucked in air and called out as loud as he could.

"Watch out, Em! Death magic, it's coming from below!" He cried out. She didn't need the warning. Emily stepped back twice as a pair of skeleton-like hands erupted from the concrete and grabbed at the air. The spell had failed entirely.

"I wonder how you could have known." Aarlam sounded quite disappointed. "Oh well. I'll just try something a little less subtle."

Chris watched with concern as darkness erupted from Aarlam's body and shrouded both Emily and himself in dark clouds. He could no longer see what was happening but could still hear their weapons clanging and clashing. Chris was worried about Emily, but she was probably just fine. She trained him on fighting in any environment and situation, including darkness, but this was the first time he'd seen this spell. Would she know what it was?

A loud *swoosh* erupted and swept away the dark clouds with a bright green flash. They soared away in all directions, revealing Emily holding her hands together with her weapon as a great sword. The mighty weapon was swept across her body as if she had just turned in a circle. Aarlam was left dumbfounded with an almost traumatized expression on his face. Chris supposed this spell was supposed to be his trump card. She then turned her head toward him and bolted in his direction, her weapon converting back into a straight sword. He tried to raise his weapon to defend but was cut clean through the torso by Emily's blade. The cut was so deep that it was implausible that it would heal fast enough for him to survive. Just how hard had Emily hit him?

"So-strong…" Aarlam managed as blood erupted from his lips, and he fell backward with an unceremonious thud. Emily stood up, converted her sword to a dagger, so it was easier to carry, and stepped over him.

"He's dead…" Chris said with amazement in his voice.

Emily breathed out as if she were de-stressing before speaking, "He gave me no choice. I'm sorry you had to see that Chris."

"Em, I've had to do the same." He explained. Emily scrunched up her face like this simple sentence hurt her somehow.

"It's not so much that, but I try to be a good example." She shut her eyes, took a deep breath, and then opened them. "We're heading inside with the others. I'll help here for a minute and then go assist in Grandham city."

"Okay." Chris agreed, staring at the dead man who was leaking blood onto the street.

"Stop looking." She approached him, placed a hand on his back, and led him away from the scene. She was rather forceful in that she was keeping him just in front of her rather than behind. As they walked up the steps which led into the rather large law enforcement building, Chris couldn't help but notice the sounds of battle dying down. "I don't want you to look."

# 13

## SANCTUARY

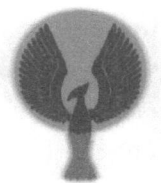

The police station's brown hard floor was littered with footsteps headed every which way. When one person took a step, another came from a different direction. The main hall's white brick walls were quite distinct and tall with signs pointing to the various parts of the station such as 'main hall' and 'community room.' Along with the front desk, which resided just at the entrance, the text 'protect and serve' could be seen in a font Chris had never seen before. At least - that's what they tried to do.

"Need a hand here!" One of the officers cried out as he tried in vain to restrain one of the Imperial soldiers. Though he was unarmed with a damaged and bloody arm, he was still quite dangerous, apparently. Two other officers rushed over, both female, and helped to take the soldier to the ground. Though he was crying out in frustration and fighting back, they did eventually manage to fully pin him on the floor and hold him in place. He continued to struggle, but that was pretty much the end of the altercation. "Stay on the ground," the officer huffed heavily.

Chris walked past the officers and spared a concerned glance. They were managing, but their training was nothing compared to the other big players here. With the city pretty much under their control, they now just needed to hold their captives until reinforcements came to take them to the Sohrann station for questioning. He wanted to help but was already exhausted from running back and forth since the initial battle. Chris hurried over to a bench in the lobby. He sat down, covering his face with his hands for a moment.

All of the exhaustion came at once. His legs ached from the constant fighting and running of the last few days. He'd gotten very little sleep and had only become more tired after the battle. Extending his legs out and sitting back, he felt a pop and winced. Chris knew his body would heal - that was no problem, but it was still not happy about everything that had occurred. Were the others going through the same thing? *She's Probably not even tired after all of this*, Chris thought to himself.

"I can't be tired too?" Penny asked in an authentic and close voice. He jumped up, removing his face from his hands and making eye contact with her. She was sitting on the bench with him and had probably been there for at least a minute. She smiled, tapped her index finger on his head, and laughed a little. "Maybe I'm just a little tired too."

Chris blew air out from his lips, "I didn't know that word was in your vocabulary after making me run those laps up and down the stairs that one time."

"You still won't let that go?" Penny asked him, setting her head on his shoulder. "Imagine if I didn't. You would be hunched over on the other side of New Hope, asking us to slow down."

"I wasn't that out of shape. I was pretty good for like thirteen." Chris reasoned.

"Tori said you fell off of a basic monkey bar set." Penny shut her eyes and sat still for a moment. She seemed fine, but her smile had gone as quickly as it had come.

"It wasn't simple..." Chris trailed off. Immediately realizing what was going on, he wrapped an arm around her shoulder as he had done many times before and pulled her close. The two sat together, silently embracing one another. The loss of her sister still weighed on her much later. Even the mention of Victoria reset her back to the moment just after it happened. All he could do was avoid her altogether and be there when her thoughts dwelled on her.

"Sir?" one of the officers had approached him and pointed to the second floor. "Ms. Spellcrafter is requesting you. She says it's urgent."

"Emily saying something is urgent," Chris said sarcastically. He gently shook Penny to let her know that they were about to get up. "This should be good."

"Yeah," Penny said. Chris cast a worried glance at her but still led the way.

Together they proceeded up the long and straight flight of stairs. Chris slid his hand along the brown wooden rails, which rode up to the top and along the second floor. Opening the door to the communication room, he was greeted by Emily, who had been paying no attention to his entrance. She was fixated on the hologram projecting from the table at the edge of the room. Her index finger was over the top of her lip, just under her nose, and the rest of her hand covered her mouth. She hit the button on the console to rewind yet again and watch for what must have been the fifth time.

"Hey, Em," Chris said, hoping to get her attention. She turned her head and looked back at them but said nothing. She just returned to this holographic recording and watched it yet again. "Is something wrong?"

"Vedi tells me that the Alliance has arrived early to engage." The hologram's audio was clear enough, but it sounded like a recording of another call. A man with black greying hair and brown eyes stood there in a crimson red and black battle garb. "And you still have not obtained the resources needed. Your element of surprise is gone."

"Yes, but we are getting close to completion—a week. Maybe a little more," another female voice said. This was a voice he recognized: Pixie. "The Alliance is making ground, but they are nowhere near the site of the operation. As soon as I have it, we'll be on our way."

"Eslena," the voice, Chaos, was stern and cold. He boomed with frustration. "Need I remind you that the Alliance seventh fleet is engaging us? Finish quickly so you can reinforce us here. We desperately need reinforcements. You have already lost a major city, an outpost, and your knight. I have given you the tools and resources for success."

"I will not fail you." Pixie – no - Eslena said confidently and very calmly. This name was indeed fake like he expected. How much of what she told him was the truth?

"If you cannot free up our ships, get the resources, and escape before the Alliance destroys you, the Empire will fall. We need this victory." Chaos lowered his head, the hologram fluttered slightly like there was interference. "Do not...spearhead..." the hologram faded to nothingness, leaving Eslena standing there instead.

"Councilor Renees?" someone out of frame said. "We've lost the signal. They've taken a direct hit to their long-range communications array."

"No matter. Our task is the same, regardless." Eslena waved her hand dismissively, and the recording ended. It started to repeat, but Emily hit the button once again to pause the hologram just before playing.

"I received this communication just after we took New Hope," Emily explained, turning her head toward Penny specifically. "It came from an unknown location in the desert. It seems we have a mole."

"That is too convenient." Penny declared with complete certainty.

"Yes, it is." Emily nodded and pressed her lips together, lowering her hand and placing it behind her back. "I will look into this, but I thought you should know."

Penny cut her eyes toward Chris, then back so fast that he almost didn't notice. She wanted him to speak up. She could hear his thoughts rambling on in his mind about Eslena. He sighed a little and opened his mouth to speak. Emily raised an eyebrow and made a face that told him she was uncertain of what could be wrong. Just what would Emily do?

"Em, I've seen this Eslena twice. She told me her name was Pixie and warned me about her knight." Chris went on, watching as Emily's eyes went wide, and she stepped toward him quickly. "Aarlam was her knight, but I have no idea why she just threw him to the wolves like that. She also said that-"

Emily had now come close enough to put both of her hands on his shoulders and squeeze just tight enough for him to feel it, "Chris. Stay. Away. From her. Shadow Councilors are dangerous. Leave her to myself and Autumn. I don't know what she told you, and I don't care."

"My concern-" Penny started to his right. Emily looked at her while holding onto him. "-Is he is able to see her when I can't. Ian can't see her either. I don't think that's possible, but if it is, then she somehow has found a way to communicate like she's his partner."

"No, anything is possible with enough time." Emily thought aloud. Penny nodded. "If you see her again, ignore her. If it is really her, you call Autumn or me. You call someone...anyone."

"I wonder if I can't see it because of my magic...come to think of it, Ian might have the same problem." Penny trailed off, but Emily must have agreed, given her tense expression. "Next time it happens, tell me. I'll try to use our link to see, but if that's the case, then it's some sort of projection."

"I have to get to Grandham, but if you see her, you tell me," Emily demanded with a look of fire. "You promise me."

Chris nodded, processing this new information, "I promise."

"Good. Good..." Emily pulled him into a hug and rubbed his back before releasing him from her grasp. Emily's eyes darted to look at Penny and conveyed something without words. Penny gave her back a similar look, and then the two broke it just as soon as it started. Perhaps it was coincidental.

"What about that transmission?" Chris asked her.

Emily smiled. "You let me handle that too. Just keep assisting here in New Hope, *where it is safe*, and make sure things run smoothly. Keep the city secure, deal with any looters, and-"

"So the unimportant stuff," Chris grunted out of frustration. Emily scowled at him. "You bet. I love it." He shifted to a seemingly cheerier tone. "So, I'm in charge?"

Emily gave him a teasing laugh and nodded, "Yes you are in charge of the basic stuff in and around New Hope. Major Lawson will also be here if you need him. Stay out of trouble."

Chris held out his arms due to this accusation. Emily turned, gave him a little grin, and then walked out.

# 14

# A NEW ENEMY

The Sohrannian sky was becoming darker by now as the sun lowered into the horizon. Chris's watch beeped multiple times as an Alliance notification was forced through. The text explained that the sun would set soon and to find a well-lit shelter if you hadn't already. Could it tell that he was in a dark zone? It must have been something that the General had pushed out to all devices on the network. He was near a well enough lit area by the police station, and the outpost in the center of the city was also illuminated. He would probably be safe, just a little bit away from the station on the parking deck's top floor.

*So. how much of what she told me was right, and how much was a lie?* Chris wondered to himself while staring off absentmindedly at the ghostly buildings looming just in front of him. None of the streetlights were on because no one had time to go and deal with the city power station, but at least they had generators for now. It put him at ease, if only just a little. So why was he out here by himself? A lot had happened, sure, but he had seen plenty and dealt with plenty. Why did he feel so overwhelmed and powerless? It was out of character even for him, and the last time he felt this way was on

Terminus when Emily had gone missing. Even with Tori, he thought he could have done something if not just stay out of her way.

"Eslena Renees." He said aloud to himself in a low voice. "Shadow Councilor. Just what are you planning? And why are you messing with me?"

"Ah, yes, the tough questions. What would you like to ask me, Christopher?" the familiar feminine voice began. Eslena materialized next to him much like a ghost and watched as he took a few steps back in shock.

"Oh, great." Chris glared at her. Remembering what Emily said, he reminded himself to treat her as a threat. "So why are you so fixated on me - *Eslena*, was it? Or should I keep calling you Pixie just for fun?"

"You don't like Pixie?" she asked sarcastically. Chris grimaced at her question but said nothing at all. Eslena's eyes squinted a little like she was just a little annoyed. "Very well, you may call me Eslena."

"Well, Eslena, why do you seem to have an obsession with me?"

Eslena's smile dropped, "Make no mistake," she said. "It is not just you. Anyone vulnerable to my magic will see images of myself from time to time. These grow in frequency, the closer I am. It's something of a curse I suppose...and a boon. I call them my Eyes."

"Is it Imagination magic?" He asked.

"Close – it is the Darker version: Psychosis. It is a spell I created myself, which I can control, but I cannot choose who is affected. It is a shame, really, but it does allow me to communicate without a need for technology. So long as I am in range." She lifted what looked like a mug of some sort to her lips and sipped it slowly. Perhaps she really was drinking something, and her hallucination reflected that. "I merely decided to speak with you directly through my Eye because you were a special case."

"Special case?" Chris repeated slowly. Eslena copied his refusal to answer by drinking from her mug, shutting her eyes. Chris balled up his fists a little. She was toying with him. "The name you used before, the Mitchell part, I've heard it before, but I don't remember where."

Eslena opened one eye and stared at him. Her pupils were spiral-like and distinct. The slightest stare made him feel like she would kill him. "I do believe you have. If you ever figure it out, you will know why I am so keen on assisting you."

"You aren't assisting me. I know you have some ulterior motive." Chris was growing impatient with her rather quickly. "This time, I know things you didn't plan to tell me. I know why you're here."

"Terrible." Eslena sat her cup down on a surface that was not there and let it fade from existence right in front of him. "That boy has put my entire operation at risk here. I told Chaos he was not to be trusted, but he is so desperate for allies that he just lets anyone join the cause. It is another reason he is not fit to rule."

"You mean-" Chris started, instantly filling in the blank before she could explain.

"Hunter Spiritbringer, yes." Eslena wore a very neutral and unreadable expression. "I'm sure you had at least a slight idea that it might have been him. I suppose it is no coincidence that he is now missing from my base. Do not trust him. He is dangerous."

"I have no idea what his goal is, though," Chris admitted to her, hoping to gain a little more information. "He doesn't want to help the Alliance or the Empire."

"I suppose it could be a personal gain or some higher master." Eslena elaborated. "I don't think anyone is capable of knowing how his mind works, which is why I think he swings his tail for another master. For a double agent, he was quite loud..."

"Eslena?" Chris asked. Eslena opened both eyes like she was surprised by his casual calling of her name. "I want to know about the Imperial operations here and what you guys are after. I also want to know why you killed your own knight!"

"My knight, hm?" Eslena asked in a clueless way. She shrugged.

"You know exactly who I'm referring to." Chris pursued with

anger. "Why on Earth did you kill your own bodyguard?! You said you wanted to help the Empire become a better place, so why?"

"To win a difficult game of chess," she began with a smile. "One must sacrifice pieces sometimes, yes?"

"You're equating killing your own ally to sacrificing a pawn?" Chris's mouth slowly formed an 'o' as terror set in. "Is it the same with all of the other Imperials who died so far?"

"Do you think it is really fair to consider my actions cruel when your own Alliance sacrifices its own soldiers and Wizards to satiate their own desire to eradicate the Empire and its people?" Chris tried looking away, but Eslena teleported directly in his face and smiled wide, showing her teeth like she was highly amused by her own point. "You, yourself, are a pawn just for a different player. So the same goes for you, Christopher Spellcrafter. The most important thing is for them to win the battle even if only one of the pieces is left standing. They would love nothing more than to eliminate all traces of the Empire."

"Maybe so, but two wrongs don't-"

"The most important thing is to win the war. People die. Planets are razed to the ground, and the war goes on. Even if I lose one knight, I've brought myself closer to victory. Besides, he was a spy, and I discovered this just before my arrival here. I merely had you assist me while also helping yourself. Mutual benefit."

"...And what exactly is the Empire trying to retrieve here on Sohrann?" Chris tried, probably pushing his luck. "What would you tell me if I asked you that?"

Eslena smiled more and stared at him wordlessly. This led him to believe that she would not respond, but then she did. "The Empire is relying on this operation to mine special resources from the planet and use them to help with space warfare. If we obtain them, it could swing the war. Right now, the Empire is on the brink of annihilation." Eslena sighed hopelessly. He couldn't help but wonder if she was lying again. Why would she tell him this? "Your Alliance is just too numerous with too many resources. Trade is a struggle now, so if we are to survive, we must take from someone else. It is that simple."

"I see."

"Is there anything more?" she asked him with a slight turn to stare at the pitch-black sky.

"Yeah. One more thing." Chris told her, stepping in front of her to speak. He mustered up all the courage he had to say these next words. "My sister already killed your knight Aarlam. She will stop your plans here and capture you, I'm sure of it. When that happens, I promise that we will do everything in our power to help the Empire form relations with the Alliance. On my home planet, the last world war nearly devastated everything and everyone because of just a few countries. I want a good resolution to this war, and if that means that I have to fight you to do so, I will. Good person or not, this war needs to end. It's gone on for two years, and that's long enough."

Eslena's smile dropped like a rock as she shut her eyes. She then reopened them; her green eyes now replaced with bright glowing yellow ones. His heart sank into the pit of his stomach as she smiled a wicked smile and laughed. "If you think a mere Wizard from Earth can follow up on that threat-" He felt differently suddenly and had no time to react to a pain that swept over his entire body. He fell to the ground, clasping his head tightly to the point where he was almost clawing at himself. "Then go ahead and see what happens to you and your pathetic Alliance. That silly girl cannot save you, and neither can the Dreadful children. They will never have the power or wisdom to face me directly."

Chris continued to suffer at her feet, the pain growing more unbearable by the second. Was she actually trying to kill him now? Fear was setting in and all he could think was just how much pain was surging through ever part of him. Chris could just barely look up at Eslena, her face blurred and distorted from this unnatural ache. Chris tried reaching out to Penny with their partner link but could not tell if she had heard him over the white noise. Was this really what someone who had mastered magic could do? A bright red glow enveloped his entire body, and a soothing calm washed over him. Had she decided to stop?

Looking up at her, Eslena had recoiled her hand and sneered, "What was that? Perhaps you are more powerful than I expected." Chris could not speak as he was preoccupied sucking in air for his lungs from the screaming; he did not even realize that he had started. "Or perhaps someone is protecting you. I will change that soon." She began to fade away rapidly into the dark night, her eyes being the last thing to go. They returned to their standard green color just before she was entirely gone.

He must have been very dazed or just was not facing the right way because Penny grabbed him up and pulled him into her arms. Behind her, Megan and Ian were rushing over too, but he could barely even make them out. Penny looked a little freaked out at the state he was in, and despite being unable to hear her, she could tell that she was pointing for Ian to stand guard in case he was attacked by demons. Megan knelt and began trying to heal him, but then said something to Penny. She could not heal an injury that was not there, specifically something mental. Instead, she started casting a spell that had a lime green color and soothed him so much that he fell asleep in her arms.

# 15

# VILLAINOUS PSYCHOSIS

Penny securely fastened the straps, which connected the tent to the hook buried deep in the concrete. She then turned to a Resistance soldier who had finished his side and gave her a quick nod. He then returned to what he was doing, like he was just a little nervous. She sighed and did the other end of the tent and then, when the job was done, stood back and made sure the construction would not fly off in the wind. She turned her head in Megan's direction. She was on the ground next to multiple injured citizens of New Hope.

Megan was going one by one, healing each of their injuries, soothing their pain, and even talking to them. She looked sleepy but still carried on with other Death and Life wizards who were present. If someone went flat, then a Storm Wizard would rush over and revive them as necessary, but for the most part, the Wizards currently on staff moved so fast that it was not required. Penny offered to help, but there was simply no need for her here with much more experienced menders on deck.

"Hey, Meg." Ian strolled over to Megan and knelt down beside her. She continued to focus on what she was doing but stopped for a moment when he put down what looked like a nutrient bar and some form of bottled beverage. "If you're not going to sleep, you need to eat and drink, okay?"

"Thank you," Megan told him softly in a tone he was probably not used to.

Ian chuckled and stretched, "Ah, Meg, I do this for you all the time. You always want to work until you drop."

"No. I meant for the other night." Megan clarified with an appreciative smile. She concluded her healing spell and placed her hands in her lap. Then, she turned and looked at him directly. "I've never had you get so protective of me, and I really wasn't sure what would happen, so thank you. It just tells me I can count on you, and that's just not something I expected from you, I guess."

"Was that an insult or a compliment because..." Ian placed his hand on his head. "I can't tell..."

"Must you ruin everything?" Megan laughed a little and turned to focus on healing again, only to tumble over. Ian caught her immediately. She was conscious, but it would be apparent to anyone that she was too exhausted to continue.

"Alright, yeah, you're done." Ian decided for her. "Hey," he called out rather loudly to a Life Wizard who was coming back from the police station. "Can you tag Megan out? She's been at this for forever."

"Sure! On my way," he responded, jogging toward them. As Ian removed Megan from her station, the other Life Wizard took her place. Ian brought her food and beverage and sat her down on the steps.

*I better check on her*, Penny told herself. She approached them at a leisurely pace but soon found herself stopping before she had even gotten close. They must have noticed her coming because the two directed their attention her way. Penny felt very strange now and couldn't bring herself to move. Just what was this? It obviously wasn't poison or anything - that much was clear, but regardless she felt weak. Then, a sharp pain came in her chest, and her head began to throb.

Ian stood up, and Megan leaned against the handrail to get up, but Ian pushed back down.

*Chris*, she finally decided. Penny turned on her heel, shoving someone out of the way that she could not see. She ran full speed toward the parking deck, which was right next to the station and only separated by a little stretch of grass. She could feel the pain getting worse every second, but the longer she took, the worse of a state he might be in. If he really was in danger and this was what she was feeling, then she had little time. *Was it a spell? No, maybe it was something blunt like a sword? But so close to the station?*

*I could fly up there. That would be faster*, Penny thought very quickly. This was an emergency, but what if he was perfectly fine and there was nothing wrong? What would he think? Penny had never shown him the truth. She decided against it. Penny could run up there fast enough and had to. She went up one floor, then another, then one more toward the top. Penny could hear him screaming over the loud reverberations of her shoes hitting the ground. Why was he screaming?

"Chris?" she called out to him. No response. He was lying on the ground of this level in a half-curled ball. A powerful red aura was fading from his body and revealing his normal green hair, white jacket, and jeans. He was still breathing like something had terrified him. Hurrying over to his side, Penny effortlessly pulled him into her arms. She wasted no time squeezing tight to get him to hold still and stop freaking out while also checking for injuries: no physical damage and no sign of an attacker. Penny decided to look around herself and remain on alert. She could be next.

"Is he alright?" Ian asked her from the lower floor.

"Get up here!" Penny called back. Megan was probably with him too. Good. She took his hand and pulled it away from his head, revealing his eyes. He looked surprised to see her, but that surprise quickly turned to pure fear. His arms came out to try and shove her away, but Penny caught both of his wrists and held them tight, pulling them around Chris's chest and keeping him from harming himself or her. "I think it's a spell."

"I'm here," Megan whispered. She must have been tired, but Penny still needed her help. She extended her hand and began healing while steadying herself with the other hand. "I don't see any-"

"It wasn't caused by a fight." Penny snapped without meaning to. "Ian, do you see anyone?"

"No, I don't," Ian answered back, stepping up onto the ledge. He grabbed the light pole and stared off into the darkness. "As if I could see if there was."

Megan gave up with her healing spell and instead swapped to a new one. Penny watched as her hand went from a dark green to more of a light color. This color surrounded Chris for a moment and then died down. His eyes shut, and his wriggling ended too. She put him to sleep. Penny just hoped that this would be enough. If it was any basic spell like a curse, it would go away on its own. That was all she could hope for.

"Do you think it was Eslena?" Ian asked, turning toward Penny. He leaped off the ledge and focused in on Chris. "How is he, Meg?"

"Eslena would have killed him." Penny reminded him with a look of concern. "Even if she didn't mean to. But I did see that Autumn's spell was set off."

"Her spell?" Ian inquired with a confused face. "Oh, right. That. I forgot that was there because Emily likes to be paranoid. So it was some form of mental attack, then. No one is here, though...odd."

"It didn't set itself off," Penny murmured to herself. She took his hand and squeezed. "If it wasn't there, would he even be here? The way he looked at me just now..."

Megan stood up in a hurry and summoned her sword. Both Penny and Ian became alert but saw nothing in the direction Megan was focused. Ian started to say something - most likely prepared to ask what exactly she was doing. Before either of them could speak any word at all, Megan let out a mighty blast of Life magic, which sent various shades of green forward in a ripple. Penny furrowed her eyebrows at this action and frowned a little. Megan really just needed to sleep now.

"What was that, Meg?!" Ian asked her. "You never just shoot off like that for no reason. Are you crazy?"

"No reason?" Megan asked, turning back to glance at him from the side of her eye. She looked around, her jaw dropped, and her chest began to rise and fall again. "Did you not see her?!"

"No one was there," Penny told her in the usual blunt and straightforward manner. "You are tired. You've slept the least out of the three of us, and so you should probably do that."

"Penny, I know what I saw," Megan promised her.

"Then why didn't we see it?" Ian asked, jumping to Penny's point immediately. "She has a point."

"I... suppose." Megan relented, holding her head, and stepping back a little. Ian was there to catch her yet again and set her down gently. "Thank you. Again, Ian."

"I can help Megan walk if you carry Chris. That will probably be easier." Penny suggested. Ian agreed.

Penny hurried over, taking Megan's arm around the back of her neck. She stood there, waiting for Ian to hoist Chris's limp self onto his back. The four made their way back toward the police station and the surrounding camp as the night became darker and colder. Normally, she would tell Emily what had happened, but she would probably just keep it between herself and the squad with such little information. Emily had a job to do, and so did they. Interrupting her would be the worst possible thing with no information on what had happened.

# 16

# AKELA

The sun rose the next day on Sohrann and once again banished the demons to the underground. There in the sand, they would remain for a few hours until night fell again in just four hours. Tents were still being set up just outside of the police station by the Resistance and the Alliance. Aid workers had also arrived by now and started preparing food, passing it out, and treating injuries. They were marked by a white and red circular symbol with a galaxy in the center. Any citizens of the city and around it were brought in to be treated as well. Some of these aid workers were also Wizards but were not affiliated at all.

Penny walked slowly down the stairs that connected to the police station, tying her hair back behind herself as she did. She sighed, staring at the tent she had set Chris in to rest for the night. She had gotten up early to tend to some of the more extensive duties with Ian to keep their partners idle for the time being. The only tasks left were the small ones, and of course, the most important of these was the power station. The generators at the checkpoint and the precinct could last another few nights. Still, with the possibility of the demon situation becoming worse or a counterattack, it was best to restore power citywide. She thought about undertaking this task herself, but that would require her to bring Chris, which she did not want to do after last night.

Penny yawned and blinked, her eyes readjusting to the sun coming over the buildings. The sun had only been up for a few minutes now, and she already was wishing that she remembered to bring better clothing. All of it was back on Salvation. What she didn't have on the station was on the Spark - which was also on the station! Still, a skirt and basic top were far cooler than a full set of armor. Ian was going to have a heat stroke here, and she would probably be stuck carrying him back to be revived.

*Chime, chime,* Penny stopped walking and lifted her watch. It was Evangeline, most likely; it was about time to check-in. Stepping out of the way of the stairs and lifting her wrist once again, Penny answered. Evangeline's voice projected out from the watch, along with her three-dimensional self sitting at her console. Penny waited while her advisor finished typing what was probably some sort of report on the situation in New Hope.

"...Advisor Evangeline to Delta One. Apologies, I was helping Miss Spellcrafter with an inquiry," she said politely with a sigh. "There is always some sort of complication on this planet."

"No problem. I'm surprised you contacted me directly, but I think I know why. You couldn't get a hold of Chris?"

"That is correct," she confirmed with a nod. "Delta Two failed to check-in, and I could not reach him. I decided to contact you instead, and if that failed, I would have contacted one of the Echoes."

"He's sleeping," Penny laughed a little. It wasn't funny or anything, but something about spelling it out for her just brought light to the situation. "I let him get some extra rest because a lot is going on here. Megan is dealing with some of the same things."

"Oh?" Evangeline raised both of her eyebrows. "What exactly happened since the battle?"

"Well," Penny sucked her teeth and spoke plainly. "Megan has seen things, Chris was terrified of something like a spell was cast on him, and the power is still out. Ian and I have been working without rest this morning to keep those two from doing a thing if possible."

"Delta One, when you say, 'seeing things,' do you mean like desert hallucinations? Fatigue? Perhaps paranoia-?" Evangeline asked, clear worry in her voice. Penny shrugged and frowned. "I see. I will not push you to contact your superior as that is going over Delta Two's head, but I advise you to inform her if the situation changes. Perhaps your partner was hit with a spell during the battle and you had not seen. Some of these do have a delayed effect. I do agree with your assessment of Echo Two, however."

"I know. I know." Penny started off at the tent again. "Other than that, we're fine. It's just the generator, a few patrol routes, and stuff like that."

Evangeline looked away at her bright screen, which flashed pink and blue for a moment. She raised a finger to Penny to say 'hold on' and then began speaking to someone else. Not long after, Penny was unmuted, and Evangeline spoke again. "Apologies. I have an update. You will be receiving mage assistance on the ground, and her first stop is New Hope City. She is already on the planet and heading toward you."

"A... mage?" Penny repeated curiously, "Oh, okay. Which one?"

"I was asked not to convey that information," Evangeline paused and made a weird face. "She wanted it to be a surprise or - at least that's what she said."

"Morgan," Penny deduced instantaneously with a head shake.

"I'm sorry?" Evangeline looked puzzled.

"Nothing. Just a thought. Have a good day, advisor. I'll tell you if there is anything else." Penny raised her free hand and did her best to smile.

"I am not used to you behaving this way," Evangeline commented with a look that was hard to read. "Good day to you too." The call ended before Penny could get a word in otherwise.

*I really am getting tired of hearing everyone say that,* she thought with an exaggerated sigh. *I guess I can see what to tackle next. Maybe even finish before Chris wakes up.*

"Good morning," Bafair said to Penny as he descended from the police station with a small squad. "I'm going out on patrol, but I'll be back in a few minutes."

"Bafair," Penny called back before he got too far. She was relieved when he turned around. "Actually, would you be okay with doing the power station while we handle the patrol?" Bafair let out a pronounced 'huh' to her question. "Something happened with Chris and Megan, so it really would be easier to just have them go on a short patrol. If not, I will split up the squad, but I'd rather keep an eye on them both."

"What happened to him calling the shots?" Bafair asked with a short laugh. He held out a hand toward his comrades to inform them to wait. "That's a big one-eighty."

"He does." Penny continued with a fiery look in her eye. "Until something happens to him. Then it's my call. If that means that he and Megan are stuck doing a basic patrol while I do the power station myself, fine."

"You know it's infested with demons because the power was out aside from the emergency lights, right?" Bafair reminded her with a scrunched-up face. "Going by yourself would be really dangerous, and I'd honestly feel accountable."

"If your team can't handle the demons and reactivate the power, then I will. I can even get a fireteam of soldiers together if that would help." She continued on, hoping to convince Bafair to allow this change of plans.

"What do you think, David?" Bafair asked him over his shoulder.

David shrugged, "I don't really care. It's busy work either way."

"Noah?" Bafair asked him next.

"I mean...you can do what you want." the Resistance fighter known as Noah answered back. "But if we get eaten then...that's all you."

"Alright." Bafair clapped his hands once and nodded at Penny.

"Done. We'll handle the power station if you give us a few people to help out. You do the patrol. The route should be pretty easy."

"Assuming we get the generator up," Noah commented from behind Bafair. "If not-"

"*Optimism*, Noah. *Optimism*. I get to use my new gun, and you get to witness it...!" David exclaimed excitedly with a laugh. "I don't get to do that on patrol!"

"*Oh, boy.*" Noah sighed heavy enough to be heard over David's excitement. "Alright. Guess we're doing the dangerous job..." David laughed maniacally at this comment and responded with a simple 'yes.'

"Good luck," Bafair saluted as respectfully as possible and then marched off toward the west.

"I should be wishing you luck," Penny said with her arms folded. "Thanks again. If he asks-"

"Asks what? I volunteered for this, and you couldn't stop me," Bafair played along with a false shrug. "And David wanted to use his new gun!"

"Ah, I've made you a troublemaker too." Penny smiled to herself and made her way over to Chris's tent. When he got up, they'd do the route together. Not only would it be something super simple and allow her to keep eyes on him, but it was just something to relax. Work or not, it was better than the constant fighting of the last few days. Maybe they could even get some real sleep after.

Penny unzipped their shared tent and entered to see him sleeping soundly in the same position she had set him down. She sat down beside him and began brushing his short hair gently. Penny knew she should wake him up now, but he actually looked the most relaxed she had seen him since they arrived. She'd let him sleep in just a little longer. What was the harm? He would always complain no matter how gently she woke him up now compared to when they first met.

Despite the grand speech of how he felt about her, he complained about her waking him and never letting him rest. Some things would never change, and that was just the truth. But one thing did change, and Penny would just have to tell him eventually. She smiled and blankly looked him over, sliding her hand down to his own and taking it tightly. He stirred a little but did not wake up. It was probably time to get him up now, but when things were like this - when he was asleep, or things slowed down, she finally had time to think about just how much she needed him too.

"Chris?" Penny asked while shaking him gently. "Chris, come on. If you're okay, I need you to wake up. We have work to do."

She waited a minute until she was sure that he was stirring a little. One more shake and he had had enough of her trying to wake him up. Chris opened his eyes, rolling on his side to look at her drowsily. She placed her hand on his head and watched as he attempted to bite her hand.

"Oh, stop," Penny lightly popped the side of his mouth and giggled. "We have a patrol to do this morning. Are you feeling up to it? You really scared us yesterday."

"Even Ian?" Chris asked sarcastically.

"Even Ian," Penny answered back thoughtfully. "We're going to have to keep an eye on you."

"Wait, you said patrol," Chris realized rightly. "What about power?"

"Oh..." Penny trailed off, pretending to think. "Bafair wanted to take it on with two other Resistance guys. They were really adamant about going, so we're doing the boring and uneventful patrol. It should be easy. Just looters and all that..."

"I feel like you had something to do with that," Chris said. Penny could tell he was trying to read her mind, so she guarded her thoughts as best as possible.

"No, I would never," Penny said in a compelling way. She placed a hand on her chest. "I'm offended, *Delta Two*." Chris stared at her, his mouth forming a bland straight line. "What? Would you prefer the name dummy?"

"You know, I just might prefer it, *Lucky Penny*," Chris replied back. "I'll meet you in a bit."

"In a bit? Am I going to have to wait an eternity for you to fully wake up? Should I ask Megan to borrow a book?" Penny stood up and smiled a little. He appeared to be okay now. Still, she'd be paying close attention to any behavioral changes.

A breeze was coming in from the eastern side of the city. It was cool and relaxing, so Penny almost didn't mind just standing outside of the tent waiting. It had not been too long, but she did not like to waste time. Penny checked her watch quickly and noted that a sandstorm was predicted to occur sometime soon but was not really concerned about it since they did not plan to leave the city. *I miss Shadehedge,* she thought absentmindedly. *Terminus reminds me of it, so it wasn't so bad, but Sohrann is just...desert everywhere.* Penny looked to the now light blue sky with white rolling clouds as her thoughts continued to go on and on. *Would you like it here, Tori?* She asked no one. *You always hated the colder climates.*

"What's that face for?" Ian asked her from his own tent, which was across from theirs. "You look so glum today."

"This is my normal expression," Penny lied to him.

Ian huffed in a half-laugh, half grunt, "I don't have to be your partner to know that's a load of crap." He folded his arms. "And it's not like you to dwell on things."

"It's nothing," Penny pressed on again. "I don't dwell anyway. I just reflect sometimes, I guess. Can we not right now?" She requested, hoping to not speak on this further.

"Can we not what?" Chris asked, finally emerging from the tent, this time without his jacket.

"Can we not take so long," Penny said, fabricating an excuse. She placed her hand on his head and smiled wide. "So slow."

"Meg took just as long," Chris tried.

"Nope. She's over by the parking garage thing reading." Ian corrected. "You're the only one who slept in! What do you have to say for yourself?"

"Something happened to him, and he needed to sleep it off," Penny quickly countered with quite the sass in her voice. "And your excuse for only helping me a little this morning?"

"...I plead the fifth." Ian held up both hands defensively.

"Do you even know what that means?" Chris inquired.

"No, but I'm assuming it's something Earth slang. I've heard you say it when you get in trouble," Ian explained.

"It just means you don't want to say anything that'll make you look bad in court," Chris shook his head slowly and held his head. "Don't say things if you don't know what they mean, buddy." Chris fiddled with his watch for a moment, most likely marking that they were headed out on patrol. "Alright. Time to make tracks. I don't really wanna see a demon ever again."

"Seconded," Penny said to him as the three of them walked toward Megan, who was still reading on the ground with her legs together. She looked really into whatever it was. Maybe she'd let Penny borrow it sometime. "Meg, we're going!"

"On my way," Megan called back, shutting her book as she said it.

Penny smirked when she placed a hand under herself, creating a powerful burst of wind that launched her up and onto her feet. She opened the heart pouch, which was on her hip, and slipped the novel-sized book inside. Megan walked as fast as she could without running to get caught up and then moved at the usual pace. Penny was about to comment on how she didn't have her hat on, but Megan swung her arm out, summoned it, and slapped it over her pink hair.

"So much laziness." Penny clapped her hands. "Please teach me more."

"Oh, you think that was lazy? Are you jealous that my magic is so useful for everyday things?" Megan sounded like she was proud of herself.

"I can too!" Chris said from the front of the group as they moved.

"Yeah, me too." Penny tried, knowing very well that she couldn't.

Ian decided to jump into this, too, "I can too!"

"Name one each," Megan said with the biggest curved smile. "Starting now."

"Cooling off my drink!" Chris said quickly.

"I can hunt with mine, I guess," Penny said very slowly. That was such a basic answer...she could have done better.

"I can make sure things die when they are killed!" Ian said in a very proud and booming voice. The group went silent. "What?"

"So, Ian is the only useless one?" Megan finally said.

"Yeah, yeah, basically." Chris and Penny said in unison.

"At least I didn't stretch my answer!" He cried out defensively. "This patrol is going to suck. I should've stayed at camp."

Penny stopped and smiled, "Where's the fun in that, Ian? You get to hang out with friends."

"Let alone three of them!" Megan continued with an evil look. She was enjoying this too much.

"You are a fortunate man," Chris said, patting his shoulder hard like Ian often did to him. "Congratulations."

---

Chris found this patrol to be going quite well. They only ran into the occasional looter, who usually dropped what they were carrying and took off. Sometimes they would attack or try to keep what they had, but typically only got a few feet away before being tackled. They never hurt or killed them; they simply ruffed them up, took a name for documentation, and sent them on their way. They were not really large enough of a squad to be taking prisoners anyway.

It was starting to rain now, which was a little abnormal considering this was a desert planet, but Chris figured there had to be some participation. He sighed, trying to remember what had happened last night, but instead found himself staring at the many vacant and damaged buildings they passed. There were homes, shops, skyscrapers, and crumbled bridges. All of it was so haunting - especially the streetlights, which were lightly swinging in the wind and flashing to perform their purpose.

*This reminds me of when Tori beat up Gatchi and her friends,* Chris thought to himself. *I left my home, but these people may not get to go back for a long time, if at all.*

"Am I the only one wondering why it's raining so hard?" Ian asked aloud over a very deep thunder crackle in the distance. He raised his hand to see the other three just ahead of himself. Chris nodded in agreement.

"It is strange, yeah," Megan noted, turning her gaze to the heavens and wincing as raindrops pelted her eyes. "At least it's cooler. The demons also don't like rain much from what I read, so there is that."

"Something the demons and I can agree on," Ian called back, drawing his hood up from his armor to cover his already soaked hair. It was a bit pointless to do this now.

"It will pass," Chris commented. Chris was using his watch to read a map, which actively updated to tell them where they were. He would click a button that sent an all clear to Evangeline and the police station forces every few blocks. No imperials, no severe resistance from people taking advantage of the chaos, and no demons. Soon, Bafair would have the power station online, and the chances of that happening would go straight to zero in an instant.

"We should be performing more thorough checks of the buildings. I don't think that popping in and out is enough." Megan shared her thoughts without a moment of hesitation when Chris quickly popped into a half-destroyed house and considered this to be enough. "There could be an ambush."

"It's unlikely, but if it would make you feel better, we can. This is just a quick run-through part of the city." Chris answered back. "It just would take too long to like check every nook and cranny."

"I suppose."

"If there is an ambush, we will handle it-" Penny stopped what she was doing and froze in place.

"Penn?" Chris questioned, lowering his arm and focusing on her. This was unusual.

Penny was staring directly at an apartment complex to their left. It had a black roof, weathered white walls, and dark text indicating level and building. This was also in a font he could barely recognize, but here at least they were big enough to make out what exactly it said: The Desert Shores. Chris spoke up again to ask her what was wrong, but she was fixated on something. She summoned her sword and shield without a moment's hesitation and started up the stairs to the second level.

"Chris?" Megan asked with concern.

"Wait there. I'll tell you if we need help, but the worst thing that can happen is we all go in here and let our guard down." Chris decided firmly. "Get under the building, so you aren't standing in the rain."

Chris could barely hear over the sounds of heavy rain slapping against the metal stairs and supports. The main thing he could hear around him was the tempo of Penny's walking and his own. The two proceeded up the stairs into a damp building that smelled thick of metallic blood and other things he did not want to think about. Either people died here trying to hide, or it was caught up in the fighting. Regardless, it was more intact than the buildings surrounding it, so he guessed that it could have just been some unfortunate soul.

The lights flickered on and off as the hum of what must have been an emergency backup generator could be heard from somewhere, but he was unsure where it could be. Perhaps it was under them, and they had not seen it, but it kept this place mildly lit. His thought was interrupted by a light splashing sound. Looking down, he expected to find a puddle, but instead found a half dried-up pool of blood which was mixing with the rain. Not too far from it was the body of someone that looked like they could be a Resistance agent. He automatically covered his mouth and stepped back, nearly falling down the stairs as he did.

Penny continued on without him, not noticing him stopping here in the corridor between stairs, rooms, and open air. Chris gently took the man by his shoulder and turned him over. Though he did not have a poncho, he did have a rifle on him as well as a pistol holster. Perhaps his gun had been taken by someone. Either he was Resistance or just someone well-armed who picked a fight they couldn't win. Alternatively, he could be a looter taking advantage of the chaos. It wasn't important, but Chris would report it no matter what. Lifting his watch, he took a quick photo, sent it back with his best guesses to the identity then moved on to find Penny.

"I heard something," Penny elaborated as he caught up to her. "I'm just not sure where yet."

"You can hear over this rain? How?" Chris asked, entirely baffled. Part of him was worried that she was experiencing the same hallucinations he was now. "Are you sure?"

"Entirely," Penny responded, placing her ear against every door one by one.

"It could be demons, you guys!" Megan cried out over the howling storm and wind. "So be careful."

"What she said!" Ian agreed.

"I doubt it. Unless one of these rooms had the lights off, and it doesn't mind running through all of the other lights outside." Penny winced a little as Chris called back to them to say this. Penny shushed him quickly. "Sorry..."

Penny nodded and hurried onward, going door to door. She would place her ear against it, and if she heard nothing, she would move on. Chris would do this too, but all he could hear was the storm. He figured Penny must have just trained herself to ignore unnecessary noises or something. Maybe she would teach him one day. Penny had now placed her hand onto one of the doorknobs while listening. She stood there for a moment like she was confirming her suspicions, then tried to open it. Locked. Penny seemed to debate kicking the door down but instead decided against it.

"Wait here," Penny decided, handing him her sword and running up to the next floor. Had she heard something else?

This was room 207 and was on the other side of the hall. He waited and waited for what must have been only a few seconds when the door suddenly unlocked on the other end. Penny's figure met him in the darkness of the room, drenched from the rain, but not tired at all. When the lightning flashed, Chris could make out an open window where she must have slipped in. He figured that it must have been hard to climb such a steep surface in the rain.

"Slowly," she whispered, raising her shield and moving slowly through the room, taking her sword back as she did.

Chris debated summoning his own sword but decided against it. He would call his weapons if needed. Even if they were attacked, what would he do? Swing and hope to hit something? It was dark, dark enough to get lost in this small living room among the fine maroon couches. Some debris had made its way from upstairs onto this floor. The wooden floor below them also didn't seem very stable anymore, so Chris was sure to follow Penny's movements as closely as possible but still found himself tripping over things. The only light in this room came from a reasonably bright electronic lantern, tossed aside haphazardly either by someone still residing here or by the various explosions and fighting.

Penny picked it up, crouching on the spot as she did. Studying the lantern for a moment, she eventually stood up, placed it on what must have been the coffee table, and moved on. Chris picked it up himself and began searching for a light to use. demons would not attack them here between the lights around the building and the rain, but he still preferred to not be entirely in the dark. Even just a few feet away from Penny, he found it hard to see, and all he knew was that she was making her way into what could be a kitchen by now.

Eventually, with some feeling along the wall, he did find the light switch. The living room lights flickered to life as the room around them revealed itself. In the kitchen, Penny could be seen still searching. Penny stopped for a moment, kneeling down in front of the kitchen sink where a pair of brown, striped, cabinet doors resided. She placed her hand on the latch, hesitating like she was preparing herself for anything. A quick gasp escaped from Penny, altering Chris immediately. He was about to charge over to check on her, but she held out her hand behind herself to tell him to wait.

A pair of small legs came out suddenly from under the sink and began to kick at Penny's torso. She didn't seem affected by it but still eventually started to block and whisper for whoever this was to stop over and over. She tried to grab at the small limbs, but they just kept coming, and it was clear that she was not trying to hurt this person. Giving up, Penny threw her shield aside and set her sword down. She then scooted a small distance away from the sink and held out both hands.

"Hey, hey...calm down. Look," Penny moved her hands up and then flipped them over to show the back of her gloves. "I'm not holding anything. I promise. I'm a friend." From where Chris was standing, he could not hear any responses to Penny's words to this person at all. He dared not to draw closer because Penny had told him to stay put. "Can I pull you out?"

"Penny?" Chris questioned from behind her.

"I said can I pull you out of there?" Penny decided to reword this to sound a little less aggressive. "Or really can you at least - can you come out on your own? You can crawl out, right? You got in there, so I don't want to hurt you trying to get you..."

"My head is stuck..." a small female voice responded just loud enough for Chris to barely make out.

"You're stuck?" Penny's voice was softer than usual, which brought Chris to the conclusion that she was speaking to a child. "Did you rush in here to hide from us? Okay. Well, I need you to help me get you out. I'm going to grab your legs and pull just a little. You just wiggle, okay?"

"Yeah," was the response she gave. Penny began to lightly pull at the pair of legs dangling from the sink.

A little girl emerged from the dark storage compartment. She had long curly black hair similar to Penny's, which was damp and bloody, dark brown eyes, and a dirty pink and blue flowered top. She appeared to be wearing blue shorts, which revealed cuts and bruises all along her legs from either hurrying to hide or something else entirely. Penny remained in a kneeling position, looking up at the girl while keeping a firm grip on her.

"There," Penny asked as she reached up and brushed the girl's hair straight again, taking a moment to note the bloody patch. "Isn't that better?"

The girl did not say anything. Instead, she lunged for Penny's chest and hid inside of it, which clearly surprised her. Chris half expected that Penny might not react for a second, but instead, she coiled her arms around the child and squeezed her affectionately. Penny could see something else under the sink just over the girl's shoulder and grabbed it carefully. She pulled away from the girl to show her a pistol. It was likely the same gun that was missing on the dead man outside.

"Why didn't you use this?" Penny asked her gently out of concern. "Did you know you had it?" The girl nodded. "But you didn't use it?"

"I was scared." That was all she said, her eyes welling up as she said this.

Penny looked down, noted something, and then spoke again. "Where are your shoes?" she asked kindly.

"Upstairs, I think..."

"Upstairs, where?" Penny asked further.

"In my room..." The girl went on. Penny nodded, standing up and pulling the girl up with her.

"Take her for me, please," Penny requested with a particular look in her eyes, which looked into Chris's. Chris extended his arms to take her into them, and though she was hesitant, she embraced him too. "I'm going to get her shoes, and then we're getting her somewhere safe."

"Okay, I've got her," Chris assured Penny.

"I'll be back," Penny assured the girl. She could feel the little scared girl's eyes following her up until she went around the turn at the top of the stairs and vanished. Behind her, Penny could hear Chris trying to make conversation with the girl as best as he could. She opened door after door, looking for the room that could be hers: a master bedroom, presumably a guest bedroom, and finally the girl's bedroom. A pair of sandals sat on the floor just under the bed. Penny went to reach for them but also noticed a pair of white shoes with blue stripes. She knew these would be better, so she got down and laid on the rugged floor, grabbing the shoes from deeper under the bed and hoisting them up as she stood.

"Are you hungry?" Penny could hear Chris ask from downstairs.

"Starving..." the girl replied finally after so many questions from Chris. Though Penny had not really been paying attention, she knew he was trying his best. "There's nothing left in the pantry, and I only know how to cook a little. I burned some stuff, and then the power went out on the stove and-"

"We're going to get you something. The stuff back at base isn't the best, but my friend Megan? Her stuff is good," Penny heard him say. Chris was rubbing her back and smiling as best as he could to relax her. "Can you tell me your name for now, though?"

"Akela..." she muttered into his shirt. It sounded more like sobbing, but she was probably trying not to cry.

"Your name is Akela?" Chris asked, gently brushing her hair, mimicking Penny as much as possible. "Well, that's a pretty name."

"I guess..." Akela hid in his sleeve and refused to come out. *I wish I could do more*, he thought to himself.

*We are.* Penny responded mentally with a quick glance. She landed at the bottom of the stairs finally and showed Akela the shoes, "Are these okay? I'm not sure if they fit. I sometimes kept shoes that didn't fit me." Akela gave a nod of approval, and so Penny got down and began to put the shoes on the girl's feet herself. She then extended her arms and waited for Akela to do the same. Picking up the girl looked rather effortless too. Akela swung herself around slowly and carefully to Penny's back. She held her legs against her, wait to keep the girl balanced.

*We need to get moving before sunset*, Penny told Chris. "Is there anything here you want?" Penny tried. Akela shrugged her shoulders and nuzzled herself into the crook of Penny's neck. She could feel her hot tears on her, and so she stopped immediately, not wanting to overwhelm her. Penny glanced back at the gun, debating grabbing it to bring with them, but instead left it. Someone would have to come for that body anyway. This train of thought led her to take the other flight of stairs near Akela's side of the complex. She waited to avoid going anywhere near the body with her in tow.

"I got the door," Chris said from behind her.

"Thank you."

The rain was slowing down a little now, and the sun was trying to shine through the dreary sky, but it was still quite messy. Ian was leaning against a vending machine, and Megan was sitting on a bench near it with her eyes shut. The two almost didn't notice when Chris and Penny had returned from their unexpected stop. Megan opened her mouth to say something, her eyes glossing over the child as the words in her throat disintegrated. She instead nodded and looked the girl over. Megan did not need to be asked to heal the girl when Penny sat her down on the bench where she was sitting. Instead, she got right to work on removing the cuts, checking for infections, and being as careful as possible.

"What are we doing about the patrol?" Ian asked Chris. Ian had now walked over to where the other three were gathered around the girl.

"Don't crowd her please," Penny requested instinctively.

"Well, the way I see it...we have two options," Chris answered back quietly. "Split up or head back. But taking her with us isn't an option, and once this rain ends, we'll be caught out at night. I'm more interested in getting her back than finishing this up. Bafair still hasn't gotten the power-up either, so that's especially not an option."

"Okay, so, what?" Ian asked, the two of them stepping away toward the edge of the complex while speaking. "We call Bafair to see if he's close to being done?"

"I'll call Eva and see what she thinks." Chris decided finally, looking back at Penny for a moment as he did. "Maybe she can round some people up to help us here. I mean, what do you think-?"

Penny continued to listen to her two squadmates discussing the situation. Though she wanted to chime in, part of her knew that if she left Akela's side, she'd panic. Instead, Penny spent this time holding the girl's tiny hand tightly in her own and remaining at her side. Even when Megan issued the word 'done' and stood up, she stayed. The girl was her responsibility - at least for now.

"We should move," Penny told her, turning in a crouched position in front of her. "Get on, okay?" The girl obeyed with much less hesitation this time and held on a lot better now that her injuries had fully gone.

"If you hold tight for a second, I'll call Eva. I'm sure-" Chris tried.

"Go ahead. I'm going to start back toward the precinct now just in case." Penny explained, marching forward into the rain with the child in tow. "You can continue the patrol. I'll see you back there."

"You don't truly expect us to leave you to head back on your own when the demons could emerge at any time." Megan directed her vision toward the sky then back at Penny. "We'll accompany you. I can't fly us with my flower very well in the rain, but I think four people can keep this girl safe better than one."

Penny looked back at the other two to see what they thought of this. Chris stepped closer to her, nodding to show that he agreed with this decision. Ian folded his arms and began walking ahead of the rest of them. He was choosing to take point just in case there was danger. Chris went next but stuck closer to Penny. Megan remained at the back of the group, watching behind them for trouble and staying near Penny and the child she had in her possession. Penny was a little surprised at their desire to remain with her since she could handle herself, but they did have a point. It was a little ironic that the most straightforward task they could possibly undertake quickly became one of the hardest instantly.

"Hey, Eva?" Chris said into his watch as the heavy rain continued to pour on. "Can you lend us a hand?"

"Advisor Evangeline to Delta Two. Are you in danger?" Evangeline's hologram jumped out from his watch but became distorted every time rain passed through it. "I was not expecting to communicate so soon."

"No. We found a kid out here...I don't even know how old she is." Chris paused, looking back at Akela, still on Penny's back. "The point is, we are heading back to camp and don't want to risk dealing with looters, demons, or whatever else could just be roaming around. Can you send us an escort or something?"

"I cannot provide you with a full escort, but I can divert a mage toward your position to meet you about halfway to the precinct base of operations," Evangeline slid her finger across her screen and watched as a notification popped up. "Continue on your current course. She will find you."

"A mage? Here? I wasn't aware..." Chris said with surprise. "I'll take it!"

"You may find her to be a handful, but she will ensure the safety of your squad and the child," Evangeline looked at Chris once again as she ended in her usual manner. "Try to avoid combat. Advisor Evangeline, out."

"Thanks," Chris concluded as the hologram fell back into his watch and the device's face went blank. This left the group by themselves for the moment.

---

The rain was slowing down now, and the sky was becoming far darker. As long as it continued raining, they'd be safe from any demonic threats, but looters would probably try to take advantage of the lack of light too. This thought went on as he wondered what the plan would be if they did get forced into a fight. He could send Penny ahead with Akela and continue fighting - maybe send Megan along with her in case there was more trouble ahead...or perhaps he could-

A bright flash erupted as the world around him went white. It was reminiscent of a time when he lost himself and was yanked into a new world. Not Terminus, but some twisted false Earth where what he wanted became reality: the Imagination Realm. Automatically, Chris raised his hands to meet his eyes and studied them, then he looked to his squad and Akela to ensure that they were all there. In the end, it turned out to just be the lights finally being activated in the city power station. Bafair was successful, so there was no worry about demons now unless they ran into a particularly dark area.

When his eyes finally adjusted, he made eye contact with a small group of looters inside a gas station. There were maybe four or five of them with two sitting outside. The two guarding the door either noticed Chris's squad or just freaked out when the lights came on. The pair bolted inside, struggling to open the door as they went. Those that were inside finished up what they were doing and hopped over counters. They knocked over shelves to get out and stumbled over each other. Three took off down the road in a hurry while the other two lagged behind, struggling to carry their stolen goods. One of these looters, a man in a red bandana, noticed them and drew his gun.

"Wizards! There are Wizards!" He cried out loudly. The others didn't really seem to want to stop and help him with a fight that they couldn't win.

Chris summoned his sword and stepped in front of the group while Penny fell behind Megan and Ian. The two of them also stepped in to prepare to fight, but it was not needed. His gun hand was surrounded by a bright pink bubble, which held almost his whole arm tightly. He tried firing to pop it, but the round just froze in time. The bubble suddenly grew about twenty times larger and consumed his whole body, entrapping him in a tight ball in which he could barely move.

"They got Yon!" one cried out, looking back at his captured comrade. "They got him!"

"Just keep running. We can still make it," was the response of one of them. Another bubble appeared around his leg and trapped him in place. "What the-!? Hey- hey, help!"

The others actually did turn around for this looter. Perhaps he was the leader of their group or just the most well-liked. This proved to be their downfall because this time, the bubble on his foot grew to about fifty times its normal size and consumed the other four, packing them together like human sardines. The bubble condensed and condensed until it was just big enough to allow basic movements. The looter on the bottom, who had now revealed his bearded face, tried stabbing down into the prison, but the knife he had pulled out bounced off, and the hilt smacked him in the jaw, causing him to yelp.

"Don't do that," a newcomer said, leaping from the top of an old apartment building. She glided down slowly in almost a hover before touching the ground. Poking the bubble, she smiled and spoke again, "Oh, don't look at me like that. I can't just let you go when I saw the whole thing."

The girl placed a hand on her hip and began twirling her long pink curly hair around her finger. She wore a reasonably long black dress with red highlights and a blue clip, large golden bracelets on either arm, red and white knee socks, and black fur-lined boots with red stripes on the top and bottom. She shut her eyes for a moment, nodding to herself as if applauding her own use of these spells. Then she held up both hands and slapped them together, colliding the bubbles and forming a giant one to hold all five, opening her eyes as she concluded.

The girl in front of them was probably about fifteen or sixteen. She raised her hand and waved in the most obvious way possible, "Hey, you guys!" she cried out happily with a bright smile. "Gee, I was right on time, huh?" Chris noted that Akela was hiding further down on Penny's back, most likely startled by Morgan, who was approaching them now.

"Morgan! Awesome entrance," Ian said to her, high fiving her as she approached. "You finally decided to try a new outfit."

"I wear what I want," Morgan said back, holding both of her hips and glaring. "At least I don't wear armor everywhere *like I'm a damn-*" She stopped herself, her eye following a small movement which had appeared over Penny's shoulder, then ducked back down when she noticed.

"Hey, Morgan," Penny said, holding out her hand to prevent her from investigating Akela and likely scaring her with her huge personality. Chris couldn't help but suppress a laugh.

"Penny!" Morgan said with the biggest smile imaginable. She held out her arms, but Penny shook her head.

"Give me a moment," she said, kneeling down to let Akela off for a moment. When the girl hopped down, Penny stood up and sighed as if she was willingly submitting herself to the death penalty. "Alright, go ahead."

Morgan attacked, hugging Penny tightly around her torso and squeezing her like a boa constrictor. Chris could have sworn that Penny had even turned a little blue and muttered the word 'ow' at least three times. When she finally let go, Penny let out an audible huff followed by a deep inhale. She didn't even have time to try to say anything before Morgan moved to the next person.

"Uh," she said, her eyes catching Akela's. The girl hid behind Penny's leg and gave Morgan a look of uncertainty. Morgan looked up at Penny, blinked a few times, and then turned back to Chris. Her eyes remained on Chris for a moment, her mouth slowly opening to say something.

"No." Chris shot these words out faster than he had ever done in his life. He could feel himself turning red now.

Morgan tilted her head and turned it toward Penny in a very animated way. She was probably trying to look intimidating or scary, but Chris found this behavior to just be silly at best, "By all means,

Penny, explain." She said in a very forced voice intended to sound dark. "Who's it?"

"I didn't have a baby!" Penny barked at her in a flustered and frustrated way. "The looks are a coincidence. We were bringing this girl back to the police station..."

"Oh, okay!" Morgan said, sighing softly and laughing it off. Suddenly she swapped to the dark tone again, "I was about to kill you both."

"Morgan, that's unsettling," Megan commented slowly to Chris's far right. "Not the voice - it's just amazing that you can threaten someone. I can't say I've seen that before."

"This is not allowed to go past innocent flirting and kissing," Morgan said to Megan while pointing at both Chris and Penny. "Only when they are thirty-five - or older!" Chris thought he heard Megan trying not to crack up hearing this. She placed a hand over her mouth and turned away.

*I am going to kill her later*, Penny said mentally. Internally, Chris could tell she was both embarrassed and ready to kill Morgan all at once, but externally she was a blushing mess, which was out of character. Her mouth was in an 'o' shape and just hanging in one position. Akela tugged on Penny's skirt a few times to see if she was okay, but Penny was more or less paralyzed by Morgan's accusation. Chris was embarrassed himself, but his partner probably had it the worst at the moment.

"If I ever see a-" Morgan cupped both of her hands together and ran them in an oval-like shape out in front of her own stomach. "-Bump like this I'll..."

Penny took a step forward and stomped hard, crushing Morgan's foot through the boot with her heel. Morgan yelped and hopped backward, holding her leg and doing an exaggerated cry. She seemed quite satisfied with her revenge on Morgan but still did not say anything. She let Akela climb back onto her back. Of course, the child asked what was being discussed, but Penny deflected by saying it was nothing important, and Chris shrugged when she looked at him.

"Morgan, I consider you a close friend, and I tell you my secrets," Penny said in a whisper, just quiet enough for herself and Chris to hear. "But if your life is in danger later, just know that I may be involved somehow. Think of it as tying up a loose end."

Morgan froze and nodded either out of loyalty for her friend or in terror. A nervous laugh followed. Chris could tell the two of them were joking around...well, mostly, Penny didn't often joke. Megan slowly shook her head as if she knew Penny was giving some sort of warning for putting her on blast. Ian just stared on with the most confused expression on his face, the situation lost to him.

"I don't want to die," Morgan said with a traumatized smile. "Chris, my will is in the mage planning room on Terminus. Ask Miyato for the documents...He'll know why."

"I wouldn't let Penny kill you!" Chris answered back, taking a moment to look past her at the looters who were still trapped in the bubble. "We should get back so we can talk safely."

"Nowhere is safe now. Not after what I've done." Morgan said, staring up at the sky, which had now turned a shade of grey, the sun fading into the horizon. "All I can do is hope it's quick."

"Quit it!" Chris protested.

# 17

# PENNY'S DETERMINATION

The police station and the surrounding area lit up like a Christmas tree in the pitch-black night. Officers and Alliance soldiers stood guard around the building while others patrolled back and forth to the checkpoint. Now that the power station was up, the whole city was safe to roam at night. Now it was just a matter of keeping it this way. It would most likely stay under their control too. Penny could not hear anything in the night now other than friendly voices - it was almost unsettling just how quiet the night was on Sohrann. Nothing wanted to be out.

Akela yawned in her ear and laid against Penny's shoulder. The girl started to lose her grip as she fell asleep, so Penny grabbed her legs carefully and held her against her back, leaning forward a little to keep from dropping her. They'd have to find out who her parents were and if they were gone, then the next step would be to figure out what other family she has. She wondered why the girl did not evacuate with the rest of the city since a majority made it out, but deep down she knew the answer. Her parents probably wouldn't just leave her like that.

Penny ducked into the tent she shared with Chris and laid out another sleeping bag between them. Then she laid the child down carefully, hushing her back to sleep when she stirred from being put down. She just stayed there with her, brushing the girl's black hair gently and watching until she was sure she had gone to sleep. Penny stood up when she was almost certain the girl had fully drifted off, but a tiny hand caught her ankle and stopped her.

"Are you going to leave me?" she asked.

"Just for a little bit. I'll be back. We both will." Penny said, referring to Chris.

"What if you don't come back?"

"I will."

"I won't sleep then."

"Akela," Penny got down on her knees and took the girl's outstretched hand. "If you don't sleep, you'll be tired in the morning. A lot is going to happen, so I need you rested for now."

"Alright." Akela said sadly, laying down in a very upset manner. She went totally silent, but Penny could tell she was not asleep at all. At least she had not started crying but it still made her feel horrible.

Sighing, Penny exited the tent and zipped it back. Chris was waiting outside and wasted no time in asking, "How is she?"

"She won't sleep." Penny answered, trailing off into almost a whisper. "How old do you think she is?"

"You didn't ask?" Chris asked her with a wide-eyed expression. "If I had to guess?" He paused and made a low humming sound in his throat. "Maybe eight? Nine?"

"She's too dependent for her to be that old, I think..." Penny turned her head to look back at the tent, watching the girl's shadow toss and turn when she left her. "I... can't always be here, but-"

"You want to be." Chris concluded, gesturing for her to walk away from the tent so Akela would not hear. She followed.

"Yeah. I do." Penny tensed up a little. "It took so much effort just to get her to eat a little. What happens when we get cycled out to go somewhere else?"

"Do you want to see if any of her family was marked as evacuated? Even if there's not I'm sure she has family somewhere." Chris said, clearly trying to be optimistic for her.

"You know how this goes." Penny gave him a side eye as they walked. "Finding her parents is just about as likely as finding a needle in a haystack. I know you don't like when I'm negative with you, but if she does have family it will take a lot of time."

"Well, what should we do...?" Chris stopped himself. "I mean what do you think will be done?"

"They'll probably evacuate her like everyone else for now but she's going to be terrified...and I doubt we will be around for her much longer. Even if by some miracle we remain in New Hope until Sohrann is under Alliance control, we won't always be over *here*. I want her to have something...anything to keep her calm."

"Like someone to stay with her or what?" Chris questioned.

Penny's eyes drifted just past Chris to the police station steps where Morgan was sitting. She was currently casting the same bubble spell over and over, connecting her thumb and index finger, and blowing out flurries of colorful bubbles. A lightbulb went on in her head suddenly as a thought occurred: who better to ask than Morgan? She was always super bubbly and enthusiastic. Morgan probably knew what could work.

"I have to go take care of something." Penny decided, her eyes returning to Chris's. "Can you watch Akela for me? I'll be back soon."

"Where are you going exactly?" Chris asked, entirely baffled.

"I'll explain later, I promise, but I want to go now while I still have time. Just trust me, alright?" Penny asked, him in her usual tone. Somehow it always worked.

"Well...alright," Chris agreed slowly. "But be careful, okay?"

"Always am." Penny said. She quickly got up on her toes and kissed him on the cheek before hurrying off to speak to Morgan, leaving Chris standing there blushing and questioning what had just happened. She would apologize for hurrying off later.

Morgan was still sitting on the steps messing around with her own spells when Penny arrived. She almost didn't notice Penny standing right in front of her because now she was trying something new. Morgan extended both hands out together and created a giant bubble. Just as she was about to blow out a gust of wind which would bring this behemoth sized creature into fruition, Penny extended a finger and popped it. "Yaaah!" she exclaimed.

Penny suppressed a laugh at this sudden noise, "Morgan?"

"Oh, hi Penny!" Morgan said, regaining her cheery deposition. "I'm surprised to see you. Are you okay?"

"Why?" Penny questioned. It was always easier to deflect with her instead of answering.

"It just seems like you want or need something." Morgan said rather vaguely while stretching in a silly manner. This was a very interesting game of neither one of them wanting to give a real answer. "Okay, I'm ready, go ahead."

"Go ahead and what?" Penny raised an eyebrow and stepped out of the way of an Alliance soldier who was hurrying up the stairs and into the building.

"Ask me to go with you." Morgan cupped her hand over her ear and crossed one leg across the other. "Come on, we're wasting time."

"Morgan." Penny sighed and stared. Morgan wasn't going to let up until she did. "...Please."

"Please help me with?" Morgan's lip curled as she sat forward like she was expecting something further. "Hmm?"

"Really? Morgan, I'm not in the mood..." Penny stopped herself when she noticed Morgan's expression. She already knew. Why was she doing this then? "Please go with me to find something for-" Penny avoided eye contact as she continued reluctantly.

"-For Akela so she can feel safe. Got it!" Morgan sat up and then finally stood, seemingly bouncing up onto her feet. "See? Was that so hard?" She beamed.

"Morgan." Penny started, turning on her heel to go off alone. She really didn't want to be teased right now.

"Okay okay! I'm coming with!" Morgan said excitedly, running just behind Penny to catch up.

The two hurried deeper into the now lit city. Now, things were quiet enough that they could hear the sound of the streetlights swinging back and forth along with their footsteps; occasionally there was a crumbling sound like a damaged building finally giving up. There was also sometimes a gunshot in the distance, but it didn't really concern either of them. Without demons roaming around freely, it was almost entirely safe to be out. Penny had slowed to a walk now instead of continuing to jog her way forward.

"So, can I ask you something?" Morgan asked. She turned and walked backwards, placing her arms behind herself in a very shy manner. They were passing the gas station as she was speaking.

"You mean like where we are going?" Penny responded with her usual sass. She really couldn't stop herself anymore.

"Well, yes, but more so about you and you-know-who." Morgan said vaguely with much intrigue in her voice.

"What?" Penny questioned.

"You know... Chris." Morgan clarified more. Penny wished that Morgan didn't pry on something that was already so difficult. "It's been two years. You said you were gonna see how you felt about him, but I can tell you're still dodging left and right. It's like you still don't know what to do about it."

"Morgan we both know why I'm putting it off, and it is entirely on purpose." Penny groaned and took a deep breath before releasing it. "It's because of me, remember? That...thing."

"Did you tell him about them?" Morgan asked, gently touching Penny's back. Penny stepped forward to avoid being touched on her upper back. Morgan recoiled her hand like she was afraid that she had harmed Penny, but then she realized that it was just because Penny was bothered by them.

"No, I have not. I probably won't either." Penny broke eye contact and hid behind her hair a little. Penny could hear the soft footsteps of Morgan moving in front of her. She thought that she had heard Morgan take a deep breath which was confirmed when she blew in Penny's face. This made her hair messy and wild but revealed her face again. As Penny fixed it, she could not help but smile at this very silly gesture. "Quit it."

"Tell him or I'll do it again!" Morgan pointed a finger as if this was some sort of ultimatum.

"Morgan...he thinks I'm human." Penny's voice lowered significantly. She did not realize that she had done it, but Morgan did. "I'd rather not, okay?"

"That's for him to decide." Morgan responded rather wisely. Penny nodded. "Trust me here, you two should have been together a long time ago. Just tell him honestly."

"Maybe. Morgan, can we focus on getting here and getting back?" Penny requested.

"Of course, but just think it over, okay?"

"I will think about thinking it over." Penny dodged as hard as she could.

"That's all I can ask for."

Penny walked faster to take the lead. Morgan followed her without argument but continued to prod Penny's emotions to try to get her to open up. It wasn't that she didn't trust Morgan so much as it was impossible for Chris to understand. Even if she had not lied, she hid the truth and now had to pay for it. It really was that simple. Not only did she not need to drag him into her family drama, which was her responsibility, but she put his life at risk almost every day.

Penny hurried up the stairs which led into the apartment building and reentered Akela's old home. Morgan was behind her but had lagged because she started looking around. The lights were far brighter now, and it was significantly easier to see. Penny stood in the foyer, wondering where she could look. Morgan confidently moved by her person and headed up the stairs. She quickly located Akela's room as if she had a GPS which directed her to the nearest girl's room. Penny followed behind her.

"This is a cozy little place," Morgan remarked. She was already on her knees looking under Akela's bed which had messy unmade blankets lying across it. "Now to find a toy."

"A toy?" Penny repeated in a half whisper.

"Yeah. Like something she can carry with her anywhere she goes. Didn't you play with toys as a kid, Penny?"

"...No." Penny answered a lot colder than she intended to. After a few moments of Morgan not responding Penny followed up with a 'sorry'. She really just couldn't help it sometimes. "Can I help?"

"You sure can." Morgan held out her hands like she was holding an object and faced Penny. "Remember: soft and fluffy. Preferably cute...not like a Grumper."

"A what?" Penny was completely lost now. She started filling through the dresser, which was filled with, you guessed it, clothes.

"It's a Lunarian thing..." Morgan said, reaching deeper under the bed. "You wouldn't get it."

Penny shrugged off her comment as she had no idea what Morgan was talking about aside from the planet being where she was from. She walked over to a small brown computer desk which was situated in the corner along with a white rug with an animated character on it. The screen was a little outdated, but still used holographic technology. Her parents must have had just enough to get her this. Penny's eye even noticed a phone next to the screen which she promptly picked up. The charge was very low and as she rifled through the messages on the notification screen, she noticed contacts labeled mom, dad, and another one named Heavenly. Would this be a good thing to take back?

"Hey, Morgan?" Penny started, holding the phone out toward her friend.

Morgan only looked for a second before answering, "One, that's not fluffy and cute and two what is she going to do with it? There's no one to call really and I doubt she'll be able to keep it charged." Morgan stopped herself. "Besides," she said as the phone illuminated in Penny's hand from her tilting it upwards. One of the messages from 'Heavenly' read: *I don't know what's going on, Akela. They made us all leave class and follow a bunch of scary looking guys. I wish you were here. I don't see my mom or my dad and I don't know where we are going.* Penny decided to set the phone down instead of continuing to pry. "They've all either left or...the other thing."

"Still," Morgan went on in a slight mumble. "It's been so long since I've seen a normal smartphone like that."

"Right?" Penny agreed as she searched around the rest of the desk. Nothing. Those text messages were bothering her more than they should have. "What do you think happened to her parents?"

"They probably made it out." Morgan said with a smile. "Not every story has an unhappy ending."

"Who leaves their daughter?" Penny asked, glaring at nothing as she said it. She had another person in mind when she shot out these words from her mouth. "A real parent protects their child no matter what with whatever they have."

"You talk like you'd know..." Morgan said suspiciously, looking back at her friend with concern.

"I don't know."

"Alright..." Morgan was seemingly fixated on the way Penny had said this.

"Morgan?"

"Yeah?"

"I'm okay." Penny promised her with a quick nod to dismiss the conversation. "Did you find anything?"

"No. I'm going to check between the mattresses. Come help me." Morgan beckoned her over with the wave of her hand. "Come on."

"Why would you check there?" Penny gave a smug look at this suggestion.

"I dunno. When I was a kid, I hid my favorite stuff under there including candy. Anything I didn't want my parents to find or friends I had over went right under there," Morgan sat up and placed both hands in her lap. "What? I wasn't always a saint."

"That explains why you're always dressed in pink...you've become the candy." Penny moved over and lifted the mattress with one hand and fished with the other gloved one. Something soft and fuzzy brushed against her index finger, so she grabbed whatever it was with her full hand and gently tugged it through. An interesting sight to behold resided in her hands: tan and fluffy fur and a curly tail which wrapped under a rabbit-like body. It also had cat-like features including the nose and eyes, but rabbit ears could also be seen. The beaded, sewn on eyes stared back at her as she held it up to get a good look.

Morgan audibly gasped in a very dramatic fashion, "Is that a Phon?!" Morgan squealed and suddenly snatched the stuffed animal from Penny to examine it. "This is one of the cutest animals on Sohrann. I saw a picture of one on my way here, oh my gosh! Look at him!"

"Will she like it?" Penny asked awkwardly.

"She'll love him!" Morgan put the Phon in Penny's face and shook it wildly, a baby face replacing her natural voice. Penny gently pushed it away from her face. "Just look at him!"

"I just hope it helps." She said, making a face at Morgan. She took the stuffed creature from her friend and attached it to her hip by slipping it under her belt. "Time to head back."

"See, aren't you glad you brought me?" Morgan placed her hands on both of her hips.

"I actually am," Penny said sincerely as she exited Akela's room and descended the stairs. "Thank you, Morgan. I appreciate it."

"...Come again??" Morgan bellowed from the top of the stairs. "Can you repeat that into my watch?"

"Just come on." Penny said, returning to her usual tone of voice because of this outburst.

The walk back toward the gas station was mostly uneventful. It was only a short walk to return to the station so long as they did not stop. On the way back though, Penny noted strange rumbling sounds in the distance like something rolling or sliding. She didn't think much of it and did not feel there was a reason to be concerned. It was probably some sort of large vehicle being brought in. She wondered if maybe she wasn't as alert as usual because she was excited to give Akela the stuffed Phon. Would it really help her? She hoped so.

"Penny," Morgan called out urgently. "Penny, look out! Look out! Look out!"

Penny felt Morgan's hands press hard against her shoulder and shove her clean out of the way. She fell onto her right side and quickly rolled to see what had happened. Morgan was hovering over a large gap in the road, which was wide enough to swallow a tank. The pink bubble surrounded her and kept her suspended perfectly. Penny scrambled to her feet and moved over to help Morgan but had no way to reach her. She glanced down into the ravine that was presented before her and noted that she could see nothing but darkness. Just how far did this go down? She was absolutely certain that it was not here before, but if so, where did it come from?

"I can't reach you!" Penny called out, extending her hand as carefully as she could. She was entirely aware that even one misstep would result in a freefall, and she was already straining to reach.

"I'll try getting closer, just grab me." Morgan said through a grunt. "I didn't have time to make a proper bubble, so this isn't going to fly if anything it wants to fall."

Morgan closed her eyes and concentrated on her spell. The bubble gradually made its way toward Penny's side of the massive ravine and slowly descended as it did. She was just barely able to keep the spell leveled with the ground and avoid going deeper. If worse came to worst and she fell, Penny would just have to go down and grab her. Morgan was close enough to reach now. She reached through the bubble with both hands, got a good grip on Morgan and as the bubble disintegrated, Morgan dropped. Penny fell onto her chest, but still had a good grip on Morgan. Together, with Morgan climbing up the narrow wall's face and Penny pulling, she was hoisted out. Morgan rolled over once she was back on the pavement, shut her eyes, and caught her breath. Penny sat up and placed her hands on her knees, staring down at the abyss.

"Are you okay?" Penny asked her while trying to peer into the solid darkness.

"Y-yeah." Morgan replied shakily. "What was that?"

"I don't know. Maybe a ground quake?" Penny said attempting to reason the situation.

"Without the Alliance knowing and being able to warn us? Right." She spoke. Penny agreed with this sentiment. This was strange but not impossible by any means. Perhaps it was always under them and the fighting finally made the ground give way.

"We'll have to take the long way to get back. I don't think it's safe this way." Penny decided, extending her hand for Morgan who took it. "I know the way back."

"Alright..." Morgan said, tossing one of her bubbles down into the abyss. The bright pink light faded not long after it was thrown. "Gosh. That was almost me."

"No, it wouldn't have been." Penny assured her. She felt around her hip to check and make sure the reason they came out here was still there. After confirming that it was still connected to her, she relaxed.

Instead of proceeding the normal way that they had intended, Penny and Morgan were forced to head back toward the hotel where she had rescued Bafair. She knew that from there, they would be fine returning to the town, and by extension, the police precinct. They moved in a hurry to make up for lost time, but Penny still dwelled on what had happened. She'd report it to the advisor when she got back. She now wondered if she could have been hearing the ground moving under her. Morgan clearly did not hear it - she saw it, but Penny could hear it before it even happened.

The lights were flickering here. They must have been damaged, but the bulbs still performed their jobs of keeping the demons away and keeping the area lit. Many dead individuals could be found this way from Alliance soldiers and Wizards to Imperial soldiers and Sorcerers. Penny even noted a few civilians - or at least people she thought were civilians since they did not appear to be affiliated with any of the factions operating on the planet. It was nothing she was not used to, but it did not make her feel any better.

"Do you still think her parents made it out?" Penny asked Morgan with a stoic expression.

"I'd like to hope so." Morgan admitted behind her.

Something told Penny to stop and check some of these bodies - specifically the ones heading back toward the direction they had come. One after another, she checked for identification of some sort and scanned it with her watch to send to Evangeline. She must have gone through thirty or so people by now. Morgan just watched and wondered why she was doing it. When she was done, Penny sent the ID data to Evangeline and waited. It only took a second for her to get back.

"What are you searching for?" Evangeline asked while sorting through the data.

"Just a hunch." Penny admitted. "Can you look at parental data for me? Specifically, to see if any of them have a child or even grandchild named 'Akela'. That's A-K-E-L-A, I think."

"Yes, give me a moment." Evangeline went silent as she continued to comb through the various information. She stopped and immediately spoke, facing to look at Penny as she did, "Yes. Aaminah and Jasper Hicks. They are the parents of one Akela Renelda Hicks."

"...I see." Penny answered back blankly.

"Where did you get this data from?" Evangeline asked.

"They're dead." Penny explained in a rather blank tone. "Thanks, Evangeline."

"I wouldn't tell her..." Morgan put forth.

"I wasn't planning to. Anyway, thanks." Penny said, focusing back on her advisor.

"One more thing, Delta One."

"Yes?"

"Are you aware that Delta Two is quite far from you at the moment? Specifically, out in the desert?"

"No? He didn't tell me." Penny raised her eyebrow. "Who is he with?"

"I'm not entirely certain." Evangeline explained. "I'll update you further as I know more. I am tracking him. For now, get yourself back to the base of operations."

"...Right." Penny said, giving Morgan a quick look to say she probably wasn't going to do that. Morgan nodded. "Delta One out."

As soon as the call ended, Penny hurried to the precinct. She'd give Akela the stuffed animal, apologize for leaving in a hurry, and go after Chris. Megan, Ian, and Morgan could watch her. Chris could be in trouble - again. The town was in view now. Penny was moving so fast that Morgan could not keep up. Sure enough, Akela was sitting next to Megan on the ground looking over her arm at the book she was reading. Megan was even reading to her and teaching her to pronounce the larger words.

"Praetorian." Megan said with a finger point. "Sound it out."

"Pretentious," Ian said from inside of the tent behind them. "Pre-tent-ious." Megan elbowed the tent, and most likely the back of his head because an 'oooow' followed.

"Idiot. I can't believe you." Megan scolded.

Megan's eyes locked onto Penny immediately and before she even had time to say anything, Akela leapt to her feet and attached herself to Penny's leg. Penny ruffled her hair for a moment and then held her close. Megan brought her legs up, closed her book, and sat attentively, "Welcome back." she said.

"Hey," Penny said in a rather hurried manner. "Akela, I got you something, but I'm going to have to show you later, okay?" Penny quickly tossed the stuffed animal behind herself with her free hand. She knew Morgan would catch it without a word of warning and she did.

"Really? What is it?"

"I'll show you when I get back. I have to go take care of something important." Akela frowned when Penny said this. "I know. I know, but I will be back as soon as possible. You stay here with Megan,

Morgan, and Ian." Penny pointed at the tent to refer to her brother. "I'm not going anywhere, okay? So don't worry."

Akela attacked Penny's torso when she knelt to check on her. Penny embraced her for a moment and then passed her back off to Megan who made a slight face. "What's he gotten into this time? He was just here."

"I don't know, but I'm going to handle it." She said.

Penny walked off, nodding at Morgan who had just finished hiding the Phon in her shared tent with Chris. She raised her watch and spoke into it just as Emily's image projected out of her watch. Penny began to explain the situation and what she had been told by her advisor. Emily wasted no time in saying 'I'm on my way.'

# O SISTER, WHERE ART THOU?

**W**hen they arrived back at the police station, Chris noted the reinforcements which had arrived. Soldiers were coming in to resupply, and he even thought he'd seen Dion but did not have time to really speak. It was quiet - almost unsettlingly so. He hated the nights on Sohrann. On Terminus, the nights were peaceful, and it was nice to go on a stroll. On Sohrann, when the lights went out, you risked instant death. Just how long would they be on this planet...?

Akela yawned in Penny's ear and laid against her shoulder. The girl started to lose her grip as she fell asleep. Chris reached out to steady her, but Penny had already grabbed her legs carefully and held her against herself, leaning forward a little to keep from dropping her. He nodded and relaxed. She was very attentive. He always found Penny to be caring, even if many would disagree, but this was a new level. It was almost like instinct. She had taken this girl with them and basically taken charge.

Penny ducked into the tent she shared with Chris and laid out another sleeping bag between them. Then she laid the child down carefully, hushing her back to sleep when she stirred from being put down. Chris watched as Penny brushed the girl's hair and lulled her to sleep. He understood why Penny felt the need for the girl to sleep with them: she felt comfortable, but why had she put Akela between them? He wouldn't question it, but perhaps he could ask about her behavior later, even if it was mentally. Feeling useless in this situation, Chris decided to slip out of the tent and wait outside for Penny. He must have been standing there at least nine minutes when Penny finally emerged.

She sighed as soon as she fully zipped up the tent. "How is she?" he asked.

"She won't sleep," Penny answered, trailing off into almost a whisper. "How old do you think she is?"

"You didn't ask?" Chris asked her with a wide-eyed expression. This was not like her. Penny was usually quite blunt and direct, regardless of the situation. "If I had to guess?" He paused and made a low humming sound in his throat, mulling the numbers over in his head. "Maybe eight? Nine?"

"She's too dependent for her to be that old, I think..." Penny turned her head to look back at the tent. Chris stared at her and frowned. "I...can't always be here, but-"

"You want to be," Chris concluded, gesturing for her to walk away from the tent so Akela would not hear. She followed very reluctantly.

"Yeah. I do." Penny tensed up and balled up her hand ever so slightly. "It took so much effort just to get her to eat a little. What happens when we get cycled out to go somewhere else?"

"Do you want to see if any of her family was marked as evacuated?" Chris asked. Even if there's not, I'm sure she has family somewhere." Chris asked himself if he was saying this because of Emily. It was probably just a weird coincidence.

"You know how this goes." Penny gave him a side-eye as they walked. Her voice lowered drastically. "Finding her parents is just about as likely as finding a needle in a haystack. I know you don't like it when I'm negative with you, but if she does have a family, it will take a lot of time."

"Well, what should we do...?" Chris stopped and rephrased. "I mean, what do you think will be done?"

"They'll probably evacuate her like everyone else for now, but she's going to be terrified...and I doubt we will be around for her much longer. Even if we remain in New Hope by some miracle until Sohrann is under Alliance control, we won't always be over here. Other cities will need help. I want her to have something...anything to keep her calm."

"Like someone to stay with her or what?" Chris questioned with uncertainty.

Penny's eyes drifted just past Chris. He turned to see what she was looking at but saw no one other than Morgan. What was wrong? He tried reading her mind like she had done many times with him but had very little success. His questions would soon be answered though, because Penny spoke up soon after. She returned her attention to him and explained very vaguely.

"I have to go take care of something." Penny decided. "Can you watch Akela for me? I'll be back soon."

"Where are you going exactly?" Chris asked, more confused than ever.

"I'll explain later, I promise, but I want to go now while I still have time. Just trust me, alright?" Penny asked him in her usual tone. *Why does this always work?* He asked himself internally.

"Well...alright," Chris agreed slowly and with much reluctance. He decided to add an addendum to this statement. "But be careful, okay?"

"Always am," Penny said with a half-smile. She quickly got up on her toes and kissed him on the cheek before hurrying off in Morgan's direction. He touched his cheek and could already tell it was burning up. Penny had really only done that a few times. Chris continued to gawk at her up until she started to speak to Morgan.

"Well, alright..." he concluded to himself.

Now he really wasn't sure what to do aside from watch Akela. It really was...strange to not be around Penny now. It felt almost as if she was always by his side - in fact, she was. What did he do without her before they became partners? Chris really couldn't remember no matter how hard he tried to. *Actually, anytime she's not around, I tend to get into trouble,* he said in a moment of self-reflective clarity. When he finished this train of thought, Chris realized that both Morgan and Penny had disappeared from the police station steps.

"And off they go." He said aloud. "Hm."

Chris debated checking on Akela, but when he noticed Megan sitting nearby reading, he figured she'd be well watched. He'd just go sit in the parking deck and think - just not as far this time, so if Eslena showed up, someone would see him. He gave a wave to her in the hopes that she would understand what he needed, but she had not noticed him because she was reading. Instead, it was Ian who waved back at him. *Thanks, buddy*, Chris thought. *Just need a minute or two.*

Walking toward the parking deck, Chris could see various flash-lights headed toward the station. It was likely Bafair returning from the station like Penny had said. The lights were quite bright and remained on, so they clearly knew what they were doing and how to do it. He smiled to himself as he entered the parking deck. A singular bike rested on the left side wall near the opposite side entrance. He wondered if that was there before, but it was quite dark the last time he had entered. Chris assumed he overlooked it somehow. He proceeded toward the ramp, which led up to the next floor but was stopped by an external force.

As he was passing, he was grabbed and pulled against the cold concrete. Someone had their hand over his mouth so he could not scream in a very familiar situation. A pistol was held up, so it was in his direct line of sight. Chris calmed himself quickly and made sense of the situation. This helped him to realize who this was. Shadow Victoria was wearing what looked like a long black half-buttoned tailed coat, dark green pants, and brown heeled boots with what looked like spurs. She also seemed to have two holsters on either side of her getup. Her black hair was swept over her right shoulder.

"You have got to stop doing that," Chris said in a startled voice.

He had his hands up, and his heart was racing. He only became more irritated when Victoria laughed and spun her pistol. She holstered it and stepped back to give him space.

"You make it too easy." She clapped back in almost a pur. "Next time, I'll be sure you don't wet yourself. Now come on." Victoria turned and headed toward the bike which he had just noticed. "I need you for something."

*I knew that wasn't there before...*He thought, realizing this situation was entirely avoidable.

"I uh - can't..." Chris said, stumbling over his words when he saw the way that she had stopped without turning. Victoria turned her head a little to where he could just barely see the side of her face.

"Oh? I recall us having made a deal. You owe me a favor, and I'm calling it in - now." Victoria answered passive-aggressively.

"Well...you see, I have to watch this kid and make sure she's safe," Chris explained as fast as he could. It felt like he was on a time limit, and when it was up, he would get shot. He could try to fight her if need be, but would he win? "I told Penny I'd watch her."

Victoria raised an eyebrow at Penny's name as if she was disgusted. "Did I ask about your personal affairs?"

"Just - right now isn't a good time..." Chris tried nervously. He felt very nervous at how she was reacting. "Later might be better-"

"She's going to be burying you later if you don't keep your word, boy." She finally snapped, turning quickly to give him a death stare.

"You gotta understand-"

"Firstly, we aren't friends, so don't ask me to understand." She quickly walked toward him and pushed a finger against his chest. "Secondly, it's been forever, so I'm sure you can make time out of your busy schedule, but seeing as you're just that busy, we can settle this little dispute..." Chris stepped back when Victoria placed a hand on her gun and pulled it partially from the holster. "One more point before I shoot you; I saved your life, so you technically owe me double."

"I'll see what I can do..." Chris said. He raised his watch and only started interacting with it when she replaced the gun and released it. "Hey, Ian." He began. "Do me a favor and watch Akela with Megan. An emergency came up."

"Need a hand?" Ian asked him eagerly. "Giving me more busywork?"

"Uh, no. No. It's nothing serious. I'll be back soon. Just keep an eye on her for me?" He reiterated.

"Done. See you soon!" Ian agreed. The call ended almost as soon as it began.

Victoria extended both arms to either side and shrugged, "See? Was that so hard?"

She climbed up onto the bike and twisted a key that was present just on the console. The bike hummed to life and began to hover just off the ground. She sat forward and made space for him to get on. When Chris didn't move, she revved the engine, performed a half donut, so she was right in front of him and patted the seat. He really didn't think testing her patience was wise, and the sooner he got back, the sooner he could get back to Akela. Chris climbed onto the back awkwardly. Suddenly he realized something. How should he hold on? It was very awkward since she was not Penny. Victoria once again caused the engine to roar as if she was telling him to hurry up and grab on; he did so, but felt quite uncomfortable.

The hoverbike flew forward at astounding speeds, cutting the corner out of the parking garage and flying out past the station. It was not long before they were so far from where he had come from that he could no longer see any recognizable buildings. Victoria had clearly ridden vehicles just as fast, if not faster than this. Her reaction times were astounding, and she had not slowed down unless she needed to suddenly take a corner. At first, he figured she was taking him to the other side of New Hope city, but they suddenly broke out into the open desert where the rolling sands were. They even shot past the outpost, which was taken during their landing assault.

"What exactly do you need me to do?" He asked her over the howling winds.

Victoria turned her head and then returned her attention forward, "I need your authorization level. At first, I was gonna just use you to brute force into this place, but then I heard you were a squad leader...meaning you have the authorization to open most Alliance owned facilities."

"I'm...not following. What are you here for?" Chris rephrased to get a better answer. "Money?"

"Ha!" Victoria snorted a little. "You've gotta be kidding me. Money?! No. I need an android to help me track someone."

"...Your sister?" Chris guessed after a moment of thought. "You're still hunting her, huh?"

"That's my business, but yes she slipped through my fingers," was all she would say in return. "Anyway, keep an eye out. The demons don't care about me, but they'll want to make a meal out of you. Just having you tagging along makes me feel like I put a target on my back."

"You're welcome," Chris said with a smug smile, which he pointed at the bike's rearview mirrors. Not even a second later, she purposefully made a slight turn to fake throwing him off. "Okay. Okay. Sorry. Can I at least go when this is done?"

"Can you drive without training wheels?" she asked him as they soared clean over a dune in a jump that made his stomach turn and drop violently.

"I haven't driven anything really," he admitted.

"Then I guess you're stuck with me. I'll take you back when this is done," she said dismissively. "You can get back to your nice little war."

Chris spoke his next words without thinking. He was just trying to make conversation. "You know, we could use your help. The war keeps getting worse, and you'd be a big help."

"Stop. Comparing me. To your Victoria." She hissed much more aggressively than usual. "I am myself. Your Victoria Dreadful is dead. I have no interest in your war or the Wizards or the Sorcerers."

"I...know she is," Chris said quietly.

Victoria's eyes cut to look at him in the mirror. She stared for a moment before saying, "Let's get this done so I can get you back to your people. These demons could try their luck any minute."

"Alright..." Chris responded absentmindedly. "So," he started, hoping to get off the topic. "That's where we're headed."

They approached a relatively large and bright building that sat alone in the middle of the desert. Perimeter lights lined the structure along with turrets that tracked them and the bike. They then turned, opened fire into the sand at something they must not have seen, and then continued to rotate as normal. It looked almost like a warehouse or a factory, but Chris could not entirely tell. About seven figures approached them with rifles. Five of them aimed at Victoria, but the other two figures kept them down.

"What's your business?" the one in the middle asked, turning a circular device on the side of his head as if calibrating his own brain. "The Alliance Wizard is allowed to be here, but you are not."

"I'm here to see Theadore Vixent," Victoria said, stepping off of the bike casually, taking out the key as she did. "You tin-cans don't scare me, so I'll cut to the chase. I need his help tracking someone so call him down here."

The figures exchanged looks, seemingly unphased by her insult. They could have almost been communicating without talking. The leader of this small squad turned the gear on his head and nodded a few times. Then, he directed two of the androids to walk to either side of Chris and Victoria while the other four fell back toward the structure. Chris opened his mouth to say something, but Victoria shut him up by waving her hand backward and mouthing, 'keep your eyes open.' A man wearing a tan buttoned-down shirt, black pants, and similarly colored shoes exited the structure from some very grand sliding doors. He was accompanied by more of these humanoids. He had curly dirty blond hair, brown eyes, and a less than stellar expression.

"He's my friend," Victoria commented. "But don't make any

mistakes here. I didn't exactly leave with the best impression...Let me talk, okay?"

"Al-right...?" Chris said with concern and a scrunched-up face. He muttered "doesn't seem like a friend to me," under his breath.

"Theo!" Victoria called out to him with a more pleasant voice than he was used to. She extended her arms out and smiled like nothing was wrong. "You have a few more grey hairs, but you still look good. Did I cause those?"

"Victoria, you have a lot of guts showing your face around my business with about a thousand androids that can gun you down," he retorted, walking directly up to her and staring her down as he did. "It's probably why you brought a Wizard with you, isn't it? And you didn't bring that captain with you, so I guess you knew that she and I would team up to shoot you."

"Probably." Victoria shrugged her arms and stepped back a little, reaching for her gun as she did. "But she'd also talk me out of this so long as I paid her back for the ship."

"The same ship you *stole* my shipment from," he clarified, his face turning beat red from anger.

"If it helps," Victoria smiled. "I crashed Aiem'y's ship not long after I did that and lost it all. The Alliance doesn't take too kindly to ships without the correct codes, and I didn't realize that *she herself* stole it. So, I'd say we're even."

"And you're here to ask for a favor, is that it?" he asked. Silence followed. "I'm lucky you came to me. It saves me the trouble of sending one of my androids."

"Actually, that's why I'm here."

"Really? For your sister, Dreadful?" He asked, drawing a pistol from his side and pointing it at her. The other androids followed suit, making Chris hop off of the bike and prepare for a fight.

"Yes, well, this time I have money so I can make it worth your while."

"I have a lot of money," he countered. "I can't say I get a lot of revenge. So if you give me the money and turn around, I might just forget all about this."

Victoria placed her left hand on her hip and got a grip on her other pistol just under her trench coat, "You never lose your charm, Theo..."

"I never get fooled the same way twice, that's right."

"I bet that's what you think," Victoria said with a head tilt.

In an instant, Victoria fired and blasted the gun clean out of Theadore's hand. She then turned, drawing her other guns as she did. The androids fell rapidly in her sweeping gunfire. Chris flinched and ducked down to avoid her gunfire, but she did not hit him regardless. Her accuracy was almost perfect. Theadore ran to retrieve his pistol. Fumbling it in his hands, he finally dug it out from the sand and turned to point at Victoria only to have it shot out from his hand again.

"Sorry about your androids," Victoria said smugly. "Now, are you ready to talk?"

"System f-f-failure. Shutting down." the android nearest to Chris said as it fidgeted in the sand before going motionless. He stepped over to his temporary comrade's side and continued to remain quiet as she did whatever it was that she was doing.

"You scum-sucking son-of-a..." Victoria interrupted his insult with a pistol whip to the face. It was probably gentler than she could have been, but Chris could feel his skull becoming tender just watching.

"Whoa, whoa easy!" Chris said, finally deciding to step in. He almost summoned his sword to swing at her for that. "Cool it!"

"Oh, I won't kill him," Victoria said with heavy sarcasm. "He's so...likable."

"You're a Wizard, right? Care to deal with the criminal attacking an honest civilian?" Theadore said while looking at Chris.

"Nice try, hun," Victoria spoke up again, waving her gun for him to stand up. "He owes me, and you do too if you don't want me to disintegrate your life's work."

"Tori-" Chris started, saying this nickname without even thinking.

"Oh, don't feel bad for him. He's just as shifty. I don't even think this was his first name change." She said, her gun following Theadore as he stood up slowly. "Now come on, Theo, old buddy. You're gonna go get me my shiny new android."

"Do you know how expensive these things are?! Goddammit, Victoria!" he exploded.

"Expensive enough to take more than three bullets," Victoria pushed the hot barrel of her gun into his back. "Now walk-ie, less talkie."

"Alright, alright! Damn..." he hurried forward, pressing a button on the wall as they approached the door. It slid upward and revealed a massive factory, with countless conveyor belts, androids assembling other androids, and a few real workers.

"You're not dumb enough to try and make them attack, are you?" Victoria asked, glancing back at Chris to ensure that he was following.

"No!"

"Okay, good!" she answered back. "Christopher, if he tries anything, turn him into a popsicle."

Chris glared a little, "I don't really want to do that."

"Did I ask what you want to do?" Victoria asked him. She answered before he even had the chance. "Just be a good guard dog."

"I thought you said that you just needed me to open something and leave!" Chris argued loudly.

"I lied. If you haven't figured that out yet, you're more gullible than I thought." Victoria sighed heavily. "You were just along in case I needed help with Theo's security or if the Alliance turned up."

"Welcome to the club, kid," Theadore mumbled in the front as he made his way up a flight of stairs. "Never trust this one unless money is involved, or you have something that'll help her."

"Yeah, Theo, I'm sorry I smacked you in the face with my gun. I only did it because you tried to kill me." Victoria responded impatiently as she pushed forward with her gun again. "Hustle. All I care about is getting my android and getting off this dust ball."

"You realize it needs something to track, right?" Theo tried as they made it to the second floor. He began pressing a few buttons on the console. "It's not just some problem-solving machine, and it's not indestructible, so I doubt it'll survive your...misadventures."

"Repeat after me: I. Don't. Care." Victoria began tapping her foot. "I already have what I need to make it work. Just give me the bot!"

"It's coming," Theadore assured her as a figure hurried over to her. "LZ-554, hurry up." He added nervously.

An android with black hair placed in a braid hurried over to them, making its way up the stairs. She stood at attention but looked nervous, her purple eyes homed in on Victoria's gun. She looked at Victoria then at Theodore. "Sir," she began in what sounded like an English accent. "Are you in danger...?"

"No, no..." Theo laughed nervously. "We're just playing a uh - game. No need to freak out. Right, old friend?"

"...Right." Victoria holstered both of her guns and dusted her hands off. "A really fun game."

"Oh...okay." She said very slowly like she had done the math on it and found that the situation did not add up. "You called me, sir?"

"Yes," he said, pointing at Victoria. "This is your new owner. You are to reassign to her immediately, LZ. Assist her with anything she needs and recognize her as your master. Do you understand?"

"I understand, sir." She said nervously.

"Good." He turned to Victoria. "It will help you find your sister and follow your exact orders from now on. Are we done?"

"We're done," Victoria smiled, looking the android over and congratulating herself. "Nice doing business with you.

"Get. Out." Theadore said with some anger but clearly knew he could do nothing.

Victoria gestured for the android to follow, and she did without a moment of delay. She kept pace perfectly and did not question her new life. Chris hurried after the two, wondering just how much of the truth Shadow Victoria had told him about what she planned to do with the android. He found himself staring at the false human only for it to occasionally stare back as if wondering why he was doing it. This manufactured person was so close that Chris would have easily mistaken her for a real person. Just how many had he run into before now?

Victoria exited the same way they came in, followed by the android and Chris. When he departed, Chris watched as the door shut on Theadore, staring down the stairs at the back of Victoria's head angrily. The android looked over the various fallen robotic bodies on the sandy floor and frowned a little. "What happened?"

"Theo got a little too excited," Victoria said vaguely. "Don't worry, I'm sure they can be rebuilt."

"Yes-" LZ said as if she was uncertain, which was odd for a robot to Chris.

Victoria silenced the two of them by drawing her gun and taking a shooting stance. "Step out!" She yelled while pointing at the bike they came on.

"You are in no position to be giving orders," Emily said, stepping out from behind the bike with her weapon. It was currently in the form of a katana. "Now, I told you to stay clear from my brother, but I will give you one chance to surrender."

"I'm not afraid of you," She assured Emily.

"Em??" Chris called out to her, completely surprised that she was here at all. How did she even know? Then a thought occurred, Eva must have told her. Great. She's always on the mark.

"It'll be alright," Emily promised him. She waved her hand as if directing someone else. "Get him for me."

Penny came out on the right side of the building with her shield raised. She was quick to grab Chris with her freehand and drag him back with her. He tried to ask her what was going on, but she would not answer. Instead, she just continued backing him up by pushing into him. She kept her guard up the whole way in case Victoria opened fire. She even prepared to block gunfire when Victoria drew her second gun and pointed at both Penny and Emily. LZ backed up nervously and looked back and forth.

"Surrender," Emily repeated once more.

"I count two against two," Victoria said in a booming voice. "I can't say I care about your track record. You haven't dealt with me. Neither of you has." She continued as if negotiating. "Now, you have your brother, and I have what I want. Let me leave, and you won't see me again. I have my own agenda."

A soft hum could be heard on the other side of the building. When it came around, Chris saw that it was indeed an Alliance tank. The white and blue chassis hovered just over the sand, blowing it every way. Soldiers disembarked from the armor and pointed weapons at Victoria. He counted about five or six. Even the tank turned the main gun on her, its flashlight marking her position as the long barrel directed itself forward. Victoria's eyes darted back and forth like she was debating what to do.

Now it was LZ's turn to act. The android shakily stepped forward and put itself between Victoria and the Alliance forces. She then whispered something to Victoria, but she clearly didn't agree as neither of them moved. Chris assumed that she was suggesting running back into the factory. The question that came to his mind next was whether LZ had any combat protocols. She seemed so afraid since the moment he met her, so it must have been unlikely.

"In my master's stead, I will apologize," LZ shouted. "This unit is not authorized to kill officials of the Alliance military or wound them, but I still must defend her."

"Shut down, and we'll reset you so that you can go back to what you did before," an Alliance soldier said loudly to Emily's right.

"I cannot do that without my master's order."

"Then your master better order you to do so," Emily said as a threat to Victoria. "Or I'll let my soldiers execute you – right now."

"LZ-" Victoria started, sighing in surrender. She raised her hands and her guns in such a way that they were dangling from her index fingers. LZ looked surprised but was prepared to do what she asked. "I'm guessing you have combat protocols, so do it," she said quickly. Emily raised her sword and prepared to block.

LZ extended both hands outward and created a very dense smoke bomb. Not only did it encompass the area in such a way that no one could see, but it also had properties like tear gas. The soldiers began coughing and falling over. Penny raised her soul barrier to shield herself and Chris from the effects, backing up the entire time to escape the cloud. Chris could not see what was happening with LZ, Shadow Tori, or Emily, but he thought he'd heard gunshots. He could also see a red orb fly forward and block gunfire from the tank and then return to Victoria's side, leaving a dense cloud of smoke in its place.

When the smoke cleared, he could see Victoria dragging LZ by the hand. She quickly mounted the bike and pulled the android along with her. She started the engine and began to drive off, but Emily was quick to catch up. She double jumped and landed directly on the bike, slashing downward at the tire. Victoria turned and fired her pistol at Emily, but she deflected without issue. She then shifted the sword around and cut Victoria across the face. When Victoria screamed out and dropped her gun to cover the side of her face, LZ acted. Latching onto Emily and bellowing a very loud apology, she began to taser Emily with her hands. Violent blue arcs of electricity flowed across her body, causing her to eventually lose her grip and fall from the moving bike.

Victoria and LZ escaped, though one of them was now slightly wounded. Demons were already advancing on Emily while she was still recovering from the sudden voltage, but Penny was quick to back her up. Just as three trolls emerged from the sand, her shield recoiled off each of them respectively and returned. Emily stood up, spinning her arm around as she did, and decapitated her attackers. The force of this attack led Chris to believe that she was furious. Emily sprinted back to the safety of the lights and headed straight for Chris and Penny, brushing off the pain like it was nothing now.

"Captain," Emily said, her voice still shaking from the electricity that was still passing through her. "Inform the general to scan for any civilian ships leaving the atmosphere. I want them apprehended."

"Ma'am," one of the soldiers said as he struggled back to his feet and tried to stop coughing. "Working on it..."

Emily advanced on Chris with nothing but purpose and anger in her eyes, "Chris, I am very disappointed in you. You not only disobeyed me, but you also worried Penny, who had no idea where you were!"

"She helped me find you in the clocktower, so I owed her." Chris reasoned.

Emily scowled. "The first rule, listen, and obey your superiors. I say what I say for a reason. Second, if your partner is saying not to do something, then maybe you shouldn't do it! What do you think we would have done if this had turned into something else?"

Chris avoided eye contact. He didn't really want to look at Penny or Emily at the moment. It was just awkward and uncomfortable for him now. He lowered his head and backed up just a little. Emily clearly noticed as her tone almost instantaneously lightened up, and she stood up straight. She corrected herself quickly and continued with, "I'm going to need you to listen to me. I only ever get one partner, and she only ever gets one partner. I came here ready to kill her over you."

"Commander Spellcrafter," the captain said from behind her. "The General says the Tenacity and the frigates are on alert and scanning as we speak."

"Very good," Emily said, turning away from Chris to speak. She didn't even notice when he slipped away to sit on the tank and wait to head back. "Now, little bro," she said, turning back to talk. "All I need is for you to-"

Penny pointed to his new position. Emily nodded and sighed, placing her palm against her forehead. "He's-"

"Go be with your partner, Penny...it's okay," Emily said, much softer. "I'll be there in a minute."

"Okay..." Penny started to walk toward the tank but stopped when Emily spoke again.

"Am I too, overbearing?" Emily asked her with a frown.

"When Tori was trying to get me to listen or stop doing something," Penny began, hoping to phrase this as best as she could. "She would remind me why she's doing it and make sure I knew that I had the choice to listen. When she would just boss me around, I usually wouldn't listen."

"Do I boss him around?"

"I don't think so, I just think-" Penny paused. What she was about to say was something she wasn't sure of, "You should be less like his superior and more like his older sister."

Emily nodded in understanding. "Can you-"

"I'll look after him as always," Penny promised. She made her way toward the tank and hopped onboard.

"Captain," Emily called out. "I'm heading to the Southern Resistance HQ to lend a hand. Get these two back to New Hope, rest up, and return to Grandham. I'll meet you there."

"Yes, ma'am." The captain said.

Chris watched as Emily said something into her watch and then waited a few moments. Just as the tank began rolling away and he'd built up the courage to bid her a farewell or say anything at all, Emily's aircraft soared in, the black armor mostly cloaked in the night. It hovered in place, blowing wind every which way while waiting on its pilot. Emily leaped up with a magic enhanced jump, kicked off of the building, and made it into the cockpit. Not even a few seconds after strapping in, she took off. Chris felt he'd given her the cold shoulder again, but there just wasn't much to say after that. Perhaps 'sorry' would be a start.

Chris turned to his right to look at Penny only to find that she was frowning. She was clearly upset about the situation too, and it definitely did not help that he could not read her mind just like always. He looked away and focused on the dark, unsettling night. Penny's gloved hand placed itself over his, her fingers curling around his own. When he turned back around to see her, she smiled.

"I'm glad you're alright." She said, scooting closer.

"You're not mad?" Chris asked, very confused.

"No. I wish you had told me what was going on so I could come sooner, though." Penny shut her eyes and lowered her shoulders. "When I got back and found out you were gone, I let Emily know and came straight here."

"Eva?" Chris inquired.

"She was tracking you the whole time, yeah," Penny told him.

"Part of me was hoping she would, but I don't think anything would have happened to me either way."

"I didn't feel like testing that Shadow's morality," Penny said, putting emphasis on the word shadow. She avoided her actual name altogether. "At least she won't bother you again."

"Are you okay? I know she kind of looks like her." Chris said, referring to the real Victoria.

"Of course. She's not my sister." Penny said to his surprise. "I'm not fazed by her."

"Alright...well," Chris decided to bring up a point of concern ever since he left. "Was Akela okay while I was gone? I left her with Megan and Ian."

Penny stared for a moment like he'd asked a stupid question, "Yes, she was fine." She spoke like something was being suppressed.

"Okay, I'm glad..." Chris said. Penny struck out suddenly, impacting his arm with her fist lightly; the noise he made was like that of a startled mouse, and his arm began to pulsate. Penny's version of lightly could be best described as a truck moving at fifty miles an hour. "Ow!"

"That was for worrying me and leaving Akela." Penny reclaimed his hand on her own and then returned her expression to a smile.

"You still hit so hard..." Chris said, rotating his arm as best as he could while she held his hand. "And I always feel it later."

"Good. Reminders prevent repeat behavior." Penny said, laying her head against his shoulder. "Now make it up to me by being a source of warmth."

"I thought you said you didn't care about the cold or anything like that." He pointed out.

"Just because I can ignore it doesn't mean I always want to, and you're warm." She clarified, pulling him closer. "Now, shh."

---

When they arrived back at the New Hope police station, mostly everyone was asleep - that was aside from Megan and Ian as well as a few others. Akela was asleep in Megan's lap, and Megan herself was reading something on her watch, which looked like demon information data. Ian was throwing a bouncy ball against the police station wall over and over while whistling softly to himself. Both of them were doing their best to remain awake despite being tired and having nothing to do.

"Meg," Ian said drowsily, shaking Megan lightly. "They're back."

Megan lifted her head and noted the tank which parked just next to the street and began disembarking soldiers. Two Wizards hurried over as well. "Well," Megan started. "You two have had a day. The advisor told me a little, but I'd like to hear the rest in the morning."

"Not now?" Chris asked her curiously.

"Chris...I'm tired." Megan admitted with a sleepy laugh. "I'll be blunt; I probably wouldn't even be listening."

"Why didn't you two sleep?" Penny asked them with a head tilt.

"Taking turns watching the kid," Ian explained. "Plus if we didn't hear from you soon, we were going to go out too." He stretched his legs and stood up. "But seeing as that's not the case, can we please sleep? I'm seeing stars, and they're not in the sky."

"Sure," Penny said, picking up Akela as carefully as she could from Megan's lap. "Was she alright?"

"She's a smart girl," Megan said in slurs. "She asked a lot of questions."

"Just be glad you got back when you did," Ian said, climbing into the tent. "Meg would've made her head explode. *Powsshhhh!*" he said, making an explosion noise.

"Remind me to smack him in the morning," Megan said, waving goodnight without thinking before climbing into her tent.

Akela stirred in Penny's arms, prompting her to hurry to the tent. She set her down on the middle sleeping bag, and when the girl woke up, the first thing she saw was Penny. "I didn't mean to wake you up," she said. "But since you're up, do you want to see the reason I was gone?"

"I want to see too," Chris said. He was just as curious as the girl who had sat up and rubbed her eyes to wake herself up more.

"What is it?" Akela asked her.

Both Chris and Akela noticed Penny fishing behind herself and under the sleeping bag. She then pulled something out and kept it behind her back. Penny removed the Phon, its rabbit-like ears and wrapped tail protruding from the body proudly. She waggled the stuffed animal in front of Akela's face just like she thought Morgan would. Penny was taken aback when Akela lunged with both arms, hooked them around the stuffed toy, and held it tight.

"You went back...?" Akela asked her, squeezing the Phon as tightly as she could.

"I wanted to make sure you had something if we were busy or somewhere else," Penny explained kindly. "So Morgan and I went looking around and found this in your room. I know it's not much, but at least until we figure out what's going to happen."

Akela smiled and hugged Penny around her torso, the stuffed toy still tightly in her grip. "Mom got me this toy," she said, holding it up high. For a moment, Chris sensed Penny's thoughts, and all he could hear was how similar she thought this girl was to Tori. "It's my favorite, but I think I'm gonna give it a new name now."

"Oh?" Penny inquired curiously. "Why?"

"What's your name?" Akela asked her.

"My-" Penny pointed at herself.

"Your name!" Akela said, jumping up and pinching Penny's cheeks.

"I can't tell you if you're doing that to my cheeks." She responded in a silly voice. Chris laughed off to the side at this spectacular display. If only he had something to record it.

"Pennelopie," Penny said with some hesitation. "Pennelopie Marie Dreadful."

"Hear that?" Akela asked the stuffed animal as she held it out in front of herself. "Your new name is...Penny Marie Dreadful. I can't say that *Pennelo-* that first name, so you're going to get the nickname! I'll call you, Penny!"

"Did...you just name it after me?" Penny raised her eyebrows and stared at the child, who nodded with glee. "My whole name?"

"Mmmhmm!" she said.

"I guess I'm not original anymore," Penny said jokingly with a shrug.

"Of course you are," Chris said with a smile. "No one is as scary as you when you're mad, and no one hits as hard."

"Is that a compliment?" Penny questioned.

"Sure, let's go with that!"

"It better be," Penny said with a smirk.

# ONWARD TO WAR

Chris opened his eyes slowly to reveal the white lowered ceiling of his station bed. His back hurt from the constant fighting, but other than that, he felt okay. It had been about a week since they had arrived and taken New Hope city, but it felt like forever. The shower he took when they arrived at the station helped tremendously, but taking a little longer to rest helped even more. He rolled onto his right side and sighed softly. He could see Penny scrolling through her watch and lying in a similar position on her own bed. Her eyes panned up and onto him after a few moments of staring, and her expression turned to a smile.

"What?" She asked him. "Can't get enough of me?" Chris chucked his pillow across the room at Penny; catching it, she sent it right back with much better accuracy. Her accuracy was so good that the pillow popped him in the mouth. "That's a yes."

Chris replaced his pillow behind himself and turned to get out of bed. Hitting his head on the low ceiling, which was always under his bed on the station, he escaped his bed and began rifling through the clothes drawer just under it. "I miss my red one," Chris said as he slipped on a grey shirt, white jacket, jeans, and black shoes.

"I think that one looks better on you," Penny told him honestly. "You look a little less like a model and more like a pilot or something."

"Was that a flirt?" Chris questioned.

"Maybe. Maybe not." Penny said, swinging herself around to get up. She stretched and yawned. "If it was, what would you do?"

"Probably flirt back?" Chris responded. She knew full well what he would do.

"Hmm. Okay," Penny shrugged her shoulders and curled her lip playfully. "Then it was." Chris turned a shade of red and immediately turned away to replace his drawer and make his bed. "Oh? I guess you were wrong about what you would do."

"I'll get you later," Chris promised with a squeak in his voice. Penny looked up from her watch with an amused expression. She leaped out of bed, dressed in an outfit similar to what she usually wore, and threw on some shoes.

"To all Allied forces, be aware of changing conditions on the planet Sohrann," Autumn's voice said over the intercom. It was also coming from both of their watches. "There are concerns related to planetary quakes occurring globally due to tectonic shifts. Be aware and pay attention to alerts from your advisor or superior officer."

"That's an understatement," Penny commented, referring to the other night when both he and Morgan were nearly eaten by the planet.

"Was it really that huge?" Chris questioned.

"That hole could have eaten a tank if it wanted to," Penny explained. "I've seen quakes, but this is something else. I'm really starting to dislike this planet."

"The people are pretty nice," Chris said, hoping to lighten the mood.

"Thank you for, once again, being my positivity, oh partner of mine," Penny said with an overexaggerated eye roll. "Now come on. I still want to get you checked out by an Imagination Wizard. If Megan ever listens to me, I want her to as well."

"Well, we know Eslena was messing with my mind." Chris

started as he approached the door and waited for her. "But Meg didn't really say much, right?"

"It doesn't matter. You see, I had a theory," Penny started as she held her hand on the button beside the door. When it opened, the two stepped out together into the crowded hallway. "Ian and I use Death magic, so we can't see Imagination magic at all. Megan hasn't been around you to see it. I'm not entirely sure what Eslena is capable of, but she trained Gatchi, so I can guess pretty well." Penny continued. "I know I am physically incapable of seeing what is going on with you, but I'm worried."

"So, what can they do then?"

"Spells can be cast on you to prevent you from seeing her," Penny explained. "I'm just not sure if it would work. If it is a curse, it'll take a bit more, but if it's a basic spell, then it should be fine."

"Why couldn't Morgan do it?" Chris asked.

"We left before I could ask her, but if we can't take care of this today, I want her to do it," Penny muttered to herself as she walked ahead and activated the elevator. "But I'm surprised the spell already on you didn't activate."

"Spell?" Chris repeated.

"I said I'm wondering if she put a spell on you," Penny lied, dodging his inquiry to guard the secret she had promised to keep.

The two stepped into the elevator and pressed the up button. Soon the elevator began moving in the direction they instructed, and the two continued their conversation. Things were calm until the elevator stopped suddenly, and the power cut entirely, leaving them in darkness. At first, Chris wasn't quite sure what to do, but he remembered that he was basically a light source. Flaring his magic, he held his hand up. Penny did the same at the exact moment he did, illuminating this tiny box in light blue and dark purple.

"What happened?" He inquired.

"I'm not sure," Penny responded to his right. She got down and pulled the panel just below the buttons off the wall. Then, she started to check the wires. "Minor power fluctuation? I hope..."

"Well..." Chris started, looking around their temporary prison. "At least I'm stuck in here with you instead of Ian or Meg. Ian would take up too much space, and Meg would lecture me on how the elevator works!"

"Neither of them would take advantage of the situation they were in to kiss you," Penny said without thinking. "At least, I hope not. Let me figure out this wiring, okay?"

"But you just-" Chris tried.

"Focused." She responded; her head buried in the control box.

A large explosion rocked the box that they were in. The two fell over respectively and scrambled to their feet, exchanging the same glance. They needed to get out of here. The station alarm chimed loudly outside of the elevator, and Chris wondered just what was happening outside. Penny, giving up on the wiring, raised her watch and explained the situation to both Megan and Ian. Ian explained that he was trapped on the hangar deck, and Megan was apparently on the command deck. Neither of them could leave.

Penny was going to suggest that one of them head for the electrical deck, but Ian was having none of it. A loud thud sounded above them and startled Chris. Not even a moment later, a sword pierced through the metal like it was cardboard and cut a man-sized hole. Ian yanked the rigid metal out of the way and extended a hand. Penny went first, jumping on the wall to give herself momentum before being hoisted out by Ian. Next was Chris, who struggled a little more, but Ian did most of the work and still got him out just fine.

"What's going on?" Chris asked him as the box they were standing on shook like it was ready to fall.

"The Empire just hit us with bombers," he explained, trying to keep his balance as he talked. "And a Behemoth class ship just jumped out into the system."

"An ambush...?" Penny said, speaking aloud to herself. "No. That can't be right. We never had the resources to attack a station and an Alliance flagship at once."

"Yeah, well, that should tell you they're desperate," Ian

responded. "We should get off of this thing." He decided, looking around for some way back up along the dimly lit shaft system.

A thick, green leafy vine fell down the shaft and landed beside him. Ian chuckled to himself as he knew exactly who it was. The three climbed their way up and only stopped when the station shook so violently that they could not keep a good grip. A minute or two later, they could see the light near the top of the shaft. Megan was indeed dangling herself out into the dark abyss and holding them up with her magic. She seemed to be struggling but had not moved an inch forward or back. Ian was first, pulling himself up alone. He grabbed the vine with both hands and yanked the other two to safety.

"Please have a plan before you jump down into a place you may not be able to get out of," Megan recommended. She released the vine and let it fall. Two Wizards who were helping to hold the door open released it and let the door shut violently.

"Now we're all trapped together," one said with a humorless grin. "Great."

"We just need to wait for the auxiliary power."

"Imperial troops are boarding!" A panicked Alliance soldier said over the intercom through his breaths. "Imperial troops have-" there was gunfire and then nothing.

"If they want a fight," Ian started. "They've picked some bad odds."

"Cornellius," Chris said into his watch. "Can you launch?"

"No. My magnetic locks were activated by the Imperials." Cornellius responded back from the hanger deck. "Still, they were gentler than you. Oh, yes, you have a boarding party coming."

"Just...hang tight," Chris said as he ran into the command deck with the other three. The station crew here was scrambling to get power online and work the defenses manually at the same time.

"But sir-" one woman said.

"I don't care about the bombers. Get us power now! We're sitting ducks." one of the Overseers said. "All of you, do your jobs so we can get out of this! We are not dead yet! Anyone not performing an essential task, grab a gun, and watch the door. The enemy may attempt to scale the elevator shaft to take this level."

Evangeline was frantically sliding bars on her screen to balance power on multiple levels. Her right hand was manually firing the guns, and on the screen, she was viewing, Chris could see that she had managed to take down two of the attacking bombers just below the station. She did not even need to look to confirm that it was them who had approached her. Instead, she continued her job and spoke as she did.

"I'm glad you are unscathed." She exclaimed. "I need you ready to go as soon as the power is up. We need fighters."

"But the boarders-" Chris started.

"Will be dealt with," Evangeline said quickly. "Emily arrived at the station just before this mess kicked off." She swiped her hand to pull up security footage of Emily sprinting forward, cutting clean through a boarding party and even throwing one out of a cracked window and escaping before the vacuum took her. The door shut behind her, and the window sealed itself with a metal plating. "I need you ready to get out there the moment the power comes on, and these shields are back online."

"Just tell us when," Penny said.

A loud and deep mechanical hum sounded as the lights flickered to life. "Now would be good," She said. "Watch yourself."

"Right," Chris said. "We can still help here; let's go!" he called out to his squad.

He was the first one out of the door and into the elevator. The elevator took them directly to the hangar deck. When the doors opened, the first thing they saw was a raging fire and various Imperial bodies. Emily had, for sure, come this way at some point. Chris also noted a few plasma marks implying that someone shot the Imperials with gunfire as well. Perhaps she had Alliance soldiers with her.

"Alright, we need to move," Chris told them as they swiftly moved left along the corridor. "I hope the planes are alright."

"Me too," Ian commented. "It would really suck if they were destroyed after all of this."

"I'm sure they are fine," Megan said, shutting down this discussion. "We need to get there before we start worrying about what happened to them."

*Boom! Crackle!* The lights flickered on and off for a moment as the station's deck shook violently. The four of them grabbed onto the ground or the wall, respectively. The sound of sliding metal could be heard outside like something detached or slammed into the outer wall - or both. Crewmembers flew across the floor and slammed into the walls. Imperials and Alliance soldiers slid across the floor, their guns discharging as they fell. Chris scrambled to his feet and looked out of the window to see not only the battle raging on the outside, but a crippled bomber headed straight for them.

"...Run for it!" Chris said as he yanked Penny to her feet and pushed her forward. He then went back for Megan and Ian. The three of them hurried along with Chris taking up the rear. When the Imperial craft slammed into the side of the station, it flew straight through. Glass flew everywhere, fire flew left and right, burning Chris as it went along. He grabbed onto the nearest edge he could find and held tight, but it wasn't enough. The vacuum began pulling him down toward the breach. Chris knew that he'd be sucked right into space if he did not act quickly, but Megan was much faster.

Extending her hand, Megan created a mess of vines just behind him, catching him like a spider's web. She then spun her hand around and produced a gust of wind that forced him forward toward her. Her hand met his, and she pulled him up to the other two. When Megan was sure he was safe, she extended her hand one more time, blasting wind outward and slamming it into the emergency button. The metal doors shut behind them, cutting off that section of the station as it was no longer safe. The four took a moment to recover from nearly being sucked out into space before shambling back to their feet and moving on. Penny was first, fighting her way forward through any remaining boarders on this level.

"I think this station is done, but let's try to defend what's left," Chris commented as they made it into the hanger. It was even more of a mess than the rest of the station. Wires hung from the ceiling and were mostly disconnected, dead mechanics littered the floor and destroyed station turrets lined the walkway. The Spark and Nighturge appeared to be just fine minus a few dents, but Emily's plane was nowhere to be found.

"That's not our call," Penny replied as she headed for the Spark. She disengaged the locks on a nearby console and rolled the plane singlehandedly onto the launching pad. Ian was doing the same for the Nighturge.

"More coming into the system! Regroup!" the General said on the Alliance channel.

Three more Imperial flagships jumped out into the system. Fighters and bombers came out of them like bees moving to attack from a hive. The General's ship, the Tenacity, flew into view from the hanger and began taking shots for the station. The Imperial ships were hammering his shields, but they held all the same. Alliance and Imperial ships and planes soared left and right, and Chris wondered just how bad things would be once they had launched. This battle was one damaged station and one flagship against about three. Suddenly, it didn't seem so easy anymore.

"The station has sustained critical damage!" a rough male voice said over the intercom. "Automated defense systems are active but failing. All hands evacuate immediately."

"Look out!" Chris heard from the other side of the hangar.

The captain known as Aiem'y ran backward into the hanger, firing her pistol as she did. Emily came just behind her and cut the door controls with her sword. Three more individuals had managed to escape just before the door shut on the Imperials and appeared to be employed under the captain. While Emily hurried over to Chris, Aiem'y began messing with the ship controls with her crew. The shuttle elevator dipped down, retrieved her ship, and came back up with it. Anyone could tell that it was the ship of a smuggler. It was a rough and older model of a heavy transport ship. It was just a commercial vessel, but she had outfitted it with weapons.

"We need to launch, now!" the captain said as she ran up into her ship. "I don't have my crew with me, so you're on the guns!"

"Em?" Chris started.

Emily took him by the shoulders, "Not now, okay? Get out there and do what Penny says. I'll be right behind you with this...character of a captain. My plane didn't make it so I'm stuck with her."

Chris looked her in the eyes and replied with an "Alright."

"You'll be fine." She concluded Emily quickly hugged him and kissed his forehead before running up into the captain's ship.

Chris climbed up into the Spark's co-pilot seat and watched as Penny lowered the canopy glass. The smuggler's ship-launched first, its heavy engines igniting and propelling it forward. It soared out into space and spun downwards (or what could be considered down in space). Next was the Nighturge, which followed suit, but headed straight for the General's flagship. Finally, the Spark took off and escaped too. Cornellius wasted no time warning them that they were surrounded, to which Penny responded with an annoyed, 'I know.'

"Advisor Evangeline to Delta Two-" Their advisor started through panting.

"Eva. Good to hear your voice," Chris admitted. "Did you make it to an escape pod?"

"No. Not yet." She admitted. Her video clearly showed that she had been injured somewhere on her hip. "Sorcerers managed to reach the command deck and I got unlucky."

"What?!" Both Chris and Penny said together.

"I have not had a chance to yet. And neither have any of the other crew on the command deck. I will soon," she assured him. "I am working on a plan, but for now, protect General Delore's ship. I'll inform you when it is ready. I will warn you; it will require some of Delta One's fancy flying." Evangeline disabled her video feed.

"Meg? Ian?" Penny said over the comms. Their images appeared on the canopy. "Let's deal with those frigates first and prevent them from swarming the Tenacity."

"We're with you," Megan responded.

"Dreadful...I see you're in the air." Violet said with the slightest bit of annoyance. Her screen shook a little. "I'll join you with the pilots I rounded up. Bomb them to pieces."

"Where are you?" Penny questioned.

"Be there soon. I've got a fighter on me, and he really doesn't know how to take a hint."

"I'll come to support you, then." Penny offered.

"I don't need your help," Violet said, cutting the communications on her end. She seemed insulted by the suggestion that Penny could help her.

Penny increased their engine's power and flew along the trench which lined the General's flagship. The turrets obviously ignored them. Chris figured that Penny wanted cover from the enemy's assault batteries, which were hammering the station and his ship. This would allow them to approach without worrying about being destroyed. Once they had gone about halfway around and the Imperial frigate could be seen, Penny unleashed a volley of missiles which the Imperial frigate's shield resistance. The guns turned on them, but Penny dodged. Changing tactics, she flew under the frigate, stripped the underside of its guns with plasma rounds, and pummeled the underside with missiles until it began to fall apart. Ian hit it from above, bombing the bridge with the Nighturge's underside weaponry while Megan swept the surface for turrets.

When they flew out of range of the frigate to come back around, Chris noticed an Alliance heavy frigate ship moving into position. Not even a moment after it came into range, it bombarded the wounded Imperial frigate and destroyed it before it even had a chance to turn and retreat. The frigate split in half, breaking off more as it did. Penny flew directly between the two separated parts of this wreck and reoriented them to pass along the General's ship. She was still remaining on the defensive. Red, yellow, and green plasma lasers flew every which way. The Tenacity fired it's rail gun at the other frigate and destroyed it in one shot, the metal disc penetrating the frigate's shield and armor. It never stood a chance against the Tenacity.

"Spark, you've got a tail!" a pilot said on the comms. Penny glanced behind herself and suddenly increased in the engines, flying past the Tenacity's bridge and trying to allow the turrets to help her.

The pilot behind them was far too good for such simple tricks. Penny would just have to try harder. She cut the engines, allowing the spark to drift. Turning hard, she opened fire behind them and directed Chris to do so as well. The Imperial plane spun to the right to avoid their fight and shot out a missile, which Chris shot down after many attempts. He was so close that Penny could just barely make out the pilot's helmet and see him push the triggers on the throttle to open fire once again. She dodged, replying with machine gun fire, which worked even in space - especially at this distance. A few of the rounds struck his plane's wings, but he was still able to fly.

This was still enough to get him to go into a retreat. Penny pursued him, firing in bursts to save ammunition. He dodged left and right and dipped behind the destroyed frigates for cover. She was still right on him, though. This pilot was not like the rest they had dealt with since they arrived. This one appeared to be out for blood and only blood. He flew even lower, attempting to force Penny to crash into the station, but she just continued to glide along the surface. No matter how fast she was going, she always seemed to be aware and ready to dodge. She only slowed down to turn hard and lead her shot into his plane, but he also avoided this attempt.

"You killed my squadron-" the enemy pilot started.

Cornellius chimed in, "He's talking on an open channel."

"-And you act like I wouldn't be back for you?!"

"You again," Penny commented under her breath. "Great."

"Me again." He said, coasting his wing along the station surface and firing at the Spark. He took out one of the guns, but they were still alright. "You would betray your Empire, kill your own people who looked up to you, and expect me to not come back? I don't care what your father wants. I'm killing you here."

"You can try," Penny responded, whipping the Spark around to give chase. "I gave you every opportunity to back off."

"And I'm giving you every opportunity to die."

"Delta One," Evangeline suddenly chimed in. "Break off. I'm ready."

"Alright," Penny said, turning hard and slowing their speed. She then increased the engines when she was ready to go.

"You think I'll let you get away?!" He bellowed, raging after them with his fighter.

The Nighturge came from above him and started pelting his plane with machine gun fire, "I think you will. Why don't you dance with me for a while!?" Ian cried out.

The pilot broke off, now having Ian to deal with, leaving the Spark to do what it needed to. "What's your plan?" Penny asked.

"The station is done for, and we have no time to repair it." Evangeline started off. "But the reactor is intact. I want you to fly into a breach I found which leads through an exhaust vent and blow up the core."

"Are you serious...?" Chris questioned. "You're still on that thing."

"I won't be when it blows," she said dismissively. "The breach is just below the medbay level near the bottom of the station."

"Alright," Penny said, taking them toward the specified location. "It will probably be a tight fit."

"It will so throttle down," Evangeline answered. "If we blow the station, it will create a large enough explosion to possibly wipe out the Imperial fleet, their fighters, and win this battle for us. I'm going to inform the fighters to retreat and for the Tenacity to jump out of the system."

"But then what?" Chris questioned with lots of concern.

"You'll fly out and head for the planet, away from the shockwave. The reactor should have a delay before exploding. I'm going to..."

Evangeline paused. "Remotely open up the ventilation so the explosion is larger and ensure you can escape."

"You can do that?" Chris questioned. Penny grimaced but said nothing.

"Just get in there and destroy the core," Evangeline ordered him. "Do not linger." Evangeline swapped channels. "General, get the Tenacity clear of the station. We're going with plan B."

"Understood." General Nicholas Delore said. "All fighters get clear of the Salvation and return to your assigned hanger. Anyone from the station, escape to the planet."

The Spark flew into the gaping maw of the station. It was where that Imperial plane had slammed into the station exterior and nearly killed them. Penny slowed down, dodging pipes, emitters, and surging electricity. Chris tried asking if she was okay, but she was so focused that she could not talk. It was a winding maze with tight corners and barely any room for error. The Spark's front lights activated in the darkness to allow her to see. Though there were lights inside of this tunnel, there were very few working ones.

"Eva? You did say you got to an escape pod, right?" Chris asked, concerned about her safety.

"Yes. I just did..." she said. Faint typing could be heard in the background. "Delta One, I've just opened the exhaust vent. Can you see it?"

Penny flew them through a narrow grating, which was just barely bigger than the Spark. They were now in a bright blue room with surging energy that circled a single structure: the reactor. Penny fired missile after missile and shot at the individual parts of this bright machine. It began to power down, and everything went dark, but then it became exceedingly bright. Circling around, Penny headed back toward the way they came.

"Get out of there!" Evangeline cried out. "It might be tricky, but you can do this. Relax. I will try to clear you a path to escape; just stay away from the walls!" Evangeline said. "The explosion may try to launch you off course, so try not to slow down. Brace yourself!"

"All Alliance ships withdraw." he heard Violet say on the comms. "Follow me!"

Penny forced the throttle all the way forward and bolted the Spark back the way they came. She dodged at blinding speeds, breathing hard as she did like she was under strain. Chris fell back into his seat and was unable to move. Penny could just barely sit forward but looked like she was fighting the force of the plane. The explosion went off and began chasing behind them; the bright yellow light was almost as fast as the Spark. Evangeline opened exhaust vents repeatedly, attempting to buy them time or get them to take another path outwards, which would be safer.

"You're nearly there," Evangeline said. "Head, right!"

"Penn..??" Chris said over the rumblings around them and fire which covered the canopy.

"You are nearly there!" Evangeline chimed in one last time. Her comms cut suddenly, possibly from the interference of the explosion.

Penny said nothing but turned right as she was instructed into a tight winding vent. The belly of the Spark scraped the bottom of the narrow passageway. Penny winced and pulled them away from it, throttling down to turn hard upon leaving the vent. The Spark exited the vent, flying rapidly down toward the planet. The Nighturge and a few other ships, including captain Aiem'y's, ducked downward toward Sohrann. The station behind them flashed and then exploded outwardly in all directions like a supernova.

The Tenacity and all Alliance frigates jumped from the system in a bright white flash. The Imperial ships were consumed by the rapidly expanding inferno. It ate through their shields, destroyed their fighters, and brought them to their knees. Only one Imperial ship was smart enough to jump out of the system, but it most likely left its fighter squadrons to perish. The station debris flew in all directions toward the planet, forcing Penny to dodge large chunks of it.

"Eva, we're clear," Chris told her. Static. Nothing but static. Prolonged, everlasting, empty static. "She's not answering..." Chris said, fiddling with the screen on his side to boost the signal.

Megan and Ian appeared as images on the canopy, but he could not seem to get Evangeline. Penny continued to fly, her mouth forming a straight line as she focused on their reentry. Penny shook her head and pushed his hand away from the console. She then returned it to the controls. Chris stared at her, baffled by this action. Megan was the one who would answer his concerns.

"She must not have launched," Megan theorized with her head lowered. "I can still reach everyone else."

"Try to stay focused." Penny urged him. "I know it's hard to, but if we die here, then all we did was waste her life. She chose to do that and give us a chance."

"Why didn't she just do it remotely?" Chris asked. "She said-"

"To work the station's core features like ventilating the core," Megan began slowly. "You have to perform it from either the core level or the command deck. She must have decided to stay behind."

"Then we killed her," Chris concluded, sinking back into his seat and releasing his gun controls.

"You didn't kill her," Ian said directly to him. "You did what she asked you to, and it worked. I'm not happy about what happened to her either, but Penny is right. Stay focused."

"What do we even do without an advisor?" Chris asked.

"We'll worry about it later!" Penny said, dodging a sudden beam of plasma. The Alliance pilot just ahead of them was not so lucky and detonated from the attack. "Behind us!"

"They don't know when to quit," Violet said, breaking off from the flock which was running for the surface. "I hope these cowards are ready for the first real fight they've had all day! They'll pay."

"Violet, not alone!" Emily hissed. The smuggler's ship broke off next, opening fire on the Imperial formation. "Chris, keep heading for the surface with your squad. Regroup in New Hope and wait for my order."

"A-alright..." Chris said. He sat up, grabbed the controls, and tried to stop his hands from shaking. He felt like he was going to vomit.

"Penny. Penny!" Ian called out loudly. "Behind you!"

"Again?!" Penny gritted her teeth and dove, dodging an Imperial fighter that soared past and missed them with its gunfire.

The fighter dove after them and desperately continued to fire. It was the same pilot from before, still driven to kill them and still just as dangerous. Penny could handle him. He just needed to get himself together. Chris returned fire to the rear and shook off his feelings of dismay. Now was not the time - like his friends had said. Megan peppered the enemy fighter with her machine gun, but Ian was busy dodging his own tail. All she could do was try to help from a distance.

"We'll have to lose him in the clouds." Penny decided. "Stay with me just a little longer, Chris." She urged.

Chris watched as Penny put the throttle to the highest setting and flew so fast that they tore a hole in the cloud layer. They were now in the middle of rolling white giants. Chris thought that maybe they had lost him, so he turned in his seat to look only to see multiple bright red missiles homing in on them. She dodged left then right, up, slowed down, and rolled. When they came too close, Penny activated the countermeasures. Tiny pellets collided with the missiles and detonated them just behind the engines.

"I'll chase you until I run out of fuel if I have to!" the voice said on the open comms. "After all, you taught me to just keep trying, right?!"

"I have no idea what you're talking about," Penny said emotionlessly as she dodged out of the clouds then back in.

"You may not remember me, but I remember you, coward!" He explained, attacking from above now. "I wanted to be a pilot, like you, and you told me to just keep trying. Just keep pushing. Don't let anyone get in your way and if they do, cut them down. You said that, Dreadful." He began laughing. "It's ironic how you're in my way now."

"I hate to be the one to say it-" Cornellius started nervously. "But we took a lot of damage from the station explosion, so systems are starting to fail."

"What?" Penny asked, narrowing rotating out of the way of a tracer missile as she said this. "Dammit. Chris, see what you can do, okay?"

"What I can-" Chris started nervously.

They stared at one another for a moment before she decided against this, "Never mind. Just sit back and breathe, okay? Shoot him if you can, but if you can't calm down, I'll make it work."

"Make it work??" Cornellius repeated. "We are going to die if enough systems fail!"

"Cornellius!" Penny snapped, giving him a hateful glare. "I will handle it. Leave him alone."

Penny threw the throttle to full once again and turned around, heading straight for the enemy pilot. She'd just end this faster than she intended. If the plane was going to go down anyway, at least she could ensure that they would land safely. The enemy pilot continued flying straight since Penny was not flying. He was silent for a moment before finally exploding out of anger.

"You're flying at me? You think I'm afraid?!" He only became angrier as he asked himself these questions. "Like I could ever lose to a spineless traitor."

He increased his own speed and opened fire. Penny dodged every shot minus a few, which caught her off guard or where the timing was too narrow to react and returned fire as well. She then began to decelerate. "Sit back..." She told Chris. "Shut your eyes if you need to. This won't feel too good. Cornellius, full power to weapons. I don't care about anything else."

"100 percent..." Cornellius started. "200...300..." he continued. "Full power achieved. I sure hope you don't kill us."

"I can help," Chris said, finally sitting forward after a deep breath.

Chris grabbed onto his gun's controls, directed it to swap to plasma, and waited for Penny to fire. She smiled at this, if only a little. Penny suddenly burst the engines so that it threw them out of control and only reactivated them when she was sure that they were behind the Imperial plane. She then reactivated them and opened fire with everything they had: missiles, machine gun, plasma gun, Chris's underbelly gun, and even dumb fire missiles which would not track him. There was no way to dodge it all. His plane was torn to pieces. All that could be heard from his side of the open communications was a frustrated 'no' over and over.

Chris watched as the plane detonated in a black puff of smoke. The pilot was dead, and the aircraft was destroyed. Penny returned power to the engines and removed the weapon systems so that they could fly easier. Chris sighed out of both relief and feeling overwhelmed from the last few moments, ducked under the seat to retrieve his tools. He'd fix the Spark on their way to New Hope from the interior and then repair anything else when they landed with whatever they had.

*Tap tap thud*, he heard. It must have been the rubble from his plane colliding with the armor. A few moments later, the pilot came into view, an oxygen mask on his face and a pistol in his hand. He slid down the canopy and stared Penny dead in the face. She turned to throw him off, but he stabbed a knife into the glass and held on tight. Then he opened fire with his pistol. Three shots struck Penny's shoulder and chest -- the final two hit her heart and stomach.

"Penn!" Chris cried out. He summoned his sword and stabbed clean through the glass until all he had left was the hilt.

The pilot dodged by leaning back and then climbed upward toward the back of the plane. Three loud explosions followed in the form of gunshots. There was a tearing noise, and finally, it stopped. Chris turned his head to see the pilot flying lazily in the wind. Another Imperial fighter came up, slowed down, and caught him. Then together, they flew away like their mission was complete.

Chris returned his attention to Penny. She was slumped down in the seat against the canopy and bleeding all over. She must have gone unconscious because no matter how much he called out to her or said her name, she did not reply. He held her wounds, and they were healing, but she was out - likely from blood loss or a combination of it and pain. An explosion happened in the engines, and the plane went into a nosedive. Chris, screaming and unsure what to do, began pulling up on the controls but could not seem to get them out of it. They were headed straight through the clouds toward the ground, and he figured they only had a few seconds. He couldn't move her to get into the pilot seat, and there was no way to repair the engines from inside if the damage was as bad as he thought.

"Oh, crap! The Spark just went dark. Where did they fly to?!" Ian said on the comms just before the sound became distorted.

"What?? Chris!" Emily screamed. "Turn this around! We have to find them!"

"Are you out of your mind?" Aiem'y shot back at her. "Not now!"

"We're gonna die!" Cornellius cried out. "You killed us!"

"Penn!" Chris tried again.

After trying to frantically work the controls on Penny's side from across the dash, Chris gave up. Chris swung his sword hard like a bat, destroying the canopy and exposing them to the cold, loud wind. He unstrapped Penny and freed her from the seat, pulling her onto himself. Then he freed himself from his own seat. The ground was coming closer now and much faster. They must have hit terminal velocity by now because he could not even will his body to move as easily. It would take one good magic boosted jump. Chris was so focused on the situation that he had not even realized that Penny was once again conscious.

"You're leaving me?!" Cornellius protested angrily. "You're going to leave me! You doomed me with your stupid flying and stupid ideas, and now you're ditching me."

"I have your backup," Chris promised him. "I need to get her out...right now."

"Let me go," Penny demanded urgently as she pushed him off.

Penny's arms locked themselves around him and held tightly. She then picked him up out of his seat and kicked hard off of the dash. The two flipped out of the plane together and into the open air. Cornellius's protests died the further he got away, and now it was just him and an unconscious Penny. There was nowhere soft to land and no way to break the fall. Wizards could take falls, but this was way too high. The fall he worried about never came through. Instead, they glided along high in the clouds and slowed down over time.

Chris, understandably shocked, turned his head back toward Penny. Relatively large black bat wings protruded from her back. The interior of them was purple, and the back of them was black. They occasionally flapped to keep them in the air but mostly only needed to glide and must have been big enough to equal his own height or at least close to it. Penny tightened her grip around his torso and flew lower. The Spark exploded violently just under them and sent shrapnel everywhere, which she avoided. Instead of stopping where the Spark landed, Penny wisely chose to keep flying away from it, as any Imperials seeking to confirm that they died would circle back around. Now, they were gliding just above the sands.

"Penny, I-" Chris was speechless and fumbling with his own words. Did she always have these wings? Were they a spell she knew or a part of her? "Where are we going?"

"Let me find someplace safe to land for now," Penny answered back shortly like she did not want to talk. "Then I'll get our emergency kit, and if we're stuck out here for the night, at least we'll be safe."

"Alright..."

# THE NIGHTFLYER

Chris felt Penny tense up as the battle continued above them. Alliance planes had flown into range and engaged some of the Imperials not far from where they were. Penny was careful to keep them clear of the skirmish and out of sight. He thought that he'd even spotted the Nighturge tearing through the enemy and occasionally flying low to scan the ground. The signals were weaker now that the station was gone. He could still hear some of what was being said during the fight with the watches.

"Hey, Ian, come back. You can't go out there! There are too many!" a pilot he did not recognize said, though the signal cut in and out.

"Shut up!" Ian snapped. Chris watched as the Nighturge corkscrewed out of the way of a missile. "I already know! I just need to check something."

"We'll be fine," Megan said, agreeing with him completely. "Ian, if we can't break through soon, we should turn around. They should be fine. I see the Spark - what is left of it, but no one is in it."

"I'll do one more sweep," Ian said through what sounded like gritted teeth. Chris watched as he expertly performed an aerial ram on an enemy bomber and let Megan color it with her machine gun. "They just keep coming..."

"We have to retreat." the pilot repeated. "I can't cover you from there! Spellcrafter is ordering a full withdrawal. We'll return with reinforcements."

"Like hell. I'll just keep shooting them until they-"

"Ian," Megan said softly from the back. "They will be okay, but we won't be if we stay. We can come back, first thing in the morning."

"...Nighturge breaking off. If you two can hear me, hold tight." Ian said reluctantly, his plane flipping around and darting off, closely pursued by the Empire. They were alone now.

Penny continued flying them as far as she could until they came upon an old shack. It looked like it could have been some sort of unique barn. The horizon was rapidly becoming golden, and so they likely did not have long to create a sanctuary for themselves. Penny dropped him gently on the sand just in front of the barn and fell to her knees. Chris tried to assist her, but she extended her hand, sucked the life out of a nearby desert plant with her magic, and held it to her heart to repair it faster. She then flipped back around and flew toward the wreck of the Spark. He tried calling out to her, but she was already out of earshot or was choosing not to listen.

He stared at the old, dilapidated building and blinked a few times. *This isn't a creepy place to spend the night at all*, he thought sarcastically. He pulled the barn doors back, the black wood chipping and cracking slightly. It seemed like there was water damage or something of that nature. Chris flared his magic in the pitch-black building. His hand gleamed blue, illuminating the barn just enough for him to see his surroundings. This only made him feel more uncomfortable because now the shadows seemed to be following him. He just couldn't win here.

"There's some hay," he said aloud, noting the abandoned haystacks set up in the corner, but dismissed using these as any form of a bed because they looked old and also rotting. Part of him was surprised that it didn't smell horrible in the barn, but he figured that there were enough holes and openings for it to air out. It probably had time as well. The worst smell in here right now could best be described as old water.

From here, he noted an old workstation that housed images of demons and other creatures he had not seen before, as well as data. They were pinned to the old wood. This led him to assume that the person who used to inhabit this place studied them demons and kept them here for some odd reason. Just behind it was a staircase that seemed to lead up to a second floor and a small room used as a bedroom. He took one step on the wooden and failing stairs, witnessed the wood snap, and decided against it. The first floor would just have to do.

"Unfortunately," he heard from outside. It sounded like Penny, so he dropped everything and headed for the door. "There was not much left of the Spark at all." Chris exited the barn to see Penny walking toward the entrance, her wings outstretched proudly and casting a shadow in the sand. "I was able to recover the long-burning flares and solar lanterns we got specifically for Sohrann. They should last the night...maybe even more if need be. I also got the panic box." Penny paused and held out a sparking electric part that looked like a microchip. "I've got Cornellius's personality matrix, but I think it's dead. I brought it so you could look." Penny walked by Chris, passing the chip off to him as she did. She pulled a blanket from the emergency kit and inspected it inside.

"Yeah," Chris said to himself in a half mutter as he inspected the burnt and bent chip. "He's done. We'll just have to use his backup when the Spark gets repaired." He kicked up some sand, unceremoniously placed the chip in the hole he created, and kicked it back. Then he patted it down. A very poor burial, but Cornellius would yell about the grave regardless. At least he wasn't totally dead - and he wouldn't remember blowing up!

Chris reentered the barn to see Penny already hard at work, trying to make a small area for them to rest using what was available. She even managed to retrieve the space heater and activated it next to the cold weather blanket. She set the blanket aside, took her shirt out of the emergency kit, and held it up. Chris figured that she probably put it in there so she could carry everything easier. She started to put it over her head, but she soon realized that she could not put it back on because of her wings. Penny, being stressed and frustrated from everything going on, cut holes in the back of the shirt and put it back on, her wings sliding easily through the holes she created with her sword.

Penny moved past him before he could speak once again, but this time with the emergency lights and flares. She began to place them around the barn's perimeter as well as a little further out to discourage anything from even attempting to come close. She did not activate them because the sun had not set but would soon. Chris tried offering his assistance, but Penny just shook her head hastily and kept working. She must have really not wanted to talk to him for some reason.

"That's good," he said. "Nice job!" There was a weird silence now.

Penny was staring at him with an expression of shock. She just frowned, lowered her face, and continued working. He joined her to help, but the moment he started on one thing, she would begin another. Chris watched her as she moved to the scent of the barn and set up the bright emergency light in the floor's center. She then activated it so that the device would emit a powerful white color. Moving to the very edge of the barn, she sat alone, far away from Chris. He figured she needed some space, so he let her be for now. Instead, he went outside to watch the sunset.

The orange horizon was now becoming black, and not long from now, it would be totally dark again. So dark that it would be impossible to see anywhere past where the lights were. He was about to go inside and tell Penny, but she must have sensed his intentions to tell her about the darkness or noticed the light fading. She activated the flares remotely, and each of them started to give off a bright blue, yellow, or red light.

*Does it really bother you that much, Penny?* He asked her mentally. No reply again. There was no way that she did not hear him. Chris looked back inside the barn and still saw no movement where Penny was. Giving up, he walked forward to where some of the bright lamps she placed were and looked at the now almost pitch-black sky. Debris from the station was raining down in fiery balls toward the planet's surface. There was also a green and blue wave moving across the dark sky, illuminating it slightly. It reminded him of the northern lights from Earth. Chris assumed this could have been caused by the space station explosion, but there was no way to be sure.

He'd almost raised his watch to ask Evangeline, but then he realized that she was no longer able to give her insight. Even if she was, the communications were so weak that it might not reach her without the station. Chris sat on the ground next to the humming device, which was sprouting out light all around itself. The lights were so bright in the sky that it was almost uncanny since he had grown used to the blank Sohrann sky. Now that he had a moment to think about everything that had happened, he found that he could not. Instead, he was worried about Penny, and his brain was almost resting. So much happened and kept happening.

"I know I annoyed the hell out of you by always getting us into trouble," Chris started, staring at the sky with a neutral expression. "But I sure hope you're resting now, Eva. You, of all people, deserve it since you never really seemed to rest when you could. I just wish you let me get a word in so I could apologize to your face before you were gone."

Chris pulled his leg into his chest and laid his head against it. He'd only worked with Evangeline for a while, but ever since Polaris, he knew he could count on her. Emily chose her as their advisor because she was good at her job and could keep them out of trouble, but he never really minded it. It was a little ironic, but Evangeline had always said how advisors usually outlived their squads. "I guess you just didn't want to lose another one." He concluded. "I never did get to find out what happened to your other one." Chris paused, making a face. "I'm talking to myself again. Going crazy already."

Half expecting Penny to be behind him and ready to tease him about his monologuing, Chris turned, but she was still inside. He frowned and turned back to face forward. "I don't care if you're not human," Chris said aloud, gripping his pants leg. "I think Ian tried to hint to me about it, but I never really cared either way. You just seemed like someone I wanted to know."

Chris reminisced on when he had first met Penny. He stopped her in a crowd of who knows how many people to ask for help on his first day. For some reason, back then, he was just drawn to her, and this could have been because of their partner link. Still, something also just told him to approach her. They went from her trying to beat him unconscious for 'breaking into her dorm,' saving an outdoor restaurant from wolves. Then fast forward, they're partners fighting Hunter in a burning clocktower to save Emily and leaping from it to safety. Throughout all of that, he never suspected it whatsoever...or cared to ask more than maybe once.

*We're a team now, so you have someone watching your back.* He heard himself say inside his head. This was not his own voice but a clear memory from back then. Soon, he could hear Penny's response to this statement. Despite two years passing, he could still remember vividly when he had gotten them trapped in that cave.

*Watching my back?* Penny was so amused at his sudden statement that she was supposedly not alone anymore.

*Yeah,* he heard himself say enthusiastically. *You've protected me, and now I'm strong enough to protect you!* The words held some merit now compared to then when anyone could squash him like a bug. He was still here by her side, causing her headaches when he got them into a mess and making her smile. Most of all, though, he was someone she could rely on now that her sister was gone. Chris needed to talk to her about this - now. She was still the same Penny to him no matter what. Whether she was a Sorcerer, Imperial, or what-ever else was irrelevant.

When Chris reentered their temporary living arrangements, he found Penny curled up in the same corner with her legs forced into her chest. She was laying her face against her knees and holding her wrist like she was in deep thought. He figured she had heard the barn door open (anyone would have been able to with how loud it was). Chris stopped halfway to her, staring at the wings moving idly behind her in a back-and-forth motion. They appeared to be bat wings - at least that was what he compared them to in his head.

The smooth wings' interior appeared to be mostly purple, with the interior being more muted than the back. Along the edges and what he could only assume were folds, the color was instead a royal blue. They came out of her back and probably stretched out just farther than her arms. They weren't huge by any means, but they could not be classified as 'small' either - they were relatively thin, looking too. He noted that these wings were more wide than tall too. Just how had Penny hid these for so long? He frowned. And why did she feel the need to? Did the others know?

Chris sat beside Penny and scooted until he was an inch or so away. He reached for her hand but drew back when she suddenly yanked it away and scooted further. Chris was not really sure what he could say or do, but he knew she was listening. "You know," Chris started with a silly face. "I can almost say that you're faster than the Spark." Penny turned her head away to face the dark wall and refused to answer. "You just picked me up and just kind of went 'woosh!' That was pretty cool."

No reply again. He decided to change tactics, "So," he tried in a more direct manner. "How long have you had these?" No reply. "You can tell me. I'm not scared."

"Liar." Penny finally said in a low voice.

"Huh?"

"You heard me." Penny continued to look away, but at least she was talking. "Humans usually don't like other species or races."

"Where on Earth-" Chris started with his mouth wide open. "Penny, come on…"

"Come on, what?" she questioned. "You guys usually aren't used to other forms of humanoids. Not to mention you're from Earth, and I hear there aren't many other species there - if any."

"If I didn't care about you being a Sorcerer, then why would I care about this?" Chris reasoned with a smile. "You told me about some of your past, and I didn't even blink. You're still you."

"Nightflyer," Penny muttered, her wings fluttered a little. This must-have annoyed her because she grabbed hold of both of them and held them tightly.

"You said 'Nightflyer'?" he repeated with nothing but confusion. Penny went quiet again. "Is it like…a human-bat kind of thing?"

"Human-bat…?" Penny scoffed a little as if this was an insult. "It's just…another type of human."

"Okay? And what's different?" He pressed on. "Besides the uh…wings." Penny grabbed hold of both of her ears and pinched them upward. "Better hearing?" she nodded, then pointed to her eyes. He did not say anything, but he assumed that she was implying she could see far better.

"So yeah, now you know," Penny grumbled, her voice very depressed. "I knew they'd come in eventually, but I was really praying that it wouldn't be for a long time like Tori. Hers hadn't come in yet, but here we are."

"They're two of my favorite colors," he said with a bright smile. "And I do like bats."

"What did I just say?" Penny said, lifting her head and glaring a little.

Seeing how she reacted, Chris decided to just roll with it, "I'm just saying that I like your bat wings. They're really cool."

"Huh??" Penny stared at him with an expression of disbelief.

"So why did you never hang upside down-" he continued with a devilish grin. Pushing her buttons somehow worked.

Pow! Penny punched him hard in the arm. "Quit it! I am a Night-flyer. Not a bat!"

"I know," Chris said, rubbing his arm and smiling at her. "And regardless, I still see you the same way."

"Yeah, as your partner," Penny concluded with a dull look. "That will never change even if we wanted to."

"No," Chris took one of her hands and squeezed hard. "I've said it once, I'll say it again: I love you, Penny."

Penny's cheeks turned a bright shade of red, and she seemingly sunk into herself. "You just keep saying that." She said softly. "I feel like you don't get what you're saying sometimes. The first time you said it, we could have died."

"And I'm still saying it now." Chris pointed out. "Even if you aren't sure how to feel, I know how I do. So, I'll be here no matter what."

"I'm sure now," she explained with a half-smile, sitting up against the wall. "-Now that you're still here, I mean. And nothing changed."

Chris raised an eyebrow. Penny brought her legs to the side and leaned toward him with a smile. Being himself, Chris smiled back but had no idea what exactly she was intending to do. Penny sighed, slipped her hand onto his cheek, and leaned forward. He froze up, his brain turning to static. All he could think at that moment was how Penny's lips were against his and how soft and warm they were. He wrapped his arms around her waist, and so she drew closer, pulling herself closer and bringing her arms around his neck. He never really expected to ever...kiss her in the first place. Though she flirted back, he thought that they would always just be friends and partners. But now he was kissing the girl who he'd come to trust more than anyone else.

Penny drew back her hair as she pulled away from his face, her hair tickling him a little. She was staring at him like she was wondering exactly what he was thinking, but they were both blushing. It should have been obvious even without the mindreading. He thought he'd opened his mouth to speak, but his mind was not quite following his body. His brain really just needed a moment to process that and ask himself why it had occurred. She tucked her hair behind her ear and shut her eyes for a moment, taking a really long breath.

"That's my answer." She said decisively when she opened them.

# 21

# FOR THE EMPIRE

The story that Penny was telling at this moment was surreal. He figured that some of the events could have been fabricated, but she explained them so vividly that it was nearly impossible. Part of him wanted to believe - no trick himself that none of it was real, that none of it was true, but the look in Penny's eyes said otherwise. As he looked over his shoulder at the girl who was telling him everything she could, he couldn't help but notice her eyes were locked on a singular spot on the wall and appeared to be very cold. Penny would likely never want to repeat any of it.

"So," Chris started in a hushed voice. "You were there in Japan? All of you?"

"...That's correct," Penny answered with a dead expression. "Myself, Ian, Tori, and even Gatchi were all there. Gatchi, Tori, and I only came sometime after it concluded, but I still did my fair share of damage."

"Surely it was in self-defense, right?" Chris tried.

"...Chris," Penny began, her eyes staring at him straight on. "Most people attacked me out of self-defense. I don't even remember how many we killed that day. Sometimes it was to instill fear and prevent an uprising, and other times it was just someone who thought they were brave. If Tori didn't step in, I'd have killed Megan too."

"Wait, but Ian didn't tell me you were all there," Chris told her. "What exactly did you do?"

Penny dragged her legs closer to herself, "Our job was just to see the damage, direct recovery efforts, and take it for the Empire. Megan tried to attack Tori, and so I almost took off her head. I actually ended up...nearly killing one of her close friends. I only stopped when Tori forced me to."

"You would have killed them?" Chris stopped himself when Penny looked away. "So why do so many people we run into give you ugly looks? You were just doing what the Empire and your dad needed. Even if it was wrong. Even the Wizards aren't always perfect-"

"*It can't be helped.*" Penny reiterated for what felt like the hundredth time. "It's my own fault that they all hate me. I never hesitated. I never questioned it, and I always did what Dad told me to. I killed my own people who looked up to me, the enemies he pointed me at, and I even attacked Tori..."

"You-" Chris started with a wide-eyed look. Penny grimaced. "I just...can't see that."

"I just did what my father said or what would benefit the Empire," Penny explained further. "I didn't care what it was or why I was doing it if it brought him closer to what he wanted and made him proud. When Mom died, Tori said Dad changed, so I decided to take it upon myself to help him achieve what he promised her to do. I promised himself if dad told me to fight - I would fight even if I had nightmares the next few years about it all."

"What's the worst thing you did?" Chris asked with nothing but hesitation.

Penny must have had a flashback or something of that nature because she suddenly tightened her lips, clawed her legs slightly, and shut her eyes, "Japan."

"But you just-"

"Japan," Penny repeated in the exact same tone. "That's all." Chris knew deep down she was lying. "I won't say everything Ian did, but...he wasn't nearly as bad as me. Tori was honestly the one with the moral compass. Mine just spun the way I was told to point it."

"Penny?" Chris tried again while she tried avoiding his gaze. "What happened?"

———

Penny ran along the destroyed streets of the village and fought as she did. She lowered her communicator, informing her sister of her progress as she went. The explosions were much louder now all around her. These terrorists were getting desperate, blowing themselves up just to take out one or two of them. It was pathetic. Her father was unifying the Shadow Realm to free them from their bonds, and here they were harming the Imperial people and his vision. *They would all pay.*

"She's in the trap! Blow it!" she heard to her right somewhere. Penny turned, drawing her gun from her hip, and fired blindly. She hit one person who fell into a bloody mess, but the trap was still sprung. The floor blew out from under her and sent her falling into a hole by the explosions. She was mostly unscathed minus a few open wounds, but it was nothing serious. It never was.

Terrorists advanced on her, firing down into the hole. She deflected their bullets back at them, hurried to both feet, and returned fire with her handgun. The terrorists she killed fell into the hole and built up at her feet. They thought they had gotten the drop on her and had the chance to kill her now, but she was just mad. Kicking off of the narrow walls, Penny leaped out of the hole, cutting down two of the traitors as she did. Then turning, she reflected gunfire and ran for cover.

Penny knew she would need to heal herself before pushing onward to eliminate the rest of the targets, and she would not call Tori for help. She never did it right. She never did what they were explicitly told to. Tori always wanted to spare someone or give them a chance to surrender. She already would have to clean up after her. She'd just do it herself. Reaching out of cover with her hand, Penny sucked the life essence out of the entire crowd of terrorists that were attacking her until they fell to the ground. All that was left of them now were that of mangled and dried up husks. Even the bone had aged, but she felt fine now. It was always such a useful spell. At least they were helpful to her at that moment.

Stepping on the weak bones which cracked underneath her heel, Penny advanced once again. Holstering her pistol and readying her sword, Penny kicked open one of the village homes and entered. No one was here from what she could tell, so she hurried upstairs. If no one was there either, then she'd move to the next one. Movement. *Thump thump thump.* It sounded like running. Penny ran as well and barraged into the room she heard it from. Seven tiny bodies could be seen huddled together under an unmoving larger one.

She hesitated for a moment, studying just what she'd come across. They couldn't have been that old, right? They were clinging to their dead father like he was some sort of shield against her. Penny lowered her sword for a moment and started to reach for her communicator to contact Tori, but then the words rang in her head again. 'Show no mercy. Leave no survivors. Show them the might of the Empire they sought to destroy,' Chaos had said. 'Any surviving cells will be back to haunt us later.' Children grew up to be monsters, too, didn't they? If you killed their parents, they always could come for you later, right?

Penny reached for her gun but was surprised when a shot fired before she had even removed it. Looking down, she saw blood spilling out from her attire. She quickly drew her own firearm and fired multiple times. She did not even see which one injured her. When she was done, none of them were moving. They were clean shots, so it was probably quick. It had to be cleaner than using her sword. *They shot first.* She thought, lifting a shaky hand to her face. *So why do I feel sick?* Pushing the feeling down until it disappeared completely, Penny moved back downstairs and into the next building.

---

"You killed the kids??" Chris blurted out with a look of concern. Penny hid her face in his shoulder and so he immediately brought himself back down to not make her feel worse, "Penny, you wouldn't."

"...We were told to wipe out everyone in the villages that were a part of the terror cells that attacked the Empire," Penny said in a nervous voice. "I just wish I could go back to that time and be the one who shot the bullet myself. They didn't shoot me where it would kill me. Maybe then they'd be alive still."

"Penny-" He murmured. What was he supposed to say to that?

"That's why I hate to ask you to stay with me." She muttered to herself. "You'll be seen as just as bad as me."

"...I always will," Chris said with a face. "I'm always with you."

"Chris, the moment we became partners, you were dragged into this." Penny interrupted. "I need to take the Imperial throne and end the war, no matter what. With Tori gone, it is now my sole responsibility to succeed my father. I have to make it all right because it's really all I can do," Penny said while staring at her hands. "To make the nightmares go away. I have to do this even if it means killing my father, fighting my own people, and dying in the process." Penny looked at him and frowned. "Emily would hide all of that from you, but it's just the truth. I can't do it without you now that I've formed a partner link with you."

"That's a lot to think about..." Chris said with a breath. He envisioned Chaos sending dancing flames toward him to burn him alive. Even Autumn could not take him when they'd first met. What chance would he have? He'd just have to trust her again and hope that they'd make a true plan. "But I'll be here. That's fine."

"Your life will constantly be in danger," Penny told him with a frown. "But I know I can do it with your help. I can't do it without you, so I'm sorry, but I have to ask you to help me.'

"I was already going to help you fight the Empire, Penn," Chris reminded her with a smile, though it was not as bright given what he now knew. "Making you Empress is just a step up."

"I just wish it didn't have to be this way," Penny told him with sad eyes. "I'd have stayed away because I know how dangerous it is. I did not want to drag you into this."

Chris shook his head and placed his hand over hers. Was this really the hand of someone who had done so many terrible things? Even if it were, he couldn't tell. He didn't really care even if he really should. This was the Penny he knew. He'd stay by her side no matter what. *It would just be a little weird to be standing beside a throne, introducing her as the new Empress. How would that even work?*

"That's not how it works," Penny said after reading his mind and laughing a little. She paused as the ground shook a little, and the air broke above the barn. "Do you hear planes?"

"I'm...not sure," Chris stood up and stared at the barn entrance, where sunlight was starting to penetrate through the tiny cracks. "Even if they are, they couldn't possibly be ours, right? We crashed in enemy territory, right?" Penny stood up and hurried to the door like there was no danger at all. "Penny, wait!" Chris urged her as he gave chase.

As he barged out of the barn doors, he shielded his face from the blowing sand and the bright sun. High powered engines whistled loudly and blew hair in his face. The Nighturge slowly lowered itself down onto the sandy floor and shut itself off. A figure vaulted out of the cockpit and landed just in front of Penny in a kneeling position. After a moment or two, Chris noticed that Penny waved her hand at her side - an action which prompted him to stand up and face her directly.

"I told you to stop that," Penny whispered just low enough for Chris to not hear.

"Right. Sorry for being late," Ian started with a grumpy face. "I wanted to come to get you the moment the two of you were shot down, but pretty much everyone said it was too dangerous to be out. Emily was going to come with me, but - a lot has happened since we last spoke."

"You're here, so it's fine," Penny assured him with a headshake. "No need for the formalities we're not in the Empire anymore. Where is our favorite Life Wizard?"

"Meg's back in New Hope. I had to make space to bring you two along back to safety." He said seriously. "I brought the Nighturge because I figured there may be Imperial patrols. I also brought Violet and a few others."

"Violet came willingly?" Chris asked with a weird face. "I want to call you a liar."

"Manipulating her isn't that hard," Ian sighed and folded his arms. "I just had to inflate her ego."

"And how did you find us?" Chris said, moving onto the very next question.

Ian stared at the sky where two other planes were flying circles around them, "Hey, I was basically raised to have a sharp eye even if Meg says I don't." He winked. "You didn't do anything to her while I was gone, did you? I'd have to kill you, you know?"

Penny snickered and looked up at the Nighturge, "Keep talking, and I'll pilot the plane, and you'll be stuck sitting in the back cramped with Chris."

"He'd be riding outside." Ian laughed loudly. "Anyways, I'm glad the both of you are okay. I was ready for anything when I came out here."

Penny snatched Chris's hand and stuck out her tongue toward Ian. She then made her way over to the Nighturge, released it, and climbed up. Chris looked back to see Ian smirking and nodding to himself like he'd had a revelation. He heard him say something along the lines of 'I see!' Before climbing into the cockpit, Ian slapped Chris hard on the back and gave a thumbs up with a bright smile. *Did he piece that together just from handholding? No way,* Chris thought to himself. Ian wasn't that quick, was he?

"So," Ian said as he buckled himself into his seat and sat back. "I see you finally showed him, huh?"

"It wasn't by choice. When the Spark got shot down, I was out for a bit, and there was no time to correct the landing or get the panic gear," Penny said with an embarrassed face. "I just had to grab him and do what I could."

"You passed out?" Ian asked, his head turned ever so slightly to look behind himself at Penny. She was sitting beside Chris in the same seat with the seat harness around both of them. "That's not like you."

"I guess I hit my head too hard," Penny lied, covering up where she'd been shot on her shirt. She must have figured he would freak out. "I really wasn't expecting him to board the plane like that."

"Well, Chris," Ian started in a more serious voice. "What's going through your mind?"

"What do you mean?" Chris asked, shifting a little as he said it. There really was no space for either of them. "Through my mind?"

"About Penny," Ian said as the plane gained altitude. "Still the same girl?"

"Still the same girl," Chris confirmed with a confident smile. Penny took his hand suddenly and laid against his shoulder. "Maybe just a little different."

"I told you," Ian said triumphantly to Penny. He looked relieved. "I don't think I asked. Are you alright, Chris?"

"I'm okay. I learned a lot," he explained while looking back at Ian. It was a little weird to be in a seat facing away from him.

"Like?"

"I told him," Penny said with a profound expression.

Ian immediately knew what she was talking about because his eyes went wide. He then shut them, nodded once, and pressed a button on the console. His image appeared on their side of the canopy. "So now you know more, huh?" Ian said, his eyes much darker than usual. "Doesn't change how you see us, does it?"

"No, I just can't really-" Chris paused, unsure of how to phrase it.

"Believe that we could do such things?" Ian concluded. "Yeah, me neither. But it happened. These are the people you're with. Never forget that and hold us to it."

Chris's jaw dropped just a little as he said this. What exactly did he mean by that? Hold them to what they did? Perhaps he meant that he wanted him to remember in case it became important? Regardless of what he intended with these words, it still made Chris think, mainly because Ian never acted this way. He stared for what felt like an eternity, but before he could say anything further, Ian's image faded from the canopy, and he focused on the sky once again. Their plane got into formation with six others, and for the rest of the flight, there would just be silence.

He never did find out what Ian meant by those words or why he reacted the way he did when Penny told him that Chris knew more about their past. The only thing he knew was that his image of them still had not changed. They were much different now than back then, and so it was irrelevant - at least to him. But one day, Chris hoped that he really could just sit down with all of them and ask why they could not just forgive themselves for what they'd done. In his mind, by being Wizards and doing what they did every day, they had made up for it a thousand times over. So why did they both always seem so sad when the Empire was mentioned?

# 22

# MEMORY GARDEN

The blue Sohrann sky only became more colorful as the sun rose higher, like canvas receiving more brush strokes. Chris couldn't help but admire it as there was not much to do while cramped in a plane. Penny moved closer to him and nudged his arm. She was acting completely different from how she did before like there was a weight lifted from her shoulders. He smiled. It really didn't bother him at all. Not even a little. In the front seat, Ian punched a button to contact Megan.

"How are things where you are?" Ian asked her. Megan's image appeared on both canopies of the plane so Chris and Penny could see too.

"Terrible," Megan said with a look of frustration. The image was bobbing back and forth like she was moving quickly. "While you were gone recovering our missing squadmates, the Empire retook part of Grandham city. On top of that, Emily isn't answering her communicator, so I'm having to give orders to prevent them from advancing on us by myself."

"You moved to Grandham?" Chris asked, sitting forward. "Isn't that north of New Hope?"

"Yeah. It is." Megan said dismissively. She really didn't want to talk about anything that wasn't important at the moment. "So what are you gonna do?"

"What do you mean?" Chris questioned with a face. "I don't even know what's going on, and Em is usually the one making the calls."

"Wait a minute, what do you mean?!" Megan stopped and began yelling into her watch. Chris and Ian winced a little as she went off. "You guys can get your butts over here, and you can come to do your job as the leader of this squad!"

"Yeah, yeah, Meg. Don't freak him out, please," Ian said as he hovered his finger over the button to cut the communications. "We'll be there as soon as possible. See you in a few minutes."

"Huh..?" Megan looked like a tea kettle ready to blow. "Ian!!" Call disconnected.

"Geez," Ian combed his fingers through his hair. "She doesn't have to yell all the time. At least I'm used to it." Ian's image appeared on their canopy. "Looks like rest will have to wait. We need to help her."

"No rest for the wicked," Penny commented.

"Never," Chris added.

"Violet," Ian started as soon as she appeared on his canopy. "We're breaking off to support Megan in Grandham. You go ahead. Thanks for the help again, all of you."

"Be careful!" A voice said. It sounded kind of like Dion. "I guess I ended up paying you back, after all, Chris - I think, was your name. Watch yourself. Grandham is a mess."

"I will," Chris said, a little taken aback by Dion's taking part in this rescue. "And thanks."

"Nothing even happened." Violet groaned impatiently. "You should've come alone. As for you, Dreadful," she said, suddenly referring to Penny. "This is why you shouldn't have had the prototype as your plane."

"Of course," Penny shot back expertly. "I shouldn't have had it because you would've destroyed it sooner all by yourself. Sorry for robbing you of the pleasure, Violet."

"Tch!" Violet cut the communications suddenly and broke formation. Chris could tell she was furious just by how she was flying.

Ian's smile vanished as they changed course and headed toward Grandham city. About thirty minutes into the ride, they were now passing over New Hope. Just North of here was Grandham city, where Megan was currently waiting for them. A convoy of Alliance tanks and transports were also headed in that direction with some Resistance forces to assist. Just how bad was it over there? Did the Empire launch a counterattack so quickly after they'd taken the city? Chris just couldn't believe it.

"Hey, Em," Chris said as her image projected itself from the watch. The "no signal" symbol crossed itself over her face, and the projection fell back into the watch. "That's not like her."

"Not like Meg to call for help either," Ian said to himself, though Chris still heard it. "Going to call her back, hold tight. Nearly there."

Megan's image appeared on the screen as if she were running from something. She took cover and pointed backward as gunfire rang on the other end of the call. "Finally." She said. "Are you almost - "Megan paused, dodged an attack coming for her face, and retaliated. "I don't care if they say they're not affected. Don't let them in under any circumstances."

"What's going on?" Ian asked her urgently. "Where are you?"

"I don't care what they say!" Megan snapped at the top of her lungs. "If they get in, then we'll be overrun. What are you doing?! You'll get us all killed! I don't care if they're not Imper-"

"Meg?" Ian repeated. The call failed and disconnected. "Hold tight, you two."

"You know where she is?" Penny asked, her brow furrowing in frustration.

"No, but once we're on the ground, I'll work on it." As Ian said this, Chris could see a much larger city than New Hope just looming in front of them, shadowed by the horizon. "Honestly, if she's alright, she'll probably find us."

Chris could see Christmas lights - or what he thought were holiday-themed lights. They reminded him a little of the decorations that one would see in a place like New York around the holidays. This wasn't nearly as important as the gunfire that was currently barraging anything flying over the city. Ian was forced to pull the Nighturge back and make a second approach at a different angle. Someone really didn't want any reinforcements to come from the air...

A sharp pain enveloped his head - a pain so bad that he felt he might just blackout. He shook it off, but it was like someone was quite literally clawing his brain to get in. It reminded him of when Eslena used the spell on him at the parking deck, but he did not see her, so it was unlikely. If it was, then both Penny and Ian were here and would be witness to it. Now was not the time to get little headaches or feel dizzy, but it really did feel like a persistent white noise now, almost like whispers.

"I'm going to open the canopy. We're landing in the thick of it." Ian warned them as he pressed two buttons. Both canopies slid open and revealed that they were flying upside down now. Chris wasn't even able to pay attention to that detail. He just had to focus, so he did not land headfirst.

Penny had begun to unlatch his harness before he even had a chance to himself. She then grabbed onto him, removed her own, and flew him straight down to the ground. Ian jumped down on his own and landed with a small crash, cracking the ground as he did. Alliance soldiers littered the street along with the occasional civilian. The damage was everywhere, and not a single inch appeared to be uncovered by a blast mark, a chunk of metal, or a long-dead fighter. The first thing Chris decided was to check the bodies, but they were dead - recently killed. Where were the Imperials that attacked them?

They were currently in what looked like a spaceport or something. Sparking wires and cables lay all around them as well as ruined tents. The tents were probably used by the refugees in the area, and judging by the Alliance flags near them, they were set up by their people and not the Resistance. All he could smell right now was smoke, and the stench was so pungent that it made his senses rather cloudy. Penny pulled him to his feet, clearly believing that checking the bodies was a waste of time right now.

*Surrender yourself to me,* he heard a voice say in his head.

"Did you say something?" Chris asked, turning to look at Penny.

She shook her head. "Listen, you're seriously starting to worry me. What exactly are you hearing?"

"It's like whispers," Chris said, completely uncertain of his own explanation. "I swear Eslena is still trying to talk to me like before."

"Ignore it," Penny demanded with a frown. "If it keeps happening, I'll have to proceed without you. She's trying to manipulate you."

"Hey," Ian said, calling out at the top of his voice. Three Wizards, one Alliance soldier, and one Resistance operative were approaching them. Ian made his way toward them, and then so much happened at once. "What's going on here?" Ian asked them in a commanding voice.

"The Empire rushed our position and has taken back most of the city. We could use your support." One of the soldiers said, his eyes shadowed by the helmet he was wearing.

"Alright. I'll let the others know." Ian said, turning back to head toward Chris and Penny.

As soon as Chris looked back to talk to Penny, gunshots rang, and Ian drew his sword after crying out in pain. He deflected the bullets over and over while back up, clearly confused at why they had turned on him. Chris hurried past him and extended both hands, freezing everyone in front of him in place. It would not last long, but it wasn't lethal...maybe just a little cold.

Penny walked by her partner and placed her hand on one of the frozen individuals. She then shut her eyes and focused for a moment. Ian did the same on another. The two must have come to the same conclusion. "They're not awake," Penny concluded with a frown.

"They're dead?" Chris asked, instantly feeling some guilt.

"No. They're alive but are quite literally asleep." Penny clarified, removing her hand from the block of ice. "Like puppets. I've only seen something like this with the Shadow Plague on my home world, but this is different. They are quite literally dreaming."

"So, sleepwalking?" Chris scratched the back of his head and raised an eyebrow.

"No like involuntary movement not being caused by their brain," Penny said, explaining in a completely different way. "And I think Ian and I are immune, but you aren't. That's why you can hear those whispers."

"We can have this discussion later!" Ian said, pushing the two of them back in the opposite direction.

Chris looked back to see multiple figures all rushing toward them. There was even an Alliance tank that hovered into view and turned the main gun on them. It then fired and missed but still threw debris up into the air, which rained down on them. Penny turned and shielded them with her soul barrier, absorbing most of the incoming fire from both the tank and the infantry. She only lowered her defenses when she saw the chance, and when it came, Penny turned and ran after the other two.

"Em?" Chris tried again. There was still no response. The other two must have been having the exact same problems as them.

"Forget it," Ian said, forcibly pushing Chris's arm down so he would not focus on the watch.

It was indeed a bad time to try to do anything other than run away. There were more of these mind-controlled fighters in this direction too. They were pouring out of what looked like a court-house, which was repurposed as a supply station. The soldiers wasted absolutely no time in opening fire at the three of them. Ian acted quickly, throwing Chris behind himself and shielding him with his armored body. Then he turned and roared at the top of his lungs. Chris had only seen him use his spell a few times, but it was always effective from what he could tell.

The soldiers held their ears and began to back away in terror as if they'd just heard a lion roar or something far too dangerous for them to handle. Some of them turned and ran, others began shaking or cowering in fear, and the rest just stood there stunned. Chris wondered if this could have caused them to return to their senses, but the answer came when they began firing again. Ian, Chris, and Penny cut through a damaged corner store. Breaking one of the windows in the back, they climbed through and headed in a random direction. Anywhere would be better so long as they were not surrounded by their own people.

"This way." Chris decided. He pointed to his right and urged the other two to follow. He just had to trust his instincts like Emily always told him. "We'll loop back around the way we came from a different direction. They should still be searching for us back that way."

"This is insane," Ian said. He looked back at Penny, who shook her head. "I feel like I just went back in time. I don't like it."

"We're not fighting or killing them, so you shouldn't feel that way. We're surviving until we find a solution and allies." Penny responded, completely shutting down this train of thought. "Don't compare it to then."

"Outnumbered, outgunned, and with no reinforcements. Sorry, but it's serious deja vu." Ian shrugged in a very animated way. "Anyways, instead of calling Megan or Emily, I'll send out a distress signal and see who bites."

"Only on Alliance channels, right?" Chris slowed down for the other two and waited for them to catch up, stepping up and over an abandoned car. "Not like to anyone and everyone?"

"Yes, Chris, because I want some random hobo to come running to save us with a shotgun screaming 'this is my moment!'" Ian said in a very sarcastic way. "P-pow. P-pow. P-pow."

"...Just put out the distress signal before I drop you." Chris said with a glare.

"Gosh." Ian shuddered and laughed nervously. He held a button and waited a few moments. A distress signal began to emit from the watch, pinging both Chris and Penny's and probably every other Alliance device within a two-hundred-mile radius. "You're starting to glare just like her too. I'm putting it out now."

"I bet Autumn will be the one to respond. Or Morgan," Penny theorized. "Regardless, we should try to find Megan. We won't last long at all without her."

"Well, yeah," Chris said with a nod. "I was always going to have us find her first, but I'm still...worried about Em too. Maybe we should..."

"We're not splitting up," Penny said, shutting down the argument with a slap on the shoulder. "You've got to stop that."

"Two against one. Sorry, but you've been outvoted." Ian said with a wink. "Now, let's move before I have to fight a hundred of our own people. Sounds fun, but also really stressful, you know?"

Chris gave Ian a quick nod and marched on to take the lead. He summoned one of his swords so it would be ready if danger came, then he spun it around and held it in reverse. It was just more comfortable sometimes. For now, they were completely invisible and had gone unnoticed. The soldiers and Wizards were more distracted by attacking one another than attacking them. It was a multiway battle, and there was not a single Imperial in sight. Were Megan and Emily also under control? Was there a limit to what Eslena could do? Why could she not take his mind over, and why did the other two not have the same question?

"On your right!" Ian warned. Chris spun around and brought his sword to meet a bullet meant for his hip. The attack flew back toward the attacker and embedded itself in him. The soldier fell out of sight. Chris was about to forget about this person, but they got back up and opened fire again from the same building, so instead, he swung his sword hard and sent an Icy arc forward, likely freezing them against some wall inside.

"They really don't care about pain..." he remarked with concern. "What we usually do to make people stay down won't work."

"Okay, so keep immobilizing them or make it so they physically can't fight. If the soldiers have to be treated, that's fine." Penny said like she was still speculating what could work. "They're not in control of their bodies - at least not entirely, so pain is really not something they care about. I wish I knew for sure, but I have seriously never seen anything about this before."

It was rare for him to hear Penny say that she did not know the answers or what to do, but she was still calm. He wished he could be more like her, but Chris knew it was unlikely. Something told him that she wouldn't want that. His thoughts droned on and on while Penny and Ian took the time to bounce ideas off each other.

Two Wizards were approaching them from the piles of rubble just in front of them. The male drew a single sword, and the other began flaring her magic. The two walked in perfect unison and fixated their eyes on Penny. Chris stepped in front of her and raised his sword as the pair stopped just short of them and stared. Then, the male spoke, his voice strained like he had been seriously injured before this.

"The runaway princess. No doubt here to aimlessly fight as if she's accomplishing something." He said in an Imperial voice. It should not have been possible since he was likely not from the Empire. He had short brown hair and brown eyes.

"I'd heard you had been shot down and were dead. Clearly, it didn't take - not that I'm surprised." The female admitted. Her face was twisted with amusement, her green eyes peering out from her blond hair. "I'm oddly pleased that you and your partner are here to witness what I can truly do."

"Eslena...?" Penny asked. Chris looked back to see her taking a cautious step back. "How..."

"I'm afraid that's something you'll never know, but I will say that you'll get to witness plenty of my power before you die." The male said, readying his sword for combat. "A living successor to the throne is actually a thorn in my plans...so if you'd please get on your knees and accept your fate, I can make this painless."

"Try not to hurt them." Chris urged the other two.

"Yes, try not to hurt them." the female said, raising both hands above her head as she did. An arc of electricity flew from her fingertips and began to collide just above her head. She then brought her hands back down toward the three and fired a powerful lightning bolt.

Penny brought her shield just in front of the blast. Then, focusing her energy, she redirected the energy in the form of a shockwave. The two Wizards stumbled but were mostly unphased by the spell. While the woman prepared another spell, the male moved in carefully and swung at Penny. He backed off when Ian attacked from his left, and Chris struck from the front. He did not seem to feel the pain at all - in fact, he only seemed to become more dangerous.

Penny broke his guard, got in close, grabbed him by the head, and kneed him in the chin. She then kicked the man over, held him down with her knee, and smacked him hard in the skull. Then, standing up, she blocked another spell coming from his partner. Chris rushed in, got in as close as possible while blocking her vicious attacks, and rammed her with his shoulder. He tried to freeze her from the legs up, but she screamed out—a terrifying surge of electricity emitted from her in all directions. Chris had just enough time to cast a spell to shield himself with Ice, but it fell apart on contact. He reached out, connected his hand with the hard street, and sprang backward onto his feet. Rotating his sword, he reflected a final lightning bolt directly at the woman and watched as her body recoiled before going limp.

"Is she alive?" Chris asked. He was concerned with his own actions at that moment. He didn't hit anything vital with her spell, did he?

"She's breathing," Penny confirmed, staring at the Wizards with a hand on her hip. "I am concerned that they can get back up, though."

"We have bigger concerns," Ian said with a finger point at a stampede.

Fifteen soldiers were charging forward toward them in perfect unison. Chris readied himself for the oncoming fight, and so did Penny. Ian rotated both of his shoulders and then took a defensive stance. It seemed like they would be overrun any second, but so long as they covered each other, it would be fine. The gunshots soared and were deflected and reflected with ease. Chris began looking for a route he could use to get in close and attack now. They couldn't stay on the defense forever. There would just be more reinforcements if they did.

Megan fell from the sky, her flower dissipating into yellow pollen, which filled the air. She landed, striking downwards with her sword, immediately taking one soldier out of the fight. The rest began coughing uncontrollably and hacking at their lungs. This allowed Megan to start cutting through the crowd with multiple spins, twirls, and swings in all directions. When she was finished, she turned toward the other three and stood with her sword at the ready. The fourteen remaining soldiers slowly sank to the ground and landed together with almost a 'pitter-patter' sound.

"You always ask to be saved but never seem to need saving," Ian howled with a few claps. "What do you need me for?"

"I ask myself that every day," Megan said with thick sarcasm. She lowered her weapon and attached it to her side temporarily.

"So, you're alright?" Chris asked her. "You look like you had no trouble."

"Now I look like I didn't." Megan corrected with a breath of air. "The squad I was with turned on me while we were trying to barricade the doors and keep our attackers out of the post office. I escaped."

"And Emily?" Chris questioned with a worried face. He was afraid of the answer.

"I have no idea. I lost communication with her when this all started," Megan recounted while rubbing her chin. "I did run into an unlikely ally who has been helping me survive."

"An unlikely ally?" Chris echoed with a look of confusion.

"Excuse the interruption," someone else said from behind Megan. His voice was familiar. "I sent the android we found to scout out the last known position of Emily. It's empty. She's alive."

The young man replaced his saber in its hilt. He had short red hair, yellow eyes, and a stressed demeanor. He also wore a white and red tunic, gloves, dark pants, and boots. Chris had the sense to punch him out right here and now. In his mind, he was grabbing this idiot by the collar and impacting his nose over and over. It really was just too bad that Emily forced him to learn to be calm and collected in these situations.

"Hunter. Good to see you again. Still alive, I see." Penny spoke in a prolonged and cold way. "Somehow, I just do not trust you to help us."

"I count four against one." Ian put forth this idea, followed by saying 'eh?' over and over like he was pitching an idea. "No Vedi to back him up."

"I could take all of you myself, but I don't want to." Hunter snapped down on all of their arguments rather quickly. "So if you want to know what is going on here, I suggest you keep your opinions to yourselves."

"He saved my life," Megan said, vouching for Hunter quickly. "So, I'd say hear him out."

"You're double-crossing the Empire now?" Chris scoffed, turning away as he said this. "And we're supposed to buy that."

"That's right. I'm also trying to save your lives; you got a problem with that?" Hunter argued, very calmly. "This is why the Alliance can't achieve anything. You are so quick to be distracted. You don't even realize what is going on right now and the first thing you think to do after seeing my message, found out I saved your squadmate, and came to warn you is debate attacking me."

"You'll have to forgive us if we don't trust you." Ian put in, wearily looking around in case of further attack.

"I don't care. Listen, this attack is a diversion to distract your leaders from the Imperial mining taking place on the other side of the planet. They don't care about the city or maintaining control," Hunter began to pace back and forth while almost thinking to himself. "They're extracting a resource called Lindinium, which would help them win the war or at least stand a chance." He turned his attention to Penny, who lowered her head as if disgusted by his very existence. "You cannot tell me you didn't see anything wrong with how few Imperials are here or how they're so quick to kill themselves rather than be captured."

"...I did, in fact, notice, but they also had reinforcements briefly." Penny conceded.

"Chaos had to lend them a hand so they wouldn't be crushed here while they performed this task. If this operation of theirs fails, the Empire falls for good." Hunter explained, stopping in his tracks. "It's why I'm here. I was tasked with finding out what they were doing - and I did, but I also found out that their mining has seriously destabilized this planet."

Megan interrupted the conversation suddenly when gunshots were heard near them, "Perhaps we should table this discussion until we return to somewhere safe. I recommend the post office. We can secure it and hold out for now."

# 23

# DESTRUCTIVE TRIGGER

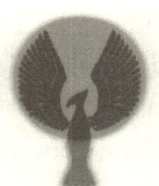

C hris pushed the heavy desk in front of the front doors of the post office building and sighed. This was the fifth one he'd found and forced against the other ones. The facility would definitely be secure. He looked to the vaulted ceiling above his head with windows that were wide enough to illuminate the building on their own and began to revise this opinion. If the mind-controlled Alliance forces had decided to do a little climbing, they could just fall through it. Perhaps they would not be smart enough to try.

Chris laid himself back against the desks and sighed. He went from flirting with Penny and... kissing her, to barricading a post office and hoping for the best. It sure would have been nice to at least have a little time to digest that occurrence. He looked over the empty building's color scheme of green, tan, and white. There were other doors, but the others would be barricading those exits. The rest went into mail and package rooms. Raising his watch, he decided to call Emily just once and received nothing yet again.

"That's not like you at all." He grumbled, his mind filling with nothing but concern.

A pit in his stomach was forming now. If this were the other way around, she'd be tearing this city apart to find him, but no one would let him leave. What was there to even talk about? Emily needed them, and they were lollygagging talking about a situation that would not change without action. The sooner he could get out of here, the better he would feel.

"Stop staring into space," Hunter demanded from across the room near one of the many benches. "We need to talk."

"Didn't I tell Megan to tie you up?" Chris asked impatiently. "Do I have to do it myself?"

"She knows I won't do anything - she's also much more mature. Now come on. You need to hear what I say."

Hunter turned without waiting and walked over to an area where multiple couches were placed together in the lobby. Then he sat down beside Ian, who scooted over a little in response. Penny stared at him with laser beam eyes like she was looking for any behavior changes or shifts in his movements. Megan was the only relaxed one and sat by herself; she tapped her foot and leaned forward while staring at her green boots. She had clearly been doing it for a while because the floor under her was scuffed heavily with black streaks.

"I wish your sister was here so I could warn her directly, but you'll have to do, I guess," Hunter said, his eyes cutting quickly toward Chris, who bit his tongue to keep from speaking. Penny must have sensed his irritation because she stood up, pulled him over to her seat, and sat down with him. She also took his hand and clung to it tightly. "The Empire is mining like I said. They've been at it for a while now ever since they found out about the rare and hard to obtain resource known as Lindinium."

"What exactly is this Lindinium?" Penny asked. She was biting the bait now too. Chris couldn't believe how quickly everyone trusted this traitor.

"It is a compound which can be used for many things from armoring vehicles and ships, to even being used as a near-infinite energy supply if controlled just right." Hunter sat back and stared at the grand ceiling blankly. "The compound is found deep underground near the core, but also helps maintain Sohrann's planetary makeup. I am not too sure how they found out about it, but I can only assume they did some research on the planet and put someone on the planet to find out more."

"Well, why not just mine one of their own planets?" Chris asked as he folded his arms tight to his chest. "What's the point in doing this to Sohrann? They're risking a lot, and this planet had nothing to do with the war anyways."

"Well," Hunter gave this some thought and then spoke up. "One, it can make the planet unstable. Two, Sohrann is the only known planet to have this compound. It is sparse but powerful. The Sohrann researchers probably never touched it because they figured it could cause planetary unrest."

"Well, yeah, I wouldn't want to touch anything that might destroy the planet I'm standing on." Ian proclaimed. "Doesn't seem smart."

"Well, it's not the Empire's planet. It is neutral to both sides, pretty much. Chaos doesn't know about the planet possibly falling apart; Eslena hid that from him," Hunter explained. He had clearly done all his homework. "Eslena knows and doesn't care about the consequences for the planet no matter how much Vedi protests."

"Wait, wait." Chris laughed a little at this absurd statement. "Vedi protested that?"

"Yeah," Hunter said without a second thought. "He did. Most of their forces don't know about it either."

"Vedi isn't heartless," Penny added, laying back onto the sofa as she said this. She actually sounded a little upset. "I've known him since I was little. He's just going...insane - from the Shadow Plague." Chris tried to say something to her about this, but the conversation went on before he could.

"Eslena is going to get a hold of every last bit of Lindinium and then leave." Hunter took a breath. "The planet might just be doomed, honestly. I've seen the readings myself, and I don't think the planet should be shifting this much. The core can't keep up with their mining. A little bit of mining might be fine, but they're extracting so much at once."

"So, we're standing on a ticking time bomb?" Megan concluded instantly, her boot stopping in place.

"I'm not one-hundred percent sure, but I'd assume so."

"And do tell, who exactly sent you to spy on them and why?" Chris inquired, standing up as he did. He began to walk over to Hunter. "You can't tell me you did this out of the kindness of your heart."

"I won't tell you who sent me," Hunter raised a hand to emphasize his words. "But my mission was to uncover more about their objective here and attempt to eliminate both Eslena and Vedi."

"You were here to assassinate them...?" Penny asked in disbelief. Her expression was painted with nothing but shock. "But that's-"

"I had a plan, but I blew it by coming to warn you all." He lowered his face and spoke further. "What's done is done, and you've been warned. I might still try to assassinate them, but I'm not really in a position to do so anymore, so instead, I'll probably leave."

"Run, you mean," Chris responded.

"I missed my opportunity, and you've been warned. Just give Emily my regards when I leave." Hunter stood up like he was about to make his exit. Chris knew he should apprehend him, but would anyone even help?

"And Morgan?" Penny inquired.

"What about her?" Hunter asked as he turned his head toward her.

"She's on the planet too; I'm sure you sensed it. Your other partner is too." Penny went on with a face. "Screw them, huh?"

"Can't be helped, but do the same for her too," Hunter answered back. "Me sticking around would be pointless now and just put them at risk. Just keep an eye on them or tell them to leave."

"As if you actually care about them," Chris said, challenging this argument in its entirety. "You risked killing them both on Terminus. Emily too."

Hunter had suffered enough of him. This back and forth finally came to a head when Hunter sprang from his seat, grabbed Chris by his shirt collar, and dragged him forward. Penny's sword appeared in her hand, almost in the exact same moment. Chris could see her preparing to attack. "When did you get the right to go telling me how I feel, you little twerp? I don't like your attitude pretending you're on the same level as Emily. I'm sick of your mouth."

"Hunter-" Penny started. She drew her sword back in preparation to attack.

*Don't,* Chris told her mentally. He could handle him by himself. He couldn't just keep relying on her to bail him out of his messes.

"You say you care so much, but Emily might be in trouble, and you'd rather tuck your tail between your legs and run off like a pathetic high and mighty coward." Chris grabbed onto Hunter's wrist and squeezed until his grip loosened on his shirt. "So, whoever you're working for is more important than my sister, the planet, and your own partners. You're a hypocrite."

"I really don't need a little kid telling me what to do." Hunter spat with a hateful glare. "Emily can take care of herself. Morgan and Jerard can manage, and you now know about the planet. If you screw that up, then that's on you."

"No wonder Emily left you," Chris said with a cocky smile. "You are so self-absorbed and don't give a damn about anyone else!"

There was a sound that was reminiscent of someone punching flesh that resonated through the post office. Hunter retracted his fist and stared down at Chris on the floor. He brought his foot back to give him a kick while he was down, but Ian caught it and threw it back to the floor. Chris wiped the blood from his chin, noted that it continued to flow, and then pulled himself to his feet using the chair. He then held himself up with it and stared back at Hunter, who was just about ready to openly fight him.

"Alright, Hunter, that's enough." Ian cautioned, placing himself between the two. Ian had summoned his sword and held it to his neck.

"Well," Chris sneered, laughing a little as he did. "It's a good thing I'm going to help the people of this planet and protect my sister. We don't need you. Thanks for the warning but you're just as crazy as them."

"You love to talk like you know it all, but you know *nothing!*" Hunter flared his magic like he might burn Ian to a crisp to get to Chris. This time it was Megan's turn to act. Just as the firebolt soared toward Ian's face, a gust of wind extinguished it. The smell of smoke still filled the air in the aftermath.

"I'm gone," Hunter said in a low hiss. He kicked over one of the chairs on his way to the door, effortlessly cleared the debris they put up to block the door and left. The door slammed hard behind him and left the four alone again.

Ian scratched the back of his head and nodded approvingly at this outcome. Megan forced Chris to sit and began casting a healing spell for his injuries. They were minor, but she still insisted on treating them and made sure he was back to one hundred percent. Chris winced a little when Megan flicked the side of his face and sighed. She then stood up, informed Penny that he would be fine, and then sat across from them with her hands in her lap.

"I'm telling Emily about that!" Ian said triumphantly as if he just watched a boy transform into a man. "I can't say I've seen you snap like that."

"Unfortunately, you two started butting heads after he proved to be an asset, but I don't blame you for your actions." Megan relented, finally. She still looked somewhat disappointed with him. "I'm sorry if that was difficult for you two."

"I had no problem with it, but when he put his hands-on Chris, I was ready to knock his daylights out." Penny recounted. "You need to stop getting beat up. Next time, I'll help even if you say I shouldn't."

"I'm not scared of him anymore," Chris said, giving Megan a thankful nod before standing back up.

"So, boss man..." Ian made his way over to the door and started to barricade it back to the way it was. "What's our next move?"

"With Emily missing, all we can do is try to contact Autumn." Chris directed them. "If Hunter is telling the truth, then we need to report this."

"And Emily?" Penny asked with a frown. Was she making that face because she was worried about him or his sister? "What about her?"

"We stay until we have her location, get her, and leave. We can't fight this many attackers -" Chris paused and then finished this thought. "And if this is a distraction, it would be best to let Autumn handle it while we look for the dig site. Maybe if we shut down the mining, the planet will be fine."

"I saw something while I was out with Morgan a few nights ago. The ground opened up, and it seemed bottomless." Penny tensed up a little. "We didn't really know what to make of it at the time, but it makes perfect sense to me. That ravine was huge."

"So the situation has changed again." Megan removed the witch hat on her head and shook her head, her hair swaying a little. "Nothing is ever simple."

"What about the Wizards and soldiers under control here? We aren't leaving them, are we?" Ian sat back against the sofa and looked at Chris.

"That's why I want to tell Autumn. If anyone can help, it'd probably be her." Chris sat down, interfacing with his watch to get in contact with Autumn. The signal was very weak, and so the only ones he could contact were basically the three sitting in front of him. With the station gone, their ability to communicate diminished. Whenever the General's flagship returned, they'd probably be just fine. "I can't get a hold of her. If only we were back on Terminus, I'd just have her pop up like she did there."

"I can fly over the city and try to spot her," Penny suggested wisely. "And I can avoid fighting if I'm quick."

"Have you been flying long enough to not get hurt?" Chris asked.

"I practiced with Megan and Morgan when they first came in," Penny said without thinking. "I mean - I'm...I'd be fine."

"You guys went through that much trouble to hide it from me?" Chris asked. "I don't understand."

"I'm just going to go on ahead," Penny said, ejecting herself from the conversation. She opened up one of the window panels on the roof and flew off at great speeds. Chris couldn't help but stare with his mouth half-open.

"It wasn't our decision, you know." Megan said, referring to Penny's wings. She stood up and began looking around the post office for something. "She insisted that we keep it from you until she was ready to tell you."

"Well, that time never came," Chris explained while going through his watch. "She kind of got forced into it, but it really didn't bother me. I mean..." Chris lowered his arm and stared blankly at the floor. "I was surprised and maybe a little startled at first, but she's still the same person."

"Must be nice," Megan commented as she ducked into one of the many doors. "But the way you talk about her, something tells me a lot more is going on."

"Does it?" Chris asked sarcastically. He had no right to give her an answer. He and Penny could discuss if that information should be shared later. All he could do now was hide his embarrassment.

"So, Meg, are you okay?" Ian asked, standing up to follow her. This left Chris by himself, which felt weird since it was rare.

"Yes, I'm fine. You don't need to keep worrying about me," Megan answered back from wherever they had gone.

Chris wasn't really listening anymore. His concentration was solely on the partner link he had with Penny. If something happened or she found Emily, she would most likely tell him this way since the signals were so strange at the moment. There was no time to get distracted. He sat back against the comfy chair, shut his eyes, and focused on nothing as best as he could. Strangely enough, he could almost feel the wind and the feeling of flight yet again by doing this. She was still in the air above the city but was quite far by now. She was fine for the moment.

*No sign of your sister,* Penny began mentally. The feeling he had a moment ago stopped, so she most likely landed. *I do see signs of a struggle headed into Augustine University. She had to have gone this way.*

*How can you be sure?* He asked her.

*Call it a hunch.* Penny answered back. *I think she's in the theater hall, so I'll circle back and meet you guys. The university isn't far. If Megan flies you two, we will be able to get there without conflict.*

# REALIZE

**M**egan's hovering flower descended onto the college campus Penny had discovered near the heart of the city. It vanished just under them and turned into pollen, disbursing into the air once more. Penny landed down not too far from them near a white gazebo surrounded by red desert flowers similar to poppies. There was quite a lot of plant life here on this campus lawn for a desert planet. Chris thought it must have taken a lot of upkeep, and even now, it still looked quite beautiful. It was just strange because he never actually had the chance to go to college.

Penny pointed just left of the lawn to a weirdly shaped building simply labeled 'Arts and sciences - Lanklen hall.' Penny led the way, her wings remaining idle on her back. The four entered the building and noted the various Wizard, Sorcerer, and soldier bodies littering the floor. According to Megan, every single one of them was alive. She only used a healing spell on the Wizards and Alliance soldiers but wholly ignored the Sorcerers. When Chris asked her to treat them anyway, she would ask him why. Penny did not try to force her, and Ian did not say a single word. Surely, they would not just leave them with broken bodies.

"I told you," Megan said, stepping over a Sorcerer to get to another Wizard as she spoke. "That goes against everything that I believe. Please do not ask that of me, Chris."

"I guess." Was Chris's response. Megan didn't really care about his disapproval. "Where do you think Emily could have gone?"

"We can rule out the classrooms." Ian deduced as he made his way down the hall, taking the lead from Penny. "So most likely, the stage room."

"You mean the theater?" Megan inquired. "I'm surprised she would retreat to there."

"I hear trouble," Penny announced. She broke into a run before anyone could say a word and left the others to chase blindly after her.

Chris could now hear it too. It sounded like a massive fight was happening in the auditorium. When they opened the doors, they could see Emily surrounded by multiple Wizards and Sorcerers. The soldiers she was dealing with were already on the ground. Emily changed her attention at great speeds from combatant to combatant, dodging swords, projectiles, and spells, and even deflecting with expert accuracy. Chris was astounded when she cartwheeled into a Sorcerer going for a high attack, stepped on his sword, and then kicked him in the throat with her heel. She turned to have her halberd grappled by two Wizards. One of them finally managed to wrench it from her grasp.

"I have her weapon. Rush her. She's defenseless!" He announced, backing away from her with it.

The others moved in for the kill but would ultimately fail. Emily dodged under multiple attacks and blocked the other with her magic. She then raised her fists and began fighting back. Emily was arguably more dangerous like this: punch, punch, dodge, duck, punch, round-house kick. Even without a weapon, Emily was just as dangerous. She caught one of her attackers' swords by the blade, jump over his head, and kicked him in the tailbone. Then after dodging another strike, she threw him into the crowd.

"What's the matter, Spellcrafter? You're looking tired!" one of them taunted as he went in to fight her. "You're not quite as quick anymore."

"Well, I'm trying not to hurt you," Emily grumbled, dropping to the stage to avoid his dagger. She then swung her legs around, knocked him to the ground, and threw herself back to her feet with him under her heel. This was the last one. She flipped over the final attacker's fire spell, landed on his shoulders and punched him. Emily finished by throwing her weight forward and sending him flying forward with her legs. Her weapon reappeared in her hand like a baseball bat and drew back as she swung a homerun! He didn't even have a chance to hit the ground before that attack landed.

"I bet that one regretted taking your weapon there," Chris said jokingly from the door. "He just made you mad, huh?"

"Chris." Emily wiped the blood from her lip and tossed her weapon aside, kicking a Sorcerer who was about to get up as she did. She jumped from the stage effortlessly and began to walk toward him. He did the same, and as soon as he was within reach, she pulled him in for a hug and would not let go. "I heard that you and Penny got shot down. Are you okay?"

"Yeah, yeah." Chris smiled a little at her concern. "I'm fine. I heard you needed rescuing."

"I don't know where you heard that," Emily responded with nothing but sarcasm. "Penny."

"Yes?" Penny asked. Her wings folded back behind her back like she was trying to hide them. "Look, I'm sorry. I've been keeping him safe..."

"Come here," Emily demanded. Penny inched forward nervously and stood in front of her. Emily pushed Chris to her left arm and then grabbed Penny with her right. Penny jumped a little but eventually shut her eyes and relaxed. "I was worried about you too. I'm glad you are both alright."

"Oh, I'm great too, thanks, Em!" Ian said from behind them both. "I'm so glad, Ian. You're so strong and smart and handsome."

"You didn't get shot down." Emily pointed her finger at Ian and gave him a playful glare. "My two babies here did."

"Babies?" Penny repeated awkwardly. Emily released her and smiled. "Uh- listen, Emily about..."

"I knew about your wings already." Emily grinned heavily. "Tori would have had them too, remember? And yes, I approve."

"Em!"

"Approve of what?" Penny asked. She was completely obvious, and it showed on her face.

Emily pulled Penny in for what seemed like another hug and whispered in her ear, "You told him about all of it, didn't you?" Penny gave her a single slow nod. "And he doesn't care, so like I said, I approve. Just don't break his heart, alright?"

"Em?" Chris repeated, unsure if she had heard him.

Emily released Penny and finally answered back, "Oh, just asking her if you two did anything you shouldn't have. It sounds like you kept it clean."

"...Quit it," Chris said, hoping to sound intimidating.

"'Quit it.'" Megan repeated behind him in an exaggerated and squeaky voice. She tipped her hat a little at Chris. "You sound like that sometimes when you get embarrassed. Like a parrot."

"Youch." Ian turned and walked backward comically. "Dang."

"Now then, little bro." Emily placed a hand on his shoulder and smiled softly. "Status report."

"Well, the General's ship still isn't back; we've been focused on finding you, we can't reach anyone outside of a small range with the watches..." Chris debated if he should tell her the next bit, but it needed to be said. "And Hunter came to warn us about...the planet possibly falling apart because of Imperial mining."

"Hunter...?" Emily repeated, a soft gasp escaping her. She regained her composure and reset. "What...did he say?"

"Supposedly, Imperial mining has destabilized the planet's core. Hunter thinks the planet may be in danger." Chris continued, observing her reactions carefully. "I'm not sure if we should trust him, but I don't think he's lying."

"And where is he now?"

"He left before I could arrest him," Chris explained with his hands together behind his back. "I would have had nowhere to put him. I have no idea where he is now."

"I..see. I think he's still trying to help us." Emily nodded with a smile. "It makes sense, but we should still be cautious."

"No. It doesn't." Chris muttered under his breath. Hearing Emily say it bothered him more than he could have predicted. "Anyways, he was supposedly here to assassinate Vedi and Eslena, but he gave up and left. He would rather warn us in what is probably a trap."

"Okay, good..." Emily's body language showed that she was relaxing now. "Well, when we get out of here, we'll look into the excavation. I'm sure that if we hurry, we can reverse the effects."

"I'm going to see if Autumn can deal with the situation here in Grandham," Chris told her. "Hunter said they're just trying to keep us distracted here."

"I may tackle this situation with her so we can just be done in this city..." Emily looked over the unconscious combatants and sighed. "I've never seen this spell before."

"I was not aware that Eslena could do this," Penny added to her right. "Especially considering the number of people under her influence. She's been trying to get into Chris's mind too."

"He told you?" Emily asked.

"I heard it." Penny clarified. She turned to look at Chris. "As long as I'm around him, I think I can cancel it out. The three of us are probably immune, and if Megan can't see or hear these things either-"

"I can, but I can clearly see that they aren't real," Megan said, jumping into the conversation. "After that one time in New Hope, I started ignoring them."

"Okay, so Chris is the only vulnerable person here, really." Penny took his hand and squeezed. "So at least until we find out how she does this, I'll need to stay with him. That's obviously not a problem."

Emily suddenly resummoned her sword and turned. One of the Sorcerers was sitting up once again but was clearly in no condition to fight. Instead, he slumped against the wall beside the stage and laid his head against the cold brick. Smiling, he began to talk in a voice that was not his own. "I am very disappointed. Hunter has forced me to speed up my timetable, but luckily, you'll all bear witness to a world's end if you survive long enough."

"You always were quite cocky." Penny mused, taking a few steps toward the wounded Sorcerer. "I don't know why father tolerated you so long."

"He found me useful, far more so than a princess who could only do the work of a dog and had an inability to think for herself," Eslena replied through the man, a smile creeping eerily across his face. "And you-" his head turned toward Ian. "You were once a knight of the Empire well regarded for doing everything it took no matter the cost."

"We can't all be like you," Ian grumbled as he turned to head for the door. He extended his hand to reach for the knob but stopped just short of it.

"You followed orders but also knew to think for yourself." Eslena sounded like she was complimenting him, but there was a hint of manipulation. "Vedi may have trained you, but you became your own person seeking a way to climb to the top. Why, you did some spectacular things in the name of making a name for yourself and being like Chaos."

"Yeah? Well, I did make a name for myself by choosing to leave." Ian shot back in a low growl. "I don't expect you to understand."

"Yes, everything changed for you after Japan, didn't it? Your whole view of the Empire turned to dust." Eslena asked. For once, she did not act like she had the answers. "What happened there, I wonder? Was it just too much or was it Victoria Dreadful?"

Ian stared blankly at the auditorium door like time had stopped. The exit sign above the door flickered and buzzed for a moment before finally going dead. Chris looked to Megan; whose face was hidden by the hat she usually wore. A straight line appeared to have been drawn across her mouth, which was the only thing he could see. Eslena cackled a little, though she could not much because the dark magic user began coughing up blood from Emily's assault.

"Japan...?" Megan stammered over her words, her back to Ian, and his back to her.

"You were there too? Interesting. Very interesting." Eslena released her control over the poor soul who fell to the ground, possibly dead from the extra strain she forced on him.

"Japan?" Megan repeated, her head turning to look over her own shoulder. "She means a few days after that, right? Or maybe just after when Penny and Tori came? Not the actual attack?" Megan started racking her brain trying to rationalize this new information. She yanked her hat down to the sides of her face and took a deep breath.

"Meg-" Chris tried to say more, but Penny stopped him. If he got involved, he just might get hurt.

"Why won't you look at me?" Megan pressed on, more and more pain and anger filling her voice. "Are you just not able to face me about it? Is she talking about the same thing!? It only sounds like the same event, right?"

Ian did not say anything, so Megan continued. "Why aren't you saying anything??"

"I can't answer that," Ian answered darkly without turning to face her.

"Then when you told me you were Imperial; did you purposefully hide that from me?!" Megan demanded, her teeth showing and clearly grinding together.

"I can't answer that..." Ian repeated much more quietly.

"Why..." Megan turned around and took a single step towards him at the door. "Why do you act as if you're in pain? Why do you act like it hurts so much?!" She finally cried out in a scream. "What gives you the right to act as if your heart is so heavy from guilt?"

"I can't answer that..." Ian answered so low that he could not be heard.

"Then why are you talking to me right now?!" Megan began yelling now as tears started streaming down her face. "Are you just incapable of saying anything else?! Why did you save me on Shade-hedge if you knew what would happen if I found out it was you??"

"I don't know," Ian answered back quickly.

"Guys-" Chris tried again in a rather small voice. "We shouldn't do this right now..."

"Are you saying you chose not to say anything? You let me become partners with you and get close to you, and now you're acting like you didn't see this day coming?" Megan began advancing on him, her boots stomping and echoing along the walls. "You just thought I'd never find out? Why?!" Megan asked in a booming voice, which reflected the pain she was feeling.

"Because when we became partners, even though I tried to keep myself reserved, I got closer to you." Ian finally answered, turning around to reveal his own tears and an angry face. "What exactly am I supposed to say? I didn't ask to be partners with you. It just happened! Then the closer I got to you, the more I realized that if I told you, then everything that happened up to that moment-"

"-I don't care!" Megan screeched, balling her hand so tightly together that she cut herself with her nails. "Everything I've done, everything I've seen, everything I've said and experienced was all so I could get revenge for my home." Megan pointed an angry finger at Ian and continued screaming. "All of it was so that one day when I found the people responsible, I could make them pay. I don't care what history we have together. All of it became irrelevant when I found out that you were the one who helped take it all away. You hunted me endlessly, helped kill my friends and family, and you think I can just act like it's all alright. I-I should kill you...You're just a Sorcerer." Megan grabbed onto her own hair and sank to the ground slowly until she was on her knees. "A Sorcerer! A Sorcerer! A murderer!"

"I..." Ian sputtered as she went on. He opened his mouth to say something, but she did not let him speak even once.

"As if you could have ever had a future fighting by my side, being my friend, or even breathing the same air as me after what you've done!" Megan finished through her sobbing. Ian, still in pain, decided to try to approach her. "Don't touch me. Don't come near me. I hate you!" Megan extended both hands out in front of her and created a powerful burst of wind to send Ian flying back. He resisted for a moment but still got sent out of the room and crashed into something loud. "I don't even know you...you bastard."

"Try to calm down," Emily said behind Megan. "Doing this solves nothing right now; wait until later. It's not safe here."

"Shut up!" She snapped suddenly as a Life spell soared toward them. Emily caught it and tossed it aside to protect Chris and Penny. "All of you knew too and hid it from me. You knew how I felt, and you still made me work with him!" Megan exploded, her eyes cutting back toward them to show rage and nothing but hurt.

"How could anyone tell you? It was his place to..." Chris began nervously.

"And you." Megan went on, gripping onto her chest. "I thought I could trust you the most because you were from Earth and you would understand. No, in fact, you *understood* what it was like to be alone and to have everything and everyone taken from you, but you still conspired with him. I thought, if anyone, I could always trust you to be direct with me." She gritted her teeth. "At least Penny didn't try to hide who she was, but he hid the truth that I would find out sometime somehow and you all helped him. I want nothing to do with you – any of you!"

"He didn't want to hurt you." Chris reasoned quickly. Penny stepped closer to him like she was ready for anything – even further attacks. "None of us did."

"I won't kill him." Megan's eyebrows furrowed in frustration as she looked to the floor. "But I'll have nothing to do with him or you. Good luck."

"Meg, wait a minute." Chris tried to be the voice of reason. "He's your partner."

"Why should I want anything to do with him?" Megan asked him with a cold glare, her tears still flowing down her face.

Megan forced herself to stand and made her way out of the auditorium. Chris hurried after her and grabbed onto her wrist tightly. He had just enough time to register Megan's sword, being drawn and swinging toward him. Penny's arm wrapped itself around him and blocked the hit. She then forcibly pulled him back while whispering in his ear, "Nothing you say to her now will matter or have an effect right now. Let her go." Chris was forced to watch Megan storm off down the hall.

"Ian!" Emily called out, heading in the direction he was thrown. "Ian, let me know if you can hear me, okay? I'll treat your injuries just don't move."

"Let her cool off," Penny said urgently. She only decided to release him when Chris's struggling, and tugging stopped. If she let him go, he would take off after her. "She needs time. Right now, I want to check on Ian."

"...Alright." Chris agreed reluctantly.

Emily was kneeling beside Ian, who had crashed into a trophy case and healing him. Her magic's shade of green was drastically different from Megan's but clearly worked the same. His glass cut wounds repaired themselves rather quickly, but Ian still said nothing. What did Chris expect him to say? His partner just said that she hated him, and his past just came back and clubbed him in the back of the head. No one even knew if Megan would come back or where she would go. The planet could be falling apart soon, and the city they were currently in was basically mind control central. Would she really be alright alone in her current mental state?

"Location readings reestablished with Spellcrafter's squadron leader. Trying to reach out to them now." A female officer said through Chris's watch. An image appeared on the watch. It only read 'audio-only.' The voice spoke further, "Oh my goodness, I'm getting so much data now that we are back in the system."

"Status update. Any response from teams on the ground?" The general's commanding and robust voice asked.

"Not yet. The signal is still a little fuzzy - oh?! The Spark was shot down while we were away, and Grandham city is once again contested."

"Focus." The general demanded quickly. "I want communications fully reestablished. They can hear us, but I need to hear them."

"General? General Nick?" Chris tried. They continued to talk over him. No use.

"Our flagship is back again." Emily guessed. She had finished tending to Ian and had come over to see. "Give them a bit. If the Tenacity can get communications back online, we may just be able to hold out until help comes."

"I can't hear them, but I have vital data online for all squad mates. Megan is rather far from the squad at the moment, but still in Grandham while Christopher, Pennelopie, and Ian are together near the college campus." The woman continued. "At this rate, we won't be able to find out what has happened, let alone get anyone down there to help. Its chaos down there."

"Forget the encryptions we had before the Tenacity left the system." The general ordered smartly. "Change the encryption and treat the ship as the new communication hub. Once that's done, we'll coordinate with the Sohrann forces and have full planetary and orbital coverage. For now, one city will have to do."

"Uh - yes, sir!" the woman responded. The call dropped five seconds later with the message 'hub terminated.'

"What about Megan?" Ian asked from behind them. Both Chris and Emily turned to see him sitting there with Penny standing beside him. "We're just leaving her?"

"We have no idea how far she has gotten, and it really isn't safe here. I'm going to inform Autumn and have her find Megan." Emily promised confidently. She extended a hand for him to stand. "Leave that to me."

"And then what?" He asked slowly. "This won't end well, Emily..."

"Leave that to me too," She said, grabbing his hand tightly in her own. She yanked him to his feet and nodded once.

## PARTY OF THREE

The city of New Hope was a refreshing sight after the madness
in Grandham and the ambush in space. It was as calm as ever -
if not more so. As they rode along the damaged road, Chris couldn't
help but notice the number of citizens who had come out of hiding or
wherever they had gone and taken shelter with the Alliance-Resis-
tance forces. It was comforting to know that their efforts were not
pointless here, but what would become of these people if what
Hunter said were to be true?

"Will we be alright without her...?" Chris asked absentmindedly.
The other two riding with him tensed up greatly - especially Ian.
Emily, who was sitting in the front seat, looked into the rearview
mirror and made a worried face. No one really seemed to want to talk
about it but him. Instead, he decided to defer his concern and focus
on the ride back. They had passed the checkpoint that they had
captured now, and after concluding a brief search of the vehicle, were
allowed to move on.

"Nearly there." The Alliance soldier in the driver's seat said.
"Once we drop the kids off, how would you like to handle this?" He
asked, his eyes glancing at Emily through his short light brown hair.

"We go back and assist the others," Emily said. She folded her arms and crossed one leg over the other. "We can discuss it when they're out of the car." Emily must have caught Chris making a face at her in the mirror because she made a face, muttered 'for your own good' or something close to it, and then returned her attention to the road.

"So now you make us 'guard' the safest city on the map?" Chris asked Emily as kindly as he could. "For our own safety, right?"

"You don't have Megan to heal you, and that also means that you're a man down," Emily explained sternly. "You are far safer here until you have a full squad. Besides, Eslena-"

"So then, it has nothing to do with your brother being in the squad?" Chris followed up smartly.

"...Well, of course," Emily surrendered with a small smile. "Like I said, I'll get her, leave that to me. I don't have to worry about you if you're here, and when we have a plan, you three can help."

"It depends on your definition of help," Penny countered quickly. "But we understand. Just don't make us do anything useless."

"So, all we get to do is guard the city?" Chris went on with nothing but disapproval. "You could use our help."

"Well, we have special representatives coming from off-planet, and they'll be situated near New Hope. Your job will be to protect them too." Emily turned to face him from the front of the armored vehicle. "I need you to do as I say right now, okay? Now is not the time to argue. A lot is going on."

"If you need us," Chris began with a glimmer of stubbornness in his eye. "I'll show up just like I did back there. I don't care."

"I'm counting on it. It's why I'll have to be more careful." Emily winked and smiled a little, but Chris could tell it dropped like a rock when she turned back around.

"You don't have to pretend." Chris suddenly said. He'd called her out so well that she wouldn't even turn around or respond. She just shook her head. "Em." Chris sighed. It was pointless. "Alright, then."

"If you made us a temporary squad for you, we can assist you in

Grandham." Penny offered. She clearly wanted to back up Chris's argument. Ian was still as silent as ever. "So why send us here?"

"You'll be doing a job that is arguably far more important than me doing clean up," Emily explained. "Easy but important. Just...be aware of the snobby personality of the person you're guarding, okay?"

"...Person we're guarding?" Ian spoke, finally. "Who exactly is that?"

"A non-combatant." Emily clarified vaguely. "You'll see. She's...a genius, just not quite right."

"We're coming up on the medical center." The driver said to Emily. She nodded and directed him to pull them over beside it.

To Chris's surprise, the medical center was the hotel where he and Penny had rescued Bafair and the survivors he had with him. Chris stared off at the grand hotel building and slowly opened his door. He stepped down onto the street level and stretched a little. Penny was next, and so Chris helped her down from the vehicle. Ian exited on the other side and walked off in a random direction. Chris wanted to speak up and stop him, but any words right now would probably be pointless. He'd just try to help later.

Emily stepped out of the vehicle only after telling the driver to wait for her. He pulled away from the hotel and parked the truck across the street. Emily approached her brother quickly and looked as if she had something to say but stopped and turned when she heard a little girl call out in a high-pitched voice. She reached for her weapon, which was currently in the form of a dagger at her side, but Chris stopped her. It was just Akela, but why was she here? Chris could see Akela running down the hotel steps with an excited face. She jumped from them on the fourth to last stair and lunged for Penny, who caught her.

"I heard you got hurt!" Akela said with a grave expression. Penny simply brushed the girl's hair and shook her head. "The people at the police place said I could come to wait here for you!"

"They did, huh?" Penny asked her with a warm smile. "Well, I'll have to thank them because you're just the person I wanted to see."

"Really?" She asked with a sparkle in her eye.

"Really," Penny answered back. Her expression lowered as Akela's hand drifted backward and reached for her wings. Penny drew back a little. "Oh, uh-"

"Pretty!" Akela said with glee. "You're like a fairy!"

"Not...exactly?" Penny giggled a little and ruffled her hair.

"That's the kid your advisor mentioned, hm?" Emily inquired. She began rubbing her chin and nodding.

"Yeah. Akela really likes Penny." Chris nodded. He continued listening to their conversation as Emily spoke to him. "We found her while doing a patrol."

"Is that so?" Emily asked him. "Well, did Evangeline ever locate her family?"

"No-" Chris answered, lowering his voice on purpose to prevent Akela from hearing. "And her parents are gone."

"Gone, huh?" Emily folded her arms and continued to look on at the scene in front of her.

"Yeah." Chris kicked the concrete, and awkwardly nodded. "I don't know what we do with kids that-"

"I'm thinking about adopting her," Emily said suddenly and with nothing but certainty. "She'd enjoy Terminus, don't you think?"

"Adopting her?" Chris echoed with wide eyes.

"Well, seeing as I probably won't have a real kid, yeah," Emily explained further. "Tori and I wanted to adopt at some point if we were still together, so in a way, I'm still doing what she wanted."

"That's all?" Chris asked. That couldn't be all, right?

"Well, you two seem to have taken a liking to her, so I want to make sure you still get to see the girl," Emily admitted with a smile. "And you can finally have a niece instead of being bossed around by me all the time. Maybe then you can see why I get onto you so much."

"Should I...tell her, or-" Chris started.

Emily patted his head. "Don't you worry about it; just know I'm going to. Now, I've got to go get shot at again."

"You say it so casually..." Chris said with a concerned face. There was no possible way that it could be natural to react this way, right? Did he do it too?

"Stay out of trouble and call if you need me." Emily smiled and opened the truck's passenger-side door. She spoke again without looking at him in a much more down to Earth way. "Oh, and Chris? If Megan comes back, keep her away from Ian for now."

"How do I do that...?" Chris asked her with a nervous face.

"Get physical if you have to," Emily buckled her seatbelt and looked down at Chris, who had now walked up to speak further. "If you aren't careful, she might try to kill him, and he may not stop her."

"Em-" Chris started with a nervous look. "You always say I can't handle things like this I-"

"You can do this," Emily ruffled his head gently and smiled as best as she could. "You're my brother, after all. You are pretty good at defusing things. I should find her long before that happens, but if it does, call me and deal with her until I arrive."

"Megan wouldn't really attack us again, would she?"

"Ian gave her plenty of reason to back then." Emily shut her door and gave him one last look. "I'm here for you. It's part of why I'm saying to stay here."

"You did have an ulterior motive..." Chris noted warily. "That must mean Megan is still in Grandham..."

"I taught you too well. You can read me now." Emily gestured for the driver, and without another word, they drove off.

"Hey, Akela, where is Morgan?" He heard Penny ask the girl.

"Oh, the pink-haired lady that talks a lot? She's back at the police place!" Akela said cheerily. "She had to handle some demons that got past them."

"That was perhaps the best description ever," Chris commented with a smug look. "Don't worry, we won't tell her. Just don't say that around her, okay?"

"It really makes me wonder what she calls you when we aren't around," Penny said sarcastically.

"Yeah, me too," Chris said, trailing off a little. Was New Hope really secure? "Hey Akela, has anything weird happened while we were gone?"

"Weird?" Akela repeated with a funny face. "No. Why...?"

"No reason." Penny suddenly said, shielding the child from the current situation. "Chris just was curious."

"Right." Chris agreed. "Hey, Penn, we should go meet this person we're guarding. Ian can catch up later."

"Can I come?" Akela asked excitedly.

"Sure, Akela." Penny surrendered kindly.

"Can I ride on your shoulders?" Akela didn't even get to finish asking the question. Penny had already hoisted her up and placed her there. "Yay!"

"We're headed back to the station, right?" Chris theorized. "Emily never said."

"Probably. It's like the safest place here." Penny led the way without a second thought.

---

A new tent had been placed inside the parking garage near the station - it wasn't really for living in. The general layout was a research station with little portable gadgets, rolling tables, and vials. Lights were scattered about the perimeter. The tent had the Resistance symbol sewn onto the top. A single individual stood there wearing a white lab coat and tan dress pants. She had dirty blonde hair, green eyes and appeared to be at least fifty.

The woman took a look at the three approaching her, became disinterested, and then went back to what she was doing. The setting sun was the only thing that gave her some pause. She was mixing some sort of solution together with a device. Chris asked himself why she would be soaking an electronic device inside a liquid substance, but he eventually gave up. Chris tried coughing to get her attention since she really did seem like the stuck-up type, but the woman ignored this. She reached for a walkie-like device attached to her belt and spoke into it.

"Murphy, I'll update you soon. Remain with the Wizard escort and stay alert." She said sternly. A response came back, but Chris was too far to hear it.

"Excuse me?" Chris tried again. Nothing.

"I think she's deaf..." Akela whispered in Penny's ear.

"Akela." Penny lightly popped the child's knee. "Shh!"

Chris finally gave in. He decided to come over and try another approach. He overlooked her science project on the table and decided to play along. "So, what's all this for?" Chris asked.

"I would explain, but I'm afraid I simply don't have time to explain basic concepts to what looks like a..." she turned, looked Chris up, down, and then turned back to what she was doing. "Fifteen-year-old."

"Did you just call me stupid?" Chris asked in disbelief, his jaw-dropping.

"I called you a child, but youth is a time where you know nothing. Of course, I bet that you want to know everything but don't put in the time to use common sense." She clarified. It didn't really make him feel better. When had this turned into a lecture? "Apologies if I made it seem that way."

"Right," Chris grunted. He took a breath and then returned to what he was going to do. "Christopher Spellcrafter."

"Ah, Christopher." The woman extended her hand and took Chris's in a light handshake. "I met your sister. She told me to expect you." She stood up straight and continued on. "Marzia Runcorn. Doctor Runcorn, to be exact."

"Are you a Resistance scientist then?" Chris questioned.

"I was until they decided that fighting demons was more important than understanding the darn critters." She snickered a little. "Anything we don't understand, let's shoot at."

"Um...some of those things are a little bigger than a critter..."

"Yes, well, someone must put in the time to understand them."

She said with a look of almost superiority. "Come now, you're a Wizard. You are supposed to value life."

"I value things that value other lives," Chris said with a sly smile. "Specifically, things that don't want to eat me."

"Fair enough, but not all demons will eat you. Some will mind control you and force you to attack other humanoid beings-" she rambled on for a few minutes, and so Chris decided to tune out.

"So, doctor," Penny interrupted from far behind him. "What did you need protection for? You seem pretty safe."

"I plan to do something very *not* safe, so I requested Wizards. Your General obliged." She said, jumping from her last sentence like it was just that easy. Chris could have sworn that she had two mouths at the rate she was going. "Yes, I need your protection from the Empire, but I plan to go underground tomorrow bright and early. You'll be coming with me."

"The demons are underground," Akela said nervously on Penny's back.

"That's why you won't be coming with us." the doctor said kindly. "I would never drag a child down into the danger."

"Tch!" Chris snickered again. "Um. You just said..."

"Except Wizards who can take care of themselves and me." she laughed a little at her own contradiction. "I plan to explore old ruins I could never enter by myself. They may reveal more about the demon population."

"Is it safe to go underground right now?" Chris asked, turning to Penny for advice.

"Not for long." She deduced smartly. "If the ground decides to shift, we'd likely not survive. Oh, and that is assuming the demons just want to let us take a walk through their home."

"Perfect. I'll see you in the morning," the doctor said dismissively while shooing him with her hand. "Now go sleep or do anything but bother me. I'd like to focus on the device that will prevent us from being killed."

The ground rumbled once more as if to signify that Sohrann was indeed still having these quakes. Chris, Penny, and Akela all stumbled back and forth and attempted to keep balance while Runcorn just continued working like it was nothing. Once it was finished, she fixed her table's belongings, cast a look at them and once again asked them to leave. Chris just had to wonder how someone like this had stayed alive so long in such a harsh environment.

# IAN'S PORTENTS

The ringing sound of gunfire woke him from his slumber. Staring up at the bleak and smoky sky, he winced. There was light there, which he thought might be the sun, but it soon exploded in a horrifying show of yellow and fiery red. He held his head for a moment and then swung himself into a sitting position upon remembering where he was. The young man's surroundings were unfamiliar - almost ghostly, but it was just because he did not want to look too closely. The massive signs atop curved buildings and the various crosswalks made it fairly obvious. How was this possible?

"Chris?!" He called out, panicked, forcing himself to stand. He turned frantically in every direction as a battle raged - if you could call it that, it was more of a massacre. Where were they? He was just on Sohrann, wasn't he? "Penny?! Pennelopie?!"

"Keep moving. Press forward." one of the soldiers said, rushing by Ian in such a way that he nearly knocked him over.

Countless others, along with a tank, followed. The black and red uniforms were hard to mistake as anything other than Imperial. There were even one or two Sorcerers with them. The Imperials cut down the Japanese military forces like they were nothing. They didn't stand a chance along against all of this - especially the magic users. One of them, a young woman, threw a grenade at a Sorcerer, only for him to run through the explosion and relieve her of an arm. The soldiers that were giving chase behind him cut her down. He knew they would. It was all like clockwork.

*Crackle crackle.* That sounded like concrete. One of the towers with a massive screen in the center was beginning to fall. The flashing sign, which read happy New Year 3023 on it, went dead as rubble crushed the frail screen. Ian turned and ran, but the shadow of the building was still gaining on him. Would it crush him?

"Double time it, Ian! Go!" He coached himself angrily. He picked up his own pace and was just barely able to jump out of the way. After sliding and cutting himself all over the street, he picked himself up.

He could hear voices to his left like someone crying for help. Ian hurried over and found a little girl and her brother trapped under rubble. They were lying on their bellies, reaching out for their unmoving mother not too far from where they were. Ian began trying to move the wreckage. He could not let these children die – he just couldn't. He crouched himself down and began to lift hard, nearly pulling his arm on all of the weight. Eventually, Ian was able to get it high enough to put his back to the structural piece.

"Crawl out!" He commanded.

...But the children didn't move. They died in the time it took him to move the debris from their small bodies. He tried. All he could do was try. Even so, he thought he could hear their tiny voices crying out yet again. Ian angrily threw down the heavy slab he had raised to rescue them and began to move down the street toward the scramble crossing again. Their voices were like phantoms but cut like a bullet through his heart. The whole way, they haunted him.

"You were too late," the little boy said in a crying voice. "Why did they kill momma?!"

Explosions tore across the sky as Imperial air support flew low to engage.

"I can't feel my leg. I'm scared..." the girl echoed.

"Stop it," Ian said. He couldn't take it anymore. He fell to his knees and shut his eyes, but the images of it all kept repeating even there. His eyelids were no shelter from this hell he helped create. Now he was crying at the top of his lungs and hyperventilating. "Stop it! I said stop it! Somebody make it stop! I didn't know! I didn't!" Ian sobbed heavily and shook his head while pulling on his own hair to the point where it would probably leave his scalp. "Shut up. Shut up! I know what I did already!"

A sharp and drawn out *shiiink* sound hissed behind him. He turned to see that it was a young man, much shorter than he was drawing a sword from the sheathing. The black, red, and grey armor was quite distinct and recognizable. No one could mistake this figure. The man removed his mask slowly, the echoed breathing subsiding. The face that had revealed itself to him was the face of a foolish boy with uniform black hair, cold - almost dead brown eyes, and the facade of a proud knight. He hesitated for a moment as if calculating his options and then suddenly drew back the sword. The knight gave him one last disgusted face before removing his head from his shoulders.

Ian's eyes drew open as his lungs began to desperately search for air. Beads of sweat rolled down his face and fell into his vision, but he could still make out the familiar yellow shade of the tent he was in. He looked to his left and noted the ordinary empty cot beside his own. The only thing he could hear inside of the tent was his own strained breathing. Outside was more of the same: footsteps and conversation. Ian sat up and brought one leg into his body while staring at the thin sheets he had pulled over himself.

His drowsy attention shifted to the fantasy book Megan had been reading over the past few days. He grabbed it. It was still lying with a page folded down on her side of the tent. The cover was of two silhouetted figures: a man and a woman with weapons staring off into the distance toward the reader. It was the second to last book in the series, according to her and the sun rising over the castle behind them was a dead giveaway that hope had returned - at least to him. The title read: The New King. Book seven of the Crucible Chronicles. He reached out for the book now that the curiosity had overtaken him. All he wanted now was something to get his mind off of what had happened yesterday.

*I don't care what history we have together. All of it became irrelevant when I found out that you were the one who helped take it all away.* A voice said in his head rather loudly. It was so distinct that it could have been a mental communication from Megan, but no, it was him. He hurriedly drew his hand back and turned away from her end of the tent, leaving the book back where he found it. Instead, he faced his armor, which was lying on the yellow-tinted floor. He could see his unkempt hair that just barely blocked his eyes. He cast a frown, sighed, and then reached out to grab it. There was still work to do... with or without her.

## LOWER THAN HELL

Penny adjusted the attachable flashlight on her top for a moment until she was sure that it would stay. Then she grabbed her gloves and carried them out of her tent. Chris was already outside, waiting for her with Morgan and Ian by the station steps. She yawned and began making her way over. Why did the doctor have to insist that they go to this place so early? Penny gave up asking herself why. People like this never seemed to have a good reason aside from theories.

Penny dragged her gloves over her hands one by one, opening and closing her hand multiple times to ensure that they were on correctly. "Good morning." She said to the others.

"Good morning," Morgan said briefly like she was in the middle of talking about something else. "Are you guys sure you don't want me to go?" She flared her magic and held up a fist. "I'm plenty useful, and if there're any freaky monsters down there, they'd think twice!"

"We should be able to handle it, assuming the doctor knows when to turn back," Penny emphasized her words to show that she did not believe this would be the case.

"You keep an eye on the people here and the city," Chris said to her again. He'd been at this since before Penny arrived. "I know you're worried, but if no one is here and something similar to what happened in Grandham happens things will get much worse. I'd feel a lot better if a mage was here protecting them."

"You guys better tell me if you get into trouble!" She demanded with a long face.

"We will," Penny said, her hand illuminated briefly in a ghostly purple. She closed her hand and nodded at Chris. "Are you sure you want to go, Ian?"

He nodded and turned to leave without them, drawing his armor's hood as he walked. Penny gestured for Chris to follow, and so he did. The three made their way into the open desert sands just outside New Hope, with Morgan watching them. She spared them one more worried glance but quickly became busy again when what was probably the thirtieth soldier was brought in because he was under Eslena's mind control. Morgan captured him in her bubble and carefully maneuvered it into the police precinct. When Autumn arrived, these people would be helped, but they were just a danger for now.

As they exited the city limits and their feet began crunching on the almost golden sands, androids began following them. If night fell and trouble came, they would have an escort that demons would mostly ignore. Metal was not exactly an excellent dietary supplement for demonic creatures. The three androids formed a triangle around them, with one in front of Ian and the other two taking up the group's rear. Ian did not say a word, his armor's cloak flowing in the heavy breeze.

"How far out are we going?" Ian asked, his voice low and muffled behind the fabric covering his face.

"She said they were ruins not too far East of the city," Chris said with uncertainty, nearly slipping and falling down a dune as he did. Penny caught his arm pretty quickly and slid down with him, balancing out the fall. "Thanks."

314

"Who willingly goes spelunking on a planet with horrors underground?" Penny asked sarcastically.

"You wouldn't do it for the Empire?" Chris asked. He quickly tried to correct himself when he realized that this sounded offensive, but Penny just smiled. "Like when you were...there with them?"

"If my Dad told me to, yes," Penny answered sincerely. She paused and then snickered. "But I would drag Tori with me, and I would be the first one out. I hate caves."

"You do?" Chris asked with some surprise. "I didn't think anything scared you."

Penny opened her mouth to say something, but was interrupted by Ian, "This is the same girl who was bawling over you when Hunter threw a rebuilt building on you," he called back at them. "Still a normal girl, remember?"

"What scares you about them?" Chris asked, hoping to pass the time as the sands continued for seemingly forever.

"Well," Penny said, giving the question some thought. "I haven't actually been in one super deep personally, but if the ground collapses or something - you're dead. If there is a flood or heavy rain of any kind, you're dead..." Penny went on and on for a bit as if this was some sort of trivia on the many ways to die underground. "Did you know that a cave is probably the least likely place to find a Nightflyer?"

"What??" Chris couldn't help but laugh just a little at this irony. "But the wings are like-"

"A bat, haha." Penny snickered. "Most Nightflyers don't actually go into caves or under trees. They just fly at night or - whenever really."

Chris was starting to worry about her now. "Will you be okay in the cave then? Since you're a - Nightflyer?"

"You'll know if I'm not," Penny assured him with a less than excited look. "It doesn't help that stalactites look like teeth or something."

"You really are afraid, aren't you?" Chris let this slip in such a way that Penny looked like she was ready to punch him. "If it helps, I'm afraid of the demons."

"Try something more irrational to make me feel better," Penny blew air out of her lips and began to flap her wings. Chris watched with wonder as she took flight and flew leisurely beside him.

"Well -" Chris smiled and shrugged. He checked to make sure Ian was far enough ahead to not hear and then spoke up. "I'm afraid of being left alone."

"Like if I leave the dorm?" Penny turned her head to look at him quickly.

"No like -" Chris paused and then narrowed his vision at nothing. "Like everyone I care about being gone like my parents. It's why I was so worried about Emily even though she's always fine. I just feel like one day, everyone will get sick of me, or worse, they'll get hurt. Sometimes I just feel powerless, you know?"

Penny blinked a few times. She landed down next to him while the others kept walking and held him in place. Grabbing hold of his wrist, she squeezed lightly. She must have wanted him to try to use his magic because when his hand began to glow light blue and emit snow particles, Penny gave him a warm smile. Her hand slid up into his own. She did the same with her own hand, and together, the two magic colors, purple and blue, danced around one another.

"I'm not going anywhere. Like I keep saying, I promise that I will do everything in my power to protect the people you care about." Penny said, the blue-ish purple glow reflecting off of her brown eyes. "So stop being afraid of that."

Chris felt himself blushing now, and he could tell she was too. He could really get used to this side of Penny - actually being open about her feelings. They almost had to be alone for it to ever happen. He nodded, accepting her promise. Penny lowered their connected hands, stopped using her magic, and began to march forward to catch up. He kept pace. Being connected to her like this was just natural now. They would be arriving at the ruins soon, so he knew he had to take advantage of any time with her that he could get.

"Hey, Penn - that was really sweet." He stumbled over his words like a fool. What did she do to him?

*I know*, she thought mentally with a wink. She knew he'd hear it. It was getting far easier to read her mind now instead of just getting back silence.

"Penn?" He spoke up without meaning to, but he just had to know now. She turned her head to listen for a moment. "She really taught Gatchi, didn't she? Eslena, I mean..."

"There it is," Ian announced to the other two.

Crumbled ruins were really all that they were. The buildings were probably made of sandstone and basic brick. They were poorly constructed, and it was clear that the weather had quickly taken its toll. How had anyone lived here in these hovels? Multiple Alliance soldiers had set up in and around the buildings to protect the doctor but would not follow them down. This was indeed a job for magic users and only those that could handle the terrors that would probably be waiting below.

The three moved through the center of this mostly buried town and looked all over. The doctor was waiting for them beside a giant hole where a rope was dangling downwards. It was so deep that Chris could not see anything but darkness, but he could have sworn that he saw eyes peering back at him. It was likely just his imagination running rampant but being paranoid on this planet would keep him alive for now. Penny rubbed his shoulder quickly to snap him out of his trance. Had the doctor been talking to him this whole time?

"Unless you want to die, you'll listen!" the doctor snarled rather angrily. She took a pen from her coat pocket and threw it harshly down into the void. If it hit the bottom, he did not hear it, but Penny might have. "You're going to need to wear oxygen masks. Do not let them break or slip. We are not leaving until I find what I'm looking for."

"Right..." Chris made a face and stepped away from the entrance to hell. "So, we're repelling? What are you looking for?"

"I'm not sure yet." She answered.

Runcorn gestured for an Alliance soldier to bring her something, and so he returned with a crate of masks with flashlights on the forehead. There were also oxygen tanks that were attached to each one. They probably would not last long. She placed her mask onto her face and then tossed one at Chris. He caught it, but he still had to resist the urge to throw it back at her face. She was already repelling down, and so he'd likely make her fall. Maybe when they got back to the surface.

He attached his mask and immediately felt a surge of oxygen hit him. The thick material hugged his face so tight that he had felt like it might crush him. He hesitated, grabbing the rope and staring down the hole. A soldier stopped him and handed him a repelling device to make his life more comfortable, but he still felt like he'd throw up. Heights were not a problem, but this was something else.

"I'll go first." Penny decided. She read his thoughts again, right? He wouldn't let her if she didn't like caves.

"No. I'll go. Don't worry." He removed the rope from her hands and lowered himself down.

Ian was next, effortlessly gripping onto the rope and zipping down. Chris hoped that his armor would not make him so heavy that they'd go flying down together to their deaths. When the light had faded enough from the sun, the mask's lights automatically activated. It nearly blinded him, but it worked. He paused to look around, get his bearings, and then kept going. At least it wasn't too claustrophobic.

"Doctor!" He called out to her from above. "How far are we going?"

"Roughly four thousand meters," she said back casually. "But that is an estimate. Please do not jump. I know you wizards are durable, but I don't need you to die before we get there."

"We don't want to die after we get there either," Ian added.

"Or die at all." Penny continued for him.

At least ten minutes passed, and he was already exhausted, but Penny kept motivating him when she could. Finally, his feet hit the ground, and because he wasn't expecting it, he stumbled into the doctor. She did not push him, nor did she protest. Instead, she stood there in awe at the view in front of her. The architecture here was far grander with thick stone-forming rounded pillars along a collapsed hallway. The hallway itself led into a massive colosseum-shaped zone. There were light blue stones embedded into the walls in certain places, which gave off a light just bright enough to illuminate just in front of itself.

"So it's true..." was all Doctor Runcorn could let escape her lips. "The Chromatic ruins were just a little deeper."

"You haven't been down here, doctor?" Chris asked as the other two finally reached the bottom behind him.

"No. We could never dig deep enough, especially because of the sand and demons. The crust disturbances opened this up, and now we can finally access it."

"And what is it?" Chris inquired. He looked around at the pale walls with green and yellow art etched into them. It reminded him of Mayan architecture that he learned about on Earth. 'Some sort of tomb?"

"Perhaps, but more likely, the ruins of a civilization that wanted to live underground." She answered back, slowly making her way forward while dragging her hand softly along the walls. "My hypothesis was correct. The cities above were just a starting point. I'm amazed so much survived."

"I feel sick," Penny mumbled as she walked up to his left. He took her hand. She wasn't joking at all. "I'm fine - just give me a bit."

"You can wait in the mausoleum," the doctor pointed to the large open room ahead of them as she entered. "We'll return for you; just be aware of the demons. They are likely all around us."

"I'll be fine," Penny said. She definitely pressed onwards like she was refusing to let anything stop her. She was always like this, but Chris wished that she'd head back to the surface. They'd manage.

The doctor removed a device, which was probably a motion detector, and began to walk haphazardly into the ruins. She really didn't care much about her safety, so he wondered how long it would take for him to hear 'save me' or something like it. Chris urged Penny to return to the surface if she needed to and then moved on with her. Ian had gone on ahead of the doctor, leaving the two of them alone on the other side of the mausoleum.

"Chris-opher?" His watch crackled a few times as the forced call failed to stabilize. "Little bro?"

"Em? Emily?" He tried. Nothing was going through, and the call soon shut down. "She's probably wondering why we're out here."

"We're still in the New Hope area. She probably sees your watch just a little further out than it should be and is confused why," Penny theorized. "I'm sure she won't be too happy-" Penny turned her head in the direction of the doctor and called out loudly. "-That her brother was sent into an old ruin that could be infested with demons!"

"She will understand once she sees my findings about the planet and the demons." The doctor called back dismissively. "I recommend you keep up. I'm detecting movement."

The group continued through the dark but tall passageways. Many of the stones and crystals that had been created to give off light had been destroyed here. The doctor looked heartbroken at all of the destroyed research she could have had but pressed on anyway. Chris was not sure what she was down here for, and neither was Penny. They were simply along for the ride. Ian was the least upset about this venture into the dark below. His mind was almost certainly still focused on Megan. He just didn't care.

"How much further are we going?" Chris asked as they began descending a ruined staircase. "A few rooms?"

"Until I find what supposedly kept these people alive down here." The doctor answered back.

They had been on these stairs for probably a minute or so. This staircase led into another staircase, which in turn, hid another staircase. Chris figured that the architect who designed these steps was some sort of masochist or hated people - perhaps even both. Once again, Chris felt eyes on him. He turned to see Penny, but it was not her. The hairs on his neck were still standing up, and it was not because of the chilly drafts which blew along the corridors here.

"Oh, there will never too many stairs," Ian complained after a minute or two. There was indeed another staircase at the bottom of this one. "Down we go. Further down. Down and down..." He sang sarcastically. "When we reach the bottom? We'll never know...no, we'll never know."

"Musical entertainment?" The doctor teased with a half chuckle. "Alright."

"Doctor? I think we're being watched." Chris said. There was no way he was just paranoid now.

The doctor made an amused noise with her throat. She responded calmly. "We are. They're in the walls, Spellcrafter."

"They're-" Chris began.

"Not all demons are rearing to kill you. Some would rather hide, and others will protect you like its own kin." She said this information like it was a fact. "The more dangerous ones would have made themselves known by now - which will be soon. I have something to deal with them, but if it should fail, you will protect me."

"What should we expect? Imps? Goblins? Trolls?" Chris asked. If that was all, they would be fine.

"Honestly? There may be new demon types down here. We haven't been able to get down here without losing lives or equipment." The doctor answered back. Her answers were so marvelously descriptive that he thought he might be able to paint what they were looking for. At this point, he missed Megan's short and witty responses that got straight to the point. If she ever decided to come back, he'd have to tell her.

"Spellcrafter? Pay attention. I'm detecting motion up ahead." The doctor said suddenly.

Penny summoned her shield and moved to the front of the group. "I see them."

"You do??" Chris asked as he tried to zone in on the wall of darkness ahead of them. "But where-"

Multiple black and purple spiders emerged from the darkness. These beings were about the size of his head, if not bigger. Chris flinched and raised a hand up to guard against two of them, but they would never reach him. Penny extended both hands and then closed them harshly. The demons withered until they were skinny little bugs and then basically popped out of existence. She had withered them away like they were candy sitting in water. Their life essence, which remained in the form of purple, flew toward her and infused themselves into her body.

"Whoa." Chris breathed out. "I've never seen you do that before. What spell was that?"

"It's a Light Magic version of a Dark Magic spell that I used to use." Penny admitted. She was glowing a little because of the infusion.

"What exactly is darker than that?" Chris questioned curiously.

"I don't really want to explain," Penny said, unwilling to disclose the information. "It doesn't heal you. That's all I'll say."

"Understatement," Ian said, drawing his sword out and preparing for further attacks.

"Chris, go in." Penny directed him. He cautiously inched forward.

She extended a glowing purple hand, which surged with energy - energy so powerful that her hand was shaking. Suddenly, the essence flew out angrily toward Chris. It flew directly into his skin and infused itself into him. Chris could feel his heart racing, and his senses were heightened. Suddenly he could see everything in front of him, and so he summoned one of his swords. Twelve demons all lurking in the darkness of various types. His eyes changed to the same color as the spell. He charged.

Chris was moving without even thinking about what came next. He clung onto the wall and blocked two swipes. Then he kicked off of the surface, spun around, and killed two demons. He flipped back upright, rolled under a scorpion's stinger, and impaled it with his blade. Then, kneeling, he swung right and sent an Ice shockwave with it. Two goblins froze in place and then were shattered by a hard kick from him. He kept going and going until the last demon was killed with a downward stab, and then he returned to his senses. He wasn't even tired. Why couldn't he move like that naturally?

"Impressive." The doctor said, her flashlight coming up behind him. "I have never seen a Wizard move like that."

"That is what the Light Magic version of that spell does." Penny rubbed his back and helped him to his feet. "But eventually, you'll get so powerful that the spell may be a little redundant."

"Is it over?" Chris asked, staring at his hands. They were not only still glowing a soft color of blue, but there was some purple too.

"Yeah. I gave you some of their energy." Penny smiled. "You did well. I was afraid it might be too much for you."

"I feel like I went on autopilot...for a second there, I could've sworn I was moving like Em." He grinned a little. "Nice. We'll have to do that more."

"Assuming there is something for me to drain," Penny added this condition to the end of his statement. "Now, come on."

They had finally reached the end of the stairs and the long corridor. There was gold everywhere in this room and other valuable rubies, but the doctor didn't seem to care. Chris was the only one really staring at it all. Instead, she moved through the sea of rich material and grabbed a staff leaning against the wall. When it made contact with her hand, it radiated a red glow. There was a crystal ball on end or something like one.

The demons were surrounding them now. Chris raised his swords, and Penny prepared another spell; Ian was already swinging and blocking blows with his armor. The doctor raised the staff high into the air and allowed it to glow brightly. The demons were suddenly kept at bay, parting like a sea to avoid the artifact. She then twirled it and pointed forward. Two of the monsters quickly turned on the others and began beating them back. The doctor ushered the other three forward into the other room and shut the old wooden door behind them.

"This is likely where we need to be. They were guarding something." She took note of the large room and waved the staff around. There was another create in here. Large flapping wings could be heard. Would it attack them? "I believe the Empire is after a mineral that the people of this planet had already discovered. If that is true, then I have all the data they do. That is what is causing the quakes."

"Wait, research?" Ian asked with wide eyes. "You were already looking into this?"

The doctor answered this question automatically. "I once worked for an Alliance company that helped me study the demons. They probably still have the data about Lindinium and its many uses for the people of this civilization." She paused and made a face. "I imagine that is why they are here in the first place."

"Hunter mentioned something about that element too, didn't he?" Penny asked.

"Yeah," Chris answered back. "I guess he wasn't lying this time."

Doctor Runcorn pointed the staff forward into the darkness and then bellowed out: "Bring me the ore!" *Yup. She's lost it*, Chris thought to himself.

*Something is coming*, Penny replied.

A long, drawn-out sound followed like a bird calling loudly. Then there was flapping and chirping. Chris nearly screamed when an oversized and colorful bird landed down in front of the four of them. It raised one of its talons and dropped a glowing object into the doctor's hand. It was the piece of something bigger, but it must have sufficed. Runcorn extended a hand and softly rubbed the creature's beak and then bid it farewell. It flew off again, but this time they could see it went to the end of the room. It landed on a tall statue of a woman holding up nothing and settled into the nest that it fashioned for itself.

"A bird?" Chris asked as he slowly began to relax.

"A demon." The doctor corrected as she turned to leave with the ore in tow. "A demon that they worshipped as a God. My theories were correct. They truly did try to live among and worship the demons as higher beings...Incredible."

"And look how that turned out." Chris said disapprovingly. "Bad idea."

"Cool, can we leave?" Ian asked with a nervous laugh. "I don't want to be that thing's treat for doing what you asked."

"We are." She assured him.

When they arrived back at the entrance they used, they found it was infested with demons. They surrounded the rope, and some were even hanging along the walls. Chris expected that Runcorn might force them to back down or that this would turn into a fight, but that did not come to pass. The demons became hostile immediately upon seeing the ore that she held in her left hand. It was like they had been trained to prevent the Lindinium from ever leaving the ruins.

"Get back," Runcorn said suddenly, raising the staff into the air.

The demons did not seem to care, but he could hear a rumbling under their feet. Stones and pebbles rumbled and rolled across the even sandy ground. Sand fell into the tunnel, and he thought that he could hear something burrowing. The doctor raised the staff even higher and stared straight ahead at the danger. Chris decided to look around to try and find what had been disturbed by her actions, only to find the giant bird had made its way up here. It lurked up behind her like a shadow and wrapped itself around them protectively, letting out an angry call from its beak.

"Oh my God-" Ian managed as the bird's giant eyes studied its prey. It sounded like it was growing, and the sound was so loud that these words were almost inaudible. Penny even covered her ears.

"Clear them." Runcorn extended her hand outwards and then pointed a finger. The bird roared a mighty roar and then bolted forward. It tore through the demons like paper, swallowed others, and crushed some under its talons. All the while, it was blocking every single demon from reaching the doctor, Chris, Penny, or Ian.

"Attached," Chris announced as he flew up the rope with the rappelling device. He held on tight as he slowly ascended.

"This is insane!" Ian called after him as he did the same.

Next was Penny. She attached herself to the rope and let it carry her upwards, but she soon shut it off. Now she was dangling a few feet above the ground and looking down at the doctor. She was getting onto the rope slowly but surely, sliding the ore into her coat pocket. She held the staff in her free hand and gave one final point to tell the greater demon to keep them busy a little longer. Together, the two ascended, but the rope was shaking violently because of the fighting down below. There was a snapping noise like something was ascending their escape method. A demon had made its way up the rope and grabbed onto the doctor's leg. Penny let go of her climbing device and dove to save her.

Chris watched with great concern as Penny built up enough speed to kill the creature with a spell, grab the doctor, and then soared back up toward the exit with her wings. She dodged demons jumping from the walls to grab them and then extended her wings further when they had cleared the danger. She was so fast that she had already gone by Chris and Ian and put the doctor back on the surface. She came back, grabbed Chris, and held him to herself, and did it again. She tried with Ian, but he insisted that he was fine. He was probably afraid she'd drop him given the armor.

"They're still coming!" one of the soldiers said as he began to fire with his rifle. Demons were indeed leaving the deep hole they used to enter the Chromatic ruins. They were even withstanding the sunlight! Chris could see their ink-like skin melting horribly, but they were still in hot pursuit. He had the sense to freeze the hole over, but would it hold?

"Seal the entrance!" The doctor ordered the demon. It soared high up out of the hole and extended its wings so wide that the sun was shrouded behind them. Then, it dove down, spinning the whole way. This was so violent that sand flew everywhere, blinding both Chris and Penny. Ian was mostly unphased through his facial covering but still shielded his eyes. The rumbling and loud blowing stopped soon after, and when they could once again see, albeit barely, the hole was once again sealed. Sand had fully covered the ground and even the rope that they used. The bird was gone too.

One surviving demon tried jumping on the doctor, its long spider-like legs flying through the air. She balled up her hand for a moment and then blasted out a beam of yellow lightning. She then stood up and leaned against the staff. Doctor Runcorn waited until the demon had fully fallen apart and sunken into the sand to turn her back to the hole. Even while heaving and trembling, the doctor was able to remove the evidence she had uncovered. She studied it for a minute and then replaced it.

"You used magic!" Chris said, vocalizing everyone's thoughts. "You're a Wizard?!"

"I used to be." She said while trembling slightly. She looked like she just might throw up, but instead just slowly made her way toward the androids that would escort them back to New Hope. "I need to analyze this and get a report...please escort me back."

"What-" Chris stared at her quizzically as she made her way between himself and Penny.

"She's partnerless." Penny indicated without much more evidence than her fatigue from the spell. "This is what happens."

The doctor was already leaving without them, the ore in tow. It hummed softly now that it was above ground as if it was reacting to the amount of oxygen in the air. Chris, Penny, and Ian followed her back toward New Hope with this new information. Chris couldn't help but wonder what Megan might have thought about this misadventure, but then he'd just made himself depressed by doing so. Penny took his hand and squeezed to dissuade the entire train of thought.

# THE BLUE EYES OF HATE

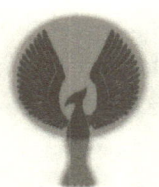

The morning sun faded behind the horizon once again. Darkness had fallen across the lands. The gentle hum of a holographic device filled the hotel lobby as multiple figures appeared in the call. Each time one would speak, they would be moved to the front. There was also a translator present in the call to assist with breaking language barriers. Chris took a seat in one of the hotel lobby chairs beside Penny and crossed his legs. General Delore spoke first, his image appearing to move forward as he did. A holographic globe of Sohrann also appeared with him and began to spin. It showed multiple cracks and breaches in the planet's crust at varying depths.

"You all understand why we found the need to contact you on such short notice." The General began. The translator beside him spoke in another language while also performing sign language for her. "As far as we can tell, the core is still stable, but according to Spellcrafter's squad, the planet is rapidly reaching the point of melting down."

A woman appeared and began signing on her hologram. When she stopped, someone else spoke for her. "Do we know what will happen when the planet reaches this point? How long do we have? I need more data than this, General."

"Fringy research labs here," an older gentleman appeared and began brushing back his greying hair. "I recommend a small scouting device. It should be sent down into one of the deepest breaches in the planetary crust and emit a pulse. This will give us all of the data we need."

Theodore appeared next. He sighed. "My androids should suffice, I suppose." Theodore began muttering to himself. "Because the best way to solve a problem is by throwing expensive and complex technology into the core of a planet to see what's what. I do expect compensation for the little...incident that happened on my business properties, though."

"I have apologized again and again for what happened." Emily's voice said as her hologram faded in beside his. The two appeared to be looking at each other. "You will be compensated, recognized, and I'll pretend that sketchy record of yours doesn't exist for your 'legit' business."

"...Yes," Theodore said with a nervous laugh. "I suppose we can just forget about the finer details. Your brother was just stopping that hooligan from uh - hurting myself of my staff."

"That's what I thought." Emily finished. She seemed to quickly look over in Chris's direction before fading out with Theodore so that the General was the sole hologram again.

"Let's try to stay on track here." The General interrupted suddenly. "Ellias? Are you connected? Borne?"

"I am." An unknown voice said. A middle-aged gentleman with short brown hair appeared in the call. He wore a long tan cloak that reminded Chris of something a warlock may wear, fingerless gloves, and a magic staff on his back. He folded his arms and spoke further, but as he did, Chris could not help but notice that he had a Resistance insignia on his back with an open eye symbol rather than a closed one. "My planet is in danger, so let's wrap this up and avoid getting distracted."

"Elias..." Penny breathed out suddenly to Chris's left. He turned to look at her, but she was fixated on the hologram.

*You know him?* Chris asked her mentally.

*Dad did. They were close; he mentioned Elias a few times.* Penny reluctantly responded back. *I hope he doesn't recognize me.*

"Let us review our situation one more time," Elias said with a serious look in his eye. He took a breath. "The Empire may have seriously destabilized Sohrann's planetary core makeup with deep mining activity. The Alliance was brought in to contain the situation and failed - this coming just after we were reluctant to even accept help." His eyes focused on something out of the camera's range. "Now you want to possibly evacuate the entire planetary population?"

"We aren't sure if evacuation is necessary yet, but it is a possibility," Autumn answered suddenly, appearing directly in front of him as she spoke. "I'd ask you to not panic as there are options, and there is the off chance that the core can once again be stabilized. I personally would recommend a wave of evacuations regardless over the course of three weeks."

"You like to lie about the situation we are in to ease others, just like your grandfather." Ellias suddenly said, attacking her words without a moment of remorse. "I believe we are past the point of easing anyone's nerves." Autumn's jaw dropped a little, and her expression saddened. "I meant nothing against you. I appreciate it, I do, but it is too little too late. Words can't save my planet, and with many of the city leaders dead or evacuated off-world, we are in a state of disarray. The Resistance was not meant to be active this long - let alone force a mass exodus."

"We should have known that when help arrived to save us from the Empire, that we would be in trouble. With Dreadful in the mix, it is not surprising. They probably just want her..." One of the Resistance officers commented suddenly. He appeared to have long cat-like ears and very thick head hair. "We might have been better off alone. Two of my operatives were tortured to the point of insanity for her location just a week after her arrival. We should let them capture her and focus on the real problems. Especially with no timetable aside from mere guesses."

Penny lowered her head and began to shut off from the conversation.

"Hey!" Chris suddenly exploded, slamming his hand down on the table in front of the hologram emitter. "Cut it out; that's ridiculous. The only ones to blame for the state of your home is the Empire, not Penny herself! Don't just toss blame when she's saved more people than you'll ever meet in your lifetime." He glared into the hologram. Everyone went silent.

"Agent Hollow, I cannot ignore what you just said. Apologize for your insensitive comment immediately." Ellias suddenly said from what seemed like a point of authority. His voice was indicative of his displeasure. Hollow's cat ears fell short as he stared at the Resistance leader with a look of shock. "They may be her people, and she may be an Imperial princess, but she now fights for us and others. The look on that boy's face should be enough of an indication of his devotion to her." He continued on while staring Chris dead in the eyes. "It is crystal clear where the blame lies, and it is not with her. Apologize. Now."

"Spellcrafter, Dreadful- I..." Hollow began nervously.

"Right. So what are we doing? The Empire still holds at least one city on the map." Chris asked dismissively, not really wanting to hear him talk further. Apologies from someone being told to say an apology always annoyed him.

Penny placed her hand over his and drew it back away from the table. Then she pulled him back to the sofa and laid against him. *I can defend myself; you know.* She reminded him. Chris nodded and shrugged without care. He always supported her so he would keep doing it. She smiled just a little but quickly let it fade. She returned her focus to the hologram projector, but he was more worried about her.

"Doctor Runcorn, what was your assessment of the demon population? You were so insistent on going underground. Was there anything worthwhile?" Ellias asked, brushing his hair with one hand and gesturing out of the camera's range with the other.

"Yes." Doctor Runcorn appeared on her own device from the upper floors of this hotel building. "The good news is I found an artifact that the original people of Sohrann used to control and direct certain demons. It even works and this will be great for future study. The bad news I've found are as follows." The doctor sat up in her bed and winced. Chris wondered if losing her partner left her in this bad of a condition, how it would be until Emily ended up the same way. "The demons can, in fact, resist the sunlight if only for a while and are entirely willing to come out during the day. I'm not sure how this is possible, but it may be that changing planetary conditions are making them more hostile and aggressive. Lastly, the ore I obtained is possibly what the Empire is mining. Those who came before us used to use the material to construct structures and also doubled as a fuel. It is possible that they are trying to protect their home – this planet and became active when Sohrann became more industrial."

"I'm sorry." someone said quickly. Chris had no idea who, but they probably were not significant. "These killing machines don't have a timer anymore? What if they come for that ore?"

"I will continue my research, but I need my assistant to bring me the notes I requested. He's gone out to study the demons in the canyons to the south but has not returned."

"Do you think he's in danger?" Autumn asked with a great deal of concern. "You said he's not a fighter, so I can go and-"

"Autumn, if you leave to go on a manhunt, we might find ourselves vulnerable up here." The general said. "Spellcrafter, I want your squad on this. Don't delay."

"Yes, sir," Chris said respectfully. Standing up, he made his way out of the hotel. Heading down the steps with Penny, he began to discuss the situation with her. "Do you think they'll find the mining site soon?"

"Probably, but for now, all we can do is treat this like we have been aside from trying to start an evacuation," Penny answered.

He nodded. "Well, I think I'll go to help the doctor's assistant. I think you should stay with Ian." Penny opened her mouth and harshly tugged his hand like she was about to flip out. "I want you to stay with Ian because he's acting more and more out of character. I don't want to leave him here alone or try to drag him out there with us."

"It might be dangerous. Without me, you'll be a lot weaker. Do I really need to keep telling you?" Penny asked. She got in his face a little and scowled harshly.

"I promise I'll be careful, and if I get into trouble; I'm sure you can come flying back faster than I can even say, 'don't worry!'" Chris pulled Penny just a little closer. "Alright?"

"One hour," Penny whispered. Her face was turning red slowly. "If I don't hear from you in one hour, I swear I will scour the desert."

"One hour. Scour the desert. Got it." Chris repeated teasingly. Penny pulled him quickly, pecked him on the mouth, and then turned to walk off. He tried asking what it was for, but she just ignored him. Keeping to Chris's wishes, she raised her watch and pressed the button to call Ian. He could hear it ringing as she walked off and not long after she was talking. He could just barely hear the 'Hey, where are you now?'.

Chris smiled and headed in the opposite direction. He could see Morgan ahead. She looked rather somber and was clearly bothered by something. At first, he was just going to walk by without saying a word, but then she stepped out in front of him and spoke up. Morgan fumbled with her words for a moment and then finally managed to decide on what to ask.

"Um, was Hunter here...on Sohrann? I sensed something like him..." Morgan frowned a little more and then awkwardly bounced a little. "I know it's weird to hear me ask this, and I know you dislike him, but I just wanted to see. I haven't felt our connection in so long. It might just be my mind playing tricks on me."

"Uh-" Chris hesitated. Should he honestly tell her? He just decided to be truthful here to avoid conflict. It was her partner, and if it was reversed, she would probably tell him. "Yeah. We ran into him in Grandham, and he told us about the Imperial plan they're discussing in the briefing right now, actually. Sorry, I didn't tell you, but I never really had time to."

"Oh." Morgan's hair shrouded her eyes a little. "Is he still here? Can I see him?"

"I think he left the planet, Morgan. He said he had no plans to stick around."

"I just thought he might come to see me or at least his other partner." Morgan sighed, and her expression became even more distant.

"Morgan..." Chris tried to think of something to say, but he was too slow.

"Thank you for telling me." Morgan smiled wide and allowed the glimmer to return to her eyes. "I wish I knew what he was up to. But his leaving might explain why I don't sense him anymore."

"If he does turn up, I'll tell you, but you know he might be dangerous. He already caused so much damage..." Chris was hoping to reason with Morgan, but she just shook her head. She would not accept the truth.

"He's still helping us. I know it. Thank you again." She said.

Morgan backed off to allow him to pass, but part of him wanted to continue this conversation further. He worried that Morgan may try to do something that she really shouldn't to help Hunter. She was kind, smart, and a good friend, but she also gave off the vibe of 'I'll just help him anyway.' He would just have to trust that she had enough self-control to handle needing to capture him. Hunter would need to be dealt with one day, and they would most likely need her.

"Weren't you going somewhere...?" Morgan asked as she placed her back against the brick building behind her and stared at him. "You seem like you have a lot on your mind-"

"Oh, I just - I'm tired." Chris lied with a half-smile. "But you know, my squad seems to get all of the fun, drawn-out missions and objectives."

"Do you need me to tag along?" Morgan asked. "I'm just going where I'm told, but I actually want to hang out with you guys!"

"Nah, it's just a basic search and rescue!" Chris said with thick sarcasm. "Nothing ever goes wrong. I'll be fine."

"Alrighty. If you need me-" Morgan tapped on her watch. "Though, I guess you're more likely to call one of your squad mates or Emily...because Emily is actually scary."

"So am I. *Ooooh*," Chris said proudly as he marched toward the search location. He could have sworn that Morgan withheld a laugh in her throat. He turned, gave her a playful glare, and then continued on his way.

---

The sun was now higher in the sky, signifying that the day was almost halfway over. Chris kept moving as he spoke to the doctor through his watch. According to Runcorn, her student was tasked with studying the canyons' demon patterns in the caves to the south. Another Wizard went to investigate his last known location, but she had gone quiet as well. Chris figured that there was a good chance that he may run into demons, but he hoped that the demons would back off in the sun. Either way, the clock was ticking. I really would be embarrassed if he had to call for help to rescue two people.

"-I'll let you know if I find anything." Chris finished his conversation with the doctor and shut his watch off. Then he broke into a run to save some time.

The dunes were a bit more level here, but now things were getting rockier. Not only was the ground getting treacherous as he neared the canyon and its caves, but there were also massive gaping holes in the ground. Sometimes they even opened up further as if they wished to swallow him up. If this canyon had decided to give up and turn into an abyss, he would most likely be in a dire situation.

Things are a mess out here, he thought to himself mentally. Chris could see multiple dead animals and signs of battle. Had the doctor come this way, or was it the Wizard? Perhaps both. The doctor may have been getting chased. He theorized to himself.

If it gets dangerous, don't overstay your welcome; just call for help. Penny answered back. She startled him a little; he didn't think she was listening.

An animal corpse was left nearby and appeared fresh. It looked like a lion but with larger, more defined features. It was certainly more imposing than any lion that Chris had seen in his life. Still, Chris inspected the very recent cuts and magic burns on its body, which was enough to tell him he was close. He hurried around the canyon's steep walls to the other side of the gap. He could hear the sound of fighting and grunting now.

Chris took a step or two toward the noise and found that the fighting was taking place on the other side of the canyon littered with cave entrances. Down below were two individuals he did not recognize. There was a young man with dirty brown hair, which was filled with sand, torn lab attire, and a blue collared shirt with a white tie. He looked like he was panicking at the debacle he found himself in. He flailed at the lion-like creature in front of him, but it backed away and focused itself on the sparking electricity of his electric baton. The other animals in this hunting group of about eight circled him impatiently, but there was someone else with him.

The young lady with him wore a long black robe with a hood drawn over her head. She had visible brown boots and what looked like a medium length grey skirt just under the black material. She certainly looked like a Wizard and was probably the one mentioned to have gone after Murphy, but he had never seen her before. Chris took a singular step backward and then dove forward. Upon landing, he rolled and took out one of the beasts with multiple swipes to the legs. It fell with a thud and began calling out in pain as it nursed its wounds.

"Another Wizard??" Murphy asked with glee. "Wonderful! If you could deal with these Otryons, I'd be in your debt."

Chris leaped over one of the Otryons and let it gallop under him, but was immediately tackled out of the air by another. Its large snout came uncomfortably close to his face and its breath smelled of the previous prey it had devoured. He swung his sword once across the creature's mouth and then kicked hard, flipped away and landed beside the other Wizard. She merely nodded at him and then continued fighting using Life magic. She wasn't much for conversation.

The ground around his Wizard ally began to illuminate green. It spread out further and further until suddenly retracting. From the sandy floor grew two venus fly traps and one that looked like a pitcher plant. They were tan and green in color. Standing up from the ground with unnatural legs, they lurched toward some of the Otryons and devoured them. The carnivorous creatures were almost unstoppable, snapping, and grabbing at the predators turned prey.

Chris was astounded. He had never seen this spell before, and it was somewhat unsettling to witness. These plants always made him feel strange on Earth, even when he had to do a project where they took care of a carnivorous plant. Perhaps the cartoons that had demonized them or just the uncanny nature of a plant could literally eat bugs, but these were eating animals bigger than him. At least she was on his side.

"Try not to hurt them! The balance of the ecosystem out here must be preserved!" Murphy insisted as he cowered behind the Wizard.

"Um, you were about to feed that balance!" Chris blurted as he rolled under one of the creatures and froze it in place as he passed. "A little bit of thanks would be nice."

"Thank you for saving me, but please don't kill them?" Murphy rephrased.

"Doing my best here..." Chris said. He caught one of the Otryons by the mouth before it could bite his arm off and held it in place. A flash of green bolted by and impacted into the creature. A flower sprouted from the point of impact and ensnared it in sharp vines. "Hey, thanks!" He called out. The Wizard nodded and then pointed to just behind him.

Chris winced. She was trying to warn him that a creature was coming right for him. The sharp teeth sank into his hip and acted like hooks to hold him in place. Murphy tried his best to taze the creature, but it did not particularly care now that it had what it wanted. He thought that Penny was calling out to him, but at the moment, he was focused on the pain. Chris tried punching the Otryon in the nose as many times as he could, but it just bit down harder. He was only freed when the other Wizard closed the distance and stabbed downward into the snout. It retreated, whimpering, and probably frustrated.

He rolled onto his side and watched as the carnivorous plants continued battle around them. She extended her hands over his injury and began healing him with great care. He could just barely make out her blue eyes, staring down at him with something of a frustrated gaze. The girl's hair was a lighter color like red, but he was too out of it to really tell, and her hood made it hard to see. The girl looked away suddenly, just as he began to piece together her face. She used her magic to yank Murphy away from one of the creatures and then finished healing him.

*Are you okay?* Penny asked frantically.

*Just a flesh wound.* Chris lied to dodge her concern.

*That felt like anything but a 'flesh wound,'* Penny answered back. She seemed really upset with him. *Partner of mine, you better get back here soon. I swear, you're going to make me have grey hairs by the time I'm like thirty.*

*I thought I was a bit more than a partner now.* Chris smirked even though he knew that she would not see it. *Shame.*

*...Get back soon, and we will discuss that.*

*What does that mean?* He asked. Would she actually answer this time?

*It means to get back soon, and we will discuss it.* Penny repeated. Nope. She was still dodgy.

The Wizard snapped her fingers in his face. Once she was sure he was paying attention, she held out her hand and pulled him to his feet. The plants had died now and successfully either killed or drove off all of the creatures. She shrugged a little and then nodded at him, but he did note that she had been careful to not show her face again. It was only now that he noticed that she was fighting with a magic staff. Could she really not speak? Why did he not listen to Emily about learning sign language?

"Uhm, thanks." He said rather awkwardly. She nodded at him. "You can understand me?" She nodded yet again. "Alright then! Did you have a plan to get us out of the canyon, or should I-"

"Thank you both!" Murphy suddenly interrupted as he hopped up and down. "That was splendid. You were so fast that I couldn't even comprehend what was happening."

"I guess you're the missing apprentice I saw on a milk carton?" Chris asked sarcastically. He extended a hand. "Are you alright?"

"Yeah, that wasn't so bad! I really am glad that it is over, though."

"For you, it wasn't so bad," Chris responded to him with a light glare. "Keep in mind, I almost got eaten for you."

The young woman stowed her staff on her back and stood in a more relaxed manner now that all was calm. Murphy smiled. "Thank you again too. If you had not arrived, this other Wizard probably would have found my remains-" He laughed nervously. "Ah, death." She did not really react to his thanks but did at least look in his direction.

Chris sighed a little and inspected one of the creatures. He had never seen it before, but it was clearly one of the predators of the planet. Perhaps it was most active in these southern regions. It was a little bit annoying to think that there were not just demons to contend with, but he should have known. Murphy approached him and smiled kindly. He appeared very awkward at first glance.

"Perhaps we got off on the wrong foot. Are you okay?" He asked Chris.

"I'm just so very tired of almost being eaten on this planet." Chris huffed as he got back to his feet. "You're nicer than Runcorn, at least."

"She's nice in her own way." Murphy laughed and rubbed the back of his head. "Sometimes she even says thank you."

Chris continued listening but moved so that might allow him to see under the hood of the woman he had just fought alongside. He was just so curious, and there was something familiar about her, but from this angle, he could still only make out that she was human, had blue eyes, and reddish hair. Perhaps it was more pink, like Megan's? He paused upon realizing that it must just be her and wanted to say something, but Murphy got his attention again.

"I don't think she has said a single word since I met her," Murphy said to him curiously. "I'd like to assume that she can't speak, but I already tried sign language and even the Arusian clicking language. I've been talking to myself throughout this whole ordeal."

"We should get you back to the doctor." Chris decided. He turned to lead Murphy to the lower end of the canyon, where it would be easier to reach the surface level. Occasionally he would hear a rumbling below his feet, and it just made him want to get to higher ground as fast as possible.

"I always knew the doctor would not leave me to the wolves! Er, so to speak." Murphy mused as they walked. As Murphy said this, a terrible flashback of being dragged by a wolf flashed into his mind. He scowled and buried this as deep in his mind as he could. "Did I say something?"

"Poor choice of words. I have had a run-in with my fair share of wolves. Replace the lion things with wolves, and that was my situation." Chris said back to him as they went along. "In front of my crush too if you can believe it. She had to save me and - yeah. Let's not discuss it."

"These Otryons are local to this area of the Badlands, but they are not normally hostile to humans. Strange...I suppose it was the quakes." Murphy pulled out a notepad and started to write down his findings. "The doctor said she could conduct her research without them even paying attention to her. Humans are not familiar prey for them, so they tend to ignore them."

Chris quickly noticed that the Wizard he had just met was following them too. She was keeping pace with them but walking somewhat slower to stay behind. Part of Chris felt a little unsettled by her constant silence. At least Myra talked a little, even if it was in fragments, and Penny communicated with him mentally, but this was just pure radio silence. She stopped when they did and kept walking whenever they did the same. He wondered if he should try calling her 'Megan,' but perhaps it was best to leave it alone. If she wanted to reveal herself - she would.

"So," Murphy began with his hand on his chin. "I assume she's with the General's forces that came to aid Sohrann? Or perhaps a Resistance Wizard?"

"I can't say I've met her," Chris lied intentionally with a small smile. "Though, her spells are kind of scary. I bet my sister could do something even more terrifying, though." Chris jumped up onto a rock formation, which led to a path that would help them escape the canyon. He helped Murphy up and then tried to do the same for his other ally, but she just levitated herself up with wind.

"Does your sister use a sword then? Like you?" He asked kindly.

"...Saying Emily likes to swing a sword around is a big understatement." Chris mimicked one of her attacks once they were on level ground. "But she does it better."

"Ah." Murphy pointed a thumb backward at what Chris assumed to be Megan. "This one sure does love her spells. I love using my fire blasts, but even I don't use them as much as her."

"Wait, you're a *Wizard*???" Chris gawked at him.

"Could you maybe act a little less surprised?!" Murphy was clearly offended. "I can help with my brain far more than my combat skills."

"I mean I am, but hey, everyone has different experience levels," Chris said wisely. "I was getting messed up my first few months as a Wizard. I couldn't even block a tennis ball."

They were nearing the top of the canyon now. Chris was going to try creating an Ice construction to allow them to reach the very top, but the Wizard they were with summoned a strong gust of wind and threw them over the top. Chris landed on his feet and caught himself, but Murphy fell hard and tumbled. He was fine and was quick to spring to his feet but was clearly far worse for wear after the event. The Wizard came soon after, seemingly hovering on something. When she climbed up and out of the canyon, pollen appeared behind her like the flower spell she often used to fly.

*I found Megan.* Chris decided after piecing together all of the clues.

*Really??* Penny asked him. She seemed happy about it. *Is she okay?*

*Yeah, I'll explain when we have a chance to talk, but just...pretend you don't know for her sake.* Chris responded. *We're heading back now. I'll think of something.*

"Which planet are you from? You look like you're from the Milky Way." Murphy continued the conversation like nothing had happened just now.

"How did you figure that out?" Chris asked with genuine surprise. "Wow."

"You look like the most default human being I've ever seen aside from your hair," Murphy said. After a pause that could have lasted an eternity, he finished with, "Not that that's a bad thing, but most humans don't look like...this."

"Okay, you're done talking." Chris decided as he continued onward, mimicking Emily to the best of his ability to sound intimidating.

## DEAR MS. FAIRYHORN

Chris watched as Murphy scurried off to Runcorn's 'base of operations' like his life depended on it. He shook his head and raised his watch to contact Emily. She would likely want to be informed of his return to the city. The sun was setting now, and the demons would be out in full force. He could see Penny approaching from the front, so he decided to hold off on this for a moment. Emily could see his location anyway. There was no doubt in his mind that she was watching it like a hawk.

"Hey." Penny started with a nervous smile. She raised her own watch to reveal an ongoing call that was currently on hold. "So Hourev called..."

*Just what I needed*, he thought. "Does he know about the Spark?"

"Mmmhmm." Penny unmuted the call.

An old man in black and blue mechanic overalls projected out from the watch between them. He had a long face, but his mood seemed to improve upon seeing that the call had resumed. He had a stubble beard, completely grey combed hair, and green eyes. Chris could tell he had oil on the side of his face, but it was being wiped off by a small cloth that the man removed from his overalls.

"Spellcrafter." He began in his usual grumpy tone. "I just wanted to call and check on you since neither of you kept tabs with me."

"We've been sort of busy...it – well, it has been crazy," Chris admitted. His stress could likely be heard in his voice. "Megan and Ian-"

"I heard from your sister." He suddenly said. Chris was surprised that Hourev even knew Emily all that well, but it made sense. He was their mechanic, after all. "Are you two kids, alright?"

"Yeah, yeah, we're okay, I guess." Chris shrugged. Penny nodded in agreement. "How are things there?"

"Calm," Hourev answered enthusiastically. "I finally finished up that other plane I was working on for the Spark line. I'm quite proud of it."

"About the Spark." Chris started awkwardly like he was admitting to a parent that he broke a plate. "We got shot down, and the plane is completely gone. Some parts were salvaged and should be coming your way, but even Cornellius's latest update was wiped out."

"You were shot down?" He repeated with wide eyes. His hologram turned back toward Penny. "I thought you were an Imperial pilot. Are you sick or something? That's not like you."

"He jumped on the plane, shot me, and disabled the flight controls." Penny snickered a little. "I should have seen it. Sorry."

"Yeah, I'm sure you are sorry." He emphasized this sentence in such a way that he caused Penny looked over at Chris as if to say 'great.' "Well, I'll send this new plane your way then."

"Wait, what about the Spark?" Chris asked him.

"Scrapped for parts or upgraded," Hourev answered quickly. He waved his hand dismissively. "I was more concerned that you were still in this life and doing alright."

"No offense, but don't you usually get onto me more than ask if I'm okay?" Chris inquired. Hourev glared in a mean way. "Sorry. Sorry. Uncalled for."

"Just don't wreck this one. It should be better than your last plane, but the AI is in default mode. I will get with you in the future to set a personality. Cornellius was flawed and needs work." He picked up a cup of coffee from off-screen and began drinking it. "Now, I believe you need to go find your other missing squad mate? The one with the smart mouth?"

"Megan?" Penny wondered.

"Yeah. Whatever her name was." He smirked. "Try not to kill her like you killed my Spark."

"Hey-!" Chris began. The call ended. "This guy."

"At least it didn't turn into a yelling competition." Penny shrugged lightly. She sighed. "I'm going to miss that plane." She continued talking despite Chris staring past her. "I should have been more careful...Chris?"

Chris subtly moved his head to point in the direction of the courthouse. In a crowd of people trying to make their way to either get food or find a tent, Ian could be seen with another hooded individual. Two were standing about ten meters from one another, but they might as well have had a sea between them. Ian drew back his hood and just stared directly at her. The hooded individual, who Chris assumed to be Megan, did the same. They said nothing, didn't move, and almost appeared frozen in time. After about a minute, Megan turned and walked off in the opposite direction, vanishing into the crowd of people. Ian walked off shortly after.

"That's really her, isn't it?" Penny frowned and turned away to avoid staring. "Do you think Ian knows it was too?"

"Yeah," Chris answered with a heavy sigh. He couldn't help but feel horrible. What if it was reversed and Penny was avoiding him or said the things Megan had said?

"I wouldn't," Penny said, destroying this train of thought. She took his hand and led him away toward the station. "Look, okay, what if we split up and talk to them individually? You talk to Megan, and I'll talk to my stubborn brother."

"I don't know what to say..."

"I don't either, but if we don't try, then not only will the squad be split up, but their partnership might not last." Penny had that look in her eye again. "We'll figure it out. There's nothing pressing going on right now, so we should do this now."

Chris made a worried face but did not say anything. Penny was quick to take both of his hands and squeeze. His heart began to race, and he got flustered again, but the concern over Megan and Ian was still there. "We'll take it step by step and help them. They need us right now. I know Ian better than you, and Megan is more likely to talk to another Earthling who isn't a Sorcerer..."

"Alright. I'll try. I'll keep you updated." Chris said. He'd try for her, but deep down, he felt that they had no place in this.

"See you in a bit," Penny said.

"Yeah." Chris agreed quickly. "Love you-" He froze. That was not what he intended to say, but it just sort of fell out of his mouth. She hugged him around the neck and waited until he had returned the embrace. Before he could even ask her what she planned to do, she flew up and away. "Still not used to the wings." He laughed a little. Chris turned, locked in on the direction Megan had gone, and broke into a run. "Okay, Meg. Please don't kill me. I'm just going to try to be a friend. Yeah..."

Chris hurried along the city streets. He could see Megan just ahead, walking alone through the eerily empty streets. She did not seem to have any problems with being alone. Perhaps she was just used to it. He called after her a few times, but she did not seem to hear him. He tried again, but this time she began moving faster. This led him to one final answer: call her by her actual name.

"Meg, wait!" Chris called out as loud as he could.

This got a response, but not the one he necessarily wanted. Megan shook her head, turned back to look at him, and summoned her flower. Chris was quick to react, running on the side of an office building on his left to get momentum. Then he launched downwards and tackled her off. *Already off to a bad start here!* He thought. The two were in freefall now, so he began thinking of spells to use. Megan pushed him off violently but also cast a spell on him, which slowed his fall just enough to not harm him. Then she began dashing between the buildings with wind spells.

"I just want to talk to you! Meg, stop!" Chris pleaded. He gave chase from street level, but he didn't have the same mobility. If only he and Penny had swapped.

"Back off!" She called back from very far ahead of him.

*I'm done with Ian. It didn't go too well. How are things with you?* Penny asked him mentally. *Wait, are you running?*

*Not good, she's flying. I'll get back to you!* Chris promised. He had to focus on catching up.

"I gotta slow you down!" Chris warned her. Extending his hand outward, he fired out multiple Ice traps, which stuck to her and froze one of her legs. "Sorry!"

"Do you want me to shoot back?!" Megan asked him angrily. She smashed the Ice with a quick slash from her sword and then kept moving.

"I didn't want to have to shoot in the first place, but you're fast. I can't keep up if you don't let me."

"Then maybe you shouldn't." She shot back angrily.

"Meg, come on." Chris begged. This wasn't going to work.

Chris watched as she summoned the flower once more. This time he was ready. He stopped running, stood in place, and rapidly fired out Ice sickles. They slammed against the flower's petals until it was littered with holes. Just before she hit the ground, Chris froze her with another spell and let the momentum attach her to the side of a building. She struggled for a moment, but he was confident that she could not get free.

"Look," Chris said as he approached her and tried to catch his breath. "I didn't want to shoot at you, but you need to listen. I want to help you and I want to apologize."

"You've helped enough." She shot back angrily. "Thanks for having my back there with Murphy, but I didn't need or ask for it. I had it under control."

"Yeah," Chris approached her and stared her dead in the face.

"But you still have friends that care about you, so at least let me come with you so we can talk. You're just going around trying to help random people, right?"

Megan smiled a little like she was in disbelief, "What exactly is there to talk about? You hid the truth from me too."

"I felt like I had to. It was Ian's place to tell you, and I didn't want to hurt you." Chris answered honestly. "Please hear me out. Please, Megan. Just for a minute."

"Get me down," Megan demanded impatiently.

"Will you listen...?" He questioned. Megan nodded reluctantly in response.

Chris swiped his hand down hard and watched as the Ice vanished from her body; she fell just in front of him. "You can tag along, and we can talk, but not a word about him. Got it?" Megan turned to face him.

"Got it." Chris agreed. He would have to backpedal on that if he hoped to solve the problem, but Chris knew that he needed to tread carefully.

Megan pointed a stern finger, "But if you ever shoot at me again, I swear..."

"In my defense, it's like the only thing I could do to catch up," Chris said quickly. "Please don't turn me into fertilizer."

"Just come on." She said, ignoring the joke entirely. She really did act like a totally different person when angry. "We'll fly and talk."

Chris nodded in agreement. He stood beside Megan and waited for her to cast the flower spell underneath their feet. As she was doing so, the ground underneath him was replaced by a soft flower's center. Suddenly, a figure appeared at the corner of his eye: a woman. Eslena was there watching him yet again with a smile. This time, Chris was ready. He pointed her out to Megan, but Eslena did not seem to care much. Megan stared at her for a few moments, her eyes turned green like she was checking for something with a spell. She suddenly sent them flying upward so violently that Chris had to grab onto the flower's center. She directed them back in the direction they had come as if she was expecting trouble.

"What? What's wrong? It's an illusion." Chris said as he grabbed onto the surface of the flower. "Slow down."

"It's not. That's really her!" Megan said. The flower violently turned left to dodge gunfire, which soared just over Chris's shoulder. "Her illusions don't have heartbeats."

Eslena was indeed on the ground behind them where they had left her. She waved her hand as if springing some sort of trap. More attackers came from the shadows in the form of mind-controlled Alliance soldiers. When she pointed upward toward Megan's flower, they opened fire with rifles. Chris deflected what he could, but one of these bullets did strike him in the chest. He fell over for a moment, his body feeling weaker and almost numb. A blue substance was embedded into his chest. *What is this?* He wondered. Chris began to drift in the wind like paper, but Megan caught him and used a spell to return his awareness.

"The bullets- they're coated with something," Chris warned her through slurred words.

"I know." Megan brought them to a sudden stop when more soldiers appeared in the direction they were heading and opened fire.

"Other way!" Chris warned her. He cast a wall of Ice just in front of them to block incoming fire, but now they were just being boxed in. "Meg, other way!"

"I know," she said through gritted teeth. "I see them. We'll head for the desert."

"But the demons-" Chris started.

"Chris, do you have a better idea? We can't make it back. I don't know who else she has under mind control."

Megan directed the flower in the direction of the desert outpost they had captured upon first arriving. It was far, but they had no choice. She continued dodging gunfire and even redirecting it with her spells to instead tranquilize the soldiers, but now some Resistance operatives were also firing on them. He could contact Penny, but would she be able to handle all of this? Even with Ian's help, this was just too much – they would just be in danger too.

"I should call Emily." he decided. Megan nodded. She did not have time to converse with him and fly through this mess.

Chris rifled through his watch's interface and pulled up Emily. The call began trying to connect, and he anxiously awaited as it did. When Emily's image appeared on screen, and it seemed like he might have a chance to tell her what was happening, a shot struck Megan in the back. The flower descended rapidly, but she could still guide them toward street level where they might land safely. The call was still ongoing, and he could hear Emily becoming more concerned, but now he was being struck by random tranquilizer rounds. It felt like every inch of his body was being pelted with paintballs that dug themselves just under his skin.

They collided with the ground, but Chris was so out of it that he could not hold onto the flower to stay near Megan. She had already recovered by casting another spell on herself to cleanse the substance's effects, but Chris was pretty much out of the fight. He rolled onto his stomach and began trying to crawl toward her, but the shots just kept coming. By now, Chris had forgotten that Emily was on the line. His mind was foggy, and he felt like he might vomit from how dizzy he was.

*Chris?* He thought he could hear Penny trying to speak to him, but his thoughts were so jumbled. Was it his imagination? He couldn't tell.

Megan was on her feet again, guarding Chris from further attacks as well as trying to protect herself. She was able to take out about twenty of the attackers firing on her with long-range Life spells that rooted them to the ground; however, she did not see the figure slowly creeping up on her from behind. Chris was just barely able to point forward and verbally warn her. Not even a second after turning to block what looked like a double-bladed weapon, Megan fell to her knees and cried out in pain. Her sword fell too - along with her severed hand. It rested not far from her. A final gunshot rang, and

Megan fell over, unconscious not far from him. Chris had to fight his eyes, which felt like weights. He had to do something. Using all of his strength, he pulled himself up from the ground just enough to see Eslena's legs calmly walking toward him. She stopped directly in front of him, said something he could not register, and then watched as he resisted the urge to fall asleep.

"Why don't we find out how long it takes the princess to come to your rescue," Eslena said to him just before it all went dark. He forced his eyes open again with all of his willpower even if they felt weighted.

Now he was just barely able to keep himself from panicking. He could not reach Penny, Emily's voice was faint and drifting despite his watch being near his ear, and no matter how hard he tried, his spells would not fire. He looked to Megan to make sure she was okay, but it was in doing this that he realized what had happened. She had actually lost her hand to this woman. Eslena picked up the severed limb and smiled down at him like it was something she had grown used to.

His first thought now was of one thing: his partner. Penny was not responding, and that led him to one conclusion. They must not have been her first targets. "Where's... Penny?" Chris asked with a look of terror.

"Oh, you're worried about your partner. We'll have her soon. She's proving to be quite stubborn," Eslena answered with a joyous smile. "You would have been harder to deal with together, so I am glad that it worked out this way. Thank you – truly."

"Who sent you after us?" Chris asked, hoping to get more out of her for Emily. Eslena kindly reached down and ended the call. Then, she removed both of their watches and set them aside.

"You act as if I cannot act on my own accord. This would have gone a lot smoother if I had been the one to go after Dreadful, though. Vedi just had to be the one to do it because he doesn't trust me!" She laughed a little. "I'll just have to tie up that loose end too."

"Loose end?" Chris managed. He forced himself to all fours and winced. He was so dizzy that he felt he might vomit.

"I'll kill the princess, blame it on the Emperor's knight, and make my move on the throne with these new resources. It was supposed to have happened by now. Simple, really." She turned to face him and gave him an expression that was subhuman. How could anyone talk about this like it was normal? "He's already killed one child, right?" *Yeah, he did.* Chris thought, though, it was hard to think at all in his current state.

"What do we have to do with this?" Chris forced himself to stand and picked up one of his swords.

"You still have some fight left?" She asked with some surprise.

"Answer me!" Chris demanded, despite the yelling making him dizzy.

"You took my apprentice from me, didn't you? It's only natural that you replace her!" Eslena spun her double-bladed weapon around to prepare for an attack. "I believe I've wasted enough time here, and I'd like to leave before this planet expires, so let's end this now."

*Even if I have no chance of winning, I won't let her hurt Penny.* Chris thought. This resilience gave him just enough energy to prepare for an attack. Eslena was walking toward him slowly now, her blades shining in the dim lights of the streetlamps. She suddenly charged. He swung low to try and catch her off guard. Eslena swiped one of her blades upward, deflecting the strike. As she passed, she turned, sliced his wrists, effortlessly knocked his sword away, and bashed the back of his head with the hilt.

# BIG BROTHER

Penny had hoped that Ian would be more receptive to the idea of trying to speak to Megan. He dodged every attempt she made and then refused to talk further. With any luck, Chris would have had more success. For the time being, she decided to just make herself useful by helping around in the city. Bafair reported a missing Resistance patrol as well as a few missing Alliance soldiers. Maybe she would look into that? It sounded simple enough, and if she flew, she would find them in no time. Penny took a moment to shrug off the yelling she had just done and then prepared for fight. Just as she was about to take off, a small pair of hands caught her leg and held onto it tightly. When she looked, she found Akela there crying and shaking.

"Hey now," Penny said as she began softly brushing her hair. "What's the matter?"

"I was playing in a building and saw a scary man..." She said through sobbing. "And he said to come get you."

"Come get me?" Penny asked suspiciously. "Akela, you know you're supposed to stay where the soldiers can see you. Where was it?"

"I don't know. I can show you..." Akela said nervously. "He was really scary."

"Did he have a gun?" Penny asked. If she could just narrow this down, she would know what happened. "A sword?"

"He just told me to get you and hurry up." She answered back. "Am I in trouble?"

"No," Penny responded. "Come on, take me to him, okay?"

"Alright..." she agreed anxiously.

"Ian." Penny began walking while recording a message for him with her watch. "I'm heading to check out a potential problem. If I don't check back in a few minutes, track my location."

Penny and Akela walked across the city, far from where the Alliance patrols would generally go at this time. She found it concerning that Akela had gone this far out but also reasoned that she was a child and wouldn't know better. As soon as this was over, Penny would have to talk to her about following directions again. As sweet as she was, Akela was hard-headed. What could she have possibly been doing out here?

"So I heard music being played, and I went to go see, and when I did, I went in there." Akela began while wiping the tears from her cheeks. She pointed at a set of buildings near a sign which said 'New Hope Civic center.' There were many strangely shaped buildings here as well as oddly shaped art. It reminded Penny of the theatre she had gone to on Shadehedge, but on a much smaller scale.

"So where was he?" Penny asked as she looked over the building. It was red and white in color. The structure almost seemed like it was glowing because of how bright the lights were. She studied the sign next to them to try to narrow down the search. "The museum, symphony, the transit station..."

"That one," Akela said. She pointed at the taller white building in the center of all of the others. "He was in that one. He was playing the drums."

"The symphony, huh?" Penny summoned her shield by swinging

her arm out and began to approach the building, but Akela stopped her. "Do you need to go back?" She asked.

"No, just be careful..." Akela urged with a large frown.

"I will," Penny promised her. "Stay behind me."

"Can't I stay out here?" She pleaded.

"It isn't safe. I'll protect you." Penny took her hand and carefully approached the symphony chambers. Akela reluctantly agreed.

The symphony lobby was large, with multiple seats that were embedded onto poles in a semicircle. It was probably a stylistic choice. Posters of a famous trumpeter were posted on the white walls and were dated for just after the Imperial invasion began. To her left, she read 'New Hope Symphony Hall,' and on the right, she saw 'Rehearsal.' There were two floors to check, but she knew that if it was like any other symphony hall, that it all led into the same room. She wondered if she should leave Akela in the lobby where the seating was but decided against it. If this was a trap, she wanted her somewhere she could be seen easily.

Penny approached the brown doors that led into the symphony hall and pushed slowly until the doors gave way to the other side. The chamber was dimly lit, with the stage being the brightest. A single individual was there sitting at a piano and studying sheet music. He adjusted it and then began to play a melody that Penny recognized all too well. It was the Imperial anthem that was written after her father came into power. She entered, lightly pushing Akela so she would hide down between the seats.

"Don't move unless something is going to hit you or I tell you to, alright?" she whispered with a serious expression. "I mean it."

"Okay..." Akela whispered back. "I'm scared."

"Don't be," Penny said as she stood up and pulled her gloves over her hands.

Penny made her way down the aisle, her boots softly pattering on the red rug. Every sound was amplified by the design of the main house. The man continued playing with a smile like he was putting on an actual performance for the audience, and all the while, Penny kept advancing on him. She was about halfway to the stage. The song was coming to an end now, and the melody was being repeated one last time. Penny was close enough to hear him humming now. He never did have a sense of pitch, but he was good at the instruments.

Vedi ended the song and stared absentmindedly at the sheet music. He had jet black hair, unnatural purple eyes with a black aura around the pupils and wore the standard Imperial knight uniform. She watched him as he adjusted his cloak for a moment and then suddenly dropped it. He must have thought that it would get in his way when fighting her. Vedi respectfully stood up, pushed in the piano chair, and bowed at the audience, and by in large Penny.

"It's good to see you again." He said kindly with his arms outstretched. A smile crept across his face. "Daddy dearest says he misses you." Penny scowled and summoned her sword without a word. "So, where's Ian? I'm supposed to get your brother too."

"He's not here." Penny took a quick look back at where she left Akela. Once she had confirmed that the child did not move, she returned her attention to Vedi. "You can tell Dad that I'm still not coming back."

"You'll be telling him yourself." Vedi summoned his straight sword and twirled it once with his wrist. "It's just too bad that Tori can't come to the reunion. She'd love it." Penny took a fighting stance and narrowed her vision on him. "Your stance changed. Is that a defensive one?"

"Come find out," Penny said. She was a little aggravated, just hearing her sister's name.

"Oh, this'll be fun," Vedi commented.

Penny twirled quickly and sent her shield flying directly at him. He caught it, but when he lowered the shield, Penny was already in his face. She swiped at his face with her sword with such ferocity that his only option was to dodge backward. Even so, he was unable to escape the follow-up shield bash from her. Her wings made it possible to move much faster than before. She went in for a stab on his arm, but his sword knocked it away from his body. He came back around to slash at her. Penny used her wings to soar upwards and over his head, using her shield to block the attack he had redirected toward her.

She swung at him from the air multiple times. Parry. Parry. Parry again. Penny tried once more, but this time Vedi kicked her hard in the stomach and sent her flying a short way back. She landed on her feet, similar to a cat, and slid across the stage's smooth brown wood. She held her gut for a moment, checked to make sure she was still good to fight, and then stood up. Her wings seemed to beat restlessly behind her as if waiting on her next move.

"You're starting to move like your mother," Vedi commented while looking at the colorful wings behind her. "Still haven't gotten the hang of them, though, have you?" He paused for a moment. "Come to think of it, that brat isn't with you. Did they scare him off? I'm disappointed in him now. Love is blind, right?"

Penny did not reply, so this prompted him to speak further. "I taught you well, huh? Nothing I say can get under your skin. Proud of you." Penny balled her hand into a light fist until her hand illuminated a ghostly purple and then threw the energy at Vedi. He caught it into his own hand and tossed it aside like it was nothing. "Did you just try to use a drain spell on me? Really? I'm the one who taught you that. Come on!"

Vedi charged at her and slid to trip her, but Penny leaped up and landed on top of his chest; she quickly sprang off and fired a different spell back at him. This time he rolled to dodge it and cartwheeled to his feet. He returned fire with his own set of attacks, which were grey in color. Instead of dodging, Penny absorbed them with her soul barrier and let the power flow through her body. Then, she transferred it into her sword and charged with her shield raised. The blade hummed with power as she swung. Vedi blocked, but every hit slammed into his blade like a truck. The last strike hit so hard that his sword tumbled out of his hand and away from him.

Vedi caught her arm and pulled her in for a quick knee to the chest. Then he tossed her aside and retrieved his weapon. "Let's start again."

Penny took a step back like she would throw her shield, but then grabbed onto the piano behind her and sent it rolling at him. Vedi vaulted over the top of it and pushed it behind himself. The piano emitted a terrible cry as it tumbled off the stage and into the floor. When he returned his attention to her, Penny was soaring through the air. She collided with him and flew rapidly until he had been thrown off of the stage. He did a backflip to recover and retreated backward to avoid her, but Penny jumped from seat to seat to keep pace. When she finally reached him, she delivered a powerful round-house kick to the face. Her wings almost sounded like a bullwhip in the wind from the sheer force of the attack.

"Sloppy as ever," Vedi said with a chuckle. He had already recovered from the blow and grabbed her ankle. "You have to think-" He began as he spun her around and let her smack into every chair around them. She winced and sucked her teeth to ignore the pain. "-Before you act, remember?!"

Vedi finally released his grip on her and sent her flying toward the high ceiling. It looked as if she might crash into it, but instead, she landed upside down and stabilized herself once again. Her wings were extended to catch as much air resistance as she could. A loud *swoosh* could be heard from them as they released all of that energy that had been built from the throw. Vedi stared up at her with a smile, and she grimaced down at him through the pain. She wondered if he was even injured from any of her attacks, but she had to keep trying.

"Oh?" Vedi held up a finger and pressed the side of his ear. "Hey, kiddo, hang on one second. Important calls." Penny descended from the ceiling and took a moment to recover on the stage while he did this. "Yeah, she's here. I got it." Vedi began pacing back and forth along the aisle of destroyed seating. "Uh-huh. Yeah. You got him? Really now?" Vedi cast an amused look at Penny. "I'll bring her too, and we should be good to go—no funny business. The big man wants her alive. That goes for her partner too."

*Chris?* Penny questioned mentally. *Chris?? What's happening?*

"I'm wrapping up here. I'll get back to you when I can." Vedi finished his conversation with a heavy sigh. "Sorry, work calls are annoying when you're with family."

"What did you do to Chris...?" Penny asked assertively. She raised her shield again now that her body had healed most of her injuries. "Where is he?"

"I'd answer, but I don't have time to play with you anymore," Vedi said as he calmly walked toward her.

"Where?!" Penny exploded. She sent out a wave of pure death magic. Vedi countered with his own, and for a moment, the air was filled with bright purple and grey colors. When the magic finally settled, she immediately noticed that he was not where she left him. He had moved so fast that when she finally got a beat on him to her right, she had no time to react. Vedi's whole fist impacted her stomach hard in a magic enhanced punch, sending her flying back against the stage wall. Then he punched her multiple times in the face, caught her by the collar, and threw her against the stage floor. Penny laid there in pain, her wings twitching from the serve injuries she had sustained.

Penny rolled onto her back and stared up at the stage lights, only for them to be obscured by Vedi. He knelt down beside her and shook his head. "Gotta take you with me now, kid. No hard feelings, alright, but this rebellious phase has to stop."

"You'll have to kill me," Penny said. She caught his hand just before he could grab onto her, but he merely smacked it away.

"I already didn't want to kill your sister. I screwed up. Come quietly." Vedi picked up Penny and threw him over his shoulder, being careful not to hurt her further as a result.

Vedi jumped down from the stage calmly and made his way toward the exit. When they were just about there, Penny turned her head to see if Akela was where she left her, only to find that she had gone missing. When Vedi pulled the door to exit, he paused. A metallic sound like a sword being picked up could be heard behind them, and Akela was at the source. She had picked up Penny's short sword and moved up behind Vedi to try to stab him. She backed up a few times as he turned and approached her but kept the sword raised.

"Kid, I just told you to find her. I'm not hurting you. You look eight or something." He said, calmly knocking the sword away with the back of his hand. "Go back to your parents." Akela's eyes cut toward Penny as he said this. "Oh. You see her as a mother or something?"

"Go hide," Penny told her weakly.

"Yeah, you heard her. Run along." Vedi coaxed. "Go on. Get."

*Boom!* A loud impact could be heard on the other side of the main doors. Someone had entered the lobby and was rapidly heading for the second floor. Then another crash sounded above them. Vedi looked up, summoning his sword as he did. He raised it right as Ian appeared from the second floor and collided his blade with Vedi's. Ian landed a short distance away when he was pushed off and readied himself again for another assault.

"You're late again..." Penny said through the pain in her chest. "Watch out for Akela."

"Akela," Ian began. He gestured for her to move out of the way with his head, preferably into the lobby. Akela frowned and continued to focus on Penny.

"There you are, Ian. Good timing. You just saved me another trip." Vedi tossed Penny aside and let her land on all fours. "Will you be more reasonable? I doubt it since you already tried swinging at me, but hey, hands slip sometimes."

"I'm not here to play with you," Ian said with angry eyes hidden just under his hood. "And don't touch my sister."

Ian sent out a wave of pure Death magic, which traveled vertically along the ground. Vedi blocked using both of his and fired back with a horizontal one instead. Ian advanced on him, blocking and firing spells until he was in melee range. Once he had reached a viable distance, Ian lunged forward with a stabbing attack. Vedi side-stepped this attempt and rotated his body to bring his sword into a position to strike again. Ian used his shoulder to knock him off balance, but Vedi could still get a firm kick in and launch Ian toward the first row.

"Set the fight up on your terms." Vedi reminisced as he approached Ian. "What was that lesson three? I taught you better than to make it obvious."

Penny tried watching the fight but could not bring herself to get up any more than she already had. Akela was with her now and checking for injuries while also urging her to get up. Penny could not stand, so instead, Akela helped her hide behind one of the many seats and rubbed her back. Akela was smart to figure out that Penny was having trouble breathing after being winded. Once Penny was ready to move, she stood up and moved with Akela toward the exit.

"You go hide; I have to help," Penny explained.

"No. You go, or I stay." Akela said assertively with the meanest face Penny had ever seen her make in the time they knew each other.

Penny turned back to see Ian trading spells with Vedi again. He was backing up over and over like he was going to be overwhelmed. Penny tried readying her own magic, but Akela caught her hand and dragged her back toward the door. "Stop backing up. You keep giving me ground that you can't get back." Vedi suggested over the fighting. Ian tried moving toward Vedi, but he found himself quickly over-whelmed with decisive strikes. Not only did they stagger him and clearly hurt more than the average sword strike, but they broke his armor apart. Most of his once shiny armor had crumbled off and fallen to the floor in metallic chips. When he tried to retreat, Vedi took the advantage, closed the gap completely, and sent Ian into the wall.

"Ian!" Penny cried out. She was done. Taking her sword from Akela and readying her shield, she moved in to battle with Vedi once more. "Sorry, Akela. Stay back!" Vedi turned toward Penny now that she was back on her feet and ready to fight, but she would never get the chance.

Ian stood up quickly and extended his hand toward Vedi. What

Penny was expecting to be another Death spell was instead an angry wall of flame. Penny watched in shock as Ian fired again and again with increasing ferocity. Even Vedi was backing off from the fire. The fire soon turned to electricity and forced Vedi to change to blocking the surges of Storm magic. Ian paused, took one good look at his hands, nodded to himself, and kept going. *Ian is a Balance user?* Penny wondered to herself. Vedi moved forward. He clearly wanted to end this quickly before Ian pulled out any more tricks. They were only basic attacks, but Ian, not knowing how to implement them and fighting like he was still using Death magic, was throwing Vedi off.

Ian blocked Vedi's first sword attack with his broadsword and then brought it around. As he swung, an arc of Ice came with the attack. Vedi slashed downwards, cutting the frozen wave in half, but another one came as soon as he had. Then Ian moved forward and slashed once, spun around, and moved into a punch. When his fist had gained enough momentum, it caught fire for a moment. The moment it touched Vedi's face, an explosion rippled across the room in a bright shockwave of red, black, and grey. Penny grabbed Akela and held her under herself. When the smoke cleared and Penny could see again, she found Vedi on the ground, barely able to move with Ian unconscious, not far from him.

"That was pretty!" Akela cheered joyfully. "Is the bad man dead?"

"Akela..." Penny said. This girl was going to pick up some bad habits from all of this.

Penny paused and turned her head toward the exit. Someone else was coming from outside. The doors opened once again opened, but this time revealed Autumn. Her curly hair and red eyes immediately set Penny at ease. Autumn wasted no time to rush over and cast a healing spell on Penny, instantly healing all of her injuries. Autumn shifted her eyes up, noted the scorches and various clear signs of magic marking the area around the stage.

"Was someone else here?" she questioned. Autumn cautiously made her way forward toward the stage. "I don't understand-" When

Autumn turned back to look at Penny, she almost went completely pale. Penny was staring directly at Ian with a stunned expression. Autumn slowly looked over Ian and noted that he showed signs of mana exhaustion. "It was Ian-?"

"It was him." She answered back. Penny could hear Vedi starting to come back to his senses again. She stood to do something about it, but Autumn effortlessly fired an Imagination spell, which created a spider web around Vedi. "Autumn, about Chris-" Penny was quick to go back to what was more important to her at this moment. "Do you know if he's okay?"

# MENTAL INSTABILITY

Chris shook his head slowly, his head pounding, and his eyes heavy. He could see his feet just below himself, but they felt far and distant. He could not focus his vision, nor could he remember what had happened. He swayed his head over to the left and then back to the right, his brain seemingly rattling around every time he moved. His senses were slowly returning to him. The room was cold, and he could hear a faint humming sound. He tried to move his hands to touch his face but instead found that his hands would not move. Some force was keeping them behind his back, binding them tightly together.

His heart was racing, and no matter how hard he tried, he couldn't focus enough to communicate with Penny mentally. *Did they take my watch?* He asked himself. Chris was just barely able to reach a hand up from his lower back to touch the arm that normally had his watch on it - gone. *Calm down. Calm down. Remember what happened.* He thought, hoping to reason with himself and not panic. *You called Emily. Someone knows where you are. Just do what she taught you.*

"Are you awake?" a shaky voice said to his left. It sounded like

Megan, but he wasn't sure since he was still coming to his senses. He turned to look and could only make out her black cloak and shoes. He shook his head to snap himself out of this groggy state. "Slowly, Chris. You just woke up from being shot multiple times with tranquilizer rounds. I know you're feeling confused, but I need you here, okay? I can't do anything without you."

"I can't really see much..." Chris said.

"You just need to calm down." Megan reminded him. She was about to say something else, but he caught her off.

"-Your hand! Is your hand okay? Are you okay?" He asked through heavy breaths.

"They let me re-attach it with a spell, yeah. So, aside from worrying about our current situation, I would say I'm doing pretty okay."

"Meg, I'm so sorry, I feel like-"

"Chris, don't you dare start. There is no way that this was your fault." Megan rolled her eyes a little and sat back. "We got ambushed. They were probably moving in to attack New Hope like Grandham. If you blame yourself, I will kick you."

"Well, what do we do?" He asked.

"I don't know right now. Calm down." Megan repeated once more. "Panicking is going to make this so much worse."

"Let me try-" Chris began pulling against the thick handcuffs behind the chair. They retaliated by shocking him violently until he brought them back together like they were. He sucked in air through his teeth and shook harshly as the electricity traveled through his body.

"I already tried that twice." Megan looked up as if she was scanning the ceiling of this small room. "I wish you'd slow down and let me update you."

"Go ahead." He surrendered.

Megan lowered her head to look at the floor and spoke slowly so he would register every word. "We were captured, and I believe we are currently on the Imperial capital ship that landed on the planet at the start of the invasion. We are also probably near the mines where they are stripping the planet. Eslena captured us, but I heard some of the guards outside our cell, talking about how Vedi was captured by Penny, Ian, and Autumn."

"Really? They got him??" Chris asked with some enthusiasm. He honestly felt that Vedi deserved a bit more than capture for what he did to Tori, but he would be tried in a court and at least rot.

"Yes, but we're still here, so they'll probably interrogate him. I don't think he will crack since he's an Imperial knight, so we should try to escape on our own." She gestured with her head at the ceiling, where a small vent was embedded. It was clear that it had been tampered with in some manner. When Chris looked at Megan, she discreetly pulled her wrists apart to show that they could no longer shock her and then placed them back together to feign helplessness. "I wore them out until they couldn't hurt me anymore. I do not recommend it though, since you can't reduce your body's response to pain like I can. It still hurt tremendously."

"So, you're free?"

"Yes."

"Then, what should I do?" Chris asked with a worried face. "You wouldn't leave me, right?"

Megan's jaw dropped a little, and at first, it seemed as if she would not reply. Eventually, she just came out with, "I'm going to pretend you didn't just say that to me."

"Yeah, but you were upset just before we were captured."

"I would never leave you though," Megan said, correcting this absurd theory. "If I didn't care, I wouldn't have tried to save you there or back when we were helping Murphy. Now be quiet. Someone is coming."

"But-" Chris tried.

There was talking outside. Someone was indeed coming. Chris began planning how to attack them, but Megan had a better idea. She hung her head low, slouched forward, and put on an act to feign weakness. Chris followed suit, remembering what they were taught about seeming like a victim. Anything they were offered should be denied unless it was food, they would avoid talking about the Alliance, and they needed to rely on each other. It was easier to learn about something like this instead of actually doing it, but at least he was not alone.

The cell door slid open and revealed Eslena clad in a black robe. At her side was a double-bladed weapon, or what Chris presumed to be one as it was currently retracted so that just the hilt was visible. She made her way down the small flight of steps that led into the cell and then waved her hand to tell the soldiers outside to shut it. For a moment, Eslena studied the two of them - likely plotting her next move. She paced back and forth with her arms behind her back, only stopping when she was sure of a plan of action.

"Are you comfortable?" She asked with a smile that seemed almost sincere for a moment. Neither of them said anything, but Chris did look to see if Megan was okay. "Are you? Thirsty, maybe?"

"You won't get anything from me," Megan said in such a way that she sounded almost pitiful. She really was a good actor when she needed to be. "You can take that water and choke on it. Thanks."

"Here I am, being as kind as I can despite recent events, and you choose to say that?" Eslena laughed at this under her breath. "I can start with you then? Oh, what about you, though, Spellcrafter?" Chris aggressively shook his head. He tried communicating with Penny, but he couldn't seem to. Was she too far away? Unless they were in space, there was no way that the distance between them was too great. He threw this concern aside. If he calmed down enough, he could probably manage it.

"Leave him alone," Megan said through gritted teeth. "You can interrogate us both and get nothing. There is nothing we would know."

"Interrogate? No, no, no." Eslena turned away and rolled her eyes. Megan had mere moments to regret these words. Their captor turned back swiftly and extended her glowing yellow hand. "I have a far better idea. This might hurt initially, but you can lessen the pain by giving in."

An unnatural force could be heard humming through the air that permeated throughout the cell. Chris watched in horror as Megan shook and writhed like she was in pain. Her head shook repeatedly, and her eyes changed to the same shade of yellow as Eslena's hand. After grinding her own teeth together and breathing heavily, she shut her eyes. It seemed like she had gone into a state of meditation, and when she reopened her eyes, her eyes were blue again.

Megan fought hard to spit out her next words: "I'm not afraid of your spells, Renees."

"It would seem so." Eslena brought her hand closer to Megan's face and forced her eyes to once again change color. "If I must break your mind, I will. A broken mind can be far more malleable than a sane one."

Megan cried out in pain and arched her back hard, but still kept her arms planted firmly behind herself. She was digging her nails into her palms to the point where they bled and sucked air in and out her teeth. Megan tried what she did before but was interrupted by something that Eslena had done. She began saying the word 'no' over and over like she was in a nightmare. Tears streamed down her face and mixed with sweat, but she kept fighting until Eslena gave up. When Eslena finally replaced her hand at her side and stopped casting the spell, Megan began to weep.

"You repressed those memories so deeply that when I finally ripped them free, your mind nearly fragmented." Eslena thought about what she had seen, but all the while, Chris was wondering what she had seen that upset her so much. "I'll return to you in a moment."

"Meg?" Chris asked. He wanted to help her, but it was about to be his turn. "Hey, Meg? Talk to me here." She was still freaking out. "What the hell did you do to her?!"

"The same thing I'm going to do to you," Eslena said menacingly.

Chris turned his head just in time to see Eslena performing the same action on him. Everything went yellow, and the world around him vanished. It seemed as if his feet had left the ground, and suddenly his arms were free. His feet sank into the dense, cold snow of a frozen forest. His hands came next and caught him just before his face was buried into the mounds of snow. Chris raised his head and tried to ignore the constant throbbing. Snowflakes fell all around. In every direction, there was snow. He had seen this before - in a nightmare just before everything that happened with Tori.

He carefully pulled his shaking legs from the snow that was so cold that it burned to touch. He knew that this was not real. Instead of fighting it, he made his way forward into the constant nothingness. The same bat from the nightmare was here again, but this time it did not die. Instead, the small creature flew circles in his cone of vision, almost as if it wanted him to follow. Having no other options, he decided to trail it. He was freezing, but if this was not real, he had no way to really die - as far as he knew.

Just like before, the little bat flew behind a tree and went missing. When Chris made his way to the tree in question and rounded it, he did not find the bat, but instead a person. She had thin, black hair in a ponytail; brown eyes which were unmoving; and a young face. Though she was covered in a thick sheet of snow, almost as if being buried, he could still make out a purple blazer, black skirt, and what looked to be black shoes. He fell to his knees beside her and gently touched her hand - freezing cold. Gone.

*I'm really sorry, Tori. It was my fault,* he thought to himself. He released her hand and stood up. The snow had stopped, and in its place, the world around him became rather hot. It was as if flames had engulfed his body. Embers rained from the dark blue sky, but the snow in front of him remained. He turned around to see the way that he had come was replaced with a cityscape. Buildings were lit ablaze, and bodies littered the streets. He was back on Terminus. Is this the invasion? Chris wondered as he turned around to see if Victoria had moved. She was indeed right where he left her. The snow had melted off and was replaced with scars and bruises.

He could see his past self taking cover as Autumn combated Vedi. All went as it had before, except he stood up and turned back toward Chris. His former self drew his sword up from the ground and charged. Though he wanted to believe that this was all fiction and none of these memories could hurt him, he still summoned his own sword and blocked. The two exchanged neutral blows back and forth, but Chris was better than his former self. He quickly disarmed the far less experienced version of himself and held the blade to his neck.

Autumn turned in a fraction of a second, defeating Vedi in one quick blast. Then she raised her hand into the air and summoned a black hole which swallowed Chris's past self whole. Once she was sure that he had been defeated, she lowered her hand and addressed Chris directly: "Do not let her invade your mind again. You will not be able to resist someone this powerful."

Chris wanted to ask her what she meant and if it was really Autumn who he was addressing, but he would not have a chance. Instead, the world around him disintegrated into a bright red flash. When it was gone, he reopened his eyes to find himself face to face with Eslena. She looked more irritated than before, like she had just witnessed something. Retracting her hand and sucking her teeth, she turned and left the room without another word.

"What?" He inquired.

Chris had seen this flash only once before: when Eslena attacked his mind for insulting her. Was Autumn connected to that as well? If so, perhaps she was closer than he thought. It was either that or she had cast a spell on him sometime before this. Either way, it was deeply concerning because now that Eslena knew about it, she would try to break it and Megan had no such protection. They needed to escape before the worst-case scenario occurred, because as far as they knew, they were on their own.

## JUDGE AND EXECUTIONER

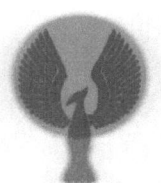

Penny flew across the city block until she found the location that Emily specified. She dove down toward the mass of Alliance soldiers who were restraining the affected and securing the area. She touched down on the street and made her way toward Emily. She could see the damage from the ambush and the handful of Eslena's mind-controlled that Chris and Megan defeated. Emily was crouched down in the middle of the street like she was examining something. Penny came closer and looked over Emily's shoulder to see two identical watches: one black and the other green and white.

"Oh no," Penny said to herself as her heart dropped into the pit of her stomach. Emily did not respond. "Em, I'm so sorry. I should have sensed it and been here."

"Eslena knew what she was doing," Emily said. She closed her hand tightly around the watches, buried them into her long white cloak, and stood up. "She tried to capture all four of you at once, but she came personally for my brother and Megan."

"Do you have any idea what she wants with them?" Penny tried.

She watched as Emily sprang to her feet and turned back in the direction of the police precinct, "No, but she has him now."

"Then we'll track them. I'm pretty sure they'd both be with Esle-na." Penny followed her, but Emily was walking much faster; her stress and anger were evident. "Emily, where are you going?"

"To have a talk with Vedi." Emily summoned her sword and began walking faster.

Penny flew with her wings until she had landed just in front of Emily. "Stop." Penny placed a hand on either of her shoulders and held her back. "What good is that going to do? I know Vedi. He won't talk even if you threaten to kill him."

"He hasn't met me." Emily tried pushing Penny back, but she caught her hands and squeezed.

"Emily, who would know him better? You or-" Penny was hoping to reason with her, but Emily was already beyond the point of talking.

"You can move, or I can *make* you." Emily's eyes homed in on Penny's, and her voice audibly shook. Only one thing was present in her brown eyes: hate. Penny knew that if she kept pushing Emily, she might lash out. Now was not the time. She stood aside and instead opted to follow her to the precinct and act as a mediator.

Emily wasted no time in getting to the police precinct. She threw the doors open and continued her angry stride to the interrogation rooms. Some of the Alliance soldiers and police officers tried reasoning with her. One reminded her that the General wanted her to stay out of this because she was emotional, but she just threw him aside with a single hand and kept going. Penny helped him up quickly and then continued to chase after Emily. Even Morgan, who would never stand for what Emily was about to do, jumped out of the way and avoided confrontation.

Emily entered the interrogation rooms, killed the cameras in Vedi's room, and then shoved the Wizard that was guarding him aside. He raised his hands and let her go. Penny followed closely and caught the door just before Emily could slam it behind herself. Vedi sat up in his seat and smiled the moment he saw her face. Penny knew that she had mere seconds to prevent Emily from committing a war crime, but she could not prevent her next actions easily.

"Oh, hello, Hand," Vedi said, mockingly using Emily's title. "Are you the next Wizard who is going to try to get me to talk?" He sat back and placed a hand on the table, his smile growing exponentially. "If you plan to appeal to my empathetic emotions, I can guarantee you that those died a long time ago."

"I'm not just the Headmaster's Hand or a Wizard, though, am I?" Emily asked as she transformed her sword into a hatchet. Penny tried reaching for her weapon, but Emily was much faster. She brought it down with so much force that the thick table cracked, and Vedi's left hand went flying away. His screams slowly turned into hysterical laughter as he sucked in air through his teeth. He took one good look at his severed hand and then met Emily's eyes once more with no fear. "I'm his sister," she finished assertively.

"Well," he said as he cupped his wrist with his remaining hand. "You have my attention! That's how you start a show."

"I will heal you - only because it will allow me to get the answers I need. If you die before I can get them, that could be problematic." Emily hissed. She performed the most basic healing spell to stop the bleeding but did not reattach the hand. Penny tried to pick it up, but Emily cast a spell to encase the separated limb in a cocoon of vines. "Now, I'll ask you nicely now that I 'have your attention'" Emily leaned in and grabbed him by his hair harshly. "Where is my brother?"

"If only we knew the answer to the mystery!" Vedi said with a mighty laugh. "Is this the part where you hit me?"

"This is the part where I decide to take you to the tallest building in New Hope and drop you off of it headfirst," Emily said. She knocked his chair back by pushing him and then picked him up by the throat. "Where is my brother?"

"Emily, I think that's enough," Penny advised from the sidelines. Emily did not seem to be listening to her at all. Emily raised her weapon once more, transforming it into a knife as she did. Penny was prepared for her this time. Penny moved to Emily's left as fast as she could and grabbed onto the arm that held her weapon. She then pushed back until Emily was forced to focus on her.

"Move," Emily demanded.

"Let me try talking to him. You need to cool off. Now." Penny held her ground but was fully prepared for a scenario where she would have to fight her. "I've known him my whole life. I need you to stop."

"She has my brother. We don't have time for you to be soft!" Emily released Vedi and began casting a spell to restrain Penny. Vines flew out from her hand to latch onto her, but Penny countered by extending her hand. A ghostly purple barrier flew out around her body and shielded her. When the spell was defeated, her soul barrier vanished.

"Five minutes," Penny begged her. "You need to let me try."

"If in five minutes you can't get their location, I'll throw you in a cell and do what I need to." Emily hissed. She turned wordlessly and slammed the interrogation room door shut. She would inevitably be watching. Penny needed to work fast.

"Are you alright?" She asked him. Penny took a moment to note his missing hand and the stub where it used to be.

"You know I'm tougher than that, my dear," Vedi said with an eye roll.

"I know."

Penny made her way around the table and stood Vedi's chair back upright. Then she helped him sit down and sat across from him. For a moment, she wondered how to get him to talk. She really didn't want to hurt him. He was already going insane from the Shadow Plague, and Emily had gone too far. Vedi was still like family to her even after what happened with Victoria. If he was still wholly sane and himself, that never would have happened.

She finally decided where to start, "Do you remember that one night when I got so mad at Tori that we got into a fight, and you had to break it up?" Penny sat up in her chair. "It was like two in the morning, and you had to come all the way to the manor to break it up because the house servants couldn't?"

"Your father was furious that you both had scratches on each other and ruined your room," Vedi said, his smile dropped a little. "I remember. What does that have to do with anything?"

"She annoyed me so much back then." Penny brought her hands together on the table and stared at them. "I couldn't stand her sometimes, but it still killed me on the inside when she was finally gone." Vedi frowned a little as Penny continued. "I left the Empire because I trusted my sister when she said that Dad had gone too far. I know he just wanted to keep his promise to mom and protect us, but in doing all of this, he's made people fear Sorcerers and the Empire even more."

"He's still your father." Vedi reminded her. She had returned him to his senses - at least temporarily. This was good enough for now. "He just wanted to create a better life for his daughters since nothing else proved to be the solution. As for your sister...I really am sorry."

"Vedi, you're sick." Penny consoled him as best as she could. "I understand. When Mom was infected, you were almost killed by her too. You're just going through the same things she was." Penny stared into his purple eyes, which almost seemed to give off a dark glow, and then continued. "When Tori died, I was lost. I felt like...maybe I had made the wrong decision, and I'd be all alone."

Vedi nodded once, "So why didn't you return?"

"I had my partner," Penny said in a single breath. "And he stayed by my side the entire time until he was sure I was okay. He was there when I needed him." She sat forward and gave him a determined look. "But now he needs me, and I don't know where he is or even where to start looking. You were here helping Eslena harvest materials to aid the Empire. You must know where she might be." Vedi's lips pressed together like he was thinking. "Please. You're the only person I think I can turn to. If something happens to him, it'll be like losing my sister all over again."

"I understand he is your partner but is it really that serious?" Vedi asked with a raise of his eyebrows. "He's just a boy. Granted, he reminds me of myself...before everything 'happened' but a boy, nonetheless. You're more important. You're a Dreadful."

*He still doesn't understand me*, she thought to herself with a sullen expression. She continued to listen to him talk on and on, and all she could think was how she felt responsible. "I really don't think you understand."

"Then help me understand," Vedi said. He was much more severe than he had ever been before.

"I just," Penny smiled a little and raised her head to look at him confidently. "I feel like I look at him the same way Dad said he looked at Mom before she passed." She finally decided to just say the first thing that came to mind. "I love him. I just don't think I'm ready to admit it to him yet because the moment I do, I'm afraid he'll go like mom did."

Vedi's mouth dropped and formed a small 'o' shape. He was speechless, and she was confident that he'd never had this facial expression before. Penny felt that she had become far lighter now that she had admitted the truth. It was no longer something that she had to bottle up or hide; even if she never told him, it was off her chest. Vedi took what felt like forever to process her words, and she was sure that the five minutes Emily allotted her had passed, but nothing happened.

"Because of my honor as a knight, I can't tell you anything related to our operations on Sohrann. It would go against everything I stand for by serving your father." He began. Vedi took a moment to debate something, possibly how to tell her without bluntly stating it. "But if Eslena is cautious, she is most likely is holding them on the Stalwart. A flagship is far more secure than anywhere else here."

"Where is it?" Penny pressed on. She had gotten up from her seat without even realizing it. "Is it still on Sohrann?"

"It hasn't taken off. As far as I know, it is still down in the desert near Conyers city. It was damaged after the battle in orbit, but by now, it has probably made repairs. You don't have long. There is an outpost there. Eslena won't let you just waltz in, though."

"You let me worry about that," Penny said with a bright smile.

"You've changed," Vedi said with a straight face.

"I know."

"I think your Chaos would be proud if he knew."

Penny shook her head. That was wishful thinking. She made her way over to Vedi's severed hand on the ground and picked it up. Emily would certainly not heal it for him, so she would just do it herself. After taking a moment to check and see if there were any plants that she could drain in the room, she placed his hand against his arm. Then she shut her eyes and focused inward. A very brief and sharp pain affected her heart and chest, but it subsided once she ended the spell.

Vedi's hand had reattached to his arm and even seemed brand new. The only evidence that remained from his injury was the dried blood along his wrist. How much time had she just taken from her own life to do that? A few days? Maybe a month? It was worth it. Vedi was stunned at this action, so she left him to think it over, bidding him a silent farewell as she did. However, just before opening the door to leave, she realized that there was one more thing she wanted to say.

"I'll find a way to fix this." She said sincerely. "All of it."

"He tried too, you know? He gave up because the two of you were conceived." Vedi said to her. She said nothing in response.

Penny shut the door behind herself and waved off the Wizard who was meant to guard Vedi. He still looked both confused and terrified but took up his post once again. She made her way back out into the police station main hall and began trying to contact Chris mentally. She could sense him and tell that he was still alive, but she could not hear anything. If he was in trouble, she should have been able to hear something. There was sometimes pain like headaches, but other than that minor detail, their link was useless. Penny wondered if Eslena had something to do with it, but partner links were immune to outside manipulation as far as she knew.

# GUARDIAN

C hris watched as Megan stood on her chair and carefully moved the vent cover up and into the metallic shaft. She lifted herself up, looked both ways, and shrugged. They would not both be able to fit, but if one of them could get free, that may be enough. The main concern now was the Imperial ship taking off and taking them with it. After fixing the vent cover, Megan hopped down and focused on Chris's restraints. She cast multiple spells on them but could not seem to apply one good enough to avoid hurting him.

"Hold still." She demanded with a yank on his wrist. She would occasionally tap on his cuffs like she was counting the minutes. "These things can kill you if you keep squirming."

"I'm trying, Meg. I can't make myself immune to the voltage like you can." Chris said through pained breaths. "Can't you just cut the-"

"We're out of time again." Megan decided. She returned to her chair, placed her hands behind her back, and continued tapping.

Minutes passed, and with every minute, Megan gave a little tap. She lowered her head again, stopped tapping, and waited. Chris did the same, but he stayed like that for what felt like an eternity. Had Megan been off this time around? She wasn't. The doors opened just as they had time and time again, and Eslena entered with the same manipulative smile as always. Chris lifted his head to look at her, but she had no interest in dealing with him at this time. Instead, she used her spell on Megan once again.

The same scene happened yet again, with Megan struggling to resist and Eslena trying to force her way into her subconscious mind. This time had lasted far longer than before, and Megan's breathing had become shallow. If she had just freed him sooner or if he could bear the pain, he would attack Eslena. Megan would be fine, of course, but for how much longer? If it was anything like what he had been through, she'd be suffering. Chris tried to force out a spell, but the cuffs shocked him so fast that it was like they had detected a sudden change. There was nothing he could do.

Eslena lowered her hand and then rotated her wrist like she was relaxing it. All the while, Megan just stared up at her without any movements whatsoever. Her face was blocked by her hair, but Chris could tell that something was noticeably wrong. "Meg? Are you alright?"

Nothing.

"Meg?" He repeated. No response. Not even an indication that she had heard him. *Penn, she did something to Meg.* He thought. She probably could not hear him, but he had to try. "Meg, you're freaking me out..."

Eslena snapped her fingers and spoke sharply, "Raise your hands for me."

Megan removed both of her hands and raised them high into the air for Eslena; the dark magician smiled and waved her hand. Megan lowered them back down and placed them in her lap. It was clear to him now that Eslena was far smarter than them both. She knew that Megan had freed herself, but how did she get Megan to follow the order to raise her arms? She was a Life Wizard, so she should have been immune to this sort of manipulation...at least, that was what he thought.

"You see, I knew she was trying to escape for a while. Her

mind read like an open book." Eslena slowly made her way over to Chris and ran her hand down the back of the chair. "She's a clever girl."

"What did you do to her...?" Chris was pleading with her now, and he didn't even know it.

"Megan, sweetie? Look at your little friend." Eslena commanded. Is she making fun of me? He wondered.

As ordered, Megan turned her head to look at Chris. Her head was perfectly straight, and her eyes were the usual blue, but something was very wrong with this image. She did not blink, nor did she take more than the occasional controlled breath. Eslena made her way over to Megan and lifted her chin to show Chris. Megan really was gone. He was alone with this lunatic now and with no way out. Chris wanted to call her again, he really did, but he knew it would do no good.

"He looks so scared and worried for you, doesn't he?" Megan nodded at her question. "Do you think he's worried for himself or you more?"

"Both," Megan answered in a very dull tone.

"Good girl." Eslena released her face and returned to Chris.

*Penn, if you can hear me, please.* He thought. There was still no response. How had so much gone so wrong so fast? Eslena would answer his pleas for attention instead of his partner. She raised her hand, cast the blinding yellow spell, and took him into the Imagination Realm once more. He fought as hard as he could to keep her out, but he was dragged in regardless - into his own mind where he wasn't safe at all. Which memory would it be this time? He almost dreaded the answer.

A loud bell could be heard before the scene around him. He fell onto his hands and nearly cut himself on the jagged wood underneath himself. The world around him was once again burning, but this time it was not the city of Terminus, but the clocktower - the clocktower where he had faced Hunter with Penny. The fires raged and spread but posed no threat to him in memory. He stood after a moment of hesitation and imagined both of his swords so they would appear in his hands.

What he had expected was Eslena again as it had been many times or corrupted memory. He would have gladly taken either of those options, but instead of either of these, it was someone else. A young woman with short red hair, a purple hair clip, and blue eyes stood in front of the shattered face of the clock. She wore a purple and black cape, a black tunic, and black boots. The girl placed a hand on her hip and smiled excitedly.

"I'm glad you could make it to my little party!" She exclaimed. "Miss Eslena is gonna be so happy when this is all over."

"Wait-" Chris hesitated for a moment but eventually built up the courage to say the name in his head. "Gatchi?"

She smiled and shrugged. "Now, did you really think that I'd turn and run after Tori won that fight?" Gatchi went on as she paced in place. "Now that's just rude. You can't just go assuming that you changed someone. That's so unappealing."

"What did you guys do to Meg?!" Chris asked in a fit of rage. He prepared a spell to attack her, but Gatchi did not flinch.

"I don't know what you mean," Gatchi stopped her endless pacing and turned away. "She's joined our big happy family. Eslena will take good care of her, and she'll take care of you too!"

"And Penny?!" He questioned quickly. He had to just hope that she was going to give more answers than Eslena. If this really was Gatchi and not a figment of his imagination, she would undoubtedly talk. "I can't hear her anymore."

"Oh, Tori's little sis?" Gatchi asked with a smile. "It's a shame, really. I kind of wanted to apologize to her for what happened between us."

"What do you mean...?" He asked slowly. He could feel his legs going weak.

"Don't worry. Penny was really important to Tori, and she was my friend. I made sure it was over quickly!" Gatchi said this in such a way that it made him want to vomit. Chris finally fell to his knees. *Is that why I can't reach her?*

"You-?" He choked on his own words. Was that even possible? Why was all of this happening?

"If it helps, I'm sorry, but she made me do it!" Gatchi protested with a depressed expression.

The bell chimed once again. The large bell kept ringing and getting louder until it finally exploded in a brilliant show of red. Autumn landed next to Chris and lowered herself to his level. She had only one thing to say: stand. When Chris just ignored her command and shook his head, she walked ahead of him and shielded him from Gatchi's view. She extended her hand and stood in a battle stance with no weapon in sight.

"Oh? You're going to fight me?" She questioned curiously. "I'm not as strong as the Headmaster's apprentice, you know?" Gatchi was talking as if this being unfair was wrong somehow.

"You act as if I care," Autumn replied with apparent irritation. "Where is your master? I warned her to remain out of this stable mind."

"I'm glad you asked! I'll let her answer for you!" Gatchi smiled and took a quick step back.

"I know how to break your spell now," Eslena informed her in a disembodied voice.

Eslena leaped out from the shadows as if she was one with them. She tried swinging high, but Autumn blocked it by snapping her fingers and creating a barrier behind herself. Autumn turned, focusing on her new target. Eslena retreated as Autumn forced ice spikes to jump out from the ground. She backflipped away from the danger and raised her double-bladed sword to Autumn.

"My warding spell can be used for more than just defending," Autumn warned her with a hateful glare. "Leave, or I'll be forced to take your life. I know you understand the rules of this realm. Your death would be final."

"Amazing! I didn't know a warding spell could attack at all! I wish you would teach me."

Eslena spun her sword around to block a fire spell and then tried making her way toward Autumn. Chris watched as Autumn used seemingly every single element of magic on Eslena. Death, Life, Imagination, Ice, Storm, and even Fire. Eslena was getting close now, but this was possibly what Autumn wanted. Just as Eslena was about to deliver what could have been a killing blow, she raised her hand and created a beautiful galaxy with a bright star in the center. Autumn slammed this galaxy down over Eslena and trapped her in the middle of the milky way-shaped structure.

"I had no idea you could use such powerful spells either. Oh well." Eslena struggled for just a moment before surrendering, but Autumn was not taking prisoners. She had given every possible warning.

"I'm just more powerful than you. Now take your curiosity for knowledge to the depths of hell. They're calling for you."

Autumn closed her hand and lowered it toward Eslena. Suddenly, the bright 'star' in the center of the galaxy expanded and ate everything around it: planets, stars, and even asteroids. Eventually, it brought Eslena into its event horizon and swallowed her up too. Nothing could escape. Not light, not matter, and not Eslena. This event counted until nothing was left of Eslena at all, and then when all had been consumed, the black hole died out into nothingness.

"Just like that...?" Chris asked her in disbelief. There was nothing of Eslena to even signify that she had ever existed.

"Autumn created me to protect you, and that is what I intend to do." She answered back with a bored expression. "She failed to breach your mind five times. I don't know what she expected."

"Created?" Chris questioned.

"You can take that up with Autumn when this is all over. I need to finish the last one off." The spell that looked like Autumn turned away from him to face Gatchi.

"You killed her just like that?" Gatchi babbled as she backed away. "I didn't think anyone could hurt Miss Eslena..."

"You're joining her." Autumn raised her hand and prepared another spell, but Chris stood in her way.

"Wait, wait! I know Gatchi. I can talk to her!" He said this, but it was strange to be defending her again. "She listened to me last time."

"I'll leave! I promise!" Gatchi begged nervously. She looked like a puppy who had realized that she had picked on a larger dog.

"Not another word." Autumn hissed at Gatchi.

"I just don't want you to hurt her if she hasn't even attacked me," Chris argued further.

Autumn turned her head to look at him with an annoyed expression. "This is not up for debate! She invaded your mind." She paused.

Chris was flung far away from Autumn by the force of a wind spell. When he landed and scrambled to his feet, he was met with a horrifying sight. Gatchi was standing directly in front of Autumn with a sword, which she had plunged directly through Autumn. She smiled calmly and sadistically as she twisted the blade over and over as if to do as much damage as possible. Autumn did not bleed, but she rapidly became fainter and fainter like a ghost leaving the corporeal world.

"I found a way around your mundane spell." Eslena's voice emitted from Gatchi's body in such a way that sent chills across Chris's skin. "Amazing how easily you were fooled by a simple change of appearance and voice." Autumn reached out like she would try one last-ditch effort to defeat Eslena but instead faded away into the air. "My student was never here, but if she was, I'm sure she would find that amusing."

"You killed her..." Chris said through nervous breaths.

"Only her spell. I haven't gotten around to her just yet and likely never will." Eslena looked at him disapprovingly. "Do you have nothing else you wish to try? Running? Fighting?"

"Would there be any point?" Chris asked her earnestly with what was probably a dead expression.

"It may prove amusing, but no." Eslena turned her back to him like she was tempting him to try something. "If it makes you feel better to try your luck-"

Chris smiled to himself. His fear was still there as well as the feeling of helplessness, but something new was there too. He took up both of his weapons and took a long, shaky breath. When he was sure that he'd done enough preparation, Chris charged and performed two quick air swipes. Eslena stopped them just inches from her neck with her magic and raised him helplessly into the air.

"Yes, yes, good. Try again." She tossed him into the ceiling once and then threw him to the ground just behind herself. "Exhaust your mind."

Chris swung low and bit his lip when he saw that she had calmly leaped over it. He brought one of his blades upward, but she stepped on it with her boot and held it down like he was a mere child. But this was how he felt right now: like a helpless child. Completely and utterly helpless. He released the sword after seeing that Eslena would not let him have it. Instead, he focused all of his energy on one last blitz.

Eslena dodged left then right and finally used her magic to stop his blade just before it struck her chest. She calmly took the weapon away from him and scoffed. "So much fire in your heart with nowhere to go. I can see why Dreadful made the perfect partner for you now. It's almost a shame that you'll be the one to kill her, isn't it?"

He'd always been able to do something, even if it was small and insignificant, but he could not even touch her. When he lost his parents, he was helpless when Emily had left Earth, and he was useless to Penny in the clocktower. What could he really do? Chris was not as capable as Penny – far from it. He was inferior to Megan and far weaker compared to Ian. If he could have at least scratched her, he would have felt better, but in the end, he was just a footnote.

"You finally realize how pointless this is?" Eslena asked him kindly. She used her magic to make him hover closer and placed a hand on his shoulder. "It's alright. All of these thoughts, these feelings will fade, and you will feel no more pain. You will be my puppet to carry out my wishes as I see fit. You should thank me for the chance to be deemed as useful."

Eslena gave him one last smug look before it all just slipped away. His thoughts left his mind like a dream that had been given up on. His desires became insignificant. The last emotion he'd probably ever feel was worthlessness, and as a tear rolled down his face, Eslena wiped it. He was not trying to call out to Penny anymore with their partner link. He was not worried about Megan or asking himself if Emily or Ian would be coming soon. He just drifted away into Eslena's green eyes and let go. The last thing he would hear was her cackling at his failure as his mind turned blank.

# THE FLAME TAKES FLIGHT

The desert outside of New Hope now looked more like a spaceship parking lot or a spaceport. Thousands of people boarded transports one after another, and as soon as they were full, the ships would take off. More vessels were coming from orbit from all corners of the galaxy as well as other neighboring galaxies. Not all of them were from the Alliance, but a majority were. The few that were had come from Earth, Mars, Neptune, and even Lunaria. Heartland Outreach was a company that had also volunteered for the evacuation, but Penny assumed that the business CEO thought it would help his image.

She helped with the evacuation as she was ordered, but her main concern was Chris and Megan. Eslena always had a way of making people bend to her will. She was also quite manipulative in the time that they knew each other. Gatchi seemed devoted to her, but Penny could tell that at least a fraction of that was fear. Megan was quite hardened, but Chris had never been in a situation like this. How long had he been trying to call for her only to go unanswered?

A hand placed itself on her shoulder and lightly tugged. She turned to see that it was Ian in a Resistance poncho. She had almost forgotten that his armor was destroyed. He stood there, watching the evacuation with her in complete silence. It was like they had both sensed something very wrong with their partners and felt the need to reach them right this moment. Something had happened, but neither was sure what it was. Penny was a little surprised that Ian was so dead set on coming with her to rescue them, but she would accept his help.

"Are you sure you want to do this?" Penny asked him. They were walking away from the large gathering of ships and heading back toward the police station. "She might still want to kill you or at least avoid you."

"I'll take whatever consequences there are," Ian answered back. He raised his hand to look at it and watched as it began to glow green. "And I think I can show her I'm someone else one day with Autumn's help."

"I knew she'd agree to train you," Penny smiled somberly. "You'll do good. It means more classes, though."

"I just wonder why we found out about it now." Ian tightened his jaw and lowered his face. "I always thought I was like you and Tori."

"Guess not," Penny said this in such a way that he thought she was dismissive, but she was just getting started. "It still is pretty cool, though. I'm just a little jealous."

"Hey," Emily marched up to them from the police station and matched their walking speed. "I spoke to the general, and apparently, we won't have much help. The evacuation is taking a lot of resources, so we'll have minimal support."

"So, it'll just be the three of us?" Penny asked with an annoyed look that hid some concern.

"No. We'll have Autumn, Morgan, Bafair, and a few other Resistance forces, and I also have another surprise that just came in."

"A surprise? Okay, but what about ships?" Penny inquired.

"No, we'll have minimal air support to assault the flagship, but our scouts say it's still on the ground. I'm going to sabotage the subsystems. Our goal should be more than rescuing my brother and Megan.

We should ground them, so they are stuck here with us to capture." Emily said, planning out their tactics as she walked. "I'll go into the ship and rescue him. You two will be a distraction."

"Emily!" Penny snapped. She was being sidelined when Chris needed her now more than ever.

"Penny!" Emily snapped back sarcastically. "Calm down. I need you in the air and I need Ian leading the attack on the ground. I can't do this alone, but I can get to him fastest if I don't have to worry about anyone else."

"Sorry, but I don't have a plane," Penny grumbled. She was quite frustrated now. "I guess that means I'm using Ian's, but I'd rather be there for him. He's my partner, remember?"

"Penny," Emily repeated. She was not used to this side of the Dreadful girl. Often, Penny would take what she was told and just do it, but now she was actively putting her foot down. "You will be there for him. You're a better pilot, so I need you to cover us and strip the ship for turrets when I lower the shields."

"Yeah, but what is she going to fly?" Ian asked curiously. "The Nighturge is still on the Tenacity getting repaired and yours blew up."

"Who said she was going to fly the Nighturge?" Emily asked. She raised an eyebrow at Penny. "Hourev sent a present."

---

Penny stared at her reflection in the aircraft's azure blue paint and slowly dragged her gloved fingers across the body. Five engines and two booster engines, large cannons on the wings and on the nose. The shape of the plane reminded her of the Spark, but more grand - like a phoenix. She made her way around to the rear of the aircraft and found that the paint had even been applied in such a way that it looked like the rear of the plane was burning with black and red colors.

The interior was different too. It had beautiful white seats with blue trim that were far closer than in the Spark, sleek curved controls on both sides, as well as new gadgets. The canopy had better call technology and an interface that would make combat smoother. There was space behind the seat for passengers as well as any supplies that they wanted to bring. When she opened it and climbed into the seat, the plane came to life and began running diagnostics. Many lines of text began scrambling in front of her on the canopy before finally settling in on one sentence: 'Welcome home, Penny Dreadful.' Penny stared at it for a moment. *It already knows me, huh?*

A new text overlay came into view as the previous one faded: 'What shall we do today?'

"We need to rescue your co-pilot." She said to herself in a low mumble.

She took a moment to familiarize herself with the controls and then shut the canopy. Emily could call her for support at any time. She had to be ready. Without Chris, she would have to do everything herself. It had been so long since she had to fly solo that she had forgotten. She folded her wings up behind herself, strapped into the seat, and grabbed the headset attached to the back of the chair. The purple construction wrapped around the back of her head and covered her ears.

'Objective added' the text continued to move across the screen as Penny put the engines into standby mode. 'Understood, retrieve C. Spellcrafter. Awaiting pilot input.'

"We need you now. The shields are down." Emily told her. Her image appeared on the canopy in a live feed that was so crisp that it caught her off guard. "Go ahead and launch. Remember, you are the one who is going to make sure we aren't cut to pieces. Autumn will help, but it's your job."

Penny smiled and nodded. It was time. She pulled up on the switch, which was placed just between the seats, and watched as it released a bright purple glow. Once it clicked into place, a message activated in bold text along the canopy 'Booster engines online.' She sat back in the seat and reminded herself over and over that this was not the Spark. It was going to go the moment that she told it to. It was a good thing that she was starting in space.

"We're going into space, activate the-"

"Interstellar mode online. Drift control active." a bland female AI responded. She would have to remember to change that later. "Begin take off?"

"Yeah," Penny confirmed. She pressed down on a petal at her foot that would distribute power to the engines and braced herself.

"The Flame is launching!" one of the mechanics warned the others in the hangar. "Maintain your distance."

Penny shot out of the Tenacity's hangar-like a bullet from a rail-gun. Her body was forced deep into the cushioned seat. She found herself wincing from the sheer force of the launch and the speed that the Flame maintained. The engines cut shortly after and instead fired when Penny wanted to change direction. As she traveled across the stars toward Sohrann and the now fractured looking surface, she couldn't help but smile. It had been so long since she was in a fighter that she could not handle initially.

The engines' constant whistle could be heard inside the cockpit, but it was probably far louder from the outside. When atmospheric reentry began, it roared louder as a thin barrier appeared around the plane. The cockpit flashed this information up on her left with the text 'Heat shield 99.77%'. The fire clouded her vision a little, but she was able to keep the plane angled just right. When the fire died down, the shields returned to max and faded from the canopy.

"Interstellar mode offline. Drift control offline.".

*Oh, he's going to hate flying with me in this!* She thought to herself. When the Flame readjusted itself to fly on the same level as the ground, Penny's stomach turned. She loved the feeling. She was coming up on the Imperial ship and admiring how fast it was coming closer. She had barely given power to the boosters, and it was already better than the Spark. She swooped down quickly, fired a missile at a cluster of surface turrets, and then moved out of range before the others could even retaliate.

Penny pulled up, brought the nose into position, and gave the engine all the power it had. Then she pulled the controls back and returned to routine flight. She was already back for another pass at the turrets. This time she fired the main guns and listened to the beautiful 'brrr' that it let out from the exterior. The nose guns riddled the turrets with holes until they were useless. She still had some time to make a difference on the ground, so she flew down to the battle taking place below the heavens and opened fire on the Imperial soldiers.

"I have Chris and Megan. What's your status?" Emily asked her.

Penny released a rambunctious laugh as she pulled up and away again. "Whooo!"

"Okay-" Emily rolled her eyes playfully. "Geez. We're coming from the main ramp. Cover us a little longer."

"I'll do more than that!" Penny said.

"Imperial fighter launch detected from the Behemoth class ship. Marking." the AI said again. "Alert, you are outnumbered seven to one."

Penny dodged a volley of missiles and then cut some of the engines. This allowed her to turn sharply while still headed in the direction that she was going. Once she was sure that the nose guns would be facing the enemy fighter, she lit them up and watched as they fell to the sandy floor. Then, she reactivated the engines and decimated the other six crafts in her way so she could return to the battle on the ground. She rotated the yoke to regain control and then reactivated the engines to build up speed.

"We're coming out. Morgan is going to fly us out of range. We need you to keep them busy."

"Any sign of Eslena?" Penny questioned. She quickly glanced out of the left window toward the ship.

"No," Emily answered over the sounds of gunfire. "I'm glad. I want him far away from her. Bafair, on your left!"

"That's strange. Eslena should be there, and if you really did sabotage their shields then-"

"Alert: co-pilot detected. C.Spellcrafter." The plane told her. It marked him escaping from the ship with Emily and Megan in real-time. "Pick up pilot?"

"Not now," Penny answered quickly. That was a terrible idea, she thought. The AI certainly was not as impressive as Cornellius, but it was more tolerable.

"Alert-" it began again.

"What?" Penny inquired.

"The Behemoth class Flagship has begun a launch." the AI said urgently.

"You won't run away. Not after what you did." Penny muttered; her thoughts focused on Eslena. She redirected the plane toward the massive spaceship and began rifling through her weapons options.

The massive engines at the rear of the ship released bright blue flames, and the flagship began gaining energy for a launch. The remaining turrets opened fire on her as well as the Imperial soldiers on the ground, but they decided to stop firing when they realized that they were being left for dead. Some made it onboard the ship, but the rest were left in the massive clouds of dust that was kicked up by the engines. The text 'Limited Visibility Mode' was activated, and the canopy dimed. Instead, the plane gave her a virtualized image of what she would have seen if there were not so many sand particles in the air.

The Flame rattled as she drew closer, and the video that she was seeing confirmed her suspicions. She was near the engines. The heat shield activated once more, so she backed off to avoid wearing them down. Another fast-moving object came from behind her, so she prepared to deal with whatever it was by lowering her own speed. Autumn flew by the Flame so fast that she had nearly lost control of the plane entirely. She was flying onwards to the Behemoth's front, so Penny decided to remain near the engines. They would have to stop it together.

"What weapons do I have for a large moving target?" Penny inquired aloud.

"For bomber sized targets-" it began.

"No, like a big easy to hit ship." Penny clarified. She yanked the controls to the right and easily dodged a piece of debris from the ship. Autumn must have been doing a number to the front.

"Because the enemy ship does not have shields, it is recommended that you use the Concussion bombs." The AI explained with a diagram on the screen. "A singular one is capable of destroying any number of engines on the Behemoth; however, getting too close could be fatal. Alternatively, you can use the heavy plasma rounds located on the wings."

"We're clear, Penny," Emily said. She sounded like she was on one of the troop transports. "Where are you?"

"I'm with Autumn. Tell the General that the Imperial ship is escaping orbit." Penny accelerated rapidly while firing carefully into the engines. Chunks of metal flew back at her, but she avoided them with relative ease.

"I already notified him," Emily responded. She trailed off into another conversation shortly after. "Are you okay, Chris?"

"Eslena wasn't that tough, Emily," Chris answered in a dull and brief way.

*When did you start acting like a bigshot, Chris?* Penny asked him mentally. There was no response again. *Odd, he should be able to hear me. We need to figure that out too.*

"The Imperial vessel has attained flight." The AI warned her. "Caution, falling debris may be accelerated by gravity."

The ship rapidly took off toward the sky, and Penny followed at a fair distance. One of the engines had failed, but they still had many more to work with, including the machines on the left and right sides. When Limited Visibility Mode deactivated, she was able to see Autumn at the front of the ship using her magic to create a giant net. She was slowing the ship down exponentially, but it was still pushing forward. This encouraged Penny to accelerate her plans and fire the concussion bombs. The bright yellow and red explosions cascaded throughout the engines but were not enough to fully put them out of commission.

"The Imperial shields have been restored from the inside. Retreat immediately!" the AI said. A bright red arrow showed her how to maneuver out of it. Penny barrel rolled out of the way just in time for the red-tinted shields to consume the air around the ship.

Autumn was thrown away from the ship, and her spell was broken. She recovered midair and began pelting the shields with what could only be described as angry saucers of fire. They distributed across the ship's shields. Upon seeing that this would not work, Autumn instead forced herself under the shields and used an explosion spell on the underbelly, the hangar decks, and did the same to all turrets in her way. She charged up a bright white lightning bolt but was shot midway through preparation. Autumn had barely managed to stop what she was doing and raise a shield but was still sent flying away.

Penny could tell that she was perfectly fine, but it was still a gun meant for ships, not people. Autumn tumbled out of control toward the ground. Penny was planning to redirect the Flame to leap out and catch her, but Autumn stabilized herself and floated in place not far from her. The two watched as the Imperial ship escaped into orbit. Penny wanted to keep chasing, but the Alliance flagships and frigates in orbit had a greater chance of stopping them than the Flame. Penny turned to head back toward the ongoing battle on the ground, but Autumn just remained there with a crestfallen expression.

# 35

## ESLENA'S PUPPETS

The evacuation was falling behind, but Penny knew that they would still get most people off of the planet. There were already massive cracks appearing throughout New Hope and randomly in the desert. It would only be a matter of time. Penny assisted when she could, but she was more concerned about Chris. She could still not communicate with him mentally, and he was very short-spoken. *What had Eslena done to him in such a short time? Torture? She barely had them more than a day.*

Penny sighed and flew away from the evacuation ships that were now going away now that they were full of refugees. She could still sense where he was, even if he wasn't responding to her anymore. It was not just that he was her partner or that he was in a dire situation, but she felt more responsible for him after finally returning his feelings. It was customary to feel sad or angry at what had happened to him - whatever it was, but it was more than that. What if Eslena had decided to kill him? Her heart felt like it had sunk directly into his stomach. *I don't want to think about that,* she thought to herself. He was fine now.

She could see Emily heading in the direction of the New Hope evacuation site, and she would definitely be going to the Grandham one next. Did she even have time to talk to Chris after they rescued him? Penny could see Emily waving her down, and so she landed in front of her. Emily looked exhausted and like she had a lot to say. Penny wasn't sure what this meant for her.

"I wanted to apologize for snapping at you over him." Emily started.

Penny interrupted her before she could say more. "If it were my sister, I'd have done the same. Don't apologize. Just - next time, do not try to shoot at me, please?"

"Ah," Emily laughed and playfully flared her magic in her hand. The bright green glow was contrasted by the sand from the desert storm blowing over. "Don't break his heart, and I won't."

"...Emily?"

"Yes?"

Penny took a breath. Who else could she confide in about the issue? She decided to just come out with the concerns she had. "I can't hear his thoughts, and I haven't been able to since he was captured. I'm not sure what that means."

"Talk to him and ask," Emily explained with a suspicious look. Did she realize something? "Go ahead and go. If anything happens, let me know."

"Like what?" She asked.

"Like what happened in Grandham. If Chris or Megan start acting strangely, tell myself, Autumn, or the General. Do not try to handle it yourself. I don't want them getting hurt."

"You think that they might have been affected? But Autumn's spell on Chris-" Penny asked with wide eyes. Emily quickly covered her mouth.

"He's my brother, and she's your squad mate, but they're still kids. So are you. Other than you and Ian, your squad mates were never taught to guard their minds against someone that powerful. It is very possible, so just stay alert." Emily whispered. She walked past Penny without another word. Penny thought it might be best to keep this to herself - at least for now. She would at least have to tell Ian of the potential danger.

Penny could see Chris standing out in the open near their tent. It had been emptied, and all of their belongings, of which there were few, were sent to the Tenacity. He appeared to just be meditating with his eyes closed. On a normal day, he'd greet her before she even came close or looked around curiously. Perhaps he was only worked up from everything that had happened, but sirens were going off in her head. As strange as it felt, she had to treat him as a potential hazard and focus on their partner link. If she felt any changes, it could be disastrous. He was not hostile like the others Eslena controlled, so she thought that he was not affected.

"Chris?" She started with a friendly smile. He was still just staring off into the sunset and watching as a sandstorm approached from the west. She decided to repeat herself. "Chris, are you okay?"

"Yes, Penny." He said in a monotone way.

"You're usually smiling when I ask you that and tell me not to worry," Penny noted with a small frown. She moved closer and took his hand in both of hers. "What did Eslena do to you?"

"Nothing." He answered. She once again focused on his thoughts and found nothing—just silence.

"I know you say she did nothing, but is it bad that I can tell you're lying?" She asked with a sad smile. "I don't need to read your thoughts to know you..."

"Oh." He said in a dull and uncaring voice.

This bothered her more than she was expecting. Chris didn't even care. "What's up with that? Did you try to even call out to me when Eslena had you?"

"Maybe. I don't remember." He said like it didn't matter right now.

"You don't remember...?" Penny repeated slowly.

"I mean, once or twice, sorry." Chris corrected himself quickly.

"Why don't we take a break and go somewhere and talk for a while? Would you like that?" Penny tried. She hoped that this would work, but she was not sure what the result might be.

"Yes!" He said in a sudden outburst. "That sounds nice!" He said urgently. Penny was taken aback by the change in attitude. He squeezed her hands and smiled, but something felt very off. So many sirens were going off in her head, but other than his strange behavior, he was harmless. Could Eslena have broken his mind like the others in Grandam?

"I want to check on Meg before we go, though, okay?" Penny said with a weird look. She was really getting bad vibes. Perhaps it was not such a good idea.

"Why?" He asked, confusion in his voice. What was confusing about this?

"...Because she was taken by Eslena too?" Penny said. "You were both there, that's why."

"Because Megan is always fine. She's always fine."

"Was she fine when she found out about Ian?" Penny asked with a look. She was actually angry at him for the first time in a while. What was with this insensitive behavior?

"You're right. I'm sorry." He looked away and sighed. "I'm just tired."

"I want to go check on her."

"We can check on her after. I want to be alone with you now." Chris said, somewhat selfishly as he grabbed her wrist. "They wouldn't mind."

"...I think they would." She said, yanking her arm out of his grip. "I'm going."

Penny turned and began making her way inside of the police station to call for Megan and Ian, but they were exiting at the exact same time. Ian had the same face that she did. They were able to convey their concerns with just a quick facial expression. Penny shrugged at him and gestured for them to all walk together deeper into New Hope. As they were leaving, Penny could see Akela heading to one of the Alliance transports with Emily. The two were deep in conversation and had likely not seen them, but Penny wondered if they were discussing her adoption.

By now, the sandstorm had picked up drastically, and so Penny imagined that the evacuation was temporarily halted in the New Hope area. She felt a little worried being out in this with both Chris and Megan. Though Penny wanted to trust them, they were both clearly exhibiting strange behavior. She could see Megan and Ian talking up ahead, which was odd given what Megan had said about not wanting anything to do with him. Was now the time to say something?

"So, Meg, about Japan-" Ian started nervously over the howling wind. It was getting harder and harder to see or hear. "I wanted to just - you know, talk about it. I know you hate me."

*Of all the times for a sandstorm this bad, it had to be now?* Penny asked herself. She could just barely see the other two, and they were not even that far ahead.

"Hate you?" Megan asked with a look of surprise. "Why would I hate you? You didn't mean to hurt me."

"But you-"

"What would I hate you for?" She continued on.

Ian stopped walking and just stared for a moment. There was silence, and only the howling wind could be audibly heard now. Ian's arm swung back to summon his sword just as Megan realized her mistake. She drew her sword using her magic and attacked high. Ian braced his sword against his arm to block. Megan bounced off and prepared for battle. The two stared one another down and waited for the other to act.

"We have to stop her!" Penny started to say this to Chris, but then she realized something was very wrong. "Chris-?"

She could feel an intense chill running down her back and neck, but more than that, she sensed Chris's urge to attack her. She turned and raised her soul barrier and watched the purple aura shield her from what looked to be black Ice. She winced a little as the Ice passed over her and flew away into the desert wind. Even though the barrier had protected her from it, her body still took a massive hit. This was not Ice magic anymore - no. She knew that this could not be any form of Light Magic he was using. This was Dark Magic...specifically Loneliness.

She turned her gaze to Chris's hand to see that he was not flaring his magic like normal. The chiaroscuro blue color in his hands was rather telling. A singular blue Ice shard floated in his hand and spun rapidly. When it was ready, Chris turned it on her. A powerful black shockwave of ice emitted from him and raced toward her. She countered with her own spell but was still nearly knocked off of her feet by the resulting explosion.

"They're using Dark Magic!" Penny warned over her shoulder. There was no response other than the howl of the fast winds. She could not see Ian, but she could see the sparks of swords colliding and the occasional dark green spell. "Dammit..."

She turned and blocked Chris's next attack by summoning her shield. He pressed down hard with both of his swords, but Penny held firm and pushed him off. They were partners, so even if he was using Dark Magic, she would still be on equal footing – it did not matter what the affinity was. He couldn't kill her, and she couldn't defat him either. This could technically go on forever. Penny advanced on him, summoned her sword, and swung twice. Once he got overconfident and swiped at her face, she turned, grabbed his arm and kicked him in the hip with all of her might.

*Sorry, Chris, I'm going to have to hurt you a little.* She thought. It was not like he would hear it, but it made her feel better. She caught his next sword attack quickly and tossed him over her head, but he recovered and landed perfectly on his feet. The two circled each other for a moment and began looking for openings. This was not like Chris at all. He liked to overwhelm his opponents and focus on sword attacks instead of using magic. This was different. He was silent, calculating, and his attacks had far more impact than expected. She bit her lip hard and cursed under her breath again.

*Crash!* Penny turned to see what this was and, in doing so, witnessed multiple bright green flashes. A singular grey one appeared, and then another loud crash followed. It sounded like one of them had been sent flying away. Penny wanted to go and help, but she knew that Chris would not allow her to escape in any capacity. She raised her shield to block a lunging attack and then stabbed forward to force Chris back with the fear of being stabbed.

"So," she said while watching his heavy breaths. "I take it Eslena really wants me dead? You don't seem to be trying to capture me."

"What gave it away?" Chris asked sarcastically through shallow breaths.

He grabbed onto his right wrist and focused all of his mana into one attack. The air itself seemed to freeze, and some of the sand particles fell to the street. Penny threw her shield hard and ducked down to prepare for the resulting explosion. Large fragments of ice were sent every which way. Penny resummoned her guard and moved through the dense storm toward his last known location, but all she could see was grey and brown.

Chris fired out another icy blast that looked more like a furious wall of arctic winds. Penny countered with her own Dark Magic but was careful to ensure that it would not kill him. She only needed to match his output. He was only using basic Dark spells, but they were spells that would hit as hard as if he had trained for years. Because of her own power, he was just as dangerous, and she needed to be mindful of it.

The two spells raged against one another, and the two partners continued advancing on one another. When the energy between the magics became too much, the two were sent flying away from one another in a grand explosion that changed the speed of the storm around them. Just when Penny was catching her breath after knocking Chris away, Megan charged out from the storm and swung at her too. Penny shielded the attack and then blocked Chris's follow up with her sword. He'd already recovered from the shockwave and began attacking her again.

She blocked them both with her shield and used her soul barrier to shield herself from anything that she had no time to block, but she could not handle the both of them alone while also trying not to harm them. Neither of the two had been phased by the pain that she inflicted, and their spells were beyond unstable. If Megan had remained focused on Chris, or she had been left to only fight Megan; then this might have been easier. Penny found herself backing up more and more until her back was against the wall. She shielded the last few chain attacks from Megan and then took a kick from Chris to the stomach. He raised his sword to strike her down as she was gasping for air from the pain, but a Death spell struck him and forced him to turn.

"They're after you, Penny! Get going!" Ian ordered her. He continued firing spell after spell to distract their mind-controlled allies, but the two quickly defended with their weapons.

Ian was charging toward them from the storm, but Chris casually used Dark Magic to freeze him in a block of ice. "I don't have time to waste on you, Ian." He hissed with a hateful glare. "I know that won't hold you, but just wait your turn."

Penny scrambled to her feet, reflected one of Megan's spells back toward her, and watched as she fell. Then, she swung at Chris as carefully as she could without hitting anything vital. Penny would just have to incapacitate them one by one. It would be difficult, but she'd need to just focus on knocking them unconscious - starting with Megan. Their bodies would still fail if she inflicted enough pain. She raised her shield a little and stood with her feet parted. She just needed to bait them into making mistakes; then she would free Ian and work with him to deal with Chris. It would be impossible to take him out alone.

A sword fell through the sandstorm and embedded itself in the ground between Penny, Megan, and Chris. Her two mind-controlled squad mates hurried backward as if they realized they'd made a colossal mistake. Emily landed in a crouched position just in front of Penny and slowly pulled the green weapon from the ground. She then swiped the sword outwards and held it in a relaxed state. Penny tried saying something, but Emily just looked away as if to say, 'Catch your breath.'

"They're under Eslena's control," Penny explained quickly. She moved away from the wall and took her place with Emily.

"Yes, I'm aware of that," Emily said coolly. She was too focused to say much at the moment. "Autumn is on her way, but she's coming from the other side of the planet. We need to incapacitate them quickly."

Penny thought for a moment. Vedi would most likely know a little bit about Eslena and how this spell worked. If he did, then this could be over faster than waiting on Autumn. "Emily, I'm going to the police station. Hold them off, okay?"

"For what...?" Emily asked, perplexed. Chris's swords collided with hers, but when Emily pushed back to knock him off, she sent him flying through the storm. Megan recoiled at the sheer force that Emily had sent him flying. His screams died down over the heavy whistling of the wind. She only regained her composure when Emily stepped toward her to continue the fight.

"Just trust me, hold them off," Penny responded confidently. She would never agree to rely on the same man that not only killed Victoria but also harmed her brother. "I'll free Ian and then go."

"I can free him without you. Focus on your plan," Emily said. She extended a glowing green hand toward Ian and started to crush the thick ice magic with vines. Chris took this time to imbue his weapon with Dark Ice energy; the blade hummed periodically "Is this...Dark Magic...? Did my brother-?" Penny nodded slowly to confirm her suspicions. Emily scowled darkly at this revelation. "Make it quick, Penny."

"I will," Penny said though she could have sworn that Emily's free hand had transformed into a fist. *Is she blaming herself* for this?

She took off through the storm and only stopped when she heard

Chris gaining on her from behind. She turned to toss her shield, but a bright green flash slammed into his shoulder and knocked him away from her. Megan was close behind, but Emily appeared from the darkness and drop kicked her before she could even think about attacking. Then, she transformed her weapon into a polearm of some sort and spun it around to point at her opponents. Emily was always so great at multitasking that Penny really didn't need to worry about watching her back. Until she returned, they would be distracted.

"Ian," she heard over the howling wind. "Warm yourself up, then help me. Remember, we're not trying to hurt them."

Penny blew through the police precinct doors and hurried to the holding cells. She earned many confused glances but did not spare them any mind. Penny hurried down the hall, to the left, and then opened Vedi's holding cell. He looked up with a surprised glance, but it turned into a smile when he saw her breathing heavily. He knew something was going on, and she was here to ask for help.

"You could at least knock." Vedi began as he laid back in his chair. "For a second there, I thought the banging was the planet finally giving up. Are they moving me soon? I don't particularly want to die on Sohrann-"

"I need your help," Penny said, straight and to the point. She grabbed onto his cuffs and then stopped herself. She didn't even know if he could help. "Do you know about Eslena's mind control spells?"

"What about them? What happened to saving your dear part-ner?" Vedi's smile faded a little.

"She did something to Chris and Megan, and now they're trying to kill me!" Penny cried out desperately. "How do I stop them? Is there a spell you can show me?"

"Stop them?" Vedi raised his eyebrows and made a strange face. He seemed confused. "Wait-they're trying to kill you? That snake!" He stood up and tossed his chair across the room, so it collided with the door. This was enough to startle Penny. "I told your father! I told him. She wants his head."

"Yeah. They only want me right now. I think they ignored Ian for the most part." Penny explained. She was trying to catch her breath between sentences. "What do I do??"

"Kid, I don't know." Penny went wide-eyed as he explained this to her. "I've never had to deal with a spell like that. The best I can do is guess how to circumvent it. This wasn't how it was supposed to go."

"'Not how it was supposed to go?'" She repeated. "You were trying to get me too." Penny reminded him.

"To help your father and protect you!" Vedi exploded angrily. "How many times do I have to tell you?!"

"That's still trying to take away my ability to choose."

"That's not what I wanted." Vedi shot back.

"Well, now my partner is trying to kill me, and so is Megan."

"You're safe down here with me. I'll protect you," Vedi promised her through gritted teeth.

"I don't want protection. I want you to save my friends." Penny argued angrily. "That's not what I came here for."

"Listen, Rabbit, you need protection," Vedi said authoritatively, hoping to convince her.

"You haven't called me that in years. I've outgrown that name, don't you think?" Penny commented. For a moment, she pictured the memories of hiding behind the gazebo on the Dreadful Manor grounds where she grew up and giggling to herself as Vedi tried to find her filled her mind, but she soon snapped back to reality. The laughter of herself and her sister Victoria died as she reopened her eyes. She knew exactly how to get him to help. "Okay, you want to protect me so bad? You have to come with me then because I'm not staying here."

"You are not going out there." He decided for her.

"You can come, or you can tell me how to try to help him, but you won't tell me what I can and can't do," Penny said. She placed her hand on the door and waited a few moments to see what he would do.

"If my trick doesn't work, I'm getting you to safety," Vedi told

Penny assertively. He approached her and extended his wrists so that she could remove the cuffs.

Penny spun her sword around and swiped downwards. The force was so great that the cuffs shattered and fell to the floor. Vedi waited a moment like he was waiting to see if Penny might just change her mind, but she did the opposite. She led him out of the police station and forced her way through Alliance forces who tried to stop them. The storm was getting lighter, but she still had trouble seeing.

*Clang, swipe, slam!* Emily brought her sword around and knocked Chris away with the back of it. Then, she turned around and blocked Megan. When Ian rejoined the fight and confronted Megan, she focused solely on Chris. He traded sword attacks with her and even occasionally landed a hit, but they were minor compared to their fight's overall state. No matter how fast Chris moved, Emily was faster. Even if the skirmish had gone on for long enough to make Emily tired, he was incapable of feeling the fatigue.

Chris dashed in to finish Emily off, but she blocked the attack as if it was a child-like swing. The two held the clash for a moment. Chris's hands began to glow a corrupted blue color like he was about to cast a spell, but Emily still tried to reach out to him. "I just wanted to protect you. Now that all of this has happened, I feel like a failure, honestly..." Emily said, their weapons sliding slightly and making an unpleasant sound. "Eslena thinks she's got you, but I know you're stronger. You're my brother, still my brother."

"Sis...?" Chris said in a sympathetic voice. He began to panic when he realized what was happening. "Em, what's going on?"

"Chris?" Emily's grip loosened as her eyes grew wide.

"Em, don't let your guard down!" Ian exploded just loud enough to bring her back.

Chris's end of the sword clash began to slack a little. He looked down at his hands and seemed to think to himself. Emily did the same, and for a moment, it seemed like he'd come back, but then he reverted. Chris gripped his singular blade hard and forced it forward into Emily's face. She tried to hold him back, but the spell that he was casting was finally unleashed. Dark ice emitted from the blade and took over her weapon. It was like a flash freeze and could not be stopped.

It was too late to do anything other than try and guard his attack. Chris's sword forced its way around hers and then collided with her face. He intensified the spell and froze part of her face in dense sheet ice. A deep cut was left traveling along her nose, eyes, and even the wound was frozen in the end. Chris attacked her further, most likely hoping to remove her from the fight entirely. She blocked a few of his attacks, but he still disarmed her and knocked her to the ground with an elbow to her jaw. She couldn't defend herself effectively without being able to see him.

Emily clawed at the pavement slightly and grasped at her face, screaming and sucking in air through her teeth. She broke the Ice with her Life magic and began healing herself but still remained on all fours. Penny knew that now was not the time to worry about her but felt concerned all the same. The best way to help her was to eliminate the threat first.

"Be lucky I didn't kill you. You shouldn't have gotten in my way." Chris said heartlessly. He picked up his other sword around the ground and rotated it to a forward grip. Emily reopened her eyes and looked around for a moment before wincing, covering her face, and writhing in pain.

"Em!? Are you alright?" Ian turned to face Chris but was quickly forced back to Megan. She was so relentless in her attacks that he really had no time to breathe. Without his armor, her attacks were consistently deadly. "Emily!" He repeated.

"Focus on Megan," Emily told him through gritted teeth and pain-filled moans. "I'm fine, give me a moment. Please...I'll handle my brother."

"No, just stay down," Penny told her. She turned her attention to Vedi. "How do we help him?"

"Just get back." Vedi pushed Penny behind himself and extended his hand. Then, he focused his mind on a spell complex. A dim grey force flew out and overtook Chris for just a moment, but it dimmed almost as soon as it connected. "What kind of spell is she using?" Vedi exclaimed in confusion.

"You can't break it?" Penny asked urgently. Chris charged at her and so Penny raised her shield, but Vedi forced her back and drew his own blade to block. He collided with Chris sword so hard that he slid back a couple of feet.

"No. It's not a spell: it's a curse. A strong one too," Vedi told her. He seemed to be thinking to himself.

"Is that Vedi?" Emily asked from the ground. She looked in their direction and tried reaching for her weapon but could not find it. "Stay away from them."

"He's not attacking us" Ian explained for her. He backed into a wall and ducked one of Megan's spells, returning fire with his own Death spell. Just when he thought he'd slowed her down, Megan summoned two giant, sentient Venus fly traps and sent them after Ian. They snapped and bit at him, but he held his ground.

"I can't help your partner, but maybe I can help you reach him." Vedi theorized while rubbing his chin and almost laughing to himself. "I can just force him to go into his own mind, and you can try to restore his memories. It's almost crazy enough to work."

"How do I do that?" Penny asked with a bewildered look. "I've never done this."

"Beats me." Vedi shrugged. "I can only assume that if I hit him with the spell, then you'll be able to help him. If not, then, hey, that sucks for him. There could be side effects, but I think you're desperate at this point."

"Do it," Penny said decisively. She would handle whatever consequences came.

Vedi brought his hand inwards and gathered energy. He held the bright grey spell in the palm of his hand and waited for Chris to get as close as possible. When he was in range, Vedi held out his hand and watched as his target collapsed at his feet. Penny dashed forward to catch him, but the moment that he landed in her arms, she too fell unconscious. Vedi watched with an amused smile.

"Now it's up to you." She heard him say just as his voice became distorted. "Your mother's spell is rather potent. Try not to lose yourself in his mind, my dear; I may not be able to help you through the resulting madness." Vedi summoned his own weapon and laughed to himself, "Keep your guard up Ian, I'm on my way."

# 36

# REMEMBRANCE

P enny opened her eyes to find herself in a classroom with shiny white floors, bland white brick walls, and dusty blinds. There was a large desk at the end of the room in front of a teaching board; smaller seats lined the floor in rows. Young minds sat in almost every single one as a lecture went on. She walked forward and then back, up and down the rows over and over. She stared at each of the students, who all were human as far as she could tell. *Is this Earth?* She questioned. *Is this a school?*

"Alright," the male teacher said aloud in an authoritative voice. "Does anyone know who Aaron Burr is? Anyone? No one?" He began looking for someone to ask to help him with the lecture. Penny watched the teacher home in on a lone boy with green hair asleep at his desk. "Mr. Spellcrafter, we spoke about this during tutoring." No reply. "Mr. Spellcrafter??" Still no reply. Penny rotated her head to the left to see Chris, or what she thought was him, him lying on the desk in front of him with his arms crossed under himself. She tried to place a hand on him and call his name, but her hand phased right through like he was some sort of ghost.

*Remember why you came here.* A voice that sounded just like her own said in her mind. *Chris needs you right now. If you let yourself get distracted, you may never find him. Remember?*

"Remember...?" She repeated to herself blankly. Penny blinked a few times and scanned the classroom. "I remember..."

"MR. SPELLCRAFTER!" The teacher boomed, slamming his book on the desk to make a loud enough noise. Chris jumped up and stared around like he was confused. Penny jumped back at this sudden reaction and watched as he sank in his seat. Pulling his hands into his jacket pockets, he tried to make himself seem small.

"I'll have to tell your parents-" the teacher paused, seemingly beat himself up about something, and then spoke again. "Just see me after class." The class began laughing, which Penny could not understand. What was so humorous? "That's enough." The teacher said to the class as a whole. "Back to the lecture."

Penny's eyes widened. A girl with black hair and brown eyes turned in her seat to look at Chris. "Tori-?" She breathed out heavily. Penny frowned, made some sort of mental note, and regained her composure. She watched as her sister brushed her hair behind her ear and started taking what looked like notes on the lectures.

Penny approached her nervously. She tried touching her, but just like with Chris, her hand phased right through. She then found herself staring at Victoria's terrible notes. Tori really didn't care about this class at all. It made sense. Why would she need to care about Earth's history? Then again, Penny figured it could just be because Chris didn't really bother to ask Tori if she actually took notes. Was this his best guess as to what she was doing? She took a moment to overlook everyone else's notes and found that they were blank. Some of the students' faces were blank, too, aside from two students in the back of the class: one male and one female. Were these the friends we always talked about?

"This isn't important." Penny decided, hurrying out of the classroom and into the empty and dimly lit hall. It bothered her, though. It truly bothered her how he saw the planet he was born on. Just how alone was he before coming to Terminus? Why did he never talk about his parents? What had happened to them and why did he not seem to care?

"I keep getting sidetracked." She said to herself.

Penny exited the classroom and entered a very bland hallway. Lockers lined the walls, and random articles of trash like paper littered the floor. The bell rang. Many faceless individuals flooded the hall and began scrambling in every direction. She became lost in the sea of people for a moment, but fortunately, they phased right through her as if she was not there. After some time, Chris became visible again, and the two individuals that she had witnessed prior took up either side of him.

For what felt like hours, Penny followed the memories. The fight with Gatchi, the flight to Terminus, and even when Chris met her. She had behaved so differently back then. How had he put up with her for so long like this? He had been so lonely and confused by everything - overwhelmed even, and the first thing she did was act coldly to him. Despite this, he was drawn to her for some reason. Even back then, despite being total strangers, a force drew her to him. She could have sworn - no, she knew that they had met before.

"*Boo!*" someone screamed behind her so loud that she nearly fell forward onto the healthy green Terminus grass. Her gaze shifted from the memory Chris had of her apologizing to him for knocking him unconscious to the girl who had disturbed her. She looked to be the same age as Penny, so she had to be at least fifteen. Her blue eyes were hypnotizing and recognizable. She had her long blonde hair in a ponytail with bangs and wore a long yellow and white dress. The girl smiled with wondrous glee as she said, "How do you do, Penny?"

"You can touch me, and you know my name," Penny observed suspiciously. She moved to draw a weapon but then quickly remembered that she could not. This was not the Imagination Realm, nor was it reality. She was defenseless.

"You were going to hurt me there, weren't you?" She asked with a giggle. "Don't worry, I don't bite."

"Who are you?"

"You don't recognize me?" She asked with a frown. Penny looked the girl up and down, but in the end, she just tilted her head and made a face. "Well, that sucks. I'm still so happy! I've been wanting to meet you, but you never let me in."

"Let you in?" Penny repeated curiously.

"I guess now that your mind is bridged with Chris's, I can finally talk to you!" She placed a finger on her chin and looked at the bright blue sky and the rolling clouds. "Though, I wish Vedi didn't have to use Mind Maze just for it to happen."

"Do I know you?" Penny was a little weirded out now, and it probably showed on her face.

She blew air out of her lips and huffed heavily. The girl seemed rather displeased. "Look closer."

The girl posed in a way that Penny could look directly at her face. Penny noticed that her appearance was slender and beautiful - familiar even. Her face looked a lot like her own and her sister's. She brushed her hair back. It was thick and reminded her a lot of her sister's. Penny looked behind the girl - her curiosity overtaking her. Beautiful white and blue wings sprouted out from her back and casually beat behind her. They were just like her own. She was a Night-flyer too.

"I really had hoped that you would recognize me, Penny," she began as Penny finally stopped looking and stared at her with her mouth agape. "I wanted my daughter to recognize me, but I understand why you might not."

Penny stared at her with various emotions: confusion, frustration, sadness, but most of all, hate. She hated her, so why did she claim to come from her mind? Chris did not know of her aside from what Penny said, and she did not want to think about her. Penny's shock turned to a glare. It must have surprised the girl because she gasped and then lowered her head. Penny was going to say something, but the girl was first.

"Why do you hate me so much?" She inquired.

"You said you're from my head, right?!" Penny screamed at her. "You already know why!"

"I want you to say it," was her declaration.

"What?"

"I want you-" she repeated. The girl raised her head and looked Penny directly in her eyes with a warm look. "-To say it to me."

Penny could feel herself getting worked up. Her upper teeth slid along the bottom ones, and she could hear herself breathing hard. She wanted so badly to punch this woman, scream at her, hate her with every fiber of her being. Penny had come here to find her partner and figure out what to do to save him, so why - why was her mother here? She did not have time for this either. Penny turned on her heel, casted a solemn look at the ground, and began walking away.

"My friends need me," Penny murmured.

"Make time." The girl said behind her with a serious look. "Or are you just that adamant about running away from everything? You act so high and mighty, but you can't even admit that you're upset over nothing. Your mind can't wrap itself around what actually happened, so you just want to give yourself a reason to hate me."

"No!" Penny snapped. She turned faster than a lightning bolt and began advancing on the girl. "I'm not running away or making excuses. I hate you because when you died, Dad went insane. I didn't want to fight. I didn't want to hurt Tori. I did not want to be in a war, and I didn't want to be this way. *You* left him when he needed you most!" Penny was in her face now. The two were close enough that Penny could choke her if she wanted, but she just couldn't.

"He needed me, or you did?" The girl said with a dull expression that showed minimal sympathy. It mirrored Penny's own - the face she used to wear all of the time. "Which one of you really needed Madelynn Dreadful? Your father, your sister, or you? Because I think-"

"I don't care what you think..." Penny breathed out in a barely audible whisper. She shut her eyes tightly and tried to tune her out.

"You felt like I abandoned all of you. Your sister talked about me, your father talked about me, and even the knight protecting you, Vedi, talked about me. They all told you how great I was and how alike we were." Madelynn said with a heart-melting smile. "But you could never admit to yourself that you weren't abandoned because believing that was easier than admitting that you'd never get to meet your mother. You'd never get to have that family that your sister talked about being so whole. This is true, no?"

Penny was speechless. She did not cry or argue further. Instead, she did the unexpected. She slowly nodded her head in agreement. Madelynn smiled to show her approval and hugged Penny tightly to herself. Even though it was not real, she was warm. It felt familiar somehow, but it was weird seeing her mother like this: not having a fit of insanity or forgetting her. Would she really have been like this, or was this just her mind imagining how it would have been?

"But you didn't come here to talk to me." Madelynn reached into one of the low hanging sleeves of her dress and removed a big book like a novel with a royal blue hardback cover and a golden spine. "You came for this. It is yours, isn't it?"

"A book?" Penny asked in an attempt at humor. "Thanks, I really appreciate it."

"You don't recognize it?" Madelynn asked with a disappointed face. "It's the memories of your partner. It's your memories. The curse may have forced him to forget who he is, but you can replace his book with this."

"It will remove the curse?! Really?" Penny asked with a surprised expression. She eagerly grabbed the book, but Madelynn refused to let go.

"Wait! It won't remove the curse. Curses can't be removed by magic or even partners. This will just restore him to how he was with your memories!" Madelynn said as fast as she could. "It is only a temporary fix, and some of his memories could be overwritten by yours."

"How do I remove the curse? This sounds just as bad!" Penny

held her head and stepped away. How could she risk removing who he was as a person?

"Didn't you study curses?" Madelynn wondered with a look of shock. Penny snatched the book from her hands and rifled through the pages. After confirming that every single page contained his memories, she exhaled. Nothing seemed to be missing from the time that she'd known him, but a few pages did seem odd. "If the woman who put the curse on him can be killed or convinced to reverse it, he will be fine. Not many spells can just make a curse go poof."

"Can't you teach me one?" Penny asked with an eager look in her eye.

"I only know what you know, sweetheart," Madelynn tapped at the book with her finger and smiled. "This will get your partner back, but Eslena should be your priority now until she is destroyed."

"Okay," Penny said as she pulled the thick text to her chest. "Don't worry, when I find Eslena, she'll wish I was just going to put a curse on her." Madelynn snickered at Penny's confident declaration. "What?"

"That Dreadful vengeance mentality is still very much a thing," Madelynn said this to herself as she waved a hand to tell Penny to get a move on. "Go save your partner, but remember until Eslena is dealt with, the two of them are connected. It is the same for your other friend. Be careful with what you say and do."

"I understand," Penny said respectfully. She turned and decided to head in the direction of the Terminus administration building. She knew that she needed to reach Autumn's library. "Thank you, mom."

Penny wasted no time in heading to Autumn's library. The world around it was white and bland. Because Chris was not around at this time, she guessed that it was only a memory fragment. However, the doors still worked; and so, she threw them open and entered. The library was far more extensive than it should have been, with books all over the shelves. There were multiple bookshelves and sections. Some of the cases were entirely empty, and others were filled to the point where there was no space.

She could see it now: a book with a color like ink. It was at eye level and looked to be spreading corruption to the other books around it. Sinister whispers emitted from the text itself. Chris might have hesitated if he was faced with a similar scenario, but she was not him. She knew that she had no choice but to do this - even if the corruption spread to her. She removed her gloves, took up the book her mother gave her, and reached out for the corrupted one.

The book's whispers turned to yells that demanded her to stop immediately. Penny pulled harder, but it was as if the book had embedded itself onto the bookcase itself. She tugged and heaved until it finally gave way, flying from the bookcase. The book's corruption attempted to leap onto her hand from the pages, and so she threw it as hard as she could against the wall. Once it had realized that there was nothing near itself to latch onto or corrupt, the book began whispering again.

Penny held the book that came from her own memories in both of her hands. She stared at the elegant design and admired it in her hands. It emitted a soft purple glow, the closer that she brought it to the bookcase. After separating the surrounding books that attempted to fall over with her hand, she slid the replacement into the gap. It sat on the shelf proudly and only stopped glowing when she stepped away.

"It'll be okay now." She said to herself with a smile. The world around her was engulfed in light, warding away the darkness. "I promise, so come back to me."

# 37

## CREPUSCULE

C hris opened his eyes to see an unfamiliar ceiling. It was white and smooth, not unlike the Sohrann space station. The soft beeping of medical equipment surrounded him. Turning his head to the right of the room, he found his vitals. Just how many times would he end up in the hospital or a hospital-like setting? He sat up and checked himself. Nothing was poking or prodding him, so he knew he was not seriously injured - at least not enough for his body to fail at healing.

He had no memories of what occurred after losing to Eslena in his mind. He was drawing a long blank, and to him, it felt like one continuous moment. Chris could once again sense Penny's presence and hear her thoughts, but she was nowhere to be seen in the room. He turned, threw the soft white sheets off of himself, and moved to the edge of the bed. It creaked slightly as his weight was applied to one side.

"Welcome back," Emily's voice said from the corner of the room. She was in a chair beside his bed and seemingly staring at the floor. "How are you feeling? Hopefully a little better after a week."

Chris cupped his forehead with his palm and winced. "Other

than a headache, I'm fine." He paused for a minute and stared at the sheets. "A week?"

"If I subtract roughly three days on Sohrann, yes." Emily responded to his right. "I'm glad you're okay, Chris."

Emily took a moment to gather herself and then slowly stood. She nearly tripped as she did, but using the chair's armrests, she was able to hoist herself from the seat. Chris was confused for a moment as to why she was stumbling around like that. She made her way to the wall that had a window that would allow one to peer out into space. He thought Emily was just looking into space, but these thoughts died when his sister slid her hand along the window and downwards until she found what she needed. The cane she had in her grip looked like it was her weapon in another transformed state.

"Why do you need a cane?" He asked with great concern. Chris tried to advance on her, but she sharply turned her head near his direction and held up a hand. "Em."

"Yes, little bro?" She answered somberly like she hated the question. *Why isn't she looking at me?* He asked himself with hesitation.

"I'm over here, Em," Chris said with a suspicious expression. "What's wrong with your eyes?" He drew closer, but Emily turned her head to avoid him. She did not want him to look too hard.

"It's just a flesh wound." She promised him with a smile, echoing something that he had said earlier to Penny. Emily tried walking toward him but nearly tripped over one of the medical instruments. He was quick to catch her and assist her in standing up.

"Em, who did this to you?" Chris asked her darkly, hoping to conceal his shaking voice. "What happened...?"

"Oh, you mean my eye?" Emily's mouth formed a thin, firm line. She gave the question some thought and then answered. "A Sorcerer caught me off guard while I was fighting you. You were under Eslena's control with a curse, so I suppose I was fixated on that. He slashed me across the eyes, and I guess the wound still hasn't healed. I'm...sure it will in time."

"A Sorcerer did this...?" Chris repeated slowly with a frown. His eyes began to well up as his voice broke out if its normal range. "Not me?"

"I told you." Emily used her cane to feel in front of her and then turned to face him. Either side of her face had a long and deep scar across it. Her nose was not spared either. When she opened her eyes, they were a milky brown color. They were looking straight ahead and not at all focused on him. "A Sorcerer caught me off guard. It was my mistake. I lost focus. If it wasn't for Penny and Ian, I'd probably have gotten much worse. It was clumsy of me to let my guard down."

"You can't see...can you?" Chris asked as the tears finally came running down his face. She reached out to place a hand on his shoulder but instead found his head, realized that there were tears, and recoiled. Emily must have decided to just go with it because she ruffled his hair, wiped his tears, and gave him a bittersweet smile.

"Not as well as I used to," was her reply.

"Will it heal?" He asked further. Chris felt as if he might vomit but did not feel sick.

"Oh, well, Autumn thinks so, but it may...it may take some time." Emily slid her hand down to his shoulder and squeezed hard. "I'm just so glad you're back to being alright. When I find Eslena, I'll make sure to-"

"To do what?" Chris asked. His eyes were beginning to well up. "You're blind."

Emily must have heard the shake in his voice because she brought him close and held him to herself clumsily. "Calm down. I'm going to handle all of that." Chris wanted to believe her, he really did, but every time he looked into her dead eyes; he felt that it would be anything but that. "I don't need to see to protect you."

"...And Sohrann? The evacuation...?" He asked shakily.

"Is ongoing," Emily answered. She extended a finger toward the wall, but he figured that she wanted to aim at the door. "You should go see Penny. I'll come too. It just may take me a moment."

"I'll help you walk," Chris told her assertively.

"No." Emily shook her head and waved her cane so he could see it. She calmed herself down and did her best to stand up straight. "I want to do this on my own. I need to be able to navigate if I'm going to fight. I may be like this for a while, remember? Fast healing and magic can only do so much, so I should try to adjust."

"What if you fall?" He persisted, hoping that she had let him help.

"Then I fall," Emily said with a smile. "I'll get back up and try again. I've already done it a few times. How do you think I got into this room and waited for you to wake up? I've been here a few times."

"I honestly figured that Penny helped you," Chris answered. His heart fell into the pit of his stomach and stayed there.

"I'm not that helpless." Emily forced out a dry laugh and then gestured for him to go ahead with a smile. "I'll be behind you soon. Just...give me time. I'll call out if I need help, I promise."

"We're on the Tenacity, right?" Chris asked her. He stopped at the door and turned to look at her.

"We are." She said while facing the wrong direction again. "So, you're safe. Please do not go anywhere. If anyone tries to tell you to head back to the planet, tell them to come talk to me."

The door opened to reveal Autumn standing there. She was clearly about to come in, but Chris was probably the one she was here for. Without saying a word, she pulled him from the room and shut the door. The two made their way a decent way away from the room and began to speak. Autumn did not seem like her natural, confident self. She looked depressed and uncertain: like she had not slept or eaten in the time he was unconscious.

"How are you feeling?" She asked him as kindly as she could. "Do you feel any different?"

"You don't have to stall, Autumn," Chris mumbled.

She frowned and took a breath before speaking, "Did Emily tell you?"

"Tell me about what?" Chris said as he recounted the depressing facts. "About how she's lying to me about what happened? How she's blind?"

Autumn was silent for what felt like forever but nodded in response. "Yes. You were the one who did that to her, Chris. Eslena put some sort of curse on you - that I've never even seen. She somehow broke my spell and- and-" She continued on but paid close attention to his facial expression. She seemed surprised that he just had a neutral one that hid all emotion. "You and Megan were trying to kill Penny, but she got in your way. You - blinded her with your sword and cast a spell into her eyes...and the wound is – its bad."

"Why can't it be healed?" He asked with almost no indication of tone or feeling. He was shaking, but he was not even aware of it and if he was, he did not care.

"I told you, magic can heal wounds, but if I'm missing what I need to fully heal the injury, I can only do a little." Autumn began twirling her hair around her finger over and over like she was nervous. "Your magic actually destroyed some of the nerves in her eyes. So-"

"She's blind," Chris concluded. "She can't see at all, can she?"

"No," Autumn stopped walking and stared at the ground. "I wasn't fast enough. If Vedi didn't come when he did, you and Megan might have killed Penny too. As for Ian, I'm not sure if he was the other target."

"Autumn, Emily asked you to put that spell on me, didn't she?" Chris inquired, though he already knew the answer.

Tears began streaming from Autumn's face, but her expression was hidden by her hair. He could only tell because they slid down her face and landed on her hands, which were still shakily messing with her curly red hair strands. She started having a breakdown right in front of him. Not only had he never seen her like this, but he did not know how to respond. For now, he would just continue to do what Penny did: veil his emotions.

"You can't be everywhere at once," Chris told her plainly even though he was not okay either. "Don't worry about me."

"I'm a failure, Chris," Autumn told him through her sobbing. "My Grandfather can be everywhere at once. He can do what I can't.

If he was here, the planet would not be at risk of destruction; if he were here, Emily wouldn't have gone blind; and you wouldn't be beating yourself up. He'd have stopped their ship too! I bet his spell wouldn't have broken!"

"Autumn-" Chris started as calmly as he could, his voice cut out halfway.

"Do you think I should resign? I thought I could be a good Headmistress one day, but I guess I am mistaken." Autumn began gesturing wildly with her hands and Chris worried that she might drive herself insane. "Every time I fix one problem and save one life, another appears, and things get far worse." Autumn brought both of her trembling hands up and covered her face. "I think it may be best for everyone's sake."

"You can't go and quit when so much went wrong so fast," Chris said as he forced a fake smile. She clearly could not tell it was not real. "The Autumn that I know would continue trying harder and harder. When you save someone, make sure you say what you always do. You'll just keep getting better and better. No one blames you for any of this." He turned to face her and winked. "If it weren't for you, I'd probably be dead or something. We need you, Autumn."

"But I'm not-"

"I think you should just keep doing your best." He said, hoping to motivate her. She couldn't help but try to smile.

"Hearing that from you means more to me than you know," Autumn said with a sad smile.

"You're still the best Wizard around." Chris reminded her with a confident smile. "Even if you don't realize it, we're all looking up to you. You'll make a great Headmistress, and we'll all be here cheering you on. Just keep picking yourself up and saying, 'it will be okay.' If you do that, I'm sure you'll find the answer."

"I never knew you could be so inspirational," Autumn admitted with a big smile. She had stopped crying now and started laughing; she never did notice that he wasn't even truly smiling. *Neither did I, but I'm glad it helped.*

"Hey, I better go find Penny, Ian, and Megan," Chris told her. He extended his hand and smiled as hard as he could. "We'll talk later."

"But are you sure you're alright?" Autumn asked with great concern. "I made it all about me when you needed someone there for you..."

"Me?" Chris's smile faded for a brief moment. He managed to regain it once more and say proudly. "Nah, I'm fine. You go ahead. I just need to process it all, I think."

Autumn nodded with a smile. "I wish I could be more like you sometimes."

"You wouldn't like it." Chris laughed off this statement, and so did she.

He turned and left her standing there in the hall. He was glad that there was a way to make her smile. It was the least he could do. Once there was enough distance between himself and Autumn, his smile dropped like a rock. His head hurt and he felt like he wanted to vomit from it all. Chris could not see his own facial expression, but he could tell that he was making a rather dark face. There was only one thing on his mind right now: Eslena.

Chris continued down the hall toward the hangar, but it was like he was on autopilot. All he could think about was finding Eslena. Making Eslena pay for what she made himself and Megan do. He would track her down, and then what would he do? Chris knew the answer to that: he would find a way to defeat her and then firmly wrap his hands around her throat. Would he kill her? Could he do this? Deep down, he wanted to, but he had never actually killed anyone without being forced to. What would it even solve? But even so, he wanted it: for his sister, for Penny, Megan, and Ian. Most of all, he wanted it for himself.

When Chris found Penny, he discovered that she was staring out of the shielded hangar entrance with many others. She said nothing but directed him to watch. His jaw dropped a little, and his shock flipped right back around to anger. Torrents of fire and heat erupted from the planet as the tan sandy surface completely disappeared under a sea of red. He could hear whispers and confusion all around him, but he continued to watch anyway. The planet, now black and red in color, began developing a scorching atmosphere. Any ship trying to escape would be eviscerated. No other ships left Sohrann, and from what he could hear all around him, no loved ones could reach anyone on the surface either.

"How could anyone do...this?" Morgan asked the blue of her eyes, reflecting the bright yellow and red colors. No one would reply to her.

"Coming in hot!" one of the mechanics warned the crowd.

Violet's craft soared through the hangar and slid across the floor, crashing into a pile of supplies. Chris was about to climb up and check on her, but she soon opened the hatch, releasing black smoke and revealing fires. Crews carrying extinguishers rushed over to help her, and as she stepped down onto the wing, she threw her helmet to the ground and held her nose. Violet looked visibly burned but far angrier than anything. Chris tried asking her if she was alright, but she ignored the question and left the landing bay.

"What happened?" Chris called after her. "Violet, hey!"

"Over half of the evacuation crews were still launching," Megan said to his left, her hat covering her face slightly. "Violet probably had to leave them."

"Where's Ian?" Chris asked her.

"I don't know, and I don't care," Megan told him in a very uncaring way. "But he's on the ship. We are not really talking, but we know that we have no choice but to work together. Don't worry, I'm not going anywhere until this Empire burns."

"You two are still going to work together...?" Chris asked her with some surprise.

"He wants to stop the Empire and make up for his past, and I want them to suffer for what they did to my home. When all of this is wrapped up, he and I will settle this." Megan turned her face away from him. "It's a necessary evil and we both benefit."

"He cares about you." Penny chimed in without even facing either of them. "Even knowing that you'd still say that?"

"It doesn't change anything." Megan turned and left the two of them alone. "He helped to take everything from me. Maybe you can forgive Penny for her past, but if it was your home she destroyed, could you still say you love her?" Penny broke eye contact with Megan when she said this to them.

"Meg." Chris tried. How was he supposed to answer that? She ignored him and left the hangar as if he had said nothing. "What about Ian?" Chris inquired with a stressed look.

"I think he's on the bridge deck," Penny answered with a long pause. "He's staying away from her and us. I sent Bafair to check on him for me, but he probably wants to be alone."

"Shouldn't I be doing something right now?" Chris asked her with a grim expression.

"Maybe." Penny turned her face to look at him. "But if you have no paths forward, all you can do is wait for one. That's what I was always told."

"Even you don't have the answers." Chris turned to leave, but Penny latched onto his hand and held him in place.

"Wait a minute."

"Yes?"

"It's just like before," Penny told him. She slowly turned her head to look back at him. "I can't read your thoughts."

"I'm just tired, Penn." Chris lied.

"And your face reminds me of how I used to look when-"

"I'm just tired," Chris repeated with no emotion. He pulled away and left her standing there with a concerned look. The last time she saw that face was when her sister died. "I'll be in our quarters, okay? I will check on Ian after I get my head on straight."

Penny was left there alone, staring at a burning planet and uncertain of the future. She wanted to chase him, but it would just go the same way as it just played out. He was not driven to kill Eslena and make her suffer for what happened. It was apparent even without reading his mind, but she could not let him do that. The Chris she cared for would be gone and instead be replaced with someone else. Even if it would make him hate her, she had to keep an eye on him. She took one last look at the dead world and then turned to follow him for what would be a very long conversation.

The Tenacity powered its large engines and turned away from the planet. Many other ships jumped from the system and went in many different directions. Once the coordinates were locked in, and the General gave the order to leave, the Tenacity jumped toward Terminus, leaving only a handful of ships behind. Soon, they too left the system. Now all that remained was a black void of nothingness and an ever-burning star that was once a thriving planet.

"This timeline-" Murphy began as he drifted through space alone in a small ship and stared at the damaged planet. "-Is far more acceptable than the last iteration. I hope it goes the way I expect. They did not die this time or get corrupted. That is good. This might just be the reality we needed!"

His body began to be consumed by blue matter, and in the blink of an eye, he left the timeline. The ship would remain adrift without a captain and no one would ever remember him. Whether it was the vacuum of space, on a dead planet, or in the middle of a battlefield, he would observe. He would observe until the best possible outcome was achieved. Would they begin to think for themselves this time, or would this timeline be another failure?

# EPILOGUE

The soft rain shower pouring onto the healthy green grassy plains finally ceased. The sun was coming up now over the horizon, rolling its rays across the land and touching everything it could from the forest far at the end of the plains, to the small little village, and finally to the city of Terminus. Along the path leading from Terminus's village, an individual with pale blue hair and a green butterfly clip traveled toward the bustling city. Villagers waved her goodbye and wished her the best on her admittedly short journey with faith that she would make it safely.

The woman's drained blue hair flowed softly in the breeze, almost annoying her because she soon brushed it aside. Her red and flowy tube top clung to her loosely, grey pants damp from the rain, and laced black boots muddy from the spoil. Her blue eyes were still adjusting to the sun, so she raised her hand to block it and continued walking down the path and across a very long wooden bridge that crossed a lake. The water splashed up against the wooden beams and made a delightful sound that seemed to loop.

She stopped and took a seat on one of the benches that sat out on the bridge. The young woman was not tired but still felt it necessary to take in the sounds and sights. It was so much more peaceful here - not just on this bridge, but on this planet. One could almost mistake this planet as uninhabited because of how natural it was. She leaned forward and watched her reflection appear in the deep water. She picked up a strand of her hair and watched her reflection do the same. This color was so strange compared to what it was before.

It was just a little further to her destination, and yet she couldn't bring herself to move away. Was she just stalling or just captivated by the lake? One could guess that even she did not have the answer. The only thing that motivated her to stand up and prepare to move were the voices approaching from the city. She stood there and waited for them, if only to seem less conspicuous in case they recognized her. They were on the bridge now. The female and the male appeared to be wearing plain white and blue robes, with the girl wearing a dress under hers to keep her tail free and the game keeping his fully buttoned with a black undershirt.

"Ahem, good morning!" the female counterpart said cheerily, her black cat ears flicking up to hear Gatchi's response. They only went down when she said nothing. "Can ya not hear me?"

"I'm like seventy percent sure she heard you. Don't assume silence always means someone can't hear you," her male partner said, his red hair covering one eye, which appeared to have an eyepatch over it. He looked like he was carrying a big barrel. "You scare people off when you yell. Remember Iris? You freaked her out."

Gatchi started to raise her hand but ultimately decided against it in case there was danger, "Oh- yes, I'm sorry I was elsewhere. Good morning."

"I see you're captivated by the lake. It is very beautiful at this hour, isn't it?" He continued on kindly. The two Wizards stopped short of her and looked out with her. "When I'm not doing something important, I sneak out here to think."

"Hey, wait," the cat girl stepped forward and circled Gatchi curiously. Gatchi flinched when she drew closer and began to sniff her all over. "Hmm...I've never seen you before! Are you a new Wizard?"

"Oh, well I-" Gatchi stopped herself and debated telling a flat out lie. "I-I'm Gatchi and..." Gatchi's hair stood on end as the cat girl began sniffing near her face, causing her hair to stand on end. "Eeep! What are you doing?!"

"You smell weird." The girl said in a direct and squeaky voice. "I've never smelled that before!"

"Excuse my rather strange and unmannered partner." The man took her by the shoulder and dragged her back. "I'm Arnaas. This is Daisy."

"Nice to meet you," she purred, her tail wagging periodically. "Are you a new Wizard then? I seriously have never seen you before."

Gatchi stared at her for a moment. The moment of discomfort faded and left her with only a feeling of depression and uncertainty. She opened her mouth to speak and shut it just as soon as it had opened. This question not only came at a bad time but was something she had not considered. Was she still a Sorcerer despite leaving? Did Penny, Tori, and Ian keep their titles? Perhaps they had renounced the label to avoid the dangers of being a Sorcerer in a Wizard environment...

"I am...really not too sure what I am anymore..." she said in a sad and yet humorous tone. "I'm just kind of me, I guess."

"I was just asking because you look like one," Daisy said kindly. "So, are you from the village? Actually, you acted like you'd never seen the lake before, so you must be an off-worlder, right?"

"...I came here to find someone," she explained nervously. "Do you know the Dreadful sisters Penny and Tori? Maybe even their brother Ian?" Gatchi paused as she formulated the final part of this question. "-A boy with green hair, maybe?"

The two partners exchanged looks like she had said something peculiar. Maybe she said it in a very suspicious way? She started to get very nervous and wondered if she should pretend to laugh it off as a joke. Their expressions together formed a thin straight line, and in the end, it was Arnaas that answered her.

"Yes. Chris and Penny - well, the boy who you mentioned are

partners, actually. Ian is in their squad, but I haven't spoken to him much, so that's about it. As for...the other one-"

"Is she not here?" Gatchi interrupted as his expression softened like he didn't want to answer that. "I'll probably be here for a while, so I can wait." Both Aarnass and Daisy made a face that was beyond telling.

"...I'm afraid Penny's sister died at the Battle of Terminus almost three years ago," Daisy explained, but soon went silent as Gatchi's face twisted into a frown. Her heart sank as she reached back, confirmed where the bench was, and slowly lowered herself into it. She then stared at the wooden floor damp from the rain and water and scowled. Gatchi just sat there, her mouth parted, and her expression fixed straight ahead. The girl she grew up with, the friend who understood her most, and the person she never had a chance to apologize to was gone - the reason she came here was gone.

"I'm sorry, are you going to be okay?" Daisy began with a stutter. "Did you - I mean...I didn't know how to say it, so I just came out and did. I didn't know you were close...You were, weren't you?"

"Where can I find them?" Gatchi asked suddenly and with weight to her voice.

Aarnas stepped out from the covered bridge and pointed upwards to the sky. A large flagship was coming in for a landing. As it reentered the atmosphere, Daisy began hopping up and down and shouting things like 'welcome back' as if they could hear her. Gatchi could feel the strong winds from the engines as it passed over them. She could feel her heart skipping as her fear took over. *They're on that, huh?* She thought to herself. I see. *Will you still hate me, Penny?*